Mike Ashley is a full-time writer, editor and researc[...] almost a hundred books to his credit. He has comp[...] fifty Mammoth books including *The Mammoth Book of Perfect Crimes and Impossible Mysteries*, *The Mammoth Book of Historical Detectives* and *The Mammoth Book of Locked Room Mysteries and Impossible Crimes*. He has also written a biography of Algernon Blackwood, *Starlight Man*. He lives in Kent with his wife and three cats and when he gets the time he likes to go for long walks.

THE MAMMOTH BOOK OF
Historical
Crime Fiction

Edited by Mike Ashley

RUNNING PRESS
PHILADELPHIA · LONDON

Constable & Robinson Ltd
3 The Lanchesters
162 Fulham Palace Road
London W6 9ER
www.constablerobinson.com

First published in the UK by Robinson,
an imprint of Constable & Robinson, 2011

A copy of the British Library Cataloguing in Publication
Data is available from the British Library

UK ISBN 978-1-84901-435-9

1 3 5 7 9 10 8 6 4 2

First published in the United States in 2011 by Running Press Book Publishers
All rights reserved under the Pan-American and International Copyright Conventions

9   8   7   6   5   4   3   2   1
Digit on the right indicates the number of this printing

US Library of Congress Control Number: 2010941547
US ISBN 978-0-7624-4267-6

Running Press Book Publishers
2300 Chestnut Street
Philadelphia, PA 19103-4371

Visit us on the web!
www.runningpress.com

Printed and bound in the UK

Contents

Copyright Acknowledgements

With the exception of the story below, all of the stories are copyright © 2011 by the individual authors, are original to this anthology and are printed with the authors' permission.

"Brodie and the Regrettable Incident" © 1998 by Anne Perry was first published in *Murder, They Wrote II*, edited by Elizabeth Foxwell and Martin H. Greenberg (New York, Boulevard Books, 1998) as "Brodie and the Regrettable Incident of the French Ambassador". Reprinted by permission of the author and the author's agent, MBA Literary Agents Ltd, London.

Introduction

Return to the Crime Scene

The stories in this anthology cover over four thousand years of crime. We travel from the Bronze Age of 2300 BC to the eve of the Second World War, passing through ancient Greece and Rome, the Byzantine Empire, medieval Venice and seventh-century Ireland, before heading for Britain and the United States.

All except one of these stories are brand new, written especially for this anthology. This is my fifteenth anthology of historical crime and mystery fiction (for those interested there is a full list on the 'Also in the series' page), and this time I wanted to feature longer stories. This allows the author to concentrate on the historical setting, character and mindset of the period, so that not only do these stories present fascinating crimes and puzzles, but you also get to know the people and their world in more detail. There are twelve stories in this volume compared to the usual twenty or twenty-five; they are almost like mini novels, allowing a greater understanding of the time.

I've also broadened the coverage. Rather than focus solely on a mystery and its solution, here we have a broader range of crimes and a wider variety of those trying to solve them. Hence you will find, among others, a young girl in Bronze Age Britain trying to understand whether a series of deaths over a period of time were accidental or deliberate; an icon-painter in ancient Byzantium, suddenly out of work when all icons are banned, who becomes embroiled in a case of deception; a priest-finder trying to track down attempted regicides; Charles Babbage and the young Ada Byron trying to crack a coded message and stop a master criminal; and New York detectives on the lookout for Butch Cassidy and the Sundance Kid.

Your guides are twelve of the leading writers in historical crime fiction who are about to bring the past alive. Let us return to the scene of the crime.

– Mike Ashley

Archimedes and the Scientific Method

Tom Holt

Tom Holt is best known for his many humorous fantasy novels, which began with Expecting Someone Taller *(1987) and include* Who's Afraid of Beowulf? *(1988),* Paint Your Dragon *(1996) and* The Portable Door *(2003) – the last heralding the start of a series featuring the magic firm of J. Wellington Wells from Gilbert and Sullivan's light opera* The Sorcerer. *But Holt is also a scholar of the ancient world and has written a number of historical novels including* The Walled Garden *(1997),* Alexander at the World's End *(1999) and* Song for Nero *(2003).*

The following story, which is the shortest in the anthology and so eases us in gently, features one of the best known of the ancient Greek scientists and mathematicians, Archimedes. He lived in the third century BC in the city of Syracuse, in Sicily, under the patronage of its ruler Hieron II. It is a shame that the one enduring image we all have of Archimedes is of him leaping out of his bath shouting "Eureka", meaning "I have found it." But it does encapsulate how Archimedes operated. When presented with a scientific problem he applied his whole self to it using scientific principles, many of which he had propounded. Archimedes unified much scientific theory into a coherent body of thought which allowed him to apply what he regarded as the scientific method. It probably made him the world's first forensic investigator.

"No," I told him. "Absolutely not."

You don't talk like that to kings, not even if they're distant cousins, not even if they're relying on you to build superweapons to fight off an otherwise unbeatable invader, not even if you're a genius respected throughout the known world. It's like the army. Disobeying a direct order is the worst thing you can possibly do, because it leads to the breakdown of the machine. You've got to have hierarchies, or you get chaos.

He looked at me. "Please," he said.

He, for the record, was King Hiero the Second of Syracuse; my distant cousin, my patron and my friend. Even so. "No," I said.

"Forget about the politics," he said. "Just think of it as an intellectual problem. Come on," he added, and that little-boy look somehow found its way back on to his face. Amazing, how he can still do that, after the life he's lived. "You'll enjoy it, you know you will. It's a challenge. You like challenges. Isn't that what it's all about, finding answers to questions?"

"I'm busy," I told him. "Really. I'm in the middle of calculating the square root of three. If I stop now—"

"The what of three what?"

"I'll lose track and have to start all over again. Four years' work, wasted. I can't possibly drop that just to help out with some sordid little diplomatic issue."

One of these days, people tell me, one of these days I'll get myself into real trouble talking to important people like that. Don't be so arrogant, people tell me. Who do you think you are, anyhow?

"Archimedes." He wasn't looking at me any more. He was staring down at his hands, folded in his lap. It was then I noticed something about him that I'd never realized before. He was getting old. The bones of the huge hands stood out rather more than they used to, and his wrists were getting thin. "No," I said.

"You never know," he went on, "it might lead to a great discovery. Like the cattle problem or the thing with the sand. Those were stupid little problems, and look where they ended up. For all you know, it could be your greatest triumph."

I sighed. You think somebody knows you, and then they say something, and it's obvious they don't. "No," I said. "Sorry, but that's final. Get one of your smart young soldiers on to it. That Corinthian we had dinner with the other evening; sharp as a razor, that one; I'm sure he'd relish the chance to prove himself.

You want someone with energy for a job like this. I'm so lazy these days I can hardly be bothered to get out of bed in the morning."

He looked at me, and I could see I'd won. I'd left him no alternative but to use threats – do this or it'll be the worse for you – and he'd decided he didn't want to go there. In other words, he valued our friendship more than the security of the nation.

"Oh, all right," I said. "Tell me about it."

*

The extraordinary thing about human beings is their similarity. We're so alike. Dogs, cows, pigs, goats, birds come in a dazzling array of different shapes and sizes, while still being recognizable as dogs, cows, pigs, goats, birds. Human beings scarcely vary at all. The height difference between the unusually short and the abnormally tall is trivial compared with other species. The proportions are remarkably constant – the head is always one-eighth of the total length, the width of the outstretched arms is always the same as the length of a single stride, and the stride is so uniform that we can use it as an accurate measurement of distance. Human beings have two basic skin colours, three hair colours, and that's it. Just think of all the colours chickens come in. It's a miracle we can ever tell each other apart.

That said, I can't stand Romans. They're practically identical to us in size, shape, skin and hair colour, and facial architecture. Quite often you can't tell a Roman from a Syracusan in the street – no surprise, when you think how long Greeks and Italians have shared Sicily. I've known Romans who can speak Greek so well you wouldn't know they weren't born here; not, that is, unless you listen to what they actually say.

It's ridiculous, therefore, to take exception to a subsection of humanity that's very nearly indistinguishable from my own subsection; particularly foolish when you consider that I'm supposed to be a scientist, governed by logic rather than emotion, and by facts susceptible to proof rather than intuition and prejudice. Still, there it is. I can't be doing with the bastards, and that's all there is to it.

Partly, I guess, my dislike stems from the fact that they're taking over the world, and nobody seems willing or able to stop them. Hiero tried, and he couldn't do it. They smashed his Carthaginian allies, and he was forced to snuggle up and sign a treaty with the

Roman smile and the Roman hobnailed boot. Not sure which of those I detest most, by the way. Probably the smile.

Needless to say, the problem Hiero had just blackmailed me into investigating was all about Romans. One Roman in particular. His name was Quintus Caecilius Naso, diplomatic attaché to the Roman delegation to the court of King Hiero, and what he'd done to make trouble for Syracuse (and perplexity for me) was to turn up, extremely dead, in a large storage jar full of pickled sprats, on the dockside at Ostia, when he should have been alive and healthy in the guest quarters of the royal palace at Syracuse.

Quintus Caecilius Naso – why Romans have to have three names when everybody else manages perfectly well with one is a mystery to me – was, at the time of his death, a thirty-six-year-old army officer, from a noble and distinguished family, serving as part of a delegation engaged in negotiating revisions to the treaty Hiero had been bounced into signing twenty years ago; in other words, he was here to bully my old friend into making yet more concessions, and I know for a fact that Hiero was deeply unhappy about the situation. However, he'd managed to claw back a little ground, and it looked as though there was a reasonable chance of lashing together a compromise and getting rid of the Romans relatively painlessly, when Naso suddenly disappeared.

I never met the man, but by all accounts he wasn't the disappearing sort. Far too much of him for that. He wasn't tall, but he was big; a lot of muscle and a lot of fat was how people described him to me, just starting to get thin on top, a square jaw floating on a bullfrog double-chin; incongruously small hands at the end of arms like legs. His party trick was to pick up a flute-girl with one hand, lift her up on his shoulder and take her outside for a relatively short time. He was never drunk and never sober, he stood far too close when he was talking to you, and he had, by all accounts, a bit of a temper.

He was last seen alive at a drinks party held at his house by Agathocles, our chief negotiator. It was a small, low-key affair; three of ours, three Romans, four cooks, two servers, two flute-girls. Agathocles and his two aides drank moderately, as did two of the Romans. Naso got plastered. Since he was the ranking diplomat on the Roman side, very little business was transacted prior to Naso being in no fit state; his two sidekicks clearly felt they lacked the authority to continue when their superior stopped talking boundaries and demilitarized zones and started singing along with the flautists and our three were just plain embarrassed. When Naso grabbed one of the girls – he dropped her, and had to use both hands – and wandered off into the courtyard with her, the rest of the party broke up by unspoken mutual consent and went home. Agathocles went into the inner room to bed. The Romans' honour guard – a dozen marines from the ship they arrived on – stayed where they were, surrounding the house. Their orders were to escort Naso back to the palace. But Naso didn't appear, so they stood there all night, assuming he'd fallen asleep somewhere. They were still standing there, at attention, when the sun rose. At this point, Naso's secretary came bustling up; the great man was due in a meeting, where was he? The guards didn't have the authority to wake him up, but the secretary did. He went inside, then looked round the courtyard, which didn't take long. No sign of Naso, or the wretched girl. The secretary then made the guards search Agathocles' house. Nothing.

The secretary and the guard-sergeant had a quick, panic-stricken conference and decided that Naso must've slipped past the guards with the girl – why he should want to do that, neither of them could begin to imagine – and was presumably shacked up with her somewhere, intending to re-emerge in his own good time. This constituted a minor diplomatic insult to us, of course, since the meeting had to be adjourned, and our side came to the conclusion that it was intended as a small act of deliberate rudeness, to put us in our place. If we made a fuss about it, we'd look petty-minded. If we said nothing, we'd be tacitly admitting we deserved to be walked all over. It was just the sort of thing Naso tended to do, and it had always worked well for him in the past.

But Naso didn't show up; not for three weeks. The atmosphere round the negotiating table quickly went from awkward to dead quiet to furiously angry. What had we done with Caecilius Naso? A senior Roman diplomat doesn't just vanish into thin air. It really didn't help that Agathocles had been the host. He'd been doing his job rather well, digging his heels in, matching the Romans gesture for gesture, tantrum for tantrum; angry words had been spoken, tables thumped, and then Agathocles had asked Naso round for drinks and Naso had disappeared. Without him, the talks simply couldn't continue. Ten days after the disappearance, the Roman garrisons on our borders mobilized and conducted unscheduled manoeuvres, as close to the frontiers as they could get without actually crossing them. Cousin Hiero had his soldiers turn the city upside down, but they found nothing. The Roman diplomats went home without saying goodbye. Their soldiers stayed on the border. Then, just as we were starting to think it couldn't get any worse, Naso turned up again.

He made his dramatic re-entry when the swinging arm of the crane winching a great big jar of sprats off the bulk freighter snapped, on the main dock at Ostia, in front of about a thousand witnesses. The jar fell on the stone slabs and smashed open, and out flopped Naso. He was still in the full diplomatic dress he'd worn to the party, so it was immediately obvious that he was someone important in the military. He was quickly identified, and a fast courier galley was immediately launched, to tell us the bad news.

*

"Presumably," Orestes said, "it was the extra weight that snapped the crane. A man's got to weigh a damn sight more than his own volume in sprats."

Orestes was the bright young Corinthian I'd proposed as my substitute. Instead, he'd been assigned to me as sidekick-in-chief. He was tall, skinny, gormless-looking and deceptively smart, with a surprisingly scientific cast of mind. "So what?" I said.

He offered me a drink, which I refused, and poured one for himself. My wine, of course. "This whole sprat business," he said. "It's got to mean something, it's too bizarre otherwise."

"Bizarre, I grant you," I said. "But meaningful . . ."

"Has to be." He nodded firmly. "Abducting and murdering a Roman emissary at a diplomatic function," he went on, "has got to be a statement of some kind. Bottling him and sending him home must, therefore, be a refinement of that statement."

"Expressive of contempt, you mean."

"Must be." He frowned at his hands. A nail-biter. "That's not good for us, is it?"

"The crane," I reminded him.

"What? Oh, right. I was just thinking, the timing of the discovery of the body. If the crane hadn't broken, the jar would've been loaded on a cart and taken to Rome. It had been ordered by—" He looked up his notes. "Philippus Longinus," he recited, "freedman, dealer and importer in wholesale foodstuffs. Disclaims all knowledge, et cetera. They've got him locked up, of course."

"Greek?"

"Doesn't say," Orestes replied, "but he's a freedman with a half-Greek name, so presumably yes. Loads of Greek merchants in Rome nowadays. Anyhow, in the normal course of business that jar of sprats would've stayed in his warehouse for months." His eyebrows, unusually thick, lowered and squashed together. "Which makes no sense."

I nodded slowly. "If you're right about the murder as a statement," I replied.

"Unless," Orestes went on, looking up sharply, "whoever did it knew the extra weight would break the crane, in which case—" He looked at me, and sighed. "A bit far-fetched?"

"As wine from Egypt," I said. "Of course," I went on, "someone could've sawed the beam part-way through."

"That's—" He looked at me again. "You're teasing me," he said.

"Yes."

"Fine. In that case, it makes no sense."

"If," I reminded him, "we approach the problem from the diplomatic-statement direction, as you seem determined to do."

He gave me a respectfully sour look. "In the circumstances . . ."

He had a point, of course. "It would seem logical to assume that it's something to do with politics and diplomacy," I conceded.

"Exactly. So we should start from there."

I sighed. "No," I said. "We should start from the beginning."

*

We took a walk. On the way there, we discussed various topics – Pythagoras, the nature of light, the origin of the winds – and paused from time to time to let me rest my ankle, which hasn't been right since I fell down the palace steps. We reached Agathocles' house just before midday, a time when I was fairly sure he'd be out.

"I'm sorry," the houseboy confirmed. "He's at the palace. Can I tell him who called?"

"We'll wait," I said firmly.

*

Of course I'd been there before, many times. I knew that Agathocles lived in his father's old house, and his father had been nobody special, a cheese merchant who was shrewd enough to buy into a grain freighter when the price was right, and then reinvest in land so his son could be a gentleman. I can only suppose Agathocles liked the place; happy childhood memories, or something of the sort. It was a small house, surrounded by a high wall, on the edge of the industrial quarter. If you stood on the street outside the front door, you could smell the tannery round the corner, or the charcoal smoke from the sickle-blade factory, or the scent of drying fish on the racks a hundred yards north. An unkind friend described it as pretentiously unpretentious, and I'm tempted to agree. Inside, you could barely move for statues, fine painted pottery, antique bronze tripods. It looked rather more impressive than it was because the rooms were so small, but even so, the collection represented a substantial amount of money, leaving you in no doubt that the great man lived where he did because he wanted to, not because he couldn't afford anything better.

It was an old-fashioned house, too; rounded at one end, with two main rooms, for living and sleeping. The upstairs room, more of a storage loft than a gentleman's chamber, was presumably a legacy of Agathocles' father's business activities, a dry and airy place to store cheeses, with a door opening into thin air, like you see in haylofts. The house stood in the middle of a larger-than-usual courtyard, half of which had been laid out as a garden, with trellised vines and fruit trees, herb beds and an ostentatious row of cabbages. The other half, shaded by a short, wide fig tree, was for sitting and talking in, and a very attractive space it made. It was surrounded, as I just told you, by a wall, and the reports said that on the fatal evening, the guards had stood all round the outside of the wall, with a sergeant minding the gate.

"Not good," Orestes said sadly. "Not good at all."

I concurred. I could see no way in which anyone could have scaled the wall – coming in or going out – without being seen by the guards, even in the dark; also there were sconces set in the wall for torches, and hooks for lanterns, and the report said that the courtyard had been lit up that night. Well nigh impossible, therefore, for Naso to have slipped out past the guards; equally implausible that anyone else could have climbed in to kill him.

"Bad," Orestes said.

"Quite. If Naso was killed—"

He looked at me. "If?"

"If," I repeated, then shrugged. "It must have been one of the people in the house at the time. Agathocles, his two aides, the two Romans, or the domestics. As you say," I added, "bad for us."

Orestes walked to the foot of the wall and stood on tiptoe. "Then how did they get rid of the body?" he said.

I smiled. "That," I said, "is probably the only thing standing between us and war."

He jumped up, trying to grab the top of the wall. He was a tall man, like I said. He couldn't do it. "Maybe they hid the body," he said, "and came back later."

I shook my head. "Naso's secretary and the guard-sergeant searched the house," I reminded him. "And it's not like there's many places you could hide a body. I'm morally certain that Naso was off the premises when the house was searched."

"But the guards were still in place. They'd have noticed."

"Yes," I said, and sat down, slowly and carefully, under Agathocles' rather splendid fig tree. My neck isn't quite as supple as it used to be, so I couldn't lean back as far as I'd have liked.

"You think," Orestes interpreted, "the body was in the *tree*?"

I smiled at him. "The outer branches overhang the wall," I said, "And it's a fact that when people are looking for something, they quite often don't bother to glance up. But no, I don't think so. Even if you were standing in the upstairs door—"

"What? You know, I hadn't noticed that."

"Which proves my point," I said smugly. "You didn't look up. I noticed that door as soon as I walked though the gate, but I don't think it's relevant in any way. It's nowhere near the wall, and it's too far for anybody, even a really strong man, to *throw* a dead body from there to the tree." I frowned, as a thought slipped quietly into my mind, like a cat curling up on your lap. "We ought to take another look inside," I said. "I believe our problem is that we've been searching for what isn't there rather than paying due attention to what is. Also," I added, "we suffer from the disadvantage of noble birth and civilized upbringing."

"What does that mean?"

"I'm not sure," I replied. "I'll tell you when I've worked it out."

★

We snooped round the house for a while, ending up in the upstairs room. Nothing obvious had caught my eye; no bloodstains, or tracks in the dust to show where a body had been dragged. I sat down on an ancient cheese press, while Orestes sat at my feet on a big coil of rope, the image of the great philosopher's respectful disciple. That made me feel like a complete fraud, of course.

"A grown man," I said, "walks out of a drinking party—"

"Staggers out of a drinking party."

"True," I said. "But he was used to being drunk. And he took the flute-girl. What about her, by the way?"

"What about her?"

"Has she turned up? Or has nobody thought to ask?"

Orestes shrugged. "I expect that if she'd been found they'd have held her for questioning."

That made me frown. Call me squeamish if you like; I don't like the notion, enshrined in the law of every Greek city, that a slave's evidence can only be admissible in a court of law if it's been extracted under torture. It gave the wretched girl an excellent motive for running away, that was for sure – assuming, that is, that she knew that something bad had happened, and she was likely to be wanted as a witness. "Let's consider that," I said. "I'm assuming Hiero's had soldiers out looking for her."

Orestes grinned. "Fair enough. I wouldn't imagine it'd be an easy search. For a start, how would they know who to look for?"

I raised an eyebrow. "Explain," I said.

"One slave-girl looks pretty much like another."

"But her owner—" I paused. "Who owns her? Do we know?"

Orestes took another look at his notes. "One Syriscus. Freedman, keeps a stable of cooks and female entertainers, hires them out for parties and functions. Quite a large establishment."

I nodded. "So it's not certain that Syriscus himself would recognise her. It'd be an overseer or a manager who'd have regular contact with the stock-in-trade."

"Presumably."

"And he," I went on, "gives a description to the patrol sergeants: so high, dark hair, so on and so forth. Probably a description that'd fit half the young women in Syracuse. So the chances of finding her, if she doesn't want to be found—"

Orestes nodded. "Pity, that," he said. "Our only possible witness."

"And if she *had* seen anything," I went on, "and if she managed to get outside the wall – if she had the sense she was born with she'd run and keep on running." I sighed. "She must've got out somehow, or she'd have been found. Now we've got two inexplicable escapes instead of one."

"Unless," Orestes pointed out reasonably, "they escaped together."

I shook my head. "A joint venture," I said. "Co-operation in the achievement of a common purpose. I don't think so. Naso gets drunk and fancies a quick one with the first girl he can lay his hands on. He carries her outside, they do the deed, and then they put their heads together and figure out a way of scaling the wall and evading the guards, something beyond the wit of us two distinguished scientists. And we're sober. No, I don't think so at all."

Orestes nodded. "So?"

"So," I concluded, "I don't think Naso got out; I think he was got out by a person or persons unknown. In which case, the girl was got out too."

"Because she was a witness?"

I shrugged. "Why not just kill her and leave her lying?" I asked. "Come to that, why disappear Naso, rather than just cut his throat and save the bother of moving the corpse over such a discouragingly formidable series of obstacles? And as for the jar of sprats—" I shook my head. "Words fail me," I said.

Orestes grinned at me. "I think," he said, "that Naso climbed out and took the girl with him over the wall. No, listen," he added, as I started to object. "I can't tell you how he might have done it, but he was a soldier, maybe he was good at silently climbing walls and evading guards. Maybe he thought it'd be a lark. Anyway, he and the girl sneak out somehow. And once he's outside, roaming around the city, that's when he's killed and stuck in the jar, which happens to be the handiest hiding-place at the time."

"Motive?"

"How about robbery?" Orestes said hopefully. "Nothing political, just everyday commercial crime. You get an honest hard-working footpad who sees this richly dressed drunk weaving his way through the Grand Portico in the middle of the night. Our footpad jumps the drunk, but the drunk's a soldier and he fights back, so the footpad hits him a bit harder than he'd normally do and kills him. In a panic, he drags the body into a nearby warehouse and dumps it in a suitable jar."

I was impressed. "Which reminds me," I said. "Do we know who the jar belonged to? We know who the buyer in Rome was, but how about the seller?"

Orestes consulted his notes. "Stratocles," he said. "General merchant."

I nodded. "I know him," I said. "He's got a warehouse—" I frowned. "Address?"

Orestes looked up at me. "Just round the corner from here," he said.

"At last." I smiled. "Something that actually makes a bit of sense. All right," I went on, "this robbery hypothesis of yours."

"It fits all the known facts."

"It covers them," I pointed out, "like a drover's coat. It's not what you'd call a tailored fit."

Orestes gave me an 'all-right, be like that' look. "It *covers* the known facts," he said. "And it has the wonderful merit of being nothing to do with politics and diplomacy, which gets Syracuse off the hook. Also," he added, with a rather more serious expression, "it's the only explanation we've got, unless we're prepared to entertain divine intervention."

I stood up. "Well done," I said. "You know, I told Hiero you'd be perfectly capable of dealing with this business on your own. But would he listen?"

"Did you really?"

"At any rate," I said, as I walked to the open door that led to nothing at all and cautiously peered out, "it's a working hypothesis. Of course, you've missed out the one thing that might just possibly prove your case."

He looked startled. "Have I?"

I grinned and pointed at the coil of rope. "You're sitting on it," I said.

His eyes grew round and wide. "Of course," he said. "Naso threw this rope into the tree!"

I picked the iron clamp off the cheese press. "Possibly using this as an improvised grappling hook."

"And they climbed along the rope to the tree, and dropped down from the overhanging branch on to the other side of the wall."

"Having chosen a spot, or a moment, with no guard present. Quite," I said. "Solved your mystery for you. Of course," I added, "you haven't yet explained how the rope and the clamp got back in here, neatly coiled up and put away."

"Damn," he said. "Does that spoil my case?"

I smiled at him. "No," I said. "It makes it interesting."

*

The next day I thought about my king, my patron and my friend, Hiero of Syracuse, and the Romans. I also thought about war, and truth. Then I sent out for a secretary – I get cramp in my wrist these days if I write much – and dictated a report on the case. It was essentially Orestes' theory, though I left out the rope and the cheese press, and a few other things. I fleshed it out a bit, for the benefit of any Romans who might read it (I felt sure that some would), with various observations of a scientific nature. Human strength, for example, and the limitations thereof. Agathocles, I pointed out, was a small man, past middle age. Even if he'd been able to murder a seasoned Roman soldier (by attacking him when his back was turned, for example), there was no way he could've disposed of the body, not without help. Such help could only have come from the domestics, since his two advisers and the remaining Romans had left the party together. As for the domestics – the cooks – they'd been thoroughly interrogated in the proper manner, were slaves, could hardly speak Greek and had never been to Agathocles' house before. They left shortly after the guests, and they all agreed that none of them had been out of the others' sight all evening. It was just possible that Agathocles, having murdered Naso, could have suborned them all – it would've had to be all of them – with bribes to help him with the body, but I left it to the common sense of the reader to conclude that it was highly unlikely. If Agathocles had wanted to kill Naso, surely he'd have laid a better plan and made sure he had his helpers in place before the event, rather than relying on recruiting slaves he'd never met before. The same, I more or less implied, held true of the servers, who were also from Syriscus' agency. As for the flute-girls, including the one carried off by Naso, they could be ruled out straight away, since mere slips of girls wouldn't have been capable of manhandling Naso's substantial body. Therefore, I concluded, if Naso hadn't been removed from the house by anybody else, he must've removed himself. That proposition established, the likeliest reconstruction of events, I suggested, was the one set forth in my report.

I concluded by praising the energy and intelligence of my colleague, Orestes of Corinth, in the investigation. I had three copies made and sent one to Hiero as soon as the ink was dry.

★

What, after all, is truth? In a court of law, it's a narrative of certain events which a majority of the jury believe to be accurate. In science, it's a hypothesis that fits (or at least covers) all the known facts without contravening any of the established laws of nature. In mathematics, it's the inevitable product of the component variables. In the subscience of history, it's the most plausible explanation of the undisputed evidence. In diplomacy, it's a version acceptable to both parties and incapable of being disproved.

★

Hiero sent my report to Rome, along with a request that the negotiations be resumed. The Romans replied with a new team of negotiators, headed by one Publius Laurentius Scaurus, a man of whom even I had heard.

"It's an honour," Scaurus said to me, having backed me into a corner at the official reception, "and a tremendous privilege to meet you. What can I say? You're my hero. The greatest living philosopher."

His breath smelt of onions. "Thank you," I said.

"Your experiment with the golden crown—"

"Actually," I really didn't want to hear him sing my praises, "I was rather taken with your latest effort. Mechanical advantage, wasn't it? The application of balanced forces in opposing vectors?"

He blushed red as a winestain. "You've actually read my paper?"

"Of course," I said. "Excellent work. And it happens to be a field in which I've dabbled quite a bit myself."

"Dabbled," he repeated. "You've only written the most significant monograph on the subject in human history. Your wonderful dictum—"

I raised my hand, not really wanting to hear my wonderful dictum, but he ignored me. " 'Give me a firm place to stand', you said, 'and I can move the Earth.' Inspirational."

I shook my head. "I didn't say that."

"Excuse me?"

"What I said was," I told him, "something along the lines of 'if a fellow had a really solid place to stand on and a long enough bit of good, strong wood, there's no reason I can see why he shouldn't be able to move something really quite big.' Not the same thing at all," I added, smiling. "Actually, I prefer your version. Much neater."

"Thank you," he said, frowning. "Of course, my little paper's really only a series of footnotes to yours. The truly groundbreaking conceptual thinking—"

"You're here as a negotiator?" I asked. "In place of poor Naso."

He sighed. "A great man," he said. "We miss him."

"You read my report," I said. "About his disappearance?"

He tried to look surprised. "That was your report? Well, I suppose I should've known. Very persuasive, of course, and the evidence presented with such clarity—"

"It was signed," I said. "Perhaps you didn't read the first line."

Eventually someone rescued me, and I hobbled away into a corner and hid behind a couple of tall colonels until we were called in to dinner.

★

On the first day of the negotiations, Scaurus raised the question of his predecessor's death.

A report had been received, he said, in which King Hiero tried to make out that Naso had been, in effect, responsible for his own death; that he'd crept furtively away from a party held in his honour, somehow evading the guards provided at his own request for his own protection, scrambling over a high wall – which Caecilius Naso could never have done, he pointed out, having been severely wounded in battle in the service of his country, as a result of which he walked with a pronounced limp, something which anybody who had ever met him couldn't possibly have helped noticing. The report, he went on, his eyes blazing with righteous indignation, was nothing less than an insult to the memory of a loyal and valiant officer, propagated by the very people who had brought about his death, in a callous attempt to disrupt the peace process which the Roman people had worked so hard to bring about.

I was there, at Hiero's insistence. I got as far as opening my mouth, but then Scaurus started up again.

Fortuitously, he continued, a thorough investigation had been conducted by a team of dedicated Roman public servants, including Naso's private secretary, the guard commander and a commission of officers of propraetorian rank – one of whom he had the honour to be. He was therefore in a position to prove that Naso was murdered, in cold blood, by a trained assassin acting on the orders of the criminal Agathocles, who in turn was carrying out the direct command of King Hiero himself, with the intention of subverting the peace process. The assassin, one Maurisca, a young woman of exceptional strength and agility, presently in custody in Rome, had been disguised as a flute-girl, in which guise she was introduced to Naso at the party. Naso, plied by his host with wine far stronger than that to which he was accustomed, was enveigled into following the assassin to the upstairs room of the house. There she murdered him. Then, with a view to covering up the crime and allowing Syracuse to evade the proper wrath of the Roman people, she proceeded to dispose of the body.

No doubt (this appalling man went on) the Syracusan delegates had read King Hiero's so-called report; in which case, they must recall that the upper room of the house was some ten feet from a substantial fig tree, whose branches overhung the outer wall. What the report neglected to mention was the presence in the loft of a number of highly significant artefacts, amongst which: a cheese press of considerable weight – the long, stout handles used to turn the screw of the said press during the whey reduction process; a coil of strong, fine rope. These apparently mundane objects, he thundered, were all that were needed to construct a rudimentary but effective crane, by the use of which the assassin shifted Naso's lifeless corpse through the open door of the upper room and into the branches of the tree. Thereafter, it was an easy matter for the assassin – previously trained as an acrobatic dancer – to leave the house, enter the courtyard, and, using the rope or a section thereof, lower Naso's body over the wall, at a distance therefrom enabling her to escape detection. Continuing, she dropped from the tree to the ground and dragged the body over a paved pathway on which she knew no trace would be left, to some point nearby, where accomplices awaited her with a cart or some similar vehicle. Said accomplices proceeded to dispose of the body by breaking into the nearest warehouse and placing it in a large storage jar, possibly with the intention of returning later and recovering it for more permanent disposal. If that was their intention, presumably they were frustrated in it by the search of the neighbourhood insisted on by the Roman delegation.

And then the obnoxious Scaurus turned round and pointed straight at me, and went on: "You may feel, fellow delegates, that such an operation, such a feat of engineering, would be difficult to achieve. The Syracusans would, no doubt, like you to believe that it would be impossible. No doubt. I believe that the very complexity – I might say the implausibility of the scheme – was a fundamental part of its design. The Syracusans want you to believe that there was no way the body, once dead, could have been removed from that place; therefore, they argue, Naso must have left the house alive, in the manner they describe in the report. But, as we have seen, their explanation is not only highly unlikely, in the light of what we know of Caecilius Naso's exemplary character, but actually impossible, because of his war wound. We have, of course, the evidence of the assassin herself, obtained and confirmed under torture before a magistrate. But even without her evidence, the matter speaks for itself. Having disproved the purportedly straightforward version offered by the Syracusans, we have no alternative but to conclude that Naso was dead when he left the house; in which case, it is an unavoidable conclusion that some form of mechanical artifice was used to remove him, and that artifice was constructed from the materials later found in the upper room. And if anybody wishes to argue that those materials were inadequate for the purpose, I say this: to any ordinary man – perhaps. To a trained engineer, even –

quite possibly. But King Hiero of Syracuse has in his service the greatest living expert, fellow delegates, the world's foremost authority on the use and application of levers and mechanical advantage; I refer, of course, to the universally acclaimed inventor Archimedes, son of Phidias, who is sitting before me as I speak; the man who once boasted, as I'm sure I need not remind you, 'Give me a firm place to stand, and I can move the Earth'. Fellow delegates—"

I'm afraid I missed the rest of the speech. Two of Hiero's men took me politely by the elbows and walked me out of the room, before I could say anything.

*

On my way home, Orestes and I stopped off at Stratocles' warehouse. It was a huge place, and the nearest uninhabited building to Agathocles' house. Inside, there were more jars than I've ever seen in my life. There were sealed jars, rows and rows of them, ready to be loaded and shipped. There were empty jars, sent back to be washed out and refilled. There were damaged jars waiting to be hauled off and dumped in the bay, and two long lines of half-filled jars, containing the preservative oil but as yet no sprats, standing by to be stoppered and sealed with pitch.

I stood next to one of these – it was about two fingers' width taller than me – and tried to imagine lifting a dead body high enough to drop inside it. It'd take several men.

"Come on," Orestes said sadly. "This part of the evidence isn't in dispute."

"I guess not," I said. "I'd still like to know why sprats, though."

"Excuse me?"

"The body was bound to turn up sooner or later," I said. "When the jar was opened. I grant you, it was sheer chance that it ended up in Rome. Even so—"

I didn't finish the sentence because at that point I slipped and nearly ended up on my face. The floor was slick with oil. Someone had tried to blot it up with sawdust, but hadn't been thorough enough.

Orestes grinned at me. "Archimedes' principle of the displacement of fluids," he said. "I read about it at school."

I gave him a look. "I'm guessing," I said, "that this is where the body was tipped in, and the displaced oil came gushing out. He was a big man, so there was a lot of spilt oil."

"Quite," Orestes said. "So where does that get us?"

I wiped oil off the sole of my sandal with the hem of my gown. "Nowhere," I said.

★

The next day, Orestes came to see me. I sent word that I didn't want to talk to anybody. He insisted. I pointed out that I was having a relaxing, well-earned bath, in which I hoped to dissolve every trace of the air I'd been forced to share with Publius Laurentius Scaurus. Orestes came in anyway, and sat down on the floor looking sadly at me and not speaking.

"I told Hiero," I said. "I didn't want to get involved."

"You're involved all right," Orestes said. "They're demanding your extradition."

I'm not a brave man. I squealed like a pig. "Hiero'll never agree."

"No," Orestes said, "he won't. And that means there's going to be a war. Which," he added, with a faint shrug of his shoulders, "we'll almost certainly lose, unless you can think of a way of blasting the Roman fleet out of the bay. Pity about that," he added.

"Yes," I said. "But it's not my fault."

"Nobody said it was," Orestes replied gloomily. "Still, that's one thing I never thought I'd see."

"What?"

"Archimedes," he said, standing up. "Outsmarted by a Roman."

He was just about to leave. I called him back. "I don't suppose," I said, "you've still got your file on Naso."

He grinned at me. "As a matter of fact," he said, and pulled out the papers from under his tunic.

I sighed. "Read them to me," I said. "My eyesight—"

So he read his notes on the life and times of Quintus Caecilius Naso, up to a point where I told him to stop and go back a bit. He read that bit again, and I asked him some questions, which he was luckily able to answer.

"You wouldn't happen to have," I said quietly, "anything similar on our friend Scaurus?"

"Wait there," he said.

★

The bath was getting cold when he came back, but I hadn't bothered to get out. I'd been too busy thinking; or, rather, bashing helplessly at the locked door of my intuition, behind which I felt sure the answer lay . . .

"Publius Laurentius Scaurus," Orestes said, peering owlishly at the paper in his hand. "A member of the influential Laurentii family, once prominent in the Optimate movement, though their influence has been on the wane for the last twenty years or so. Married to the second cousin of the celebrated Aemilius—"

There was a lot more of that sort of thing. I was partly listening, the way an old married man partly listens to his wife. At the same time, my mind was hopping, flapping, until suddenly and quite unexpectedly, it soared.

"Got it!*" I remember shouting. "Here, help me out, I've got to see Hiero."

Which I did, refusing to wait, or see anybody else. I barged my way into the royal presence and told him all about it. Then I said, "Well?"

A pause; then Hiero said, "You're right."

"Yes," I said. "I am."

Hiero nodded slowly. Then he lifted his head and looked at me. "Archimedes," he said.

"Yes?"

"Why haven't you got any clothes on?"

*

In contrast to our previous encounters, my third meeting with Scaurus was distinctly low-key. There were just the three of us, in a small garden at the back of the palace. We sat like civilized men under a fine old beech tree, and a boy served wine and honey cakes.

Hiero – he was the third member of the party – wiped his lips delicately on a linen napkin and gave Scaurus a friendly smile. "I asked you here," he said, "to see if we can't work something out. Something sensible," he added. "Just the three of us."

Scaurus nodded gracefully. "I can't see why we shouldn't be able to," he said. "If you're prepared to be realistic."

Hiero nodded. "And since you're such an admirer of my

---

*   In Greek, *Eureka*

cousin's work," he went on, "I've asked him along. I know you've had your differences, let's say, but I feel sure that deep down, both of you men of science, you can really *talk* to each other. Wouldn't you say?"

"Of course," Scaurus said. "And you're right. The very greatest admiration."

I acknowledged the compliment as best I could. "Maybe," I said, "we could have a chat about scientific method."

A slight frown crossed Scaurus' face. "I'd have thought we had rather more urgent—"

I raised my hand. "Method first," I said, "then the specifics."

He shrugged. "If you like."

"What I admired about that paper of yours," I went on, "wasn't the actual conclusions, which are fanciful, or the empirical data, which is deeply flawed. No, what I liked was the *approach*. Confronted, you said, with various different explanations for an observed phenomenon – all of which fit the facts equally well – logic requires that we choose the explanation that calls for the least number of new assumptions. Is that right?" I asked nicely. "My Latin's nothing special, but I think that's what you said."

He looked at me as if he didn't like me nearly as much as he used to. "More or less," he said.

"In other words," I went on, "the simplest explanation is likely to be the right one."

"That's not actually what I—"

"Near enough," I said firmly, "is good enough. In which case," I went on, "try this. The simplest explanation for what happened to Naso isn't that he climbed the wall on his own, or that this mysterious and wonderful flute-girl of yours winched him over the wall on an improvised crane. The simplest explanation," I said, beaming at him like the rising sun, "is that when he came outside to shag the flute-girl, he found the sergeant of his honour guard waiting for him. The sergeant killed him, and a couple of squaddies lugged him out through the open gate and put him on a cart, to be disposed of later in a nearby warehouse. Well?" I asked him. "Simple enough for you?"

Bless him. He didn't say a word.

"And why would the sergeant do such a thing?" I continued. "Because he was ordered to, or paid, or both. Who by? Well, that's a subject for speculation, I grant you. It could have been a member of a rival political faction – let's see, Naso was well up in the Popular party, just as you're quite well thought of among the Optimates, aren't you? Or maybe it was someone who reckoned the best way to make sure there'd be a war would be by manufacturing a serious diplomatic incident. Mind you," I added, "they'd have to be a Optimate, since the Populars don't want a war right now. Or it could simply have been the uncle of Naso's first wife; you know, the one who died in mysterious circumstances, falling down the stairs or something like that, thereby making it possible for Naso to marry that rich and well-connected heiress. Or maybe it was just that someone whose career's been nothing special lately simply wanted his job. We just don't know. I'm sure," I added sweetly, "that once we've shared our theories with Naso's friends in the Populars, they'd have no trouble thinking of someone who answers one of those descriptions. Or maybe all of them, even."

He gave me a look that would've curdled milk. "Have you finished?" he said.

"Yes. Almost," I added. "I'd just like to give you a new dictum for your collection."

"Well?"

"Give me a firm place to stand," I said, "and I can kick your arse from here to Agrigentum."

*

Later, Orestes asked me, "So why sprats?"

"Ah," I said, smiling like a happy Socrates. "My guess is, the Romans had chosen poor old Stratocles' warehouse well in advance as a good place to lose the body. They wouldn't want it found, not ever, because a disappearance was just as good for breaking up the peace talks as a visible murder, and a body might just've given the game away; no rope-marks or anything like that to support the crane theory. There might have been some trifling clue they'd overlooked, but which might've been picked up by one of our sharp-as-needles Syracusan investigators. Attention to detail, you see, a typically Roman trait."

"But?"

I grinned. "But when they got to the warehouse – it was dark, remember, and they wouldn't have risked a light – they made a slight mistake. They'd been intending to put the corpse in one of the damaged jars we saw there, earmarked for dumping in the bay. Instead, they dumped it in a half-filled jar, which is how come it ended up in Rome." I shook my head sadly. "Too clever by half," I said, "and basically just careless."

★

There was no war. Scaurus went home, and was replaced by a polite old Optimate who explained that the girl Maurisca had confessed that she'd been bribed by the Carthaginians (nice touch, everybody hates the Carthaginians) to tell a parcel of lies in order to get Hiero into trouble. The charges were, therefore, withdrawn, and the negotiations proceeded to a long, drawn out, meaningless conclusion.

And that, I sincerely hope, was the last time I'll ever have anything to do with the Romans. They may have their stirling qualities, but I don't like them. They have absolutely no respect, in my opinion, for the scientific method.

Something to do with Diana

Steven Saylor

Over the last twenty years Steven Saylor has been carving a sizable niche for himself in the world of ancient Rome. He has recently embarked on a colossal history of Rome told in fictional form, starting with Roma *(2007) which charts the growth of Rome from its earliest days to the time of Julius Caesar, and* Empire *(2010) which takes us through to the Emperor Hadrian. But Saylor is probably best known for his stories featuring Gordianus the Finder, who lives by his wits and, because of his acquaintanceship with Cicero in* Roman Blood *(1991), the first book in the series, frequently finds himself involved in the higher level of politics and intrigue in Republican Rome. Other books in the series include* Arms of Nemesis *(1992),* Catilina's Riddle *(1993),* Rubicon *(1999),* The Judgement of Caesar *(2004),* The Triumph of Caesar *(2008) and two collections,* The House of the Vestals *(1997) and* A Gladiator Dies Only Once *(2005).*

Saylor is working on another volume featuring Gordianus but this time set during his early years, against the backcloth of the original Seven Wonders of the World. The following story, set in 92 BC, *takes place at the Temple of Diana (know as Artemis to the Greeks) in Ephesus. Gordianus, aged just eighteen, is on an extended journey accompanied by his former tutor, the poet Antipater of Sidon, who was one of the first to list the Seven Wonders.*

Marina
If fires be hot, knives sharp, or waters deep,
Untied I still my virgin knot will keep.
Diana, aid my purpose!
Bawd
What have we to do with Diana?

—Shakespeare, *Pericles, Prince of Tyre*

"Ah, Ephesus!" cried Antipater. "Most cosmopolitan of all Greek cities – pride of Asia, jewel of the East!" He stood at the prow of the ship and gazed with glittering eyes at the city before us.

As soon as the ship left the open sea and entered the mouth of the Cayster River, Antipater had used his sharp elbows to force his way to the head of the little group of passengers, with me following in his wake; despite his wrinkles and white hair, the old poet was neither shy nor weak. Our first glimpse of Ephesus came as we rounded a little bend and saw an indistinct mass of buildings clustered against a low mountain. Moment by moment we drew nearer, until the city loomed before us.

The harbour was pierced by a long mole that projected far into the water. So many ships had moored alongside, that it seemed impossible we should find a spot, especially because other ships were arriving ahead of us, with their sails aloft and colorful pennants fluttering in the breeze. By the Roman calendar this was Aprilis, but in Ephesus this was the holy month of Artemision, marked by one festival after another in honour of the city's patron goddess, Artemis. Antipater had told me that the celebrations drew tens of thousands of visitors from all over the Greek-speaking world, and it appeared he had not been exaggerating.

A harbour-master in a small boat sailed out to inform the captain that there was no room for our ship to dock at the mole. We would have to pitch anchor and await a ferryboat to take the passengers ashore. The ferrymen would have to be paid, of course, and Antipater grumbled at the extra expense, but I was glad for the chance to remain for a while in the harbour and take in the view.

Beyond the crowded wharves rose the famous five-mile walls of Ephesus. Where the mole met the shore these walls were pierced by an ornamental gate flanked by towers. The tall doors of the gate stood wide open, welcoming all the world into the city of Artemis – for a price, Antipater explained, for he anticipated that we would have to pay a special fee to enter the city during the festival. Beyond the walls I saw the rooftops of temples and tall apartment buildings. Further away, clustered on the slope of Mount Pion, were a great many houses. Some were like palaces, with ornate terraces and hillside gardens.

The most prominent building to be seen was the enormous theatre built into the hillside. The semicircular tiers of seats that faced the harbour were filled with tens of thousands of spectators; apparently they were watching a comedy, for every now and then I heard a burst of distant laughter. Scores of towering, brightly painted statues lined the uppermost rim of the theatre; these images of gods and heroes appeared to be gazing not at the stage below them but across the rooftops of the city, straight at me.

"I see the famous theatre," I said, shading my eyes against the late-morning sun above Mount Pion, "but where is the great Temple of Artemis?"

Antipater snorted. "Gordianus! Have you forgotten the geography I taught you? Your head is like a sieve, boy."

I bridled at being called a boy – I was eighteen, after all – then smiled as the lesson came back to me. "I remember now. The Temple of Artemis was built outside the city, about a mile inland, on low, marshy ground. It must be . . . somewhere over there." I pointed to a spot beyond the steep northern slope of Mount Pion.

Antipater raised a bushy eyebrow. "Very good. And why did the builders chose that site for the temple?"

"Because they decided that building on marshy soil would soften the effect of earthquakes on such a massive structure."

"Correct. To further stabilize the ground, before the cornerstone was laid, they spread a deep layer of crushed charcoal. And then what?"

"Atop the charcoal they put down many layers of fleece, taken from sheep sacrificed in honour of the goddess."

"You are an apt pupil after all, my boy," said Antipater, gratifying and irritating me in the same breath.

The sun was directly above our heads by the time a ferryboat arrived. Antipater again elbowed his way to the front, with me following, so that we were among the first to be ferried ashore. As soon as we alighted on the mole, a group of boys swarmed around us. Antipater chose the two who looked most honest to him and tossed them each a coin. They gathered our travelling bags and followed after us.

We strolled up the mole, which seemed like a small city itself; the crowded ships were like dwellings along a broad thoroughfare. I saw people everywhere, heard babies crying, and noticed that many of the masts were strung with laundry. A great many of the visitors to Ephesus, unable to find accommodations in the city, were apparently residing aboard ship.

"Where will we stay in Ephesus?" I asked.

"Years ago, when I lived here for a while, I had a pupil named Eutropius," said Antipater. "I haven't seen him since, but we've corresponded over the years. Eutropius is grown now, a widower with a child of his own. He inherited his father's house, about halfway up the hill, not far from the theatre. Eutropius has done rather well for himself, so I'm sure our accommodations will be quite comfortable."

We reached the end of the mole and arrived at the open gate, where people stood in long queues to be admitted to the city. I was unsure which queue we should get into, until one of the gatekeepers shouted, in Latin, "Roman citizens and their parties in this line! Roman citizens, queue here!"

As we stepped into the line, I noticed that some in the crowd gave us dirty looks. The line was shorter than the others, and moved more quickly. Soon we stood before a man in a ridiculously tall hat a bit like a quail's plume – only a bureaucrat would wear such a thing – who glanced at my iron citizen's ring as I handed him the travelling papers my father had secured for me before I left Rome.

Speaking Latin, the official read aloud: " 'Gordianus, citizen of Rome, born in the consulship of Gaius Marius and Lucius Valerius Flaccus' – that makes you what, eighteen years old? – 'of average height with dark hair and regular features, no distinguishing marks, speaks Latin and some Greek' – and with an atrocious accent, I'll wager." The man eyed me with barely concealed contempt.

"His Greek accent is actually rather good," said Antipater. "Certainly better than your Latin accent."

"And who are you?"

"I am the young man's travelling companion, formerly his tutor. Zoticus of Zeugma." Antipater gave the name under which he was travelling incognito. "And you would not be speaking to us this way if my friend were older and wearing his toga and followed by a retinue of slaves. But Gordianus is no less a citizen than any other Roman, and you will treat him with respect – or else I shall report you to the provincial governor."

The official took a long look at Antipater, made a sour face, then handed my documents back to me and waved us on.

"You certainly put that fellow in his place!" I said with a laugh.

"Yes, well . . . I fear you may encounter more than a little of that sort of thing here in Ephesus, Gordianus."

"What do you mean?"

"Anti-Roman sentiment runs deep throughout the province of Asia – through all the Greek-speaking provinces for that matter – but especially here in Ephesus."

"But why?"

"The Roman governor based at Pergamon taxes the people mercilessly. And there are a great many Romans in the city – thousands of them, all claiming special privileges, taking the best seats at the theatre, rewarding each other with places of honour at the festivals, sucking up the profits from the import and export trade, even sticking their fingers into the treasury at the Temple of Artemis – which is the great bank for all of Asia, and the lifeblood of Ephesus. I'm afraid, in the forty years since the Romans established their authority here, a great deal of resentment has been stirred up. If even a petty document-checker at the gate feels he can speak to you that way, I fear to imagine how others will behave. I think it might be best if we speak no more Latin while we're here in Ephesus, Gordianus, even among ourselves. Others may overhear and make assumptions."

Somewhere in the middle of this discourse, he had switched from Latin to Greek, and it took my mind a moment to catch up.

"That may be . . . a challenge," I finally said, pausing to think of the Greek word.

Antipater sighed. "Your words may be Greek, but your accent is decidedly Roman."

"You told the document-checker I had a good accent!"

"Yes, well ... perhaps you should simply speak as little as possible."

We followed the crowd and found ourselves in a market-place thronged with pilgrims and tourists, where vendors sold all sorts of foodstuffs as well as a great variety of talismans. There were miniature replicas of Artemis's temple as well as images of the goddess herself. These images came in various sizes and were fashioned from various materials: from crudely made terra cotta and wooden trinkets, to statuettes that displayed the highest standards of craftsmanship, some advertised as being cast of solid gold.

I paused to admire a statuette of the goddess in her Ephesian guise, which seems so exotic to Roman eyes. Our Artemis – we call her Diana – is a virgin huntress; she carries a bow and wears a short, simple tunic suitable for the chase. But the manifestation of the goddess here – presumably more ancient – stood stiffly upright with her bent elbows against her body, her forearms extended and her hands open. She wore a mural crown, and outlining her head was a nimbus decorated with winged bulls. More bulls, along with other animals, adorned the stiff garment that covered her lower body, almost like a mummy casing. From her neck hung a necklace of acorns, and below this I saw the most striking feature of Artemis of Ephesus: a mass of pendulous, gourd-shaped protrusions that hung in a cluster from her upper body. I might have taken these for multiple breasts, had Antipater not explained to me that these protrusions were bulls' testicles. Many bulls would be sacrificed to the virgin goddess during the festival.

I picked up the image to look at it more closely. The gold was quite heavy.

"Don't touch unless you intend to buy!" snapped the vendor, a gaunt man with a long beard. He snatched the little statue from my hand.

"Sorry," I said, lapsing into Latin. The vendor gave me a nasty look.

We moved on. "Do you think that image was really made of solid gold?" I asked Antipater.

"Yes, and therefore far beyond your means."

"Do people really buy such expensive items for keepsakes?"

"Not for keepsakes, but to make offerings. Pilgrims purchase whichever of the images they can afford, then donate them to the Temple of Artemis as an act of propitiation to the goddess."

"But the priests must collect thousands of talismans."

"Megabyzoi – the priests are called Megabyzoi," he explained. "And yes, they collect many talismans during the festivals."

"What do the Megabyzoi do with all those images?"

"The offerings are added to the wealth of the temple treasury, of course."

I looked at the vast number of people around us. The open-air market seemed to stretch on forever. "So the vendors make a nice profit selling the images, and the temple receives a hefty income from all those offerings."

Antipater smiled. "Don't forget what the pilgrims receive – participation in one of the most beloved religious festivals in the world, an open air feast, and the favour of the goddess, including her protection on their journey home. But the donation of these trinkets is only a tiny part of the temple's income. Rich men from many cities and even foreign kings store their fortunes in the temple's vaults and pay a handsome fee for the service; that vast reservoir of wealth allows the Megabyzoi to make loans, charging handsome interest. Artemis of Ephesus owns vineyards and quarries, pastures and salt-beds, fisheries and sacred herds of deer. The Temple of Artemis is one of the world's great storehouses of wealth – and every Roman governor spends his tenure trying to figure out some way to get his hands on it."

We bought some goat's cheese on a skewer from a vendor and slowly made our way through the crowd. The crush lessened as we ascended a winding street that took us halfway up Mount Pion, where we at last arrived at the house of Eutropius.

"It's larger than I remember it," said Antipater, gazing at the immaculately maintained façade. "I do believe he's added a storey since I was here."

The slave who answered the door dismissed our baggage carriers and instructed some underlings to take our things to the guest quarters. We were shown to a garden at the centre of the house where our host reclined on a couch, apparently just waking from a nap. Eutropius was perhaps forty – with a robust physique and the first touch of frost in his golden hair – and wore a beautifully tailored robe spun from coarse silk dyed a rich saffron hue. He sprang up and approached Antipater with open arms.

"Teacher!" he exclaimed. "You haven't aged a bit."

"Nonsense!" Antipater gestured to his white hair, but smiled, pleased by the compliment. He introduced me to our host, and we all exchanged pleasantries.

The air above our heads resounded with the sound of a great many people laughing.

"From the theatre," explained Eutropius.

"But why are you not there?" asked Antipater.

"Bah! Plays bore me – all those actors making terrible puns and behaving like idiots. You taught me to love poetry, Teacher, but I'm afraid you were never able to imbue me with a love of comedy."

"Artemis herself enjoys the performances," said Antipater.

"So they say – even when they're as wooden as she is," said Eutropius. Antipater cackled, but I missed the joke.

Antipater drew a sharp breath. "But who is this?"

"Anthea!" Eutropius strode to embrace the girl who had just entered the garden. She was a few years younger than I, and golden haired like her father. She wore a knee-length purple tunic cinched with a silver chain tied below breasts just beginning to bud. The garment hung loosely over her shoulders, baring her arms, which were surprisingly tawny. (A Roman girl of the same social standing would have creamy-white limbs, and would never display them to a stranger.) She wore a necklace of gilded acorns and a fawnskin cape. Strapped across her shoulder was a quiver filled with brightly painted, miniature arrows. In one hand she carried a dainty little bow – clearly a ceremonial weapon – and in the other an equally dainty javelin.

"Is it Artemis herself I see?" whispered Antipater in a dreamy voice. I was thinking the same thing myself. The exotic Ephesian Artemis of the talismans was alien to me, but this was the Diana I knew, virgin goddess of the hunt.

Eutropius gazed proudly at his daughter. "Anthea turned fourteen just last month. This is her first year to take part in the procession."

"No one in the crowd will look at anyone else," declared Antipater, at which the girl lowered her eyes and blushed.

As lovely as Anthea was, my attention was suddenly claimed by the slave girl who followed her into the garden. She was older than her mistress, perhaps my own age, with lustrous black hair, dark eyes and a long, straight nose. She wore a dark blue tunic with sleeves that came to her elbows, cinched with a thin leather belt. Her figure was more womanly than Anthea's and her demeanour less girlish. She smiled, apparently pleased at the fuss we were making over her mistress, and when she saw me looking at her, she stared back at me and raised an eyebrow. My cheeks turned hot and I looked away.

"Look at you, blushing back at Anthea!" whispered Antipater, mistaking the cause of my reaction.

Another burst of laughter resounded above us, followed by long, sustained applause.

"I do believe that means the play is over," said Eutropius. "Teacher, if you and Gordianus would like to wash up a bit and change your clothes before the procession begins, you'd better do it quickly."

I looked up at the sky, which was beginning to fade as twilight approached. "A procession? But it'll be dark soon."

"Exactly," said Antipater. "The procession of Artemis takes place after sundown."

"Roman festivals happen in daylight," I muttered, lapsing into my native tongue.

"Well, you are not in Rome anymore," said Antipater. "So stop speaking Latin!"

"I'll call for the porter to show you to your quarters," said Eutropius. But, before he could clap his hands, the slave girl stepped forward.

"I'll do it, master," she said. She stood directly in front of me and trained her gaze on me. I realized, with some discomfort, that to meet her eyes I had to look up a bit. She was slightly taller than I.

"Very well, Amestris," said Eutropius, with a vague wave.

We followed Amestris down a short hallway and up a flight of stairs. Her shapely hips swayed as she ascended the steps ahead of us.

She showed Antipater to his room, then led me to the one next to it. It was small but opulently appointed. A balcony offered a view of the harbour. On a little table I saw a basin of water and a sponge.

"Will you require help to bathe yourself?" said Amestris, standing in the doorway.

I stared at her for a long moment. "No," I finally managed to say, in Latin – for at that moment, even the simplest Greek deserted me. Amestris made an elegant bow that caused her breasts to dangle voluptuously for a moment, then backed away.

"Amestris – that's a Persian name, isn't it?" I blurted, finally thinking of something to say.

For an answer, she merely nodded, then withdrew. I could have sworn I heard her laughing quietly.

After we had refreshed ourselves and changed into our most colourful tunics, Antipater and I rejoined our host in the garden. Eutropius had been joined by another man about his own age and of his own class, to judge by the newcomer's expensive-looking garments. Anthea had also been joined by a friend, a girl attired exactly as she was, in the guise of Artemis the huntress, but with flowing red hair and plainer features.

"This is my friend and business partner, Mnason," said Eutropius, "and this is his daughter, Chloe, who will also be taking part in the procession for the first time." Under his breath he added, to Antipater, "The two of us are both widowers, sadly, so quite often we take part in festivals and civic celebrations together with our daughters."

The six of us set out. Amestris came along as well, apparently to make sure that all was perfect for Anthea and Chloe's appearance in the procession. I deliberately kept my eyes off her, determined to take in the sights and sounds of the festive city.

A short walk brought us to the main entrance of the theatre. There were a great many people in the square, and the crowd was still issuing out. Everyone looked quite cheerful, and, for those who needed more cheering up, vendors were selling wine. Some in the crowd had brought their own cups, but the vendors were also selling ornamental cups made of copper, or silver, or even gold set with stones; like the talismans for sale in the market, these precious objects were destined to be offered to Artemis at the end of the procession.

As darkness fell, lamps were lit all around the square, casting a flickering orange glow across the sea of smiling faces. The crowd suddenly grew hushed. A way was cleared in front of the theatre entrance. I assumed some dignitary, perhaps the Roman governor, was about to make his exit. Instead, a statue of Artemis emerged, carried aloft by a small group of priests wearing bright yellow robes and tall yellow headdresses.

Antipater spoke in my ear. "Those are the Megabyzoi, and that statue is *the* Artemis of Ephesus, the model for all the replicas we saw in the market-place."

The statue was made not of stone or bronze, but of wood, probably ebony to judge by the few areas that were not adorned with bright paint. Her face and hands were gilded. An elaborately embroidered robe with broad sleeves had been fitted over her body, and a veil covered her face. A wagon festooned with wreaths and strings of beads approached, drawn by bulls decorated with ribbons and garlands. The Megabyzoi carrying the statue gently placed it upright in the wagon.

Suddenly I understood Eutropius's pun about the wooden statue watching a wooden performance. Artemis herself, brought from her temple and specially dressed for the occasion, had been the guest of honour at the play.

The wagon rolled forward. With Artemis leading the way, others began to take their place in the procession. Musicians with flutes, horns, lyres, and tambourines appeared. Eutropius gave his daughter a kiss on the forehead, and Mnason did likewise, then Anthea and Chloe ran to join a group of similarly dressed girls who took a place in the procession behind the musicians. The girls performed a curious dance, leaping in the air and then crouching down, looking this way and that, mimicking the movements of birds. Then the hunted became hunters, as in unison the girls raised their little bows, notched miniature arrows, and shot them in the air. Women in the crowd laughed and rushed forward, trying to catch the harmless arrows as they fell.

"The arrows are tokens of childbirth," Antipater explained. "The women who catch them hope to enjoy a quick conception and an easy delivery."

"But how is it that a virgin goddess is also a fertility goddess?" I asked.

Antipater's sigh made me feel quite the ignorant Roman. "So it has always been. Because she herself does not conceive, Artemis is able to act as helpmate to those who do."

The dancers put their bows over their shoulders, pulled the little javelins from their belts, and began a new dance, forming a circle and rhythmically tapping their javelins against the ground inside the circle and then outside. Even among so many young and lovely girls, Anthea stood out. From others in the crowd I overheard many comments about her beauty, and more than one observer echoed Antipater's observation that she appeared to personify the goddess herself.

The wagon bearing Artemis rolled out of sight around a corner. The musicians and dancing girls followed. Close behind the girls came a large contingent of boys and youths wearing colourful finery; these were athletes who would be taking part in various competitions in the days to come. Cattle, sheep, goats, and oxen destined for sacrifice were herded into the procession by the representatives of various trade guilds and other organizations who carried aloft their symbols and implements. Antipater explained to me how all these diverse groups figured in the long and fabled history of the city, but most of what he said went in one ear and out the other. I was distracted by the presence of Amestris, who followed our party, keeping a discreet distance. Every so often our eyes met. Invariably, it was I who looked away first.

At the very end of the official procession came the Megabyzoi, a great many of them, all wearing bright yellow robes and headdresses. Some carried sacred objects, including knives and axes for sacrifice, while others waved burning bundles of incense. The scented smoke wafted over the vast crowd of Ephesians and pilgrims that moved forward to follow the procession.

"Aren't the Megabyzoi eunuchs?" I said, recalling something I'd once heard and trying to get a better look at the priests over the heads of the crowd.

Eutropius and Mnason both laughed, and Antipater gave me an indulgent smile. "Once upon a time, that was indeed the case," he said. "But your information is a few centuries out of date, Gordianus. The ritual castration of the priests of Artemis ended many generations ago. Even so, the goddess still demands that those in her service, both male and female, be sexually pure. Though his manhood remains intact, each Megabyzus takes a vow to remain unmarried and celibate for as long as he serves in the priesthood of Artemis."

"That seems practical," I said.

"What do you mean?"

"With all the wealth that flows into the temple coffers, it's probably a good thing that the priests aren't married men. Otherwise, they might be tempted to put their own children ahead of their sacred service."

"Gordianus is wise for his years," said Eutropius. "What father doesn't do all he can for his child? The chastity of the Megabyzoi should, in theory, make them less greedy. But sometimes I think it only makes them more grumpy. And it certainly doesn't keep them from meddling in politics."

Mnason raised an eyebrow, glanced at me, then gestured to his friend to be quiet. Did he feel the need to be discreet because I was Roman?

Antipater ignored them. "How can I explain this to you, Gordianus? Think of the Roman goddess Vesta, and how vital it is for the well-being of Rome that the Vestals maintain their virginity. So it is with Ephesian Artemis. Chastity is absolutely essential for those who serve her, and not just her priests, or the women who work in the temple, called hierodules. All the girls who dance in the procession today must be virgins. Indeed, no freeborn female who is not a virgin may so much as step foot inside the Temple of Artemis, upon pain of death."

We followed the procession out of the square and down a broad, paved street called the Sacred Way, lit all long its length with torches. After we passed though a broad gate in the city's northern wall, these torches were set farther apart and in the intervening patches of deep shadow I could see the starry sky above our heads.

The Sacred Way took us gradually downhill. In the valley ahead, at the end of the winding line of torches, I saw our destination – the great Temple of Artemis. A huge crowd of pilgrims, many carrying torches, had already gathered at the temple to welcome the procession. The structure had the unearthly appearance of a vast, rectangular forest of glowing columns, afloat in a pool of light. Though it was still almost a mile away, the temple already looked enormous. Antipater had told me it was the largest temple ever built by the Greeks – four times the size of the famous Parthenon atop the Acropolis in Athens.

The temple loomed larger with each step I took, and the closer I drew to it, the more astonished I was by the perfect beauty of the place. Gleaming marble steps led up to the broad porch. The massive walls of the sanctuary were surrounded by a double row of columns at least sixty feet high. White marble predominated, but many of the sculptural details had been highlighted with red, blue, or yellow paint, as well as touches of gleaming gold.

Even to my untrained and untravelled eye, the elegance of the columns was breathtaking. The bases were decorated with elaborate carvings, and each of the capitals ended in a graceful spiral curve to either side.

"It was here that the order of columns called Ionic originated," said Antipater, following my gaze. "The architects deliberately imbued the columns with feminine attributes. Thus you see that the stacked marble drums ascend not to a plain, unadorned capital, but to those elegant whorls on either side, which mimic a woman's curls. The whole length of each column is fluted with shallow channels, in imitation of the pleats of a woman's gown. The proportion of the height to the circumference and the way each column gently tapers is also meant to give them a feminine delicacy."

My eyes followed the columns to the pediment high above the porch, where I saw something I was not used to seeing in a temple – a tall, open window with an elaborate frame around it. I assumed it was there to admit light in the daytime, but, as I was about to discover, this window had a far more important purpose.

In front of the temple, some distance from the steps, a low wall enclosed an elegantly carved altar for sacrificing animals. As the procession arrived before the temple, some of the yellow-robed Megabyzoi broke away from the larger contingent and took up places at this altar, producing ceremonial daggers, ropes for holding down the animals, butchering knives and axes, and other implements for the sacrifices. Other Megabyzoi stoked the pyres upon which the carved and spitted meat would be roasted. Others unloaded the statue of Artemis from the cart, carried her up the steps and into the temple. Yet another group of priests unyoked the garlanded bulls that had pulled the cart and led them towards the altar. A great many other animals, including sheep, goats, and oxen, were already being held in pens in the enclosure. They were to be sacrificed and roasted in the course of the evening, to satiate the appetite of the vast crowd.

The first of the bulls was led up a short ramp on to the altar, pushed to its side, and securely trussed. Megabyzoi intoned prayers to Artemis and walked among the crowd, carrying bowls of smoking incense. One of the priests – apparently the foremost among them to judge by the special embroidery on his robe and the height of his headdress – mounted a platform beside the altar where everyone in the crowd could see him. He raised his arms aloft.

"That's Theotimus," whispered Eutropius to Antipater, "head priest of the Megabyzoi." A certain edge in his voice caused me to look at Eutropius, who scowled as he gazed at the priest. So did Mnason.

The musicians ceased their playing. The girls stopped dancing. The crowd fell silent.

"People of Ephesus," cried Theotimus, "welcomed visitors, all who have gathered here for the love and adoration of the goddess, the sacrifices are ready to begin. If our rituals in your honour are pleasing to you, great Artemis – protector of virgins, supreme huntress, patron of wild places, benefactor since its beginning of the grateful city of Ephesus – we beg you, Artemis, to step forth and witness our propitiations to you."

The expectant crowd turned its gaze from the priest to the window set high in the temple. From within came a flicker of light, and then the goddess appeared at the window, her outstretched hands open in a gesture of acceptance. The apparition was so uncanny that it took me a moment to realize that I was seeing the statue that had been paraded in the cart. Unless Artemis had propelled herself, the priests had somehow managed to get the image all the way up to the window. Her veil had been removed and her gilded face shone brightly, reflecting the light of the torches and the roasting-pyres around the altar.

As the crowd erupted in cheers, Theotimus strode to the altar, lifted a dagger high above his head, and plunged the blade into the bull's heart. The bound creature bellowed and thrashed, then fell limp. With a single, deft movement, the Megabyzus sliced off the bull's testicles and held them aloft. The crowd again erupted in cheers.

"For Artemis!" shouted Theotimus, and others took up the cry: "For Artemis!"

Eutropius saw the dumbfounded expression on my face. I was used to seeing animal sacrifice, but I had never witnessed a post-mortem castration. "The sacred testes are reserved for the virgin goddess; the rest will be for us," said my host matter-of-factly. "I'm rather partial to the meat of the flank myself, especially if it's nicely grilled."

One beast after another was slain, with Artemis looking on from her high window, and the process of carving and cooking the meat began. The crowd gradually broke into groups, moving forward to receive their portion according to rules of rank and seniority determined by the Megabyzoi, who moved among the crowd to keep order – especially among those who had imbibed a great deal of wine. Clouds of smoke enveloped the crowd, and the smell of roasting meat mingled with the sweet fragrance of incense.

"Unless the two of you are terribly hungry, Teacher, this would be a good time for your young Roman friend to have a look inside the temple," suggested Eutropius. "Anthea and Chloe and the other virgins will be performing more dances."

Antipater declared this a splendid idea, and together we followed our host and Mnason up the broad marble steps and to the porch. Amestris came with us. Did that mean she was a virgin? Then I recalled Antipater's precise words – that no *freeborn* female could enter the temple unless she was a virgin. Perhaps this stricture did not extend to slaves . . .

I shook my head and put aside this train of thought. What business was it of mine, whether the slave was a virgin or not?

Striding between the towering columns, we entered the grandest space I had ever seen. The sanctuary was lit by many lamps and decorated with many statues, but was so vast that no part of it seemed cluttered. The floor was of shimmering marble in a dizzying array of patterns and colours. High above our heads was a ceiling of massive cedar beams, alternately painted red, yellow and blue, outlined with gold and decorated with gold ornaments. Adorning the marble walls were paintings of breathtaking beauty. Surely every tale ever told of Artemis was illustrated somewhere upon these vast walls, along with the images of many other gods and heroes.

Antipater drew my attention to the most famous painting in the temple, the gigantic portrait of Alexander the Great by Apelles. By some trick of colouring and perspective, the conqueror's hand and the thunderbolt it held appeared to come out of the wall and hover in space above our heads. The effect was astounding.

The acoustics of the space were also extraordinary, amplifying and somehow enhancing the tune being played by the musicians who had taken part in the procession. They stood to one side, while in the centre of the vast space, the virgins dressed as Artemis performed another dance with a crowd looking on.

"They're enacting the story of Actaeon," whispered Eutropius, leading us closer. I saw that one of the girls had put on a Phrygian cap and wrapped a cloak around herself to play the part of the young hunter; from her red hair, I realized it was Chloe. Other girls, with dog pelts over their heads and shoulders, played the part of Actaeon's hounds. Others, holding bits of foliage, acted as trees. Actaeon, thirsty and eager to reach a pool hidden by the trees, pushed aside the leafy branches – at his touch the dancers yielded and twirled away – until, suddenly, the goddess Artemis was revealed, bathing in the imaginary pool.

Beside me, Antipater drew a sharp breath. I stifled a gasp and glanced at Eutropius, who smiled proudly. It was Anthea who played the startled goddess, and there was nothing imaginary about her nakedness. The milky white perfection of her small breasts and pale nipples seemed to glow in the soft interior light of the temple, radiating an almost supernatural beauty.

The music rose to a shrill crescendo. The hunter looked as startled as the goddess. Artemis reached for her tunic to cover herself, and Actaeon moved to avert his eyes, but too late. Anthea threw her tunic into the air and raised her arms; the garment seemed to float down and cover her nakedness of its own volition. She whirled about, waving her arms wildly and mimicking a furious expression. Suddenly her whirling stopped and she froze in an attitude of accusation, pointing at Actaeon, who drew back in terror.

As Chloe darted this way and that, the forest closed around her, concealing her. The music abruptly stopped, then resumed with a new, menacing theme. The dancers playing trees drew back, revealing Actaeon transformed into a stag. Chloe now wore a deerskin, and completely covering her head was a mask of a young stag with small antlers.

The dancers playing the forest dispersed; those playing the hounds converged. To a cacophony of yelping pipes and agitated rattles, the hounds pursued the leaping stag until they surrounded it. Around and around they whirled, tormenting the stag who had once been their master. Chloe was completely hidden from sight, except for the stag's-head mask with antlers, which whirled around and around with the hounds.

The frenzied music changed. The hounds drew back. The stag's head fell to the floor, trailing blood-red streamers. Of Actaeon – torn to pieces in the story – nothing more remained to be seen.

Amid the whirling crush of the dancing hounds, Chloe must have removed the stag's head, pulled a dog's hide over her costume, and disappeared among the hounds. It was a simple trick, but the effect was uncanny. It seemed as if the hounds had literally devoured their prey.

Nearby, Anthea looked on with a suitably stern expression. Artemis had exacted a terrible vengeance on the mortal who had dared, however inadvertently, to gaze upon her nakedness.

Suddenly, one of the dancers screamed. Other girls cried out. The company began to scatter.

The music trailed off and fell silent. In the middle of the temple, one of the dancers lay crumpled on the floor. By her red hair, I knew it was Chloe.

Mnason rushed to his daughter. Eutropius hurried after him. I began to follow, but Antipater held me back.

"Let's not get in the way, Gordianus. Probably the poor girl merely fainted – from excitement, perhaps ..." His words lacked conviction. Antipater could see as clearly as could I that there was something unnatural in the way Chloe was lying, with her limbs twisted and her head thrown back. Mnason reached her and crouched over the motionless body for a moment, then threw back his head and let out a cry of anguish.

"She's dead!" someone shouted. "Chloe is dead!"

There were cries of dismay, followed by murmurs and whispers.

"Dead, did someone say?"

"Surely not!"

"But see how her father weeps?"

"What happened? Did anyone see anything?"

"Look – someone must have alerted the Megabyzoi, for here comes Theotimus."

Striding into the sanctuary, the head Megabyzus passed directly by me. He reeked of the smell of burning flesh and his yellow robes were spattered with blood.

"What's going on here?" His booming voice reverberated through the temple, silencing the crowd, which parted before him. Even Mnason drew back. The Megabyzus strode to the girl's body and knelt beside it.

Amid the hubbub and confusion, I noticed that the stag's-head mask was still lying on the floor. Chloe was the focus of all attention; no one seemed interested in the mask. I walked over to it, knelt down, and picked it up. What instinct led me to do so? Antipater would later say it was the hand of Artemis that guided me, but I think I was acting on something my father had taught me: *When everyone else is looking at a certain thing, turn your attention to the thing at which they are not looking. You may see what no one else sees.*

The mask was a thing of beauty, superbly crafted, made from the pelt of a deer and real antlers. The eyes were of some flashing green stone; the shiny black nose was made of obsidian. The mask showed signs of wear; probably it had been handed down and used year after year in the same dance, performed by many different virgins at many different festivals. I examined it inside and out – and noticed a curious thing . . .

"Put that down!" shouted the Megabyzus.

I dropped the mask at once.

Theotimus turned from his examination of Chloe, rose to his feet and strode towards me. The look on his face sent a shiver up my spine. There is a reason men like Theotimus rise to become the head of whatever calling they follow. Everything about the man was intimidating; his tall stature and commanding demeanour, his broad shoulders and his booming voice, and, most of all, his flashing eyes – which seemed to bore directly into mine.

"Who are you, to touch an object sacred to the worship of Artemis?"

I opened my mouth, but not a word would come out. Latin and Greek alike deserted me.

Antipater came to my rescue. "The boy is a visitor, Megabyzus. He made an innocent mistake."

"A visitor?"

"From Rome," I managed to blurt out.

"Rome?" Theotimus raised an eyebrow.

Antipater groaned – had he not warned me to be discreet about my origins? – but after giving me a last, hard look, the Megabyzus snatched up the stag mask and seemed to lose interest in me. He turned to the crowd that had gathered around the corpse.

"The girl is dead," he announced. There were cries and groans from the spectators.

"But Megabyzus, what happened to her?" shouted someone.

"There are no marks upon the girl's body. She seems to have died suddenly and without warning. Because her death occurred here in the temple, we must assume that Artemis herself played a role in it."

"No!" cried Mnason. "Chloe was as devoted to Artemis as all the other virgins."

"I am not accusing your daughter of impurity, Mnason. But if Artemis struck her down, we must conclude that the goddess was sorely displeased with some aspect of the sacred ritual." He glanced at the mask in his hands. "I take it the dance of Actaeon was being performed. Who was dancing the part of Artemis?"

The dancers had drawn to one side, where they huddled together, clutching and comforting each other. From their midst, Anthea stepped forward.

The Megabyzus approached her. Eutropius moved to join his daughter, but the priest raised a hand to order him back.

Theotimus towered over the girl, staring down at her. Anthea quailed under his gaze, trembled, and bit her lip. She began to weep.

The Megabyzus turned to address the spectators. "The girl is impure," he announced.

"No!" shouted Eutropius. "That's a lie!"

There were gasps from the crowd.

"You dare to accuse the head of the Megabyzoi of lying?" said Theotimus. "Here in the very sanctuary of Artemis?"

Eutropius was flummoxed. He clenched his fists and his face turned bright red. "No, Megabyzus, of course not," he finally muttered. "But my daughter is innocent, I tell you. She is a virgin. There must be a test—"

"Of course there will be a test," said Theotimus, "just as Artemis decrees in such a terrible circumstance as this. My fellow Megabyzoi, remove this girl from the temple at once, before her presence can pollute it further."

Priests moved forward to seize Anthea, who shivered and cried out for her father. Eutropius followed after them, ashen-faced. More Megabyzoi picked up the body of Chloe and bore it away, followed by her distraught father. The dancers dispersed, looking for their families. The musicians stared at one another, dumbfounded.

I turned to Antipater, and saw tears in his eyes. He shook his head. "How I looked forward to this day, when I might stand once again in the Temple of Artemis. And how I looked forward to showing it to you, Gordianus. But not like this. What a terrible day! What a disaster!"

I felt someone's eyes on me and turned to see, some distance away, amid the dwindling, dazed crowd that remained in the sanctuary, the slave girl, Amestris. Her gaze was so intense, it seemed to me that she must have something she wanted to tell me, or to ask. But for the first time that day, it was she who looked away first, as she turned and hurriedly left the temple.

The atmosphere was gloomy in the house of Eutropius that night. I imagine the mood was little better in all the other households of Ephesus, for the death in the temple and the accusation against Anthea had put an end to the feasting and celebration. The Megabyzoi had instructed the people to return to their homes and to pray for the guidance of Artemis.

In the garden, Amestris served a frugal meal to Eutropius, Mnason, Antipater and me – though I was the only one who seemed to have any appetite.

"A youth of your age will eat, no matter what the circumstances," said Antipater with a sigh. He passed his untouched bowl of millet and lentils to me.

"No one will ever convince me that it was the will of Artemis that Chloe should die," muttered Mnason, staring into space with a blank expression. "Our enemies are behind this, Eutropius. You know whom I mean."

Eutropius looked not at his friend, but at me. I felt like an intruder.

"If the rest of you don't mind, I'll finish this in my room," I said, picking up my bowl.

"I'll go with you," said Antipater.

"No, Teacher – stay. We could use your advice," said Eutropius He issued no such request to me, and avoided meeting my eyes. I took my leave.

Alone in my room, once the bowl was empty, I found it impossible to simply sit on the bed. I paced for a while, then took off my shoes and walked quietly down the hallway to the top of the stairs; the conversation from the garden carried quite well to that spot. I stood and listened.

"Everyone knows that Theotimus is completely in the grip of the Roman governor," Mnason was saying. "He's determined to bring down all who oppose him – those of us who believe that Ephesus should be free of the Romans."

"But surely you're not saying the Megabyzus had something to do with Chloe's death," said Antipater.

"That's exactly what I'm saying!" cried Mnason, with a sob in his voice.

After a long silence, Eutropius spoke. "It does seem to me that his accusation against Anthea was too well-timed to have been spontaneous. As unthinkable as it sounds, I have to wonder if Theotimus played some part in your daughter's death, and then used it as an excuse to make his foul accusation against Anthea – an accusation that will destroy me as well, if the test goes against her."

"This test – I've heard of it, but I've never witnessed it," said Antipater.

"It's seldom used, Teacher. I can count on the fingers of one hand the occasions it's been performed in my lifetime."

"I seem to recall it involves a cave in the sacred grove of Ortygia," said Antipater.

"Yes. Until the test takes place, the accused girl is kept by the hierodules, the female acolytes who serve under the Megabyzoi.

On the day of the test, they escort the girl to the grove of Ortygia, which is full of wonders and manifestations of divine will. One of the most sacred spots is a cave near the stream where Leto gave birth to Artemis and her twin brother, Apollo. In that cave, hanging by a chain from the ceiling, are some Pan pipes; there's a story that explains how they came to be there, but I won't recount it now. Long ago, an iron door was put in place across the opening of the cave, and only the Megabyzoi have the key. This is the test: if a maiden is accused of having lost her virginity, the truth of the matter can be determined by shutting her up in the cave, alone. If she is truly a virgin, the Pan pipes play a melody – whether Pan himself performs on the pipes, or a divine wind blows through them, no one knows – and the door opens of its accord, allowing the virgin to emerge with her reputation for purity intact."

"And if the girl is not a virgin?"

"Then the pipes are silent, and the girl is never seen again."

"She dies in the cave?" said Antipater with gasp.

"The door is opened the next day, and the Megabyzoi enter, but no body is ever found. As I said, the girl is simply . . . never seen again." Eutropius spoke with a quaver in his voice.

"So the sacred cave is exclusively in the keeping of the Megabyzoi?" said Antipater.

"Of course, as are all the sacred places of Artemis."

"But if you suspect Theotimus to be capable of murder – indeed, of profaning the very Temple of Artemis with such a crime – then might he not contrive to somehow falsify the virgin test, as well? You must protest, Eutropius. You must come forward with your suspicions."

"Without proof? With no evidence at all, except for Theotimus's animus towards Mnason and myself, because we hate the Romans? The Roman governor certainly won't help us, and if we dare to impugn the validity of the virgin test, the people will turn against us as well. We'll be accused of sacrilege and put on trial ourselves."

"And subjected to some other supernatural test equally under the control of Theotimus, no doubt." Antipater sighed. "You find yourselves in a terrible situation."

"It's the Romans who've turned the priests against their own people," muttered Mnason. "The Megabyzoi should be the champions of the people, not their enemy."

"To be fair," said Eutropius, "there are divisions within the Megabyzoi. Most are as loyal to Ephesus and to the Greek way of life as you and I, Mnason. Theotimus is the exception, but he also happens to be the head priest. He always takes the side of the Romans, and he does all he can to silence those of us who oppose them. That sorry state of affairs will all change when Mithridates comes."

Mithridates! No wonder they dared not speak openly in front of me, a Roman. Mithridates was the King of Pontus, which bordered Rome's territories in the East. For years he had been positioning himself as the rival of Rome, offering his rule to the Greek-speaking peoples of Asia Minor as an alternative to the Romans. Everyone in Rome said that an all out war with Mithridates was inevitable. It was clear which side Eutropius and his friends would take. Perhaps they were even agents for the king.

"Mithridates may indeed drive the Romans out of Ephesus someday," said Antipater quietly, "but that is of no use to us here and now. What can we do to save Anthea?"

"We must pray that Artemis is more powerful than the corrupt priest who speaks in her name," said Eutropius quietly. "I must pray that the virgin test will give a true answer, and that Anthea will be vindicated."

There followed a long silence from the garden. I suddenly felt that I was being watched, and turned to see Amestris behind me.

"Did you need something, Roman?" she said.

"How long have you been standing there?"

"About as long as you have." She flashed a crooked smile.

I swallowed hard. "Then you heard everything that I heard."

"Yes."

"This grove called Ortygia – where is it?"

"Not far from the city. You take the Sacred Way, but you go in the opposite direction from the Temple of Artemis, to the south. Outside the city walls, the road turns west and goes up a steep hill, where a cliff overlooks the harbour. Go a little further, and you arrive at the sacred grove."

"And this cave they spoke of?"

"The Sacred Way leads directly to it."

"I see."

"Why do you ask, Roman?"

I shrugged. "Antipater says I should learn the geography of all the places we visit."

"You'll see where the cave is, soon enough. The whole city will march out there tomorrow, to see the test performed." There was a catch in her voice, and she lowered her eyes. "Poor Anthea!"

"Do you not believe that she's a virgin?"

"I know she is. My mistress and I have no secrets from each other. But I fear the test, even so."

"Yes, so do I," I said quietly. There was more talk from the garden, too low to make out, and the rustle of men rising from their chairs. "I should go back to my room now."

"And I should see if my master requires anything else."

I watched her walk down the stairs, then returned to my room. A little later I heard Antipater enter the room next to mine. The old fellow must have been completely exhausted, for only moments later I heard the sound of his snoring through the wall.

I rose from my bed, slipped into my shoes, and pulled a light cloak over my tunic. The front door would be barred, with a slave sleeping beside it; might there be some way to descend from the balcony outside my bedroom? By the bright moonlight, I saw a good spot to land, should I jump. I had no idea if I could climb back up again, but I decided not to worry about that.

The jump and the landing were easier than I had hoped. I found my way to the front of the house, and from there retraced the route we had taken to the theatre, where I had no trouble locating the Sacred Way. The torches that had lit the street so brightly earlier had gone out. According to Amestris, my goal lay in the direction opposite to the one we had taken to the temple, so I turned about and headed south. Bathed by moonlight, the unfamiliar precinct seemed at once beautiful and eerie. I passed the elegant façades of grand houses, gymnasia, temples, and shopping porticoes, but saw not a single person. The goddess had been gravely offended on her feast day, and the people of Ephesus were keeping to their houses.

I had worried that I might encounter a locked gate in the city wall, but the high doors stood wide open, and a group of officials, including some Megabyzoi – the first people I had seen – were conversing in a huddle to one side of the Sacred Way, discussing preparations for the trial that would take place the next day, when thousands of people would pass through this gate.

I stole through the opening and kept to the shadows, following the Sacred Way through a region of gravesites and then up a hill, where the road became more winding and narrow, and the paving more uneven. Now and again, beyond the rocks and trees to my right, I caught glimpses of the harbour. The woods became thicker; cypresses towered above me, and the smell of cedars scented the cool night air. I heard the splashing of a stream nearby, and gasped to think that I might be standing on the very place where Artemis and Apollo had been born.

I came at last to an opening in the woods. Across a meadow bright with moonlight, in the centre of a rocky outcrop, I saw the door of the cave. The polished iron glinted in the light.

I circled the meadow, keeping in shadow, until I reached the door. From my tunic I took out a small bag my father had given me before I left on my travels. In it were some tools he had taught me to use; some were quite old, veritable antiques, while others he had invented himself. While other fathers were teaching their sons to barter in the market, or build a wall, or speak in the Forum, my father had taught me everything he knew about picking locks.

I was happily surprised to discover that no guard of any sort had been set on the door; the whole meadow and the grove all around appeared to be deserted. Perhaps the place was considered too sacred for any mortal to inhabit except on ritual occasions.

Still, I dared not strike a flame, and so I had to work by moonlight. The lock was of a sort I had never encountered before. I tried one tool, then another. At last I found an implement that seemed to fit the keyhole, and yet I could not make the lock yield, no matter how I twisted or turned the tool – until suddenly I heard a bolt drop, and the door gave way.

The fact that I might be committing a crime against the goddess gave me pause. I was poised to enter the cave – but would I ever step foot outside it? I took heart from something my father had told me: *The threat of divine punishment is often invoked by mortals for the sake of their own self-interest. You should always evaluate such claims using your own judgement. I myself have made a lifelong habit*

*of violating so-called divine laws, and yet here I stand before you, alive
and well, and at peace with the gods.*

I stepped inside the cave, leaving the door open behind me
as my eyes adjusted to the greater darkness. The cave was not
completely black; here and there, from narrow fissures above
my head, shafts of moonlight pierced the darkness. I began to
perceive the general shape of the chamber around me, and saw
that it opened on to a larger one beyond. That chamber was
illuminated by even brighter shafts of moonlight. Dangling from
a rocky roof three or four times the height of a man, suspended
from a silver chain, I saw the Pan pipes. They were in the very
centre of the chamber and I could see no way to reach them.

A third chamber lay beyond. It was the smallest and the darkest.
Only by feeling my way around the walls did I discover a small
door, hardly big enough to admit a stooping man. I attempted
to pick the lock, but I dropped my tools, and in the darkness
despaired of retrieving them. As I was searched about, my hands
chanced upon several objects, including a knife and an axe of the
sort the Megabyzoi used to sacrifice animals, and a sack of some
strong material, large enough to accommodate a small body.

Then I touched something bony and pointed, like a horn,
which seemed to be attached to an animal's hide.

I gave a cry and started back, hitting my head on a outcrop
of stone. By the dim light, I saw the glinting eyes of some beast,
very close to the ground, staring up at me. My heart pounded.
What was this creature? Why did it make no noise? Was this the
guardian of the cave, some horned monster set here by Artemis
to gore to death an impious intruder like myself?

Gradually, I perceived the true shape of the thing that seemed
to gaze up at me. It was the stag's-head mask that had been worn
by Chloe in the dance of Actaeon.

I picked it up and carried it into the larger chamber, where I
could examine it by a better light.

Suddenly I realized that I had never shut the door by which I
had entered. I returned to the antechamber, pulled the door shut,
and heard the bolt drop into place inside.

Taking my time, I retrieved the tools I had dropped and
eventually managed to open the door in the third chamber.
Fresh air blew against my face. I ventured a few paces outside

and found myself in a rocky defile overgrown by thickets. No apparent path led away from it. Clearly, this was a secret rear entrance to the cave.

I stepped back inside the cave and locked the small door behind me. I returned to the large chamber and tried to find a comfortable spot. I had no worries that I would fall asleep – I kept imagining that the stag's-head mask was staring at me. Also, from time to time I imagined I heard someone else in the cave, breathing softly and making slight noises. I remembered another of my father's lessons – *His own imagination is a man's most fearsome enemy* – and assured myself that I was completely alone.

Eventually I must have dozed off, for suddenly I awoke to the muffled sound of women lamenting, and the discordant music of rattles and tambourines from beyond the iron door.

A ceremony was taking place outside the cave. The words were too indistinct for me to make them out, but I was certain I recognized the stern voice of Theotimus, the head Megabyzus.

At length, I heard the iron door open, and then slam shut.

The music outside ceased. The crowd grew silent.

The sound of a girl sobbing echoed through the cave. The sobbing eventually quietened, then drew nearer, then ended in a gasp as Anthea, dressed in a simple white tunic, stepped into the large chamber and perceived me standing there.

The light was too dim for her not-yet-adjusted eyes to recognize me. She started back in fear.

"Anthea!" I whispered. "You know me. We met yesterday in your father's house. I'm Gordianus – the Roman, travelling with Antipater."

Her panic was replaced by confusion. "What are you doing here? How did you come to be here?"

"Never mind that," I said. "The question is: how can we get those pipes to play?" I gestured to the Pan pipes dangling above our heads.

"They really exist," muttered Anthea. "When the hierodules explained the test to me, I didn't know what to think – pipes that would play a tune by themselves if I were truly a virgin. But there they are! And I *am* a virgin – that's a fact, as the goddess herself surely knows. These pipes will play, then. They must!"

Together we gazed up at the pipes. No divine wind blew through the cave – there was no wind of any sort. The pipes hung motionless, and produced no music.

"Perhaps *you're* the problem," said Anthea, staring at me accusingly.

"What do you mean?"

"They say the pipes refuse to play in the presence of one who is not a virgin."

"So?"

"Are *you* a virgin, Gordianus of Rome?"

My face grow hot. "I'm not even sure the term 'virgin' can be applied to a male," I said evasively.

"Nonsense! Are you sexually pure, or not? Have you known a woman?"

"This is all beside the point," I said. "I'm here to save you, if I can."

"And how will you do that, Roman?"

"By playing those pipes."

"Do you even know how to play them?"

"Well . . ."

"And how on earth do you propose to reach them?"

"Perhaps you could play them, Anthea. If you were to stand on my shoulders—"

"I'm a dancer. I have no skill at music – and even if I did, standing on your shoulders wouldn't raise me high enough to reach those pipes."

"We could try."

We did. Anthea had a fine sense of balance, not surprising in a dancer, and stood steadily on my shoulders.

"Try to grab the pipes and pull them free," I said, grunting under her weight. She was heavier than she looked.

She groaned with frustration. "Impossible! I can't reach them. Even if I could, the chain holding them looks very strong."

From out of the dim shadows came a voice: "Perhaps *I* could reach them."

Recognizing the voice, Anthea cried out with joy and jumped from my shoulders. Amestris stepped from the shadows to embrace her mistress, and both wept with emotion.

I realized Amestris must have followed me to the cave, had slipped inside while the door was still open, then concealed herself in the shadows. It was her breathing I had heard in the still darkness.

Amestris drew back. "Mistress, if you were to stand on the Roman's shoulder, and I were to stand on yours—"

"I'm not sure I can hold both of you," I said.

"Of course you can, you brawny Roman," said Amestris. Her words made me blush, but they also gave me confidence. "And *I* can play the pipes," she added. "You've said yourself, mistress, that I play like a songbird."

From outside, after a long silence, the sound of lamenting had gradually resumed. Women wailed and shrieked. Hearing no music from the cave, the crowd assumed the worst.

Anthea put her hands on her hips and gazed up at the pipes, as if giving them one last chance to play by themselves. "I suppose it's worth a try," she finally said.

She climbed on to my shoulders. While I held fast to her ankles, she extended her arms to steady herself against the rock wall. Amestris climbed up after her. I thought my shoulders would surely collapse, but I gritted my teeth and said nothing. I rolled up my eyes, but was unable to lift my head enough to see what was going on above me.

Suddenly I heard a long, low note from the Pan pipes, followed by a higher note. There was a pause, and then, filling the cave, echoing from the walls, came one of the most haunting melodies I had ever heard.

The wailing from outside ceased, replaced by cries of wonderment – and did I hear the voice of Theotimus, uttering a howl of confusion and disbelief?

The strange, beautiful tune came to an end – and just in time, for I could not have supported them a moment longer. Amestris scrambled down, and Anthea leaped to the ground. I staggered against the wall and rubbed my aching shoulders.

"What now?" whispered Anthea.

"Supposedly, the door should open of its own accord," I said.

"If it doesn't, the Megabyzoi have the key," said Amestris. "Perhaps they'll unlock it."

I shook my head. "I wouldn't hold my breath waiting for that to happen. But I wouldn't be surprised if Theotimus joins us soon."

"What do you mean, Gordianus?" said Anthea.

I hurriedly explained that there was a secret entrance in the chamber beyond – and told them what I wanted them to do.

Only moments later, there was a sound from the rear entrance, and a flash of light as it was opened and then shut. I heard a stifled curse and an exclamation – "By Hades. The axe, the knife, the mask; where are they?" – and then Theotimus stepped into the main chamber. In one hand he held his priest's headdress, which he must have removed in order to duck through the small doorway. He stopped short at the sight of Anthea and Amestris standing side by side, then gazed up at the dangling Pan pipes.

"How did the slave girl get in here?" he said in a snarling whisper. "And how in Hades did you manage to play those pipes?"

He was unaware of my presence. I stood behind him, my back pressed against the wall, hidden in a patch of shadow. At my feet were the knife and the axe – the deadly implements with which he no doubt had intended to kill Anthea.

I had moved the weapons deliberately, so that he could not pick them up when he entered – and also so that I could use them myself, if the need arose. Theotimus was a large, strongly muscled man – he had a butcher's build, after all – and if we were to come to blows, I would need all the advantages I could muster. But, before resorting to the weapons, first I wanted to try another means of dealing with him. In my hands I held the stag's-head mask.

While the sight of the two girls continued to distract the Megabyzus, I stole up behind him, reached high, and placed the mask over his head. His head was larger than Chloe's, and it was a tight fit. I shoved downward with all my might, and through the palms of my hands, I imagined I could feel the impact of the short, needle-sharp spike fixed inside the top of the mask as it penetrated his scalp.

I had glimpsed the spike the day before, in the temple, when I looked inside the mask. If my guess was correct, the spike had been covered with a poison which had caused the death of Chloe; her motions of panic and dismay had not been acting or dancing, but death-throes, as the poison entered her skull and worked its evil on her. After the mask was removed, the puncture mark and any traces of blood amid her lustrous red hair would not have been visible to anyone unless they closely examined her scalp, and there had been neither time nor reason to do so before Theotimus arrived and took control of the situation. No wonder the Megabyzus had expressed alarm and moved so quickly to take the mask from me after I picked it up; and he then had afterwards brought it to this hiding place – along with the implements with which he intended to put an end to Anthea, and the sack for the disposal of her corpse.

No doubt it had been his intention to wait until the grieving crowd dispersed, and then, at his leisure, to return to the cave, come in by the secret entrance, and deal with Anthea. Before killing her, what other atrocities had he planned to commit on her virgin body? A man who would commit murder against one of Artemis's virgins in the goddess's temple certainly would not stop at committing some terrible sacrilege in the sacred cave of Ortygia.

Theotimus was a monster. It seemed fitting that his own murder weapon should be used against him.

But did enough poison remain on the spike to work its evil on him? The puncture certainly caused him pain; he gave a cry and reached up frantically. Clutching the antlers, trying desperately to remove the mask, he lurched this way and that, looking like a dancer playing the role of Actaeon. He ran blindly against one wall, butting it with the antlers, and then against another. Convulsing, he fell to the ground, kicked out his legs – and then was utterly still.

The three of us stared down at his lifeless body for a long moment, hardly able to believe what had just happened. I had never before caused a man's death. I had done so deliberately and without compunction – or so I thought. Nonetheless, I was gripped by a succession of confusing emotions. I became even more confused when Anthea grabbed my shoulders and kissed me full on the mouth.

"My hero!" she cried. "My champion!"

Beyond her, I saw Amestris gazing at me. Strangely, her smile meant even more to me than Anthea's kiss.

"Come, Anthea," I said, stepping back from her embrace, "there's no reason for you to remain a moment longer in this terrible place. I can open the iron door from the inside, using the same instruments I used to get in. The door will open, you will step into the daylight, and the door will shut behind you. The trial shall end just as it should."

"What about you and Amestris? What about – him?" She looked at the corpse of Theotimus.

"Amestris and I will leave by the back way. And later, after we've talked with your father, we'll figure out what to do about Theotimus."

So it happened. Staying out of sight, I opened the iron door for Anthea and then shut it behind her. Through the door, I heard a loud cry of joy from Eutropius, and the cheering of the crowd.

Amestris and I headed towards the back of the cave. Under the pipes of Pan, Amestris grabbed me and pressed her mouth to mine. Her kiss was very different from the one Anthea had given me.

It was she who broke the kiss, with a laugh. "Gordianus, you look as if you've never been kissed that way before."

"Well, I—"

She gazed up at the pipes and frowned "What do you think? Would the pipes have played if I hadn't come along?"

"What do you mean?"

"Did the presence of one who was not a virgin prevent the pipes from playing? I worried about that when I decided to follow you inside. But a voice in my head said, 'Do it!' And so I did. And surely it was the right thing to do, for only with the three of us working together were we able to save my mistress."

"I'm sure we both did the right thing, Amestris. But are you saying that you're not . . ."

She cocked her head, then smiled. "Certainly not! No more than you are, I'm sure." She laughed, then saw my face. Her smile faded. "Gordianus, don't tell me that *you* have never . . ."

I lowered my eyes. "I don't know how these things are done in Ephesus, but it is not uncommon for a Roman citizen to wait until a year or so after he puts on his manly toga before he . . . experiences the pleasures of Venus."

"Venus? Ah, yes, that's the name you Romans give to Aphrodite. And when did you put on your manly toga?"

"A year ago, when I turned seventeen."

"I see. Then I suppose you must be due to experience the pleasures of Venus any day now."

I didn't know what to say. Was she making fun of me?

Feeling suddenly awkward, I led her to the rear door and we made our exit from the cave unseen.

That night, after the initial joy of his daughter's salvation subsided a bit, Eutropius conferred with Antipater and Mnason and myself. The others were at first shocked at my impious behaviour in breaching the entrance of the cave of Ortygia – "Crazy Roman!" muttered Mnason under his breath – but Antipater suggested that perhaps Artemis herself, driven to extreme measures to rid her temple of such a wicked priest, had led both Amestris and myself to the cave, and to Anthea's rescue.

"The gods often achieve their ends by means that appear mysterious and even contradictory to us mortals," said Antipater. "Yes, in this matter I see the guiding hand of Artemis. Who else but Gordianus – a 'crazy Roman,' as you call him, Mnason – would have even thought of breaking into the cave and entering ahead of Anthea? Theotimus was counting on our very piety to doom the girl, knowing we would do nothing to stop or affect the trial. Yes, I believe that Gordianus and the slave girl were nothing more or less than the agents of Artemis," he declared, and that seemed to settle the matter.

As for the body of Theotimus, Antipater said that we should do nothing and simply leave it where it was. Either the Megabyzoi would soon find it – especially if some were in league with Theotimus, in which case they might or might not perceive the cause of his death, and either way would be unable to implicate Anthea or anyone else, and would almost certainly conceal the fact of his death – or his body would not be found for a very long time. In either case, it would seem that the head of the Megabyzoi, after making a foul and false accusation against Anthea, had vanished from the face of the earth. The people of Ephesus would draw their own conclusions.

"Everyone knows Theotimus was a puppet of the Romans," said Mnason. "People will see his downfall and disappearance as a divine punishment, and a sign that the rule of the Romans and the traitors who support them is coming to an end. Perhaps . . .

perhaps the death of my dear Chloe will serve a greater purpose after all, if it brings her beloved city closer to freedom."

Antipater laid a comforting hand on the man's shoulder. "I think you speak wisely, Mnason. Your daughter was a faithful servant of Artemis, and she will not have died in vain." He turned to Eutropius. "I had hoped to stay longer in Ephesus, old friend, but the situation here makes me uneasy. With all that's happened, I fear that anti-Roman sentiments are likely to turn violent. The faction that favours Mithridates will be emboldened; the Roman governor will feel obliged to react – and who knows what may happen? For my own sake, and for that of my young Roman companion, I think we should move on, and sooner rather than later."

Eutropius nodded. "I, too, had hoped for a longer visit. But you're right, Teacher – neither of you may be safe here. Tomorrow, let us all go together to the Temple of Artemis to make a special sacrifice of thanksgiving, and another sacrifice to ask the goddess to bless your travels, and then I shall see about booking passage for you and Gordianus to sail to your next destination."

We all retired to our separate rooms for the night.

I was unable to sleep. The room was too bright. I drew the heavy drapes to shut out the moonlight and went back to bed. I tossed and turned. I stared at the ceiling. I buried my face in my pillow and tried to think of anything except Amestris.

I heard the door open quietly, then click shut. Soft footsteps crossed the room.

I looked up from the pillow. All was dark until she drew back the drapes and I saw her naked silhouette framed by moonlight. Before I could say her name, she was beside me in the bed.

I ran my hands over her naked body and held her close. "Blessed Artemis!" I whispered.

"Artemis has nothing to do with this," said Amestris, with a soft laugh and a touch that sent a quiver of ecstasy through me. "Tonight, we worship Venus."

And so, in the city most famously devoted to the virgin goddess of the hunt, I killed my first man, and I knew my first woman.

After our visit to the temple the next morning, Antipater and I set sail. Amestris stood with the others on the wharf. We waved farewell. Gazing at her beauty, remembering her touch, I felt a stab of longing and wondered if I would ever see her again.

As I watched the city recede, I made a silent vow. Never in my travels would I pass a temple of Artemis without going inside to light a bit of incense and utter a prayer, asking the goddess to bestow her blessings upon Amestris.

"Gordianus – what is that strange tune you're humming?" said Antipater.

"Don't you recognize it? It's the melody Amestris played on the Pan pipes."

It haunts me still.

Eyes of the Icon

Mary Reed and Eric Mayer

Since 1999, Mary Reed and Eric Mayer have been charting the investigations of John the Eunuch, starting with One for Sorrow. *These novels, and related short stories, are set in sixth-century Constantinople. The following story shares the Constantinople background, but takes place nearly two centuries later, during the turbulent reign of Emperor Leo III. There had been much debate across the eastern Mediterranean about the depiction of Christ on coins and icons, and, in or about the year 726, Leo banned the use and worship of such images. His most significant act was to remove the image of Christ that stood at the giant bronze Chalke Gate at the entrance to the Palace of Constantinople. The upheaval that this caused is the starting point for the following story.*

1

My first mistake was eating the Lord's eyes.

I didn't mean to. I woke up hungry, freezing, and cursing Emperor Leo.

"Damn you, excellency, for banning religious imagery and destroying my livelihood. Damn you for pulling down the Christ over the Bronze Gates. Why didn't you just throw Victor the icon-painter into the bonfire as well?"

As if the emperor even knew I existed. But me carrying on like this made me forget my troubles, until the pensioned soldier in the apartment below started banging his broom handle against my floorboards. If only he and his colleagues had wielded their spears as enthusiastically against the Persians. Maybe the empire wouldn't be in such a sorry state.

When I opened the shutters to dump my pot of night soil I had a look around the alley below. A brawny fellow dressed in a labourer's leather trousers slouched by. For some reason I had the impression he might have just started in motion at the creak of the shutters. I tossed the slop as far as I could but the man was already out of range.

I started cursing again.

They were watching, I was sure.

I could feel their gaze all the time.

Whoever they were.

Or was it just the painted saviour propped up against the wall on his pine board, staring at me?

I went to the table where my dry pigments were laid out in ceramic containers. I was determined to get to work, even though I wasn't sure where I could sell an icon these days. There was a rime of ice around the bowl into which I'd cracked open my last remaining egg the night before.

I picked the bowl up, intending to separate the yolk from the white. The faint odour of food woke a demon who twisted my guts and forced my hand upwards. Before I could help myself I was lowering the bowl from my lips.

Over the rim I saw the Lord glaring at me. His eyes were formless gouges. I hadn't finished them. I hadn't yet refined the lines around the irises, or painted in the pupils.

As the egg went down in one painful gulp, I remembered a colleague who had slipped off the scaffold high up under the vault of the atrium at a mansion we were decorating. When I got to him he was face down on the floor, surrounded by green tile fish. The blue tile ocean had not lessened the impact of his fall. I pulled his shoulder. He flopped over like a half empty sack of wheat and stared at me.

Both his eyeballs had burst. Blood-flecked matter oozed out from the eye sockets and ran sluggishly down the crushed cheeks.

The cold, congealed egg stuck in my throat; it felt as if it had the consistency of that ooze. I should have used the egg to moisten black pigment for the icon's eyes. Now I couldn't give the icon eyes. I had swallowed his eyes.

I gagged. Nothing came up.

I was still hungry, and thirsty too.

And the Lord wasn't likely to give much assistance to someone who'd just eaten his eyes.

2

"The fact of the matter, Flaccus, is that I don't have so much as a copper follis to my name."

Flaccus sat placidly sipping his wine on the other side of the tavern table. He didn't offer to buy me a cup. "I'm lugging bricks myself, Victor. Plenty of work in that line."

Easy for him to say. He was a big, broad bull of a man, unlike myself.

"Yes, I'm sure," I replied. "The earthquake left plenty of rubble. Cheap construction material."

"Leo's a frugal sort."

"Imagine, a frugal emperor. What's the empire come to? What would Justinian the Great say if he could see us here, two hundred years in his future, his glorious Constantinople half deserted and in ruins? No work for artists like ourselves. Unless you happen to know someone who—"

Flaccus shook his head. "I haven't found a buyer for months. I had a few patrons commission work under the table, until Leo ordered the Chalke Gate Christ replaced by that hideous cross. Now everyone's frightened."

"No doubt the idea of Patriarch Anastasius. Does anyone take this nonsense seriously? This idea that veneration of images amounts to idolatry?"

Flaccus shrugged. "Whatever God in heaven might think about seeing his son depicted in egg tempera, here on earth it's the emperor's opinion that counts."

He started in on his bread and cheese. I looked away, over his wide shoulder, but the mosaic on the wall tormented me with a plate piled high with fruit.

If Flaccus with his enormous ego and artistic pretenses was resigned to hauling bricks, perhaps it was time for me to finally put my plan into action. Except I didn't exactly have a plan. And, even if I did, I needed an accomplice. Or, rather, a partner. Not Flaccus, certainly. He'd just turn me in for the reward. So would everyone else I knew. What could you expect from men who made a living painting martyrs for wealthy aristocrats? Men like me?

His stool squeaked as Flaccus stood. "Good seeing you, Victor. Remember what I said – bricks. I'd be happy to put in a word for you." He belched and left.

A couple of young men in good but threadbare cloaks entered the tavern. They might have been clerks from the palace. Shouldn't they have been at work by now? Did they have a shifty look about them or was that just my imagination? I got up hastily and went back out into the cold.

What did I need a partner for anyway? If I could sell the thing, the buyer could do the donkey-work.

But the idea of working alone scared me. That was it, if I was honest about it.

Or possibly it was just an excuse to do nothing.

I kept looking behind me for the fellows who were posing as clerks but didn't see them. Which didn't mean they weren't trailing me.

I couldn't put a plan in motion while I was under surveillance, could I?

3

A winter wind off the Sea of Marmara groaned under colonnades. No one who had anywhere better to go was out on the streets.

When I got back to my room, as hungry and thirsty as when I'd left, but colder, I found I'd been locked out.

My landlady answered her door at the first knock. "Don't try to apologize," she croaked before I could speak. "This time you have to leave. I'm a charitable woman, young man, but I need to eat too." Her face was as brown and wrinkled as her robes.

"But I'm sure to have the rent soon, Macedonia. I've almost finished a new icon. All I need is a buyer." I had begun to shiver. I didn't want to go back out into the wind.

Macedonia only frowned, deepening the creases in her face.

"I'll give you the icon," I told her. "It's worth far more than a month's rent. Or will be, once this all passes."

"Another icon? My back room already looks like the Great Church did before that devil Leo got started. This folly won't pass until the emperor does."

"In dark times those of the true faith find comfort in the glow of sacred images," I argued.

"Especially an admirable pious woman such as myself. Isn't that what you always tell me? I'm surprised you don't gild your paintings with your tongue!"

"This new image is a fine portrait of the saviour. But if you'd prefer, say, John the Baptist, I can easily change—"

"I already have a room full of saints. Every morning and every evening I pray to Saint Paul and Saint Stephen and all the rest: 'Please let my lodger the painter of icons pay his rent, Amen.' And look what it's got me."

"Maybe the Lord means for you to have this new image, rather than a few paltry coins?"

Macedonia laughed. She sounded like a starving gull. "And you think I shouldn't question the will of the Lord? Do you know what I heard about that earthquake a few weeks ago? The ground started shaking at the exact moment the workmen put their hands on that statue up by the amphitheatre – the one everyone says is Empress Theodora." She lowered her voice, as if we might be overheard. "Really, it's some pagan goddess. Athena, probably. Been there forever. She likes looking out over the sea. Didn't like the City Prefect trying to move her; the fellow who repaired the crack she put in my kitchen wall told me. That's what a thousand-year-old goddess can do. Your painted saints can't even find my rent."

4

As I left the apartment building a figure leapt up from the doorway and lurched off out of sight.

Only a beggar, I told myself, to judge from the man's rags. I could feel my heart leaping against my ribs. Why should I be startled at a beggar who'd taken shelter? If I was going to start being alarmed by beggars, I'd be jumping out of my skin every time I turned a corner.

I was gutless was what it amounted to. If I had any courage I would have acted by now. Then again, if I had any courage, would

I be making my living by lurking in my room painting saints on boards?

I had always thought of myself as a Christian. I even went to church sometimes. And where had it got me – or any of the thousands of other good Christians trapped in the rotted carcass of the empire?

It started to rain. Black clouds rubbed their bellies against the countless crosses bristling from Constantinople's rooftops – a view of Calvary multiplied a thousand times.

And here I am imagining I'm being crucified, I chided myself. Macedonia was right. Icons wouldn't put a roof over my head or food on my plate, or even supply me with a plate.

Not the icons I painted, at any rate.

Now that I didn't even have a room to shelter in, maybe the time had come to take the chance I'd been holding in reserve for weeks. What choice did I have?

I cut through a square I crossed almost every day – a deserted place surrounded by boarded-up shops – and went towards a sculpture that stood under one corner of the square's colonnade.

For once, the stylite who lived atop the granite column rising above the two-storey brick buildings was silent. Probably he was too cold to cry out to humanity or heaven, or both. If it got much colder, with the rain coming down, he'd be covered in a glimmering sheen of ice, like the gold leaf I put on my images.

Living in the city, you learn to ignore holy men the same way you ignore stray dogs, gulls, and beggars. Not to mention I was busy looking over my shoulder in case those clerks – or whoever they were – had followed me from the tavern.

Which is why as I ducked under the colonnade I ran smack into the girl. She would've ended up on her backside but she grabbed two handfuls of my cloak and clung to me, radiating warmth and exotic perfume.

"Sorry," I said, disconcerted. "I was thinking." As if I couldn't watch where I was going and think at the same time.

The girl smiled faintly. There was just a touch of red on her slightly parted lips. Beneath a sodden blue wool cloak she wore a stola of faded green silk. Not a whore. A servant wearing household hand-me-downs who'd stolen a couple of dabs of her mistress's make-up and perfume.

Her triangular little face was nothing special except for the enormous brown eyes. They were outsized, their gaze piercing.

An icon's eyes.

I'd seen her before. How could I forget a face like that? But where? It came back to me. At Florentius's house. Yes, the last time I'd futilely tried to sell him one of my icons.

I kept the knowledge to myself.

The wind picked up, blowing rain under the colonnade.

The girl glanced around. Her gaze slid over the metal sculpture in front of the spot where we had collided.

"What is that thing?" she asked. "It's horrible."

"It's a hound. Or at least that's what I've been told." The larger-than-life image, made of iron and covered with rusty mange, didn't look like much of anything. Its shoulder was roughly the height of my shoulder. It wasn't doing anything, just standing there looking out into the square towards the stylite's column.

The girl frowned. "Was it stuck in this out of the way spot to keep anyone from having to look at it?"

"Not very handsome, is it? They say it was once part of a group with a hare and a statue – said to be of Pan – but the last person who knew why it's here or what it represents probably died decades ago."

The girl wrinkled her nose. "What an eyesore. Someone ought to remove it."

"Might not be a good idea. You can never tell how these old statues are going to react." I didn't mention Macedonia's tale about Athena and the earthquake.

It was making me nervous, the way she kept examining the hound. Was it that interesting? "Look," I said, "Let's find somewhere dry. I know a place."

I started to walk away, expecting her to follow. Instead I heard a clatter. When I whirled around the girl wasn't in sight. I saw a board lying underneath the hound. The board I'd used to cover a gap in the wall.

I scrambled under the statue and through the gap, ripping the sleeve of my tunic on a sharp-edged broken brick.

She was already at the bottom of the rubble incline leading down from the gap, on the floor of what had been a shop that had collapsed, so that watery light and rain poured in.

She pointed to an archway in the far wall. "We can stay dry in there," she called up to me.

"No, wait!" I yelled. I slid frantically down the rubble, hoping to stop her.

Too late. By the time I'd reached the archway she had vanished through it.

After hundreds of years of fires and earthquakes, not to mention emperors intent on remaking the city in their own images, Constantinople sits atop a labyrinth of abandoned foundations, sub-basements, tunnels, and cisterns, many linked together over the centuries as a result of incessant construction and reconstruction. There are entrances to this vast underworld hidden all over the city – some man-made, but mostly being the result of accidents, fires, earthquakes, decay.

You never know where one of those entrances might lead. Until you've been through it.

I'd been through this one.

Which is why I sprinted across the dusty sub-basement trying to catch the girl. I knew she would spot the place where the bricks had fallen out of a wall, leaving a cave-like entrance above a waist-high pile of debris. As I reached her side she was stepping up on to the pile of shattered bricks and craning her neck to see into the cave.

She shrieked.

We were looking into an alcove or possibly the gap between the inner and outer walls of an ancient, buried building. The monstrous thing that had made her scream loomed over us, twice my height. There was no doubt it saw us. It was staring straight at us.

A gigantic face of Christ.

5

"This is the image from over the Chalke Gate!" I said.

"But Leo had it taken down! They burned it in front of the Golden Milestone, by the Augustaion!"

The vast open square of the Augustaion – from the Milestone all the way back to the Great Church – had been packed with gawkers. I'd gone there after hearing rumours about Leo's

planned desecration, but hadn't been able to get near enough to
see anything of the icon's destruction.

"This is only the icon's face," I pointed out. "Maybe what they
burned for the crowd was the body."

The girl shivered and pulled her wet cloak tighter. I couldn't
blame her. A black, pointed beard framed the icon's gaunt
visage. The lips were not merely closed, as tradition required,
but drawn in a taut, angry line. The eyes were merciless. This
was clearly the Christ who, like an emperor, had come with a
sword.

Which was why Christ and the emperor had succeeded while
most of us fail.

Could I be merciless?

I'd protected my treasure once.

That had been different. I'd simply reacted in anger and fear. I
hadn't had time to ponder what I was doing.

"You can't be sure it's the real icon," the girl was saying.

"No, this is definitely the Chalke Christ. I've seen it hundreds
of times, whenever I passed the palace gate. Look at the way the
shadows round the eyes are formed, and the highlights in the
irises. Very distinctive. See how the pupils aren't quite as close
to the upper eyelids as would usually be the case? That was to
give the impression he was looking down from above the gate,
meeting the gaze of anyone approaching."

"How would you notice all that?" She asked, gazing at me with
her huge brown eyes.

"I paint icons for a living. At least I used to. Now most of my
patrons are afraid to do business with me. My name's Victor, by
the way."

"Arabia," she said absently, her mind obviously not on
introductions. "It's very strange. My employer, Florentius,
collects icons."

"Florentius! You mean the wine merchant with the house near
the Great Church?"

"That's right."

"Why, I've done work for him! You must have seen my painting
of Saint Laurentius?"

"Oh, hardly. I've only been there a short time. I mostly scrub
floors. He keeps the icons locked out of sight. Thinks nobody

knows about them, but servants gossip. That's how I know about his collection. This one must be worth a fortune!"

"All it's worth right now is the head of anyone unfortunate enough to be caught with it. Possessing any image is a crime, let alone the most famous one in the empire. In fact, we probably shouldn't stay here."

I turned as if I intended to go back the way we had come but Arabia remained planted in front of the icon. "We can't leave it here, Victor. Can't you see, it isn't just chance that we found it. It's a miracle. We can't turn our backs on a miracle."

It sounded funny for her to say that. But why not? I knew nothing about Arabia. Just because a woman steals a dab of her mistress's lip colour doesn't mean she has no religious beliefs.

"There's nothing either of us can do with it. At least nothing I can think of," I lied.

"Florentius is already hiding icons. Why not one more?"

"He would probably turn us over to the authorities as soon as we approached him. Even if he didn't, we'd be putting ourselves in danger for the rest of our lives. The emperor would be bound to hear about the icon sooner or later and—"

Arabia screwed her face up in thought. "Of course we couldn't stay in the city. Florentius would give us enough to leave, to buy a farm, maybe. Just enough for us to get going again. It wouldn't be much for a man of his wealth."

It was the sort of plan I'd been thinking about, in a general way, for some time. Maybe Arabia could be of some assistance; the partner I needed. If I dared to trust a partner.

"Have you ever held a solidus?" she asked me. Her eyes glittered.

"Not often." My transactions rarely involved silver, let alone gold.

"I did, once. Florentius dropped it. He let me hold it. It was heavy. There was a picture of Emperor Leo on the front. He has the same narrow face and the same pointed beard as that icon. There was a cross behind his shoulder. It was such a lovely coin. Do you know what I did? I couldn't help myself. I kissed the emperor."

The icon's gaze bored into me. I felt a gnawing pain in my stomach. I'd almost forgotten I had eaten nothing that morning, except the egg. Land was cheap in the countryside. A few solidi would buy a farm. There would be plenty of eggs on a farm.

If I could force myself to go through with it.

6

"We'll need to wait for a few days," I said. "Florentius will have to make some preparations. He'll have to be careful. He can't just send a couple of servants to drag the icon along the street."

I didn't mention my fear that I was being followed. If I was, when I failed to return to my rooms tonight, they'd start looking for me.

I'd need to deal with Florentius at some point. A servant girl couldn't approach her wealthy employer and ask him to buy an illicit icon, let alone vouch for its authenticity. I could do both. Florentius knew and trusted me, to the extent any aristocrat knows and trusts the artisans he hires. But I'd need to be patient, give my pursuers time to shift their search to another part of the city.

Who was I fooling? I needed time to get my courage up.

At any rate, I told myself, it would be safer for Arabia to be out and about than me. She might prove very useful in that way. And, if anything went wrong and I had to stay in hiding for an extended period, she'd be able to keep me supplied with food.

I explained some of what I had in mind and sent her off. She returned with a wine skin and a sack.

"Praise be to God for what he provides," she said. I'm not sure whether she was being ironic, or where exactly the Lord had left the provisions. It appeared to be the army barracks in what used to be the Baths of Zeuxippos, judging from the hard biscuits underneath the clay lamp, the iron striker and flint, and the jar of lamp oil.

I had a biscuit halfway to my mouth when Arabia leaned forward and kissed me lightly on the lips. Then she was gone, leaving behind a wraith of her perfume.

And a thought that persisted in thrusting itself forward.

Something that really needed attention.

I lit the lamp. The rats scrabbling nearby quietened down and the painted icon opposite where I sat resumed staring at me. I returned its gaze. Had I been a more religious person I would have taken some comfort in the holy presence. The Lord was here with me. Even though he was everywhere at once, yet, like the saints, he was even more strongly where his icons or relics were – or so they said.

But on the other hand how forgiving was he?

He didn't look very forgiving at all. The flickering lamplight animated the giant features. At times the taut lips appeared ready to snarl, and at other times about to quirk into a sardonic smile.

The face was so large that, had the mouth opened, it could have snapped my head off with one bite. A rat peeped out from around the corner of the panel. I found a bit of brick and flicked it at the rodent, which scuttled away. The movement had made barely a sound but immediately I heard a noise coming from outside my little niche.

No. It had to be my imagination.

I sat and listened, feeling my muscles tighten until my legs began to cramp. I had to know. I crawled out of my hole, lamp in hand, took several steps forward, and listened.

Nothing.

I went a few paces further, then quickly on into the cavernous space beyond, a dry and abandoned cistern. Darkness swallowed the feeble lamplight. Several toppled columns, piled together, partly blocked the way in.

From a distance came the loud sound of cascading water. It was raining again and getting in somewhere. That must have been the sound I thought I had heard.

All the same, I checked behind the columns.

Philokalas was still there.

Or rather the tunic full of bones and scraps of rotted flesh that had once been Philokalas. The rats and whatever else lived down here had devoured most of him, which made the stench less than it might otherwise have been.

Still, I knew I should move him. It would be better if Arabia didn't stumble across the body. I bent down but my stomach lurched at the thought of touching the thing. I hadn't eaten much for days, and the biscuits weren't sitting well.

I returned to my hiding place. Now I could almost swear the icon was smiling benignly at me, as if to say, "Don't worry about

Philokalas. You acted without thinking. You're only human." Or maybe it was just smiling to itself. Finding the whole thing funny.

I dozed.

After being awakened countless times by phantom footsteps, I finally woke to Arabia gently nuzzling my neck.

She had whiskers.

I came fully awake, flailing at a rat.

By the time I had my wits about me, my assailant was gone. In the dim lamplight I noticed the biscuit sack had moved. I started to pull it back towards me and rats boiled out and streamed behind the holy image.

The rest of the night I stayed alert.

So far, things had gone reasonably well. But I brooded over all the things that might go wrong.

Then I thought about the gnawed bones that used to be a labourer named Philokalas.

After which I thought about Arabia who had showed quick intelligence and a certain amount of cunning.

More to the point, if things went wrong I could deny everything. After all, she was only a servant and I was an artist, a craftsman well-known to Florentius. That was another good reason for me to work with her.

When Arabia arrived the next morning she wore a blue embroidered cloak and a yellow stola. She'd pinched a deeper shade of lip colouring and had pulled her glossy hair into neat coils at the sides of her head. She looked more like a lady than a servant.

"What are you looking at?" she asked, as if she didn't know. Her eyes shone. The eyes are where life shines out. In my icons I tried to capture that in paint with bright lines and detailing. That was part of what I had left unfinished on the eyeless Christ back in my room. Yet I'd never managed to hint at eyes like Arabia's.

"I'm glad to see you," I told her. "It's a relief, after having that thing glowering at me all night." I nodded towards the icon.

She had brought a basket with her. This time the Lord had provided bread and cheese. I ate and described my restless night and some of the conclusions I'd drawn before the unseen dawn arrived overhead. Farming was fine, but the empire stretched a long way and so did the grasp of the emperor. Besides, what were the chances Florentius would agree to buy the icon rather than report us immediately to the authorities?

I just wanted to plan for all eventualities but she took it the wrong way. Her face darkened. "Don't lose courage before we've even started. It's lack of sleep, that's all."

"The rats never stop running," I complained, around a mouthful of bread. "They come out from behind that thing."

She went over and stood beside the giant image. "We're not going to be stopped by rats." She put a finger to her lips and then dropped a piece of cheese near the icon. "They love cheese even better than biscuits," she whispered.

She didn't move for a long time. She had all the patience in the world.

Finally a beady-eyed head poked out from behind the panel. The neck extended slightly, the nose twitched towards the cheese. Arabia brought the heel of a yellow shoe down sharply. I heard the rodent's skull pop.

"There," she said. "See how easily that's dealt with? Now we'll deal with something else."

She shrugged off her heavy cloak, tossed it on to the floor, and began to loosen her stola.

7

The bottom of a wine cup isn't the only place men find courage to overcome doubts. After Arabia helped me overcome mine, she straightened her hair, stood, and quickly pulled the stola back over her head. The flickering lamplight flung the trembling shadow of her body up over the holy visage.

"When we have our farm, we won't have to rush," I said. "We'll be able to lie together all morning if we want."

She slapped the dust off her cloak. "How did you come to paint icons, Victor? Are you a religious man?"

"I'm a Christian. Who isn't? But I can't say I'm particularly religious. My family were killed by a pestilence when I was a child. My mother died screaming in agony."

"I wouldn't think you'd be inspired to paint icons."

"I wasn't inspired. It came about because I was apprenticed to an artisan's workshop. I used to paint frescoes too. Frescoes have to be done in warmer weather, so the plaster and paint set right. I realized that in the summer, when most painters are decorating frescoes in churches and mansions, an icon-painter could find plenty of commissions. I've always been practical."

"Is my lip colour smudged?" She leaned forward into the lamplight so I could see.

"Not a bit. You have a beautiful mouth. And what about you? How long have you worked for Florentius?"

"Not long."

"You've always done the same thing?"

"Been a rich man's servant, you mean?"

"You don't like being employed by Florentius? He strikes me as a man of decency. He's always shown me respect in our business dealings."

She laughed. "You really think a rich man like Florentius respects people like us?"

"He's told me he admires my skills."

"Unless you're rich you're just a thing to be used. Did Florentius offer to lend you any money to tide you over?"

"Well—"

"What about your other wealthy patrons? What would a month's rent be to them? Or a year's? Have they offered?"

"They haven't," I admitted. I hated seeing her angry. It worried me. It could ruin everything. "You aren't from Constantinople, are you?" I said, to change the subject.

"No. I was born in the countryside. I thought it all very boring – dirt and pigs as far as you could see – so I ran away to the big city. Not a very interesting story."

"Until now!"

"Yes, until now. The best stories are the ones we make up for ourselves. You can't trust others to make up your story for you. You're never the hero of someone else's story."

She smoothed down her stola and patted her hair. "I'll be back this evening," she said. "You can tell me how it goes with Florentius. And then . . ." When she kissed me before leaving, I wondered whether she was thinking about kissing the emperor on the solidus.

8

I felt distracted. I attempted not to look at the red blot on the floor where the dead rat lay. I avoided the icon's eyes. From those monstrous windows, was there some theological lesson to be gleaned, into the spirit above and the crushed verminous body below? Would Chrysostom, he of the golden tongue, have penned a Homily on a Dead Rat?

The thought reminded me I had things to do and had better get them done.

For a start, it was time to visit Florentius again.

After going through the archway and climbing the rubble slope up to my entrance to the underworld, I peered through a knothole in the board Arabia had replaced. It was not exactly the great bronze gate to the palace. The space under the iron dog was clear. I crawled out and scanned the square from between scabrous canine forelegs. There wasn't a living creature in sight except for the stylite high up on his pillar, leaning against its rusted railing like a lifeless icon, and an emaciated cat sniffing the empty donation basket hanging to the ground from a rope attached to the stylite's railing.

I scuttled away as fast as possible.

I had instructed Arabia to take similar care but could only trust she had taken heed of my warning.

Once out of the square I tried to tidy my clothing. I smoothed wrinkles and shook off dust and cobwebs, but I wasn't really in any state to present myself to a wealthy patron.

I intended to cut across the Augustaion in front of the Great Church but I began to have the sensation I was being watched.

Possibly I still felt the gaze of those colossal eyes. It wasn't the painted eyes that bothered me so much. It was what they represented. That 'being' up in the sky, seeing everything, all the time. Looking and looking, but never doing anything about what it saw.

A beggar sat slumped at the base of the towering column atop which the Emperor Justinian endlessly rode his chariot.

The beggar who had been sitting in Macedonia's doorway.

No. Constantinople was filled with beggars and there was nothing to distinguish one pile of rags from another.

Nevertheless, I veered on to a side street just in case.

I went through an abandoned space where a mansion or church or an imperial building had once stood. Statuary – and pieces of statuary – stood and lay amidst brown weeds jutting through the crumbling pavement. My friends and I had come here when boys and played catch with the heads of ancient philosophers. Sometimes we convinced ourselves we saw demons darting in and out among the frozen figures. I had soon learned that there really are demons in the world, but all of them are human beings.

You just have to stay one step ahead.

When I got to my destination I was sure I had lost anyone who might have been following me. Glancing up and down the street, I noticed nothing suspicious. The large, luxurious house where I had delivered more than one icon showed passers-by only a plain brick front without windows at street level. Beyond its roof loomed the vast dome of the Great Church. When the interior of the dome was lit at night, it must illuminate the whole third storey of the house.

My patron agreed to talk to me. A few servants passed through the atrium while I waited, but I didn't see Arabia.

Florentius was a heavy-set man with thick lips and a red nose. He looked more like a bacchant than a pious Christian. He led me through his office, where we met in the past, and along the peristyle, bordering what had been an ornamental inner garden in more prosperous times. Now the space was filled with pigsties. Several monstrous hogs – mounds of undulating flesh – drank from a basin, overlooked by a marble Aphrodite. Chickens scattered in front of us.

Florentius kicked a plump marble foot out of our path. "Cupid," he told me. "He keeps turning up. Pieces of him, that is. Fell into a pigsty during the earthquake. Must have surprised the pig."

As we passed under the peristyle and into the rear of the house, he frowned at several labourers busy with trowels and mortar in the hallway.

"Did you suffer much damage?" I asked.

"Enough to keep too many unwashed labourers tracking mud around. Don't like having such people underfoot. At least a man knows his own servants; and labouring types can never be counted on. Worse than donkeys. The job's only half finished and they vanish and need to be replaced. On the other hand, I've tripped over the brutes wrapped around my serving girls in the storeroom."

"It must be vexing for a man like yourself."

"Indeed. But I thank the Lord it wasn't worse. I hear there are cracks in the foundation of the Great Church and the Patriarch lost most of the wine in his cellars."

We came to a metal-banded wooden door which Florentius unlocked. "It's a sin to keep my holy men hidden away back here. Every day I pray we will soon be rid of the beast who sits on the throne."

Perhaps he felt safe expressing treasonous thoughts to an icon-painter.

After all, I was a criminal in the eyes of the law.

I had never seen his private bath. Doubtless he had kept it locked even before he used it to store illicit icons. The frescoes on the walls and domed ceiling of the tiny room depicted ancient gods embroiled in an Olympian orgy in garishly coloured detail.

"I bought this place from a bishop," Florentius explained.

Icons were stacked in the dry bath. Several hung on the painted walls, including my depiction of Saint Laurentius being martyred on a red-hot grid.

Florentius noticed the direction of my gaze. "An exquisite work! The saint's pain is palpable. How it pleases me! What can such a young man as yourself know about pain, to capture it so perfectly?" He stared fondly at the image.

Demonic figures, seen in twisted profile, prodded Laurentius' bound, blackening flesh with tridents. I wondered what a man with as much wealth as Florentius could know about pain to appreciate it so much, but I only smiled modestly.

Florentius looked away from the icon and towards the artist. "What fools they are to claim we venerate the wood and paint itself. I venerate your skills. Your talents help me to understand how we must face suffering. How perfectly you capture the saint's beatific demeanour! After my wife died last year I often looked to this painting for comfort, for a lesson in the way a Christian endures, secure in the knowledge that all is God's will." He wiped his glistening eyes. "And now, young man, for what reason have you come to see me?"

9

"I knew Florentius would agree," Arabia put the plate of honey-cakes she'd brought on the dirt in front of the Chalke Christ. It made me think of a pagan offering.

"It took all my powers of persuasion," I said.

"You have a golden tongue."

"I must have. Florentius suspects Leo and the Patriarch know the icon was salvaged in some fashion and spirited away. Naturally they're outraged."

"If it was seen again, people would think it was a miracle, a sign the pair of them are the real heretics."

"That's about what Florentius told me. They're having the city watched. Spies are everywhere. So he needs time to make arrangements. Or to change his mind."

"He won't change his mind," Arabia replied.

"You think not? We're to meet tomorrow at an early hour at the Golden Milestone to discuss the matter further."

Arabia clapped her hands together like a child. "How very appropriate. Right where the icon was burnt. Or supposedly burnt. Sit down and try these sweets."

Florentius probably hadn't chosen the Golden Milestone for the symbolism but rather because people often lingered beneath it to talk. We would attract no attention, nor would either of us be able to resort to treachery in such a public spot.

All the same, I was uneasy about the arrangement. For one thing whoever was following me could conceal themselves in the crowds. I would need to be careful. I hunkered down and took one of the sticky cakes. It was very sweet indeed. I noticed the plate was silver.

"It was difficult to get away," I said. "He kept talking."

Arabia's large brown eyes narrowed. "What did he want to talk about?"

"Religion. He wanted to know whether a painter could depict Christ as both divine and human at the same time. According to Emperor Leo and the Patriarch, that can't be done in paint. Another good excuse for destroying icons! The icon will either depict Christ's physical nature only – which is one sort of heresy – or show his physical and spiritual natures mixed, which is another sort."

"That's stupid." Arabia stretched up on her toes to tap the gilded halo behind the giant head, then rapped her knuckles against the sharp tip of its nose. "There's your spiritual and there's your physical. It's plain to anyone."

"All the same, I hate to think of him telling the emperor about an icon-painter who—"

"And Leo, of course, wanting to know who this icon-painter is!"

"Exactly."

Arabia shook her head. "I wouldn't worry." She sat down on the floor, leaned against me, and began nibbling a cake.

"Florentius might see this as an opportunity to gain Leo's goodwill, by turning us and the icon over to him," I said. What I was thinking was that maybe I could arrange for Arabia alone to be turned over, if it came to it.

"Is that why you look so shifty? You're expecting the emperor's guards or the urban watch to barge in?"

"I didn't realize I—"

"Oh yes, I've noticed." She smiled at me as she carefully licked honey off her fingers. Her pink tongue darted in and out and her moistened fingers glistened in the lamplight. "But remember Florentius doesn't know where the icon is or where we are."

"At some point, though, we'll have to trust him. We can't move the icon above-ground ourselves. If we cleared some of the bricks in front of that hole we might be able to squeeze it out of this place, since clearly whoever hid it here heaped those bricks up to help conceal the entrance. But it will never fit through that gap under the hound. Someone would have to make an opening somewhere in the outside wall, fast, and get the icon away faster, before the urban watch showed up to see what was causing the commotion."

"You've thought of everything, haven't you?" Arabia leaned her head on my shoulder and I was enveloped in her warmth. "Have you painted many images of Christ?"

"A few. The last one is still back in my room. I'm afraid I left him eyeless."

"He doesn't need eyes, does he? If he wants to see without them, he could see with his hands or his nose."

"There's a lot of extra work to be done on eyes. But then you probably aren't interested in egg tempera techniques."

She didn't dispute the statement so I shut up.

"Don't worry so much," she told me. "Everything is going to work out perfectly. It's been preordained. Don't you see? Our running into each other, taking shelter from the rain, finding the icon, both of us working for Florentius, who collects icons . . . it's all too much to be a coincidence. We're being guided by the hand of God. Have faith, Victor!"

I didn't have a chance to reply. There was a scrabbling noise outside our hiding place.

I went over and looked into the dimness, but saw nothing.

I was turning away, chiding myself for my nervousness, when there was another scuffling sound and a figure appeared out of the gloom.

At first I thought it was a feathered demon or a giant bird. Then I saw it was a man, waving his arms wildly, flapping the tattered garment he wore.

A beggar.

He shouted in a voice as ragged as his clothes. "Ye who gaze upon the great face of the Lord, repent! Repent! Repent!"

Arabia screamed.

The ragged man turned and scuttled away towards the cistern.

I went after him. He must have seen the icon, not to mention Arabia and me.

He scrambled over the fallen columns and I followed him into the darkness beyond.

I could hear his feet slapping across the stones better than I could see him. More than once I heard him fall. I shouldn't have been able to catch him otherwise, since he was surprisingly nimble. It was like trying to catch a desperate beast.

The man kept crying out to the Lord. Down here, the Lord was the only one likely to hear. I didn't want him to get back above ground where he could tell his tale to anyone who would listen.

I began to gain on him. I managed a burst of speed born of desperation, and my cold-numbed fingers brushed a fluttering scrap of cloth. I leapt forward and dragged him down.

He was stronger than I expected, and more agile. Claw-like nails tore at my neck. A sharp knee caught me in the stomach.

Teeth sank into my shoulder. It felt as if I was being attacked by a pack of feral dogs.

I tried to get up and he slammed me backwards. My head hit the ground and lights flared behind my eyes.

Then there was a loud thud and the beggar grunted. I couldn't feel him flailing at me any longer.

There were more thuds. I blinked. We were surrounded by the orange glow of the lamp Arabia held in one hand. In the other she gripped a bloody half brick.

I pushed myself up.

The beggar lay crumpled face down.

His skull had been caved in.

My chest burned from exertion and I hurt everywhere. If Arabia had arrived too late it would have been me lying there.

She'd saved my life.

I couldn't take my gaze off the corpse. She'd hit the man again and again. Bloody shards of bone jutted through the matted hair.

Arabia started to sob. "I was so frightened, Victor. So frightened for you." She threw the brick away. Her narrow shoulders shook.

I put my arm around her. "We'll go back now. I'll hide his body later."

By the time we were back at our hole in the wall we were both shivering uncontrollably.

"Your clothes are ruined," Arabia said. "I'll bring you new ones."

"Steal them from Florentius, you mean! That's where you've been finding the food you bring me, isn't it? I noticed his household seal on the plate."

"We're not stealing. It's an advance payment."

"Then again, what's theft compared to murder?"

"We were only defending ourselves. We had to kill him."

We? I hadn't killed the beggar. But, on the other hand, there was Philokalas. I didn't correct Arabia. We thought alike. "No," I said, we're not guilty of murder or theft, or greed or coveting another man's possessions either, since all we want from Florentius is enough to keep us safe. And as for worshipping graven images, that's a matter of opinion anyway."

Arabia laughed. She gave me an appraising look. "You're forgetting lust," she said. "And I'm afraid that's a sin you can't deny."

10

Arabia left, returned with food and the clothes she'd promised, and departed again. I set the clean clothing – plain garments of the type servants wear – to one side, for my meeting with Florentius next day. Then I sat down and tried to avoid the gaze of the icon.

Sometimes, when I painted an image, I had the uncanny sensation that the saint in heaven was also right in front of me, under my brush. At such times I felt I was painting a hole in the world and an otherworldly presence was stepping through.

Yet paints were paints. Pigments, wine, water, egg. There wasn't anything else. Just raw materials and artistic technique.

I tried to keep my gaze on the floor. The crushed head of the rat still poked out from behind the icon. I got up and pushed it out of sight.

What time was it? The middle of the night? Probably earlier. It seemed as if I'd been sitting alone, in the cold, with my thoughts, forever.

Possibly Florentius would have me arrested when I showed up at the Golden Milestone.

I could feel the icon looking down at me. I looked up into those cold, bottomless eyes.

The girl is nothing more than a miserable sinner, the icon seemed to say. Not in words, but in my own thoughts. I swear it spoke to me in my thoughts, stirring them into a resolve I could not have reached on my own.

She is no better than yourself, the thing counselled. A killer. If Florentius betrays you, pretend your intent all along has been to turn over to the authorities a treacherous servant named Arabia who unwisely led you to the hidden icon which you wanted returned to the emperor for proper disposal.

"But Arabia saved my life," I whispered.

By killing a man, brutally, the icon countered. She was no innocent. But would Christ offer such advice? Why not? He had administered to men's human needs when he walked the earth. He had fed the starving. Wasn't I starving?

There are things that need to be done, the icon told me.

I walked back into the cistern and slung the body of the beggar over my shoulder. I'd had no reason to cross the cistern before but now I followed a line of pillars into the darkness, staggering under the dead man's reeking weight, balancing my lamp in one hand, until I came to what remained of a concrete wall that had exploded inward, scattering massive chunks of masonry over a collection of chariots beyond.

I must be underneath the Hippodrome. There were ranks of chariots, all in good repair, except where portions of the ceiling had fallen on them. How long had they sat here? When had there last been a chariot race in Constantinople?

When I was done with the beggar I went back for Philokalas.

What was left of him wasn't as heavy as the beggar, but I was shaking with revulsion by the time I'd shoved most of his bones under a chariot. A few had fallen out of his robes and rattled on to the floor of the cistern. I'd left them there. In the unlikely event the bodies were found, the natural impression would be the men had taken shelter during the earthquake and picked the wrong place.

Technically I was a murderer but I didn't feel like one. It had been an accident. Taking my usual route early one morning, I'd seen Philokalas scuttle under the iron hound, and followed out of curiosity.

True, thieves were known to hide stolen goods in the abandoned depths of the city and it may have occurred to me that, if I discovered an illicit collection, who could fault a starving icon-painter from taking sustenance from a criminal's hands?

Honestly, I had formed no particular plan as I slunk behind him, through the archway at the bottom of the rubble slope.

I saw the gigantic icon at the same time Philokalas saw me.

If only he had not been so hot-tempered! How else was I supposed to respond when he drew his dagger?

I used a piece of jagged brick, the same as Arabia. Luckily I had thought to pick one up as I followed him, just in case.

I didn't hit him as many times as Arabia had hit the beggar.

The one crunching blow sickened me so much I dropped the

brick and if I hadn't hit Philokalas in exactly the right place – purely by chance – he'd still be alive.

As soon as I had examined the icon I recognized it but couldn't work out how to use the knowledge to my advantage.

Now, standing beside the chariot that concealed the dead men, I wasn't anxious to hurry back into the icon's stern presence.

Why not explore?

Beyond the storage room lay an area which had been shaken by the last earthquake, or possibly previous tremors, until it resembled a natural cavern strewn with jagged boulders and stones. It might have been a basement or several basements. Dark passageways led off in different directions.

What drew my attention was the stone stairway leading upwards.

The stairs must have traversed more than one floor, but the floors were gone. I climbed to the top and peeped out through a small space between enormous double doors.

Scattered torches illuminated an otherwise dark courtyard. A grist-mill of the sort powered by a donkey sat in the middle. What I could distinguish of the surroundings told me nothing, although the little I could see of it showed that the building rising behind the courtyard looked uncommonly large. Twisting uncomfortably and craning my neck to see upwards I had a shock.

Over the roof the sun was rising.

How had I managed to misjudge time so badly? How could it be dawn already? I wouldn't be there to meet Arabia when she arrived! I wouldn't be on time for my appointment with Florentius!

Understanding arrived a step behind panic.

The orange glow was not the rising sun but the flames of a thousand lamps. I wasn't far from the Great Church with its lighted dome. I might be looking into the rear courtyard of the Patriarch's residence for that matter. At any rate, if I was close to the Great Church, I was close to Florentius. Here was the answer to how he might transport the icon.

A donkey brayed in the night as a dark figure moved across the courtyard.

I ducked away and started back down.

That was when the stairway tried to shake me off.

11

One instant my foot was coming down on the next step, then I'd lost my balance and was stepping into space. I flung my arms out in time to regain my balance and managed to keep hold of the lamp even as it splashed hot oil across my hand.

It was another earthquake. As frequent as they are, my surprise at their onset has never lessened, neither did my horror at the unnatural spectacle of solid earth rippling and walls bulging.

The stairway remained intact. So did I. I reached the bottom and stumbled over the heaving floor and into the chariot room. Clouds of dirt, dust, and plaster whorled out at me.

Half-blinded, coughing and choking, I staggered through the chariots, barging into wheels, tripping over yokes. The shaking made the chariots rattle and creak. I could have been threading my way through a cacophonous, ghostly race.

Finally, I was back at the cistern. As I started across the vibrating abyss there was a hollow boom. Then another. And another. If the ceiling came crashing down would I even know it or would the world just instantly end?

Suddenly a section of a column, several arm-breadths in diameter, rolled out of the Stygian depths. It roared towards me with terrifying speed. I threw myself out of the way and two rotating, leering satyr heads almost took my nose off.

My lamp hissed and guttered. I'd spilled most of the oil. I started to run.

The floor shook underfoot and I feared at any instant I would step into a freshly opened chasm.

By the time I arrived back at my starting point, the shaking was over.

Luckily the alcove had survived.

Arabia arrived some time later. I described my explorations, leaving out the part about moving corpses, and went on to formulate a more or less clear plan.

"Presuming Florentius can use that courtyard safely, you can meet him at the stairway and lead him through the chariot room and the cistern," I told her. "If Florentius violates the arrangement

– if he brings armed men, for example, or if you sense danger – take him somewhere else. Tell him the icon is hidden above-ground, show him down an alley, and bolt."

The arrangement also had the advantage of keeping Arabia and myself apart which, I calculated, might make it easier for me to disown her if the need arose.

"Of course, Florentius will need to bring our payment in person," she said. "He won't cause trouble since he'll be in the middle of it. And he knows if he's caught with an illicit icon, Leo is unlikely to believe any excuses he might have."

"And we take the money and run."

Her huge eyes flashed. "Not run. Ride, Victor. We'll be rich. We'll buy the first horses we see! Then we'll be off to Greece or maybe Italy. Anywhere we want. In a couple of days this dreary city will be nothing but a nightmare."

"I hope so." I couldn't help thinking there was only one way that it can turn out right, and endless ways it could go wrong. And if it turned out right . . . what about Arabia? "Do you really want to risk your life for a few coins?"

She took hold of my arm and I smelled her perfume and felt her heat. "Not just coins, Victor. Gold coins. Lovely solidi with the emperor's face on them. Imagine what fine things they'll buy. Farms and jewels and silks."

"Silks won't do you any good if Leo has us hunted down."

Arabia's reddened lips curved into a scimitar of a smile. "Silk makes a better winding sheet than linen."

Well, I thought, if that's how she feels about it, nobody can blame me for what I might need to do.

12

There wasn't time for sleep before my meeting with Florentius, but I didn't need any. I just wanted to get it over with and away from the city.

I crept out from under the iron hound, making certain there was nobody around except the resident stylite, and trotted off to my appointment.

I was halfway there when someone called my name.

"Victor! Stop!"

My first impulse was to flee, but could I elude a company of armed guards? I hesitated and turned to face my fate.

My former landlady waddled in my direction. "Victor, why haven't you been home?"

"You locked me out."

Macedonia snorted and waved her hand. "And why did I lock you out? I thought you'd want your paints badly enough to find a few folles for a poor old woman. I didn't mean anything by it. It's just business."

"I'm giving up painting icons," I said.

"Giving up painting? But why? Such a talent! Such a service to the Lord! How do you intend to pay what you owe me if you give up painting?"

"He doesn't need me to paint icons. He can put any icons he wants anywhere, including on top of the dome of the Great Church or next to the moon."

"And why would he do that for such a wicked race? He's kept busy punishing us now that devil Leo has taken over. The butcher told me there's plague in the Copper Market."

"And there was another earthquake a few hours ago. Not much of one this time, fortunately."

Macedonia shook her head. "No, that was Athena stamping her foot again. The old gods liked shaking the ground. They used to frighten the farmers that way. Heaven prefers a good pestilence in the city. And where are you staying now? If you are paying rent to someone else, you'd be better off paying me. I'll give you a month before I go to the magistrate."

I kept peering this way and that, to see if we were being watched. I didn't like standing in one place. "I'm in a hurry," I said. "I have to meet someone."

"That man who was asking about you this morning?"

"A man was asking about me this morning?"

"He was asking about a painter of icons. I denied there was any such person under my roof, which was quite true at the time. He didn't believe me and insisted I show him your room."

"Did he know my name?"

"No, but he described you. Do you owe him money too?"

It must have been someone sent by Florentius, I thought. Did the fool think I had the Chalke icon hidden under my bed? All the same, it was disturbing. And why not ask for me by name?

"What did he look like?"

Macedonia pondered the question. "Nobody. A labourer. A big, broad-shouldered man, like the one who showed up looking for you a few weeks ago. Philokalas, wasn't it? The man this morning asked about him. Had he been to see me? Do you suppose he was a friend of the first man?"

So, I thought. Probably the man who had called on Macedonia was not from Florentius but rather a friend of Philokalas. "I can't imagine who it was," I said.

What a shock that had been when I discovered that Philokalas had been looking for me an hour before I killed him. I'd returned from defending myself and Macedonia had told me that a man, meeting the description of the fellow who had attacked me with the dagger, had just been to her door. A man named Philokalas. At least that was the name he'd given her, which was the only reason I knew his name. I'd never seen the man in my life.

He had never seen me either because, when I surprised him during his visit to me with the icon, he didn't show any recognition.

To be honest, I hadn't given him time, on account of the dagger.

I soon realized that his friends – his accomplices – knew he had come for me, for whatever reason. They'd been following me ever since.

Or so I imagined.

Macedonia must have seen the worry in my face. "Don't worry. I showed him the room belonging to the leather worker on the top floor. Not an icon to be seen, and he certainly looked!"

I didn't want that final, unfinished icon. I could practically feel its eyeless gaze, piercing the wall of my former room, groping down streets and through squares, probing under colonnades, trying to find me. "You can have the icon I left, Macedonia. Or perhaps it would be best to burn it."

"I already did," she said with a sniff. "It was cold last night, not to mention safer for everyone if someone else comes sniffing about. Now remember what I said about extending you some extra credit."

I thanked her and took my leave. She looked put out that I wouldn't tell her where I was living, but what was I supposed to say?

After we parted I continued, more nervous than ever, to my meeting with Florentius. He was waiting just inside one of the Milestone's four arches. As I drew nearer I saw he was pretending to study inscriptions on the marble, as if he cared what the distance was from where he stood to Thessalonika or Antioch or Alexandria.

I called out a greeting.

Three armed guards emerged from the shadows and moved towards me.

They continued past, laughing to each other, arguing about which tavern to patronize.

"You look pale, my friend," Florentius said. "Are you cold? Had you been here when they burnt the great icon you could have warmed yourself. Look, you can still see where the heat scorched the stone. How the flames must have raged!"

"Did you see the burning?"

"No. After all, it would not have been seemly for me to be observed here. And there was violence. Some of the mob joined our saviour in the flames, or so I have heard. I can't imagine it."

The way his eyes sparkled it looked to me as if he were trying hard to imagine the scene. We got down to business, looking over our shoulders all the time.

"Yes, I know where you mean," he said when I described the courtyard with the door to the stairway leading underground. "It's been empty some time with just a watchman living there. A few coins will ensure he looks the other way."

I lingered after he'd gone so we would not be seen walking together.

Everything was arranged.

My gaze wandered across the Golden Milestone. Over the centuries, one emperor after another had mounted his own garish ornaments on the monument.

I found myself studying a group of three statues. Women. They blazed in the sunlight. While some might dream of having gold stitching in their hems and gold medallions pinned to their stolas, these three far exceeded such dreams for they were, themselves, entirely gilded.

From where I stood I could read the inscription on their plinth. They represented Sophia, the wife of Emperor Justin II, Justin's niece Helena, and his daughter, Arabia.

The name was surely a sign.

I was confident by the next evening, Arabia and I would be in very different circumstances.

I was not mistaken.

13

Arabia brought the final meal I would consume in our underground hiding place. I ate smoked mackerel and described my meeting. She took the news that arrangements were in place as a matter of course but didn't linger. She had to be up early to be on hand to guide Florentius.

"Then we shall have a long day ahead, putting the city behind us," she said, leaning forward to give me a last kiss.

When she was gone, I began on the biscuits she'd brought. As I chewed, I noticed reddish flakes on the half-eaten portion in my hand. I brought it up to my eyes. The flakes were paint which had blistered off the icon.

I looked up into the monstrous face. Whereas before, the visage had been stern, now it seemed absolutely malevolent. It radiated hatred. The black pupils of the gigantic eyes were pits, opening on to some illimitable void.

The quibbling of theologians notwithstanding, it was clear Christ had walked the earth in recognizably human form, but the painted Christ before me was not human. Why hadn't I noticed? The eyes weren't human. They were out of proportion. All the features were the wrong size. The shape of the skull was unnatural. There was something very wrong with the mouth.

This was not Christ but something else.

Of course. It was the devil who had presided over the city for so many years. Was that surprising when you considered what went on in the alleyways and the mansions? The horror and depravity? Why would anyone think otherwise?

And wasn't the distorted visage similar to those I painted? Did any of those supposed holy men look human? It had been Satan directing my hand, using it to fill the city with painted demons.

Demons who were human beings were already there – and I among them.

The darkness in the eyes stirred in the trembling lamplight. I thought I could see lights in the depths. The faint glow of an unimaginably distant conflagration.

There came into my head a soft sound like that made by a flame leaping from a bonfire.

The sound resolved into words. Why do you think of Satan or Christ? As if there is any difference. There is no good or evil. There is simply what is. Do you truly want to share your reward with the servant girl? Is she to be trusted any more than Philokalas?

Then I felt my hand close around a jagged chunk of brick, felt myself draw the deadly weapon into my robes.

"No," I whispered. "I won't. I can't."

But you can, the icon told me. Have courage.

I fell back and lay there, arguing in my mind with the icon, with myself, and after an eternity dropped into blessed unconsciousness.

Voices woke me.

I scrambled stiffly to my feet. I was aware of the weight of the brick I had concealed inside my tunic.

Was it already morning?

The voices came nearer.

"Here we are." It was Arabia.

She appeared in the irregular entrance to our lair, smiling. Her impossibly brilliant eyes widened a little as if to tell me, "See, just as I promised, we've done it. It's all right now."

She carried a bulky leather satchel. Florentius was right behind her and I backed up to make room.

Florentius gasped and his florid face grew redder. He stared at the huge image. "Oh, magnificent! To be so close! Oh, wonder of wonders! The poor maimed thing. Ah, the pain he suffers! How can I ever reward you, my dear girl?"

"You already have." Arabia hefted the satchel and shook it until the coins it contained jingled. "Should I have asked for more? I didn't want to be greedy!"

"Do you want more? You shall have it!"

I was standing with my shoulder-blades almost pressed to the icon, but as far as Florentius was concerned I might as well not have been there.

"My men will haul this treasure up the stairs and out to the hand-cart," he told Arabia.

Just then three big men squeezed into the already crowded space. I thought Florentius must be very cautious to arm his servants with swords. Also, it violated our understanding.

One of the newcomers glanced at me, then at Florentius. "You two heretical traitors are under arrest by order of the Patriarch."

Florentius looked around in confusion as if he'd suddenly awakened in some strange place. "What? What is this?"

I probably looked as dazed as he did. "Arabia!" I cried. "Run!" She didn't move. She appeared inexplicably serene.

Florentius gaped at her. "Arabia? Is that what you call yourself when you're not in my bed? Where did you get a name like that?"

Arabia laughed at him.

I hadn't realized she could make such an ugly sound. It made me sick to hear it.

"You, marry a servant?" she sneered. "Do you think I'm a fool? And by the way, that lazy clod of a workman, Philokalas, who never finished patching your basement wall, the one who previously worked for the Patriarch? He won't be coming back."

She directed her horrible gaze at me. "You thought I didn't find his body? Philokalas and I took turns coming down here to make certain the icon was safe, but I always used the door you were so proud of finding. He was careless. I warned him about going in under the hound, but he took no notice."

Florentius's face contorted with agony. "And to think you used to work at the Patriarch's residence! He gave you his recommendation! What kinds of servants does he employ?"

I stood there unable to speak. I couldn't believe . . . didn't want to believe. I could have reached into my tunic, pulled out the brick, and killed her on the spot. But I didn't.

The guard apparently in charge of the other two said, "Young woman, the Patriarch wishes to express his gratitude for helping to apprehend this godless pair. He hopes the small financial arrangement he has made for your earthly needs is suitable, and will be happy to continue to offer you spiritual guidance at the usual times."

The woman I had known as Arabia departed without another glance in my direction. I expected a final word, but the performance had obviously ended.

Florentius babbled about the emperor and the Patriarch. I paid no attention. Neither did the armed men.

"This opening needs to be widened," said the commander. "We don't dare damage the icon. Make sure you keep clear of the broken bricks. We don't want any scratches."

"Ah," Florentius sighed. "Will those monsters consign the Lord to the flames again? Let poor Florentius burn with him!"

"Out of the way," grumbled one of the men. "We've got work to do." He pushed Florentius, who stumbled towards the hole.

"He's trying to escape," the commander casually remarked, and ran Florentius through with his sword. "Make sure the other doesn't get away." He nodded in my direction.

A guard raised his blade and stepped towards me.

I threw myself to one side and yanked with all my strength at the edge of the heavy wooden panel. It toppled forward and crashed down on everyone else in the chamber. I scrambled up and across the back of the icon and was out of it before anyone could react.

Then I ran.

So you, big painted demon, you saved me in the end, I thought. For a while at least.

I didn't have time to be angry at Arabia. Not then. Later there would be more than enough time.

As I burst out from beneath the iron hound, shouts echoed from underground.

I started across the deserted square. Even in my panic, I realized something was different.

What?

I looked up at the stylite's pillar.

The stylite was gone.

But the rope dangling the basket used to send up food hung between the pillar's railing and the ground.

The shouts behind me sounded louder.

I took hold of the rope and pulled myself up, hand over hand. Normally it would have been an impossible feat but my life was at stake.

By the time my pursuers clambered out into the square I was a distant figure in dishevelled clothes, head bent, half leaning against the railing.

The men rushed straight past the pillar.

Nobody notices stylites.

14

I would have been out of the city before nightfall if a guard hadn't been left beside the iron hound. No one notices stylites, but a guard wouldn't miss seeing one of those holy men sliding down a rope off his pillar.

Before dark the watchman was relieved by two more who set up torches along the colonnade. Perhaps they hoped I would return to try to hide myself in the underground maze.

I was in a bad spot. Sooner or later somebody was going to check the pillar. But at least I had time to think and I'd always survived by my wits.

Admittedly I'd made a few errors in judgement the past couple of days. It was obvious now but could I have known then that Arabia was waiting for me that morning near the hound?

In retrospect I was able to piece the story together. Arabia and Philokalas had been working together. Arabia had seen me at Florentius's house and knew I could help her and Philokalas sell the icon, something they couldn't do themselves – one being a servant, the other a lowly labourer.

She probably met Philokalas when both worked at the Patriarch's residence. Philokalas must have come upon the hidden image while in the course of repair-work in the Patriarch's cellars following the earthquake. In fact, the earthquake might well have revealed the icon's hiding place.

Had Arabia and Philokalas carted it together to the underground hiding place where I found it, and she pretended to see it for the first time? She could have let Philokalas into the Patriarch's house at night; the only way to get the icon down underground was through the door I had been so happy to find. Or had Philokalas's other accomplices helped him move it? Were there others? Perhaps the men following me had been all my imagination and the fellow who asked Macedonia about Philokalas was simply a worried friend to whom he had unwisely let drop a word or two about an icon-painter he was seeking?

At any rate, once Philokalas vanished, Arabia began looking for the useful icon-painter herself. And now she'd double-crossed me. Not only was she running off with my share of Florentius's payment, she also had whatever the rival collector had paid her.

How could she? It didn't seem fair. I would never have killed her. Even if I'd had the chance. I swear I wouldn't have killed her.

There had to be a rival collector, the way I saw it. Despite what they said, the guards and the man who had killed Florentius weren't sent by the Patriarch – who was well known to be violently opposed to icons. That was why Leo made him Patriarch. He wouldn't be concerned if the image were damaged when transported, as his supposed men had carelessly indicated he would.

Not everyone would have noticed that little slip, but I did.

It could only mean those men were sent by someone else who had heard about the icon's survival or been informed about it by Arabia. Doubtless she'd managed to get the collector's name from Florentius, who'd evidently been taking advantage of her by his own admission.

I was exhausted, but there wasn't enough room on the pillar's platform to lie down, so I leaned against its railing and looked out over the city. The glowing dome of the Great Church seemed to throw orange sparks along the streets and into windows and on ships in the harbour. I could almost feel the gaze of monstrous eyes staring down out of the black vault of the heavens, but there was nothing to see up there except the glittering cold points of stars, and ragged wraiths of cloud fleeing before a rising wind.

People say Hades is underground, but I found it up there in cold loneliness.

And it was the iron hound who guarded the entrance to the path I took that led me there.

I wouldn't have killed Arabia. When I wasn't looking up I looked down at the piece of brick beside my feet, the unused symbol of my mercy.

15

At dawn I began to cry out for Patriarch Anastasius.

People pay no attention to stylites, but then most stylites don't demand to see the Patriarch and shout about stolen icons.

I'm not certain what I expected. After days down there in the dark with a gigantic demon staring at me, and then a frigid night atop a pillar too close to that big being in the sky, I was probably not in my right mind. But I could not be certain I was not still being sought in order to silence me forever.

The one result of my plea I didn't expect was for Patriarch Anastasius himself to appear.

Yes, possibly it was a vision. The other day I saw Satan perched like a huge bat on Justinian's statue atop the column in the Augustaion. I'm fairly certain that was a vision. And I've seen other things as well. You get a new perspective from one of these stylite's columns.

But whether the visitation was real or not – and what difference does it make to someone in my position? – a regal-looking man, swathed in layers of heavily embroidered robes, entered the square accompanied by a company of retainers, most carrying lances.

The Patriarch climbed up stairs concealed inside my pillar – a feature I wished I had known about when fleeing – and emerged on the narrow, windswept platform.

He was not an old man. He wore a beard, cut in the manner of the icon with whom I had recently grown acquainted. His eyes were not as large as the image's, but they were almost as deep and his mouth was as cruel.

"Excellency," I began, having no idea how you addressed a Patriarch. "A traitor rescued the Chalke Christ you wished destroyed, another found it, and yet another traitor—"

He put up a hand. "We can speak freely here since nobody will hear us except, perhaps, heaven. I was informed that the watchman I ordered stationed on this pillar was behaving oddly. Since he had already been relieved of his duty once my icon was retrieved, I was curious."

"Watchman? Your icon? What happened to the stylite?"

He smiled but did not answer all my questions. "Have you noticed there's a good view of that scabby dog from up here?

And there's no other way into that part of the labyrinth apart from through a door in a certain courtyard."

"But you ordered the icon burned!"

"What choice did I have? The holy image had been taken down and brought to stay overnight in my residence. Then when the splintered remains were brought out to be set on fire, the pile of bits of painted boards was so large that nobody realized part of it was missing."

"And you concealed the upper portion? But why?"

"We must always think of the future, in this world as in the one to which we will go in due course. The next emperor may have different notions and wish icons to be restored. You see I speak frankly. If I realized the earthquake had fractured the wall of the vault in which that upper panel was hidden, I wouldn't have allowed the workman down there. He stole it. Carted it off and hid it."

"Those were your men who came for the icon? It was you who paid Arabia?"

"My former servant, you mean? The girl who went to work for Florentius? A lovely girl. I've come to know her quite well. A pity about Florentius. He was found murdered in an alley not far from here. Such is the state of the city, no doubt the villains responsible will never be apprehended."

The Patriarch looked away and scanned the panorama around us. "I've often wondered what you holy men could see from here. It's magnificent."

"But I'm not a holy man!"

"I disagree. I believe you are. Look, your hands are blue with cold. Suffering sharpens faith. The more tenuous our connection to our pitiful fleshly husks, the closer we are to heaven. You are blessed, my friend. It is difficult to feel the holy presence while wrapped in fine robes and surrounded by luxury." He gave a sorrowful shake of his head and smiled faintly. "Yet can those of us who choose to serve him refuse the harsh sacrifices as we are asked to make?"

He fixed me in his demon's gaze. "You know too much to ever descend from this pillar. I shall allow you to stay here and glory in the presence of the Lord. I will arrange to have acolytes, armed for your protection, stationed below day and night."

It took an instant for me to understand the horror of my situation. "No, excellency," I cried. "Why not kill me? Why leave me here?"

"Because," the patriarch said as he turned to go down the stairs, "it pleases me."

16

"Did you truly believe you would never see me again?"

Arabia smiled sweetly up at me. As usual, my armed guards retired out of earshot when she waved them away.

A warm dawn breeze ruffled her brightly coloured silks. All around, the ruins and vacant spaces of Constantinople were coming alive with the myriad greens of spring. I could almost smell her perfume.

"After the Patriarch left, I wondered," I said. "I considered throwing myself to the ground, but a colleague of mine died in a fall, and, well . . ."

"A nasty death," she agreed.

"Yes. I could never bring myself to do it though I would at least be lying down. Sometimes I long for a doorway to lie in and be out of the rain."

Her lips formed a red pout. "Then you did doubt me."

"Oh, yes, I did at times. The morning I woke up with ice in my hair, and the night the angels descended from the clouds and set the sea on fire. Those were the worst."

"It's a fine house, isn't it?" she said. "Even if it isn't a farmhouse."

"Yes, though I can only see the corner of it, just past the Great Church and the Patriarch's residence."

"It's very convenient to the Patriarch's house, that's true."

I yanked on the rope and hauled the basket up. Arabia waved to me before pulling the curtain of her litter shut. Her attendants picked the chair up and trotted away across the square. But she would be back. She visits often.

She always brings me a big basket full of boiled eggs.

I wished I'd had a boiled egg that long ago morning. Maybe if I hadn't eaten the eyes of the Lord, things would have turned out differently.

Night of the Snow Wolf

Peter Tremayne

We move back a century from the previous story and the Byzantine world, to the Celtic world of seventh century Ireland and the time of Sister Fidelma. She is a dalaigh, *or advocate of the law courts of Ireland, and was the daughter of the King of Muman, ancient Munster. As Tremayne reveals at the website of the International Sister Fidelma Society (http://www.sisterfidelma.com/), "Her main role could be compared to a modern Scottish sheriff substitute whose job is to gather and assess the evidence, independent of the police, to see if there is a case to be answered." Fidelma has been conducting her investigations through nineteen novels, so far, and two collections of stories. The series began with* Absolution by Murder *(1994) set in the year 664. The nineteenth novel,* Chalice of Blood *(2010) has reached the year 670, and Fidelma is still only 34 years old, so there's scope for many more stories. The following, which takes place in the winter of 670, is set in the Silvermines Mountains of north-west Tipperary.*

Sister Fidelma realized that she had taken the wrong turning the moment the track began to ascend at an unusually steep angle. By this time she knew that she should be on level ground, as her intended route passed along the valley floor between the mountains instead of ascending towards the higher reaches. But the snow was still falling, cold, thick and blinding, so that she saw only whiteness shrouding everything around her. She realized, too, that nightfall was not far off.

She adjusted her woollen cloak closer around her neck in a vain effort to keep out the cold, before halting her horse for a moment to consider the situation. Night and the snow were falling too fast for her to have any hope in finding the right track, even if she turned back. The route that she was taking seemed to lead in the same general direction, perhaps parallel to the track along the valley floor along which she had intended to follow. There was always the expectation that the path she was on might descend and rejoin her original route; although that was a slim expectation, indeed.

Whichever path she took, she would have to find shelter very soon for there was no chance of her reaching her destination before dark. She wondered if Brother Eadulf was already at the settlement of Béal Átha Gabhann, "the mouth of the ford of the smith", for it was there that she had arranged to meet him in order that they might travel back to Cashel together. She shivered again. The oncoming night was bringing a cold wind with it. There was no doubt that she could not ride much further without seeking shelter. Even if she could find her way down to lower ground, she had to cross a valley and a broad river before negotiating another pass through Sliabh an Airgid, the Silver Mountains, before arriving at her intended objective.

The mournful cry of a wolf came faintly, muffled by the barrier of falling snow. It was taken up by an answering cry but, in these conditions, it was difficult to judge the direction and distance of the sound.

Fidelma's horse started nervously, tossing its head with its thick mane.

"Steady, steady there, Aonbharr," Fidelma called, leaning forward and patting its short neck encouragingly. The horse calmed immediately. Aonbharr was of an ancient breed, a gift from her brother, bought from a Gaulish trader. It was usually of a calm temperament, intelligent and agile. She had named him 'the supreme one" after the horse of Manannán mac Lir, the god of the oceans, who had been worshipped before the coming of the New Faith. According to legend, the horse could run across land or sea, fly across mountains, and could not be killed by man or god. Fidelma smiled softly. At this moment she wished that Aonbharr had the same abilities as his mythical namesake so that she could reach her destination before nightfall.

There came another plaintive cry, both beautiful and chilling. The mournful wolf-call that, although she had heard it often enough, sent a shiver down her spine. This time it seemed closer and slightly above her, somewhere up on the higher reaches of the mountain.

She urged her horse forward gently along the snowy track, blinking against the icy pellicles that blew against her face in the gusting wind. They hit her face like hurtful darts.

She was conscious now of the darkening sky, even through the falling snow, which made the oncoming night more of a curious twilight.

Then there came a new sound, a new cry, from somewhere above her. It was not the cry of a wolf, but something like a woeful bellow. Frowning, she tugged slightly on the rein and obediently her horse came to a halt. She listened carefully, head to one side, trying to analyse the sounds that mingled with the gusting wind. The bellow came again. She was right. It was the distressed cry of a cow. She glanced up the hill, screwing up her eyes to penetrate the driving snow, trying to locate the beast, and wondering what kind of a farmer would leave his animal outside on such a night as this.

The snow flurries eased for a moment and she saw the dark outline of some buildings just a short way up the hill. She suddenly relaxed and smiled. The cow must be in one of the sheds, and the buildings indicated it was a hill-farm. That meant shelter, warmth and hospitality for the night. All she had to do was find the path that led upwards to the farmstead. It was not far away but the precipitous slopes were dangerous unless one followed a path. But it was a question of finding the path.

She slid from her horse and, leading it by the reins, began to walk slowly along the track, peering carefully at the ground and bordering embankment. It did not take her long to spot a depression through the snowy banks, that indicated where a path left the main track and wound up the hillside towards the buildings. Even then, Fidelma would not endanger her horse by returning to its back. She walked carefully forward, leading the animal upwards along the path. In this manner it was some time before she arrived at the buildings, which, by their outline, appeared to be a *bóthan* or large cabin, and a barn beyond that – containing a chicken run, by the sound of the angry clucking.

But the buildings were all in darkness and, apart from the sounds of the animals, there seemed an uncanny silence.

Fidelma paused and shouted: "*Hóigh!*"

The only answer was the cries of the animals. There was neither sound nor movement from the *bóthan*.

Fidelma took a step forward towards the door of the *bothán* and found that Aonbharr was tugging on the reins, pulling backwards. The sudden tug hurt her arm and she turned round in surprise. The horse's eyes were wide, eyeballs rolling and nostrils flaring.

"Steady, boy, steady," she coaxed, reaching out a hand to rub his muzzle. He calmed down a little, standing still but trembling. She peered round, trying to find what had upset the horse. She noticed a mound of snow before the door. Whatever lay beneath, she realized there was a dark red stain there. Blood! The mound was too small to be that of a human. She turned and led Aonbharr towards the barn, where she noticed there was a stretch of fencing and a rail. She secured the reins to the fence and turned back to the mound.

Bending down, she scraped some of the snow away. It soon became clear that it was the short, leggy body of a dog. It had a dense, wiry coat and wore a collar with a leash attached. When she tugged at it, Fidelma found the leash was also attached to a metal ring by the door. The dog was a terrier. Such a breed was commonly used to hunt small game in this area but they were also alert and courageous guard dogs. What was immediately obvious were the facts that someone had smashed the skull of the animal with a blunt instrument and that it had happened not very long ago, as the blood was not yet congealing.

Fidelma's mouth compressed in a grim line and she rose to her feet, glancing around with eyes narrowed. There was no movement anywhere. Aonbharr stood patiently tethered. The cow was still plaintively lowing, the chickens clucking. As she turned towards the dark door of the *bóthan* she heard, once more, the nearby cry of a wolf.

Unconsciously, she squared her shoulders ready to face the unexpected, and moved towards the door. She raised her fist and hammered on it twice and paused. As she expected, there was no sound of movement, no answer. She lowered her hand to the door-catch and raised it. To her surprise – for she fully expected to find it locked or bolted – the door swung inwards into the blackness.

"Is anyone there?" she called, feeling a little foolish at the question.

She hesitated on the threshold a moment or so and took a pace inside. Within the curious twilight from the reflected snow outside, a gloomy half-light that permeated from the door and a single small window, there was little discernible. The chill was almost as bad inside as it was outside. She hesitated a moment before stepping towards the outline of a table where she could just make out an oil lamp.

From her shoulder she removed the strap from which hung her *sursaing-bholg,* her girdle bag, which she always carried on journeys. In it reposed various items, including her *cior-bholg* or comb-bag that contained toiletries which all women carried. But, more importantly, it was also where she kept her *tenlach-teined,* the means of producing "hand-fire"; a flint, steel and a tinder-box. As part of their training, warriors had to practise the art of swiftly lighting fires and Fidelma, growing up among those whose task was to guard her family – for was she not the daughter of Failbe Flann, King of Muman – she would often pass happy days being taught this art by kindly warriors until she was as adept at it as they were. Indeed, it did not take her long to ignite the tinder and light the oil lamp; it was a rough earthenware pot with a snout to support the wick.

Now she had a better light she took it in her hand and peered round the inside of the cabin. Its walls were of dry stone and its roof was of timber. It was poorly furnished. The stout wooden table, on which the oil lamp had sat, also had two earthenware bowls and wooden spoons nearby, as if in preparation for a meal. Two chairs were at the table. A cot stood with blankets near the far corner of the fireplace, which contained grey ash, but there was faint warmth coming from it. There was plenty of kindling and logs piled near the fireplace. A large lantern hung unlit over the fireplace, a sturdy type of lamp, whose wick was protected so that it could be used outside, even in a high wind. Also by the fire, to one side of the pile of logs, stood a hunter's bow and a sheaf of arrows. Even as quickly as she made the examination, Fidelma knew that they were not of good quality workmanship, but of the sort a hill-farmer might make himself and use for hunting. Apart from an old wooden chest and some cupboards, there was nothing else in the cabin. Nor was there any indication of why or when the occupants had left, except that it was less than a day or so ago because the fire, with its smouldering ashes, could not have lasted much longer before dying entirely.

She stood, undecided. Then she became aware again of the whistling wind, saw the snow flurries beyond the door, and heard the bellow of the cow and the nervous whinny of her horse. Abruptly, she stirred herself into action. She went to the fire and placed some kindling on it, reaching for the small bellows. It took a minute or two before the kindling began to spark and flame and she was able to place a couple of large pieces of wood on it. Satisfied, she stood up and lit the heavier storm-lantern from the oil lamp, turned, and headed outside, closing the cabin door behind her.

She glanced sorrowfully at the dead terrier before passing on to the barn. Aonbharr gave a plaintive neigh, turning his head in her direction, as if comforted to see her again.

"First things first, boy," she said, as if he could understand. She opened the barn door and passed in quickly, closing the door behind her, lest any of the animals escaped. The animal making the most noise was a large bay-coloured cow that turned mournful eyes on her and began to make a lowing sound. Fidelma saw immediately what the problem was: the cow needing milking as well as feeding. In another corner, two goats came towards her bleating. They were partitioned in a pen but it was clear they needed feeding, as did the half-a-dozen chickens squabbling in a run along one side of the barn.

She stood looking at them and shaking her head. Then she hung up the storm-lantern from a hook on one of the rafters, for the roof was very low and the barn no bigger than a small room.

"Very well," she addressed them. "I'm not much good at this but . . ."

She glanced around. There was a bucket and milking stool to one side. But first she turned and searched for the grain that would be used for the chicken feed. There was a sack nearby. That task over, she turned her attention to the goats. There was a stack of hay, which she knew to be the primary source of nutrients for goats during the winter months, and she distributed it in their feeding trough, making sure that neither of the two does were in need of milking. There was still water available. It did not take long to place the cow's feed ready, but the animal was still lowing and it was obvious what the priority was.

With a sigh, she placed the three-legged stool and took the bucket. She had not milked a cow since she was a young girl but she had not forgotten the technique. Finally, with the cow content and the bucket full of warm milk, she turned to her next task. Aonbharr would have to accept being stabled next to the cow. She led her horse in and unsaddled him. Then, finding a soft brush, vigorously took the snow from his coat and dried it as best she could with handfuls of hay. Then she spotted a heavy, ageing horse blanket tucked away in the corner of some rafters. She covered Aonbharr with it and managed to find a small sack of oats, making sure that he was able to reach the trough of water. A contented quiet had descended on the inhabitants of the barn and so, with tasks fulfilled, she took the storm-lantern and the bucket of milk and went outside, closing the door behind her.

Night had fully descended now but the wind was still gusting and howling, causing the snow to come almost horizontally across the valley. She stood for a moment, storm-lantern in hand, head to one side listening to the sound of the tempest. Now and then she turned, thinking she detected the cries of the wolves amidst the mountains. That reminded her, and she retraced her steps back to where the body of the terrier lay. She paused, shaking her head sadly before she passed into the *bóthan* and placed the milk on the table. The fire was blazing away now. She searched quickly hoping to find a spade or any similar implement.

She was tired now, cold and hungry. The task would have to wait until morning, but she had a practical duty first. She went outside again with the storm-lantern. She set it by the dead animal, untied the leash and wiped the falling snow away as much as she could. Then she examined her surroundings. There was little choice. She had half-dragged, half-carried the carcass of the animal to a depression she could see a little way down the hill from the cabin, and pushed the body into it, before looking around for rocks and stones under the covering of snow. These she placed over the remains, packing them with as much snow as she could.

"Sorry, boy," she said grimly. "That's as much as I can do this night."

Her main purpose was to prevent scavengers from savaging the body, until she could bury it properly. With wolves in the vicinity it was dangerous to leave a carcass in the open, especially when there was a barn of live animals nearby.

Her duty to the livestock complete, she collected the storm-lantern and returned to the cabin, securing the door behind her. She went to the fire and placed more logs on it. Then, glancing round to ensure all was secure, she stood before the fire, took off her clothes and drew a blanket she had taken from the cot around her, using it to rub her cold limbs vigorously. Finally dry and warm, she turned, took an earthenware mug and helped herself to the fresh milk.

One of the cupboards revealed some slightly stale bread, cheese and cold meats. They seemed completely edible. She made herself a meal then, drawing a large wooden chair with arms on it before the fire, sat there eating her frugal meal and staring into the flames. As she did so, she allowed her mind to consider the problem that confronted her.

What had happened to the occupants of the *bóthan*?

She used the plural because she had discovered female items of clothing and toiletry as well as male. She presumed that they were husband and wife, existing in this lonely hill-farm. They had deserted the place for no more than a day or so before her arrival, leaving the cow to be milked and the animals unfed. Why? She could accept the idea that the man had gone off to look for one of his animals in the snowstorm and come to some grief. That was not impossible in these mountains. Perhaps his wife, in desperation, had gone to look for him.

There was only one thing that made her uncomfortable about that explanation. The dead guard dog; the terrier outside the door with his skull smashed in.

She moved forward and placed another log on the fire, watching it crackle a little with the sparks flying upwards into the chimney. She meditated on the problem for a while, listening to the whispering wail of the wind around the eaves of the cabin and, now and again, the lonely howl of the wolves.

Sleep crept up on her unawares.

When she awoke she felt suddenly cold and with that half-dreaming, half-waking sensation that there were other people in the room talking to her; a laugh, a cry, a strange thumping sound. She lay for a moment, that moment between sleep and waking when dreams seem as real as actuality. Then she stiffened. She was fully awake and she could hear people talking; again she could hear an odd thumping sound. Her eyes stared into the semi-gloom around her. The embers of the fire lighted the cabin for she had extinguished the oil lamp. She could see nothing. The interior of the cabin was as empty as when she had arrived.

Slowly she sat up, feeling stiff and uncomfortable, took the oil lamp and, igniting it from the embers of the fire, stood up holding it high, and peered round again.

She distinctly heard a laugh. It was far away but not outside the cabin. It seemed to come from under her very feet. It was harsh, without humour, almost . . . almost evil. Fidelma hardly ever applied that word to anything. Then there came two thuds, in quick succession, which seemed to cause the very cabin to shake. The floor seemed to vibrate. She waited, lamp in hand, every nerve tensed, her senses alert. But there was quiet now. An eternity seemed to pass and she could hear nothing more than the wailing of the wind. She moved quietly to the small window but it was blocked with snow. She hesitated a moment, placed the lamp on the table and went to the door, removing the wooden bar which fastened it.

Outside, the snow was still gusting in the wind but it remained dark. She could not tell how near dawn it was, only that there was no glimmer of light in the sky. The snow-clouds hid the moon as well as the stars. Then, near at hand, came the eerie howl of a wolf and, so it seemed, another animal close by answered the cry. She peered forward, suddenly nervous. The cry started again, and was answered again. It was clear that this was no lone wolf, weak and banished from the pack. These sounds were of hunting wolves, which meant perhaps as many as ten. She knew that country folk were liable to exaggerate the stories of wolf attacks on livestock and on people. Tradition painted the wolves as the incarnation of evil and malevolence, and, while Fidelma knew more than most about woodcraft, she admitted to having respect for ancient tales. She swiftly pushed the door shut again and put the bar back in place, making certain that it was secure.

She stood for a moment in uncertainty. Finally she turned, to build up the fire again before sitting down in the chair and pulling the blanket around her for more warmth. Somehow she had no inclination to go to lay down on the bed of the absent occupants.

There were only two possibilities for what had occurred. She had either imagined things or they had been real. And if they were real, then there must be an explanation. She had not been imagining things. Of that, she was absolutely sure. She *had* heard voices, and she had heard the thuds that shook the cabin.

Even before the coming of Christianity, her people had implicit belief in the Otherworld. Gods and mortals could pass freely between the Otherworld and this world. The old religion was based on the unchanging nature of the elements of this visible world as well as the invisible Otherworld. They were part of one entity. Both worlds were without barriers for, although parallel, they were not mutually exclusive. Fidelma did not reject the concept for it was still a living faith in many parts of the country in spite of the changes put in place by the advocates of the New Faith. When a soul died in this world, it was reborn in the other, and when a soul died in the Otherworld, it was reborn in this. A constant interchange of souls was taking place. And yet, it was said that at midnight on one special day of the year, the Otherworld could be both seen and heard. She shook her head. She had been raised with reason – taught that only facts counted, that everything could be explained by logic if one had sufficient information to do so. Just because she did not have the information to make an explanation, it did not mean to say that an explanation did not exist.

In trying to analyse the matter, sleep stole up on her again.

She woke feeling stiff and uncomfortable. She stretched and eased her limbs before rising to her feet. A faint light was filtering through the snow-covered widow and she could her the distant clucking of chickens. It was past dawn. She took some wood and placed it on the dying fire. Then she found the bowl of cold water, its edges showing where it had begun to freeze. She had used it on the previous night. She splashed her face – used the items from her *ciobhog*, her comb-bag, to freshen herself – dressed, and looked for something to eat. The milk was cold and still drinkable.

Feeling thus refreshed, she went to the door, unbarred it and looked out.

The gusting winds of the night had blown away the snow-clouds and, amazingly, the sky was azure with the pale sun hanging above the eastern peaks. The snow carpeted the mountains, lit in bright white and, seemingly, undisturbed. Everything seemed calm and peaceful. She made her way to the barn to attend to the animals. While she was feeding them, she turned her attention yet again to the mystery, and what she should do next. There was no choice but to ride on to Béal Átha Gabhann although it meant abandoning the animals. Also, if the occupants had come to mishap on the mountains and survived the night, it meant abandoning them too. But what else could she do alone? She was not even sure exactly where she was except that she must be somewhere in the Sliabh Eibhlinc mountain range, an area she did not know except for the main route through them which, with the snows of last evening, she had managed to miss.

Outside the barn she stood and examined the shapes of the mountains but there was none she recognized. Not that she was expecting much, for she had only travelled this route a few times, but thought she might have retained some memory of the shape of the hills that were always an important guide to travellers.

She returned to the barn and saddled Aonbharr in readiness. The sooner she left, the sooner she might be able to find someone who could help either look after the animals or find the missing occupants.

She made her way back to the cabin to collect her *sursaing-bholg*, the girdle bag with her belongings. She opened the door and froze abruptly. In the chair before the fire – the chair where she had slept for a few uncomfortable hours – sat a man. He turned his head sharply in surprise at her entrance.

He was tall, thin and with a shock of white hair but without beard or moustache. His high-domed forehead accentuated a thin nose with strangely arched nostrils and high bridge. His pale skin stretched tightly over his sharply etched features. Indeed, there seemed no colour in his cheeks at all. He seemed a man who avoided the excesses of the weather but, in spite of his thin features, the pale hands that spread palm downward on his knees, bespoke strength.

Controlling his surprise, he rose from the chair and stood regarding her with pale, almost colourless eyes.

"Who are you?" Fidelma demanded, also recovering her poise.

"I should ask you that question first," the man replied, with a thin smile. "What are you doing here?"

"Are you the owner of this farmstead?" she persisted, not put off by his counter question. Then she relented a little. "I am Fidelma of Cashel. I was on my way to Béal Átha Gabhann last night when I lost my way, saw this cabin and came here to seek shelter."

At her name, the man showed some recognition.

"Fidelma the *dálaigh*?" he asked sharply. "The lawyer and sister to the King?"

"I am an advocate of the law courts," she confirmed. "And now it is your turn to identify yourself."

"I am . . . I am brother to Cianat, wife to Cuilind, who owns this farm," he replied, shortly. "I came to visit them. I tend goats on the far side of this valley? You say that you came here last night?"

"I found this cabin deserted. There is no sign of the occupants. The animals were in need of tending and, most worryingly, the guard dog was laying by the cabin door, still tethered, but its skull crushed in."

It was impossible to judge the man's expression in the shadows of the cabin; he breathed out sharply but said nothing.

"You say that you are kin to the people here?" pressed Fidelma. "What is your name?"

"I am known as Fáelur," he replied. "What do you know of . . . of the disappearance of Cianat and Cuilind?"

"I have told you all I know," responded Fidelma. "I suppose that you know these mountains well? They might have had an accident in the snowstorm."

Fáelur pursed his lips as he thought about it.

"Maybe they have gone to visit someone else in the valley. It would be unusual for anything to happen, because Cuilind knows the mountains well, as does my sister."

"No matter how well a person thinks they know mountains, in a snowstorm mistakes can be made," Fidelma assured him. "*Cotidiana vilescunt*," she added the Latin phrase automatically, meaning that familiarity breeds contempt.

Fáelur nodded slowly in agreement.

"Perhaps you are right. One thinks one knows the land well but snow obliterates the features, no matter how familiar they have been. Indeed, they may have come to grief on the mountain in the snowstorm. Anything could have happened, a broken leg or some such accident."

"I presume there are people here who could form a search party for them?"

"I can certainly raise some . . . some local people."

"The one thing that bothered me was that I found the dog still tied up and killed, its skull smashed. I dragged it from the door and piled stones and snow over it as there were wolves in evidence in the mountains last night."

Fáelur glanced at her quickly. "That is worrying. What do you make of it?"

"There is nothing I can make of it without information," replied Fidelma. "Anyway, I suggest that if there are others living in this valley, you should organize a search for your sister and her husband. Alas, I cannot stay longer. I must try to find the way to Béal Átha Gabhann for I was expected there last night."

For a passing moment, it seemed a look of relief came into the man's eyes and then he sighed.

"I will take care of things now."

"I have fed the animals. But they will need tending to later on. The cow particularly."

"That is no problem. I will collect some friends and look after things here. As you say, a search must be organized." There was a hesitation. "Are you rested well, for it will be a hard ride to Béal Átha Gabhann?"

"I was warm and comfortable in the cabin last night. I wish I could stay to help in the search for the owners. I will endeavour to make amends for their hospitality once I have completed my business."

Something had made her withhold telling Fáelur about her disturbed night. She did not know why. Perhaps it was because he seemed anxious about her having had a good rest.

She moved to the table and collected her things, her comb-bag, and placed them all in her *sursaing-bholg* and hung it over her shoulder. She turned to the man with a smile.

"Now I will get my horse and if you can point me in the right direction . . . ?"

The man came with her to the door of the cabin and waited while she collected Aonbharr.

"There is a path down there that leads back to a main track," he said, pointing in the direction she had climbed to the cabin from on the previous night. "Best lead your horse down to it. Then you turn northwards," he indicated the direction. "You see that peak there, on the far side of the valley? That is Sliabh Coimeálta, Keeper's Hill. Keep that on your left and this track comes down through a valley, at the end of which you'll find the streams that rise in these hills, all converging into a broad stream called Glaise an Ghleanna. Follow the bank and that will lead you directly to the main river, the Mhaoilchearn. You'll see a small stone circle by it. It is easy to ford the river there and beyond it you will see the pass that will bring you through the mountains called Sliabh an Airgid. Once through the pass, you will find your destination."

Fidelma thanked him and offered her best wishes that his search for his missing sister and brother-in-law would prove successful and that all would be well with them. He nodded thoughtfully and stood by the cabin door watching her as she led her horse back down the path to the main track. It was difficult, as the snowfall of the previous night had completely covered any recognisable signs of where it lay. It was only when she reached a flat area of snow that ran in both directions that she realized she had reached the main track. She mounted Aonbharr before glancing back. It was as if the man had not moved, for he still stood watching her. She raised a hand in acknowledgement and set off at a quick walking pace northward on her journey.

It was only sometime later that she realized what had been causing an irritation in the back of her mind. As she had led Aonbharr from the cabin down the path to the main track, the path had been completely covered in snow, so that she had to feel her way down. It had been completely covered in the snowfall, smooth and white, except where a single set of tracks followed it. They could have been the tracks of a dog but Fidelma knew that they had doubtless been made by one of the wolves that had been howling near the cabin during the night. But that was not what was causing the growing unease. It was the question, how had a man called Fáelur come to the cabin? Surely he would have left tracks in the snow? And there were none.

★★★

"We were worried about you, Fidelma. We were afraid that you were lost in the snowstorm. Eadulf was very concerned." It was Fidelma's cousin Scoth, the daughter of Prince Gilcach of the Eóghanacht Airthir Chliach, who chided her as she ushered her into the hall of her father's hunting lodge.

Fidelma had reached the settlement at Béal Átha Gabhann by mid afternoon, when the sky had already begun to darken again. There she had found not only Eadulf, waiting anxiously for her, but also her cousin. Prince Gilcach kept a small hunting lodge at the settlement and Scoth was currently in residence, insisting that Eadulf and Fidelma stay with her. Soon Fidelma was relaxing in a chair before a crackling log fire with a glass of mulled wine. Seated by her were Eadulf and Scoth.

Scoth was younger than Fidelma by five or six years; an attractive girl with golden-red hair who seemed to treat everything and everyone with an intense curiosity. Her family shared a common descent with the Eóghanacht of Cashel from Óengus – the first Christian King of Muman. Scoth was always lively and loved nothing more than to gossip.

"Scoth suggested that we should form a search party for you," admitted Eadulf, Fidelma's stoic partner, "for there were violent snowstorms across the peaks last night."

Fidelma glanced at Eadulf with a quick, reassuring smile.

"There was no need to worry on my account. I found shelter for the night."

"Where did you find hospitality?" demanded Scoth in surprise. "These mountains are sparsely populated and the tracks are few and far between." When Fidelma explained the route she had taken, a worried expression formed on the face of her cousin. "I know where you went wrong. You must have left the main track in the valley and headed through the high pass between Sliabh Coimeálta and An Cnoc Fionn. You should have remained in the valley and followed the track to the east of An Cnoc Fionn."

They were interrupted by a knock on the door and one of the female attendants entered.

"Excuse me, my lady," she said, speaking directly to Scoth. "A messenger has arrived and needs a private word."

Scoth looked irritable. "I am with my cousin. Can't they wait?"

"They told me to tell you that it is news of Rechtabra."

Scoth rose quickly with an apologetic expression. "Rechtabra is my wayward cousin," she said to Fidelma. "You may remember him? I will be but a moment."

She was, indeed, back before hardly any time had passed. "What were we talking about? You said that you missed the valley track east of An Cnoc Fionn."

"It was in the blizzard that I lost the path. There was no track to follow," countered Fidelma.

Scoth looked serious. "But no one lives up along that high pass. There is scarcely a track you can follow on foot, let alone one to ride."

Fidelma smiled thinly. "I found that out for myself."

Scoth seemed clearly worried. "So where did you find shelter? It is said that there are caves in those mountains but they are thought to be the lairs of wolves that haunt that area. Surely you didn't shelter in a cave?"

Seated before the roaring fire with Scoth and Eadulf, and the warming mug of mulled wine in her hand, Fidelma felt rather embarrassed by some of the fears that had passed through her mind during the previous night. She relaxed and told her story with a smile.

"A curious tale," Scoth commented reflectively.

"The place being so deserted, I am wondering if we could raise some people and ride back to the valley tomorrow to see if we can help with the search. I was considering passing back that way on my return to Cashel. Of course, with this weather it may well be bodies that we would be searching for, if the woman's relative has not found them before."

"There is no need for you to be troubled in that matter," Scoth insisted. "A trip back through the high pass will take both you and Eadulf out of your way. It is not the best route back to Cashel." She glanced through the window. "Nightfall will be on us soon otherwise I would suggest my warriors should go to help the search for this missing couple. Who did you say these hill-farmers were, Fidelma? Ciarnat and . . . ?"

"Ciarnat and Cuilind," repeated Fidelma. "And the man who was the brother of the woman said his name was Fáelur."

Scoth started nervously. The involuntary movement was not lost on Fidelma.

"Do you know these people?" she asked with interest.

The girl shook her head. "In truth, I have never heard of Ciarnat and Cuilind before . . . except . . ."

"Except?" pressed Fidelma when she hesitated.

The girl regarded her with an odd expression.

"You know the meaning of the name Fáelur, surely?"

Fidelma shrugged. It had not occurred to her to think of its meaning. "It means . . ." she paused. A frown crossed her features as she realized what was passing through Scoth's mind. "It means 'wolfman'."

"What of it?" asked Eadulf, curiously. "Our son is called Alchú – little hound. It's common enough to use such names, surely? I knew a man called Onchú, which means fierce hound."

Scoth was still serious. "We do not couple the name of a wolf with a personal name. Not in these mountains. There is a legend . . ."

"Ah! A legend," Fidelma smiled, trying to lighten her cousin's ominous tone.

Eadulf shook his head in rebuke at her, missing the point. "Didn't you once say that legend is but half-remembered history?"

Fidelma shrugged and asked: "What is the legend?"

"The old ones say that there is an evil wolf-pack in the mountains that is led by a being who is half-wolf and half man. A being called Fáelur – the wolfman." There was suppressed awe and excitement in Scoth's voice.

Fidelma leant back and chuckled. "Are you suggesting that the man I met was no man but a werewolf? Come Scoth! I thought better of you than to give credence to ancient legends."

The girl remained serious. "It is no ancient legend. People here have been talking about such things during the last week or two."

"The last week? Why?"

"They say the Fáelur attacks the unwary and carries them off to the lair of his were-folk. About this time, so the locals say, there is a particular full of the moon that they call 'the night of the snow wolf'. This is when the were-folk are most active."

Fidelma smiled mischievously. "Well, he didn't carry me off to his lair, which must prove that this Fáelur wasn't the wolfman of the legend. Besides, this encounter was in broad daylight. Come, Scoth, these ancient stories . . ."

"I told you that they were not so ancient. Why, only last week . . ." she paused and her lips compressed.

"Last week?" Fidelma pressed with interest. "What happened?"

"The people here say that one of their number was carried off by the Fáelur and has not been seen since."

Fidelma's expression showed ill-concealed sarcasm.

"And did anyone witness this wolf-man carrying off this person?"

Scoth raised her shoulder and let it fall in negative fashion.

"All I know is that he went up into the Sliabh na Airgid, the Silver Mountains, and was never seen again. He came from a settlement near here."

"There are several reasons, apart from phantom wolves, why a man going alone into the mountains in winter might not return," Fidelma observed shrewdly. "Was a search made for him?"

"It was but no sign was found of him. People said they heard wolves howling."

"Not unusual," Fidelma replied. "But I did not come here to talk about Otherworld creatures." She dismissed her fears of the previous night and thought about the mystery of the disappearance of the occupants of the cabin in the high pass. She did not believe in such things as phantoms. They did not exist. But the couple were missing. "Eadulf and I can start back to Cashel early tomorrow and go through the high pass to find out whether the farmer and his wife have been found or not. It is not such a great detour."

"Tomorrow?" Scoth was frowning. Clearly there was something worrying her which she was finding difficult to articulate.

"What brings you here, Scoth?" Fidelma tried to change the subject. "I expected you to be at your father's fortress, An tAonach, during this inclement weather."

The girl pursed her lips. "These days I prefer to spend time under the shadows of the mountains than out on the plain at the Place of Assembly. I was surprised when Eadulf arrived here and told me that he was due to meet you." She hesitated and glanced at the blackening sky through the window. "You still intend to travel back to Cashel tomorrow?"

"If the weather clears," confirmed Fidelma.

Her cousin hesitated for a moment or two and then sighed. "I confess that your coming here is rather fortuitous. I need your knowledge."

"You have a legal problem, Scoth?" Fidelma was surprised.

Her cousin nodded solemnly.

"My father and his Brehon are absent, giving judgements at the abbey of Brendán in Biorra. They are not expected back before the Feast of Brigit. So you may be the very person to consult while you are here."

"What advice do you need that it cannot await the return of your father and his Brehon?"

"I mentioned our cousin Rechtabra earlier. Do you remember him?"

Fidelma frowned, trying to recollect. "A dirty, uncouth little boy who threw mud at me when I came visiting here with my uncle many years ago? I was only thirteen summers and was very sensitive about my appearance, as I recall."

Scoth grimaced. "He is still uncouth and dirty, but you remember him as a child. Now he is full grown to manhood. He has not improved his personality. He maintains his vicious temper and is even more arrogant."

"So there is a problem between you? The messenger that just arrived brought you word of him. Something serious?"

"For me, it is serious," confirmed the girl. "I inherited some land near here from my mother. The land contains a silver mine. Rechtabra has occupied it and claims that I should not inherit."

Fidelma was surprised. "On what basis does he make that claim?"

"That he believes a woman could not inherit a silver mine."

"You have the necessary evidence that it was left to you as a *banchomarba*, a female heir? Such inheritance is within the law."

"Of course. My father's Brehon has the evidence and my father knows the story well. But they are not here. It was not by chance that Rechtabra waited until my father and his Brehon had left for the tour of judgements before he occupied the mine and started to work it. By the time they return, he will have denuded the mine of most of its wealth."

"Then what of your father's *tanist*, his heir apparent? Surely he has the authority to stop Rechtabra?"

Scoth's lips compressed sourly. "Rechtabra is my father's tanist. And that is my problem."

Fidelma gazed thoughtfully at her for a moment. "So, what you are saying is that he has moved on to your land and claimed it in defiance of the law? But he must know of the consequences when your father and his Brehon return?"

"He probably means to extract as much as he can before they return. With such riches, I am told that he could buy protection, even travel where retribution is of no consequence. I was wondering what I could do. I do not have enough warriors loyal to me to overthrow him."

"Well the answer is simple in law. According to the *Din Techtugad*, if he remains in defiance then you can institute the procedure of *bantellach*, a legal means of pursuing a claim for female rights of land-ownership. You do not have to resort to force. It would be best, however, if your father's Brehon gave the judgement. But is it certain that Rechtabra is fully aware that he will have to pay you compensation and fines for his presumption?"

"I do not know," Scoth replied with a shrug. Then her eyes lightened. "Would it not be possible for you to give him a warning before you leave?"

"We mean to start back first thing in the morning," she glanced at Eadulf, who shrugged.

"A word from you might stop him," Scoth went on persuasively. "Tomorrow we could ride to the mine. It is not far to the west of here and you could warn him so that he understands the consequences of what he is doing . . . Please?"

Fidelma sighed with resignation. "I suppose that I could explain the law to him, if that is all that is needed."

Scoth relaxed with a smile. "I would appreciate it. Rechtabra might give this matter more serious thought if he knows that the King's sister is watching his actions."

"I presume Rechtabra has men working at the mine with him? If I remember that evil little boy, he might not like his cousin lecturing him on the law. Alas, silver seems to turn people's minds."

"Are there are many silver mines in this district?" asked Eadulf.

"Those mountains you have to pass through to Cashel are called Sliabh an Argid, the Silver Mountains," Scoth replied quickly. "The mountains are rich in silver and thus my father is able to pay the *gabal na rígh*, the king's tribute, in *unga* weights, grams of silver rather than cattle as some princes do."

"And do many people here work in the silver mines?" asked Eadulf, who was always interested in learning about people and places.

"That is why this settlement is called the Mouth of the Ford of the Smith," replied Scoth. "The smiths, however, that work here are silversmiths. This is where most of the silver in the mines is worked."

Fidelma suddenly stretched, yawned and rose. "Forgive me, Scoth. I have had a hard journey these last few days and no bath last night. Let me rest before the evening bath and meal and, I promise you, first thing in the morning, we will ride out to find our wayward cousin. We will delay our journey a further day."

"It is good of you, Fidelma," Scoth reached forward and placed a hand on Fidelma's arm. "I am sure Rechtabra will take notice of you. Eadulf knows where the guestroom is. I will order water to be heated for your bath after you have rested."

Eadulf led the way to the door. As she reached it, Fidelma hesitated with a slight frown and glanced back to her cousin.

"As a matter of interest, that man who disappeared ... you said he was local man? Did you know him?"

Scoth shook her head. "I did not. But I heard that he worked for Rechtabra."

"In what capacity?"

"He was a *cerd*, an expert silver-worker."

***

They awoke the next morning to find the snowstorm had returned with a vengeance. From a short time after midnight, the wind was howling outside, hurling the snow this way and that with an intense fury, and daylight brought no respite.

Eadulf regarded Fidelma with a wry expression as they sat at the early morning meal. Of Scoth there was not yet any sign.

"I hope your cousin does not expect us to go tracking through the snowstorm to meet this wayward cousin Rechtarbra."

Fidelma smiled. "I think not. We will wait until it abates."

"It seems a curious business."

Fidelma raised her eyes from her plate and looked at him with interest. "What does?" she asked.

"I heard Scoth talking to one of her attendants this morning. You recall the messenger that arrived yesterday with news of Rechtabra? Apparently, he was sent away immediately, even though the wind was already getting up then. He was sent back to the silver mine. I presume the man was spying for her."

Fidelma sniffed. "No harm in that. If Rechtabra is flouting the law then it is wise for someone to watch him."

There was a sudden noise outside and the door was opened abruptly. Scoth came quickly through, slamming it shut behind her. Her eyes were wide as if in fearful anticipation

"It's Rechtabra!" she gasped, glancing quickly over her shoulder as if the man was behind her. "He and his bodyguard have just arrived."

Fidelma looked up without surprise at her apparent trepidation.

"I presume that he comes seeking shelter from the snowstorm? After all, this is your father's hunting lodge and, presumably, as tanist, he has rights to shelter here?"

"But perhaps he has heard that you are here . . ." began Scoth, still agitated.

"Does he have a residence near here?"

"He does not. He usually camps at the mine workings."

"Then why would he come here for any reason other than the obvious one, which would be to escape this snowstorm and the gusting winds? Are you on such bad terms with him about this mine that he would not seek shelter here or that you would refuse him such?"

There was a sudden noise of stamping feet outside the door and it was flung open again as two men entered, shaking the snow from the fur outer garments that they wore. They halted in surprise at the company. Then one of them closed the door and both newcomers stood gazing at Scoth and her companions.

The leader – a young man, quite handsome in a way, though with blue eyes perhaps too close set, and burnished copper-coloured hair – peeled off his fur and grinned at his cousin.

"Greetings, cousin Scoth!" He inclined his head to her. "I trust we are welcome from the unrelenting chill?"

Scoth edged away to stand by the fire and did not reply to his bantering humour.

Fidelma had risen from her seat, standing to face the newcomer and his companion. Eadulf followed her example.

"Rechtabra," Fidelma greeted him quietly. "Do you recognize me after all these years?"

The young man examined her closely, frowning a little, and then a broad grin shaped his features.

"By the blessed saints. It is cousin Fidelma . . . Fidelma of Cashel." He moved forward and embraced her. Then he stood back. "I have not seen you since I was eleven years old." He turned to Eadulf. "So you must be Eadulf of Seaxmund's Ham?" He thrust out a hand. "Well, it seems we have a family gathering." He gave an exaggerated shiver and peered round. "Surely someone can offer frozen travellers some *corma* to drive out the wolf from my stomach."

Scoth pouted disapprovingly. "It is too early for strong drink."

Rechtabra grinned at his cousin. "I swear that you are becoming a prude. We have spent an hour riding in this weather and will surely expire without something to warm our bellies. Oh," he turned to his companion, who was removing his fur coat. "This is Máen the Silent, my right hand. Máen, this is my cousin, Fidelma of Cashel, and her husband, Eadulf, of whom I am sure you have heard."

Máen, true to his name, merely bowed his head in acknowledgement but said nothing.

Rechtabra was looking round. "Now, that drink."

Eadulf had spotted the flagon of *corma*, the strong liquor, and poured out two measures in earthenware goblets for the young man and his companion. Rechtabra raised it in silent tribute, before taking a seat by the fire. Scoth remained standing, while Fidelma and Eadulf resumed their seats. Máen took a seat a little farther back.

"Well now, what brings you here of all places in this little corner of your brother's kingdom?" Rechtabra asked. "And in such winter weather."

"I had arranged to meet Eadulf here so that we could journey back to Cashel together," explained Fidelma. "It seems the weather has decided that we must stay longer than we had anticipated."

"A strange little spot for your paths to meet," commented the tanist. Eadulf wondered if there was suspicion in his voice.

"A logical spot," he intervened. "Fidelma was coming back from the port of Luimneach, through the mountains, and I was coming from the abbey of the blessed Cronan at Tuaim Gréine. What logical meeting point for our two paths to cross but here?"

Rechtabra glanced at Eadulf with a smile. "Quite right, my friend. Quite right," he said gently. Then he glanced at Scoth. "And more company for you for a while?"

The girl blushed furiously. "I am not lacking in company."

"Of course not. At least your father will approve of the company of our cousin from Cashel." The tanist's voice was gentle but hinted at something else.

"And why are you here?" Fidelma asked, seeing the hot colour on Scoth's cheeks, and changing the conversation.

Rechtabra chuckled. "Our presence is dictated by the weather."

"But to come here to escape from it, you must have set out from somewhere," Eadulf said with a smile.

"You are sharp, Eadulf. Máen and I were encamped in the foothills of the mountains, a short way off. We decided we would seek more warmth and comfort than a wind-blown tent and a blanket until this chilly storm has passed."

Scoth sniffed, made to speak, and then suddenly made for the door. "You will excuse me. I have several things to attend to."

When she had gone, Rechtabra shook his head and turned in confidential manner to Fidelma, though still with a smile on his face.

"A strange one, that. I think she resents that I am heir apparent to the chieftainship. She also resents the fact that her father wanted her to marry me. Well, the feeling of repugnance between us is mutual."

"Is there anything else that would make her dislike you?" pressed Fidelma gently.

Rechtabra stared searchingly at her for a moment before he re-assumed his grin.

"I can think of several things, cousin. I am honest about my faults."

"Shall we speak of silver mines?"

Fidelma was aware of the silent Máen suddenly leaning forward intently in his chair.

"Silver mines?" Rechtabra said, almost sharply. "What have they to do with likes and dislikes?"

"I suppose that you know that I am a *dálaigh* . . ."

"You reputation in the kingdom is well known, cousin Fidelma. There is even a rumour that King Colgú may make you his Chief Brehon. And so?"

"Scoth believes that you have appropriated a silver mine and some land that she should rightfully control."

Rechtabra gazed at her a moment, turned to Máen with a shrug, and sighed deeply before turning back.

"And therefore . . . ?" he queried.

"Therefore, I should remind you of the law. If this is Scoth's property then it cannot be appropriated. It cannot be alienated from her control as a *banchomarba*, a female heir. Any illegal use of the mine would bring forth fines, compensation and reimbursement of the estimated amount of silver removed from it."

Rechtabra was nodding as if in agreement.

"Cousin, there is one word that you have used in that. A most important word. I am sure you can guess at what the word is . . . if."

Fidelma regarded him thoughtfully.

"Do you deny it?"

"Assuredly I do."

"She wanted us to ride with her today to where this mine was in order to warn you that she will take legal action."

Rechtabra chuckled with amusement. "And what legal action could she take? If our Brehon were here, then he would tell her. If Prince Gilcach, her father, were here then he would not take the matter as lightly as I do. The silver mines here are the wealth of our people, and Gilcach shares that among them on the great annual festival at An tAonach. We jealously guard the wealth of the mines for they are our joint wealth and not owned by one person, whether it be Scoth or even myself."

There was an honest intensity in his voice that surprised her.

"Then you are willing for this matter to be heard before a Brehon?"

"If that Brehon is aware of all the facts," confirmed the tanist.

"But if this is not the truth, why would Scoth make it up?"

"Because of her dislike for me."

"That does not seem a strong reason."

"Nevertheless, it is the only one I can think of. Not only did she hate me when her father suggested marriage but it seemed that Gilcach was not in favour of a man she *did* want to marry." Rechtabra's tone was indifferent. "Anyway, it is a silly accusation and could only be made during the absence of Gilcach and his Brehon."

"Then we must leave this matter until it can be judged competently by Gilcach and his Brehon. But remember, Rechtabra, that, in the interim, all the silver taken from the mine in question must be accounted for."

Rechtabra smiled grimly. "So it has been and so it shall be. I am answerable to the Prince Gilcach for the well-being of the mines and he shall have a full accounting."

"Speaking of the well-being," – Fidelma felt it time to change the topic, for the matter was leading to a stalemate between Rechtabra and Scoth – "I am told that one of your mine-workers has disappeared."

To her surprise it was Máen who suddenly laughed grimly and then exchanged an apologetic glance with the tanist.

"Only one?" Máen said in answer to Fidelma's scrutiny. "More like a dozen good men have disappeared in this area."

Fidelma's eyes widened a fraction at the news.

"A dozen? All workers in the silver mines? During what space of time have these disappearances taken place?"

"From the time of the last full of the moon."

"The locals call that one 'the night of the snow wolf '," added Máen. "There are rumours, of course, which have been set abroad by silly, superstitious people. Stories of the men lured to their doom in the mountains . . ."

"Lured? By whom?"

"Ancient legends say there is a monster dwelling there," Máen said. "Some creature called Fáelur, the wolfman, who feeds upon the unwary traveller. So people tell you not to ride through the mountains during these days."

"And what do you say happened to these men? Twelve, you say? All strong mine-workers."

This time Rechtabra replied. "I am not good at making

guesses, cousin. Maybe the local superstition is right. All I know is that their disappearance is an inconvenience. I have the mines to run."

It was later that Fidelma put Rechtabra's denials to Scoth.

"He is a liar! I tell you, he is a liar!" she cried angrily.

"The matter must be judged," returned Fidelma. "When my brother, the King, learns of the return of your father and his Brehon, he will summon everyone to attend him at Cashel. You and Rechtabra must defend your claims. That will be an end to the matter. Will that satisfy you?"

"But meanwhile he will go on stealing the silver that belongs to me."

"He has been warned that, if guilty, the amount will be estimated and that will be reimbursed with compensation and fines. Perhaps I can persuade my brother to send some warriors of his bodyguard to observe Rechtabra's activities. That must satisfy you."

"I suppose it must satisfy me." Scoth did not sound convinced.

"Well, I do not think that Rechtabra would have confessed to me immediately as to any wrongdoing – especially if he is guilty," Fidelma pointed out. "It is the best judgement I can make in the circumstances."

That night the snow continued to fall.

***

The snow continued to fall for two more days, spreading from the west in the darkened skies. There was little point in looking at the track beyond the gates of the hunting lodge for the wind-driven snow was blinding and freezing. It was an uncomfortable two days, for Fidelma and Eadulf were forced to spend them in the main hall – albeit before a roaring fire – in icy atmosphere between Scoth and Rechtabra, which almost matched the atmosphere outside. In fact, two fires had been lit, each at opposite ends of the great hall, so no one encroached on anyone else.

Eadulf passed much of the time playing *fidchell*, or wooden wisdom, with Rechtabra. Eadulf had found himself quite adept at the game that was popular among the people of the five kingdoms. It was the equivalent of chess in other lands. The object of the game was to protect the single High King piece, standing in the centre of the board that was divided into squares. His protectors were the four provincial kings. The attacking pieces could mount their attack from any of the four sides of the board with the eventual task of trapping the High King so he was unable to move. It was a game of skill and forethought.

Scoth had retired to a corner not too far from one of the fires but by one of the snow-blocked windows that gave a little light. Mostly the oil lamps were lit to provide illumination. Scoth had taken out her *iadach*, a workbag in which needles and threads and materials for embroidery were carried. Using various coloured balls of thread called *certle*, she bent to her task. Embroidery was a recognized art in which all royal ladies were proficient. It was said that every chiefly household maintained a chief *druinech* or embroideress. Even the Blessed Patrick had three embroiders in his household – his own sister, Lupait, Cruimtheris, a princess of the royal house of Ulaidh, and Erca, the daughter of the prince who gave land to Patrick at Ard Macha so that he could build a church there.

Fidelma passed the time with the silent Máen, playing *brandubh* – another board game, called 'Black Raven'. They set up their board at the far end of the hall by the other fire. Máen was not a brilliant player and eventually Fidelma tried to draw him into a little conversation about himself and his service to the tanist. They spoke in low, whispered tones, so as not to disturb anyone else. Little by little she learnt that he had been fostered with Rechtabra, trained as a warrior and thenceforth became his *trenfher* or champion, a term meaning chief bodyguard.

"Do you spend all the time in this part of the territory? Among the mines?"

Máen shook his head. "As tanist, Rechtabra's task is to frequently go on a circuit of the territory, much like the Brehon, to be watchful over the people and the property of Prince Gilcach."

"What do you make of this argument between the lady Scoth and the tanist?"

Máen looked about him quickly but, seeing Scoth intent on her sewing and Eadulf and Rechtabra concentrating on their game, he realized they could not be overheard if he spoke softly.

"It started when Prince Gilcach made his wish known that he wanted Scoth to marry Rechtabra. Rechtabra accepted the idea

– not that he was in love, but it was a logical move for the good of the chieftainship."

"And the lady, Scoth?"

"She was enraged. If the truth be known, she had met someone else. I do not know who it was, but rumour had it that he was from Bréifne but not of a chiefly family. The more her father tried to persuade her against it, the more she fought and the more her dislike of Rechtabra increased."

"And what did Rechtabra think of this?"

"He was not happy. He knows that Prince Gilcach indulges his daughter. Moreover, the petty chieftains want to curry favour with Gilcach, and it had occurred to Rechtabra that Gilcach could call a meeting of his council and persuade them to elect a new tanist and one which he could persuade his daughter to marry. I think Rechtabra is very insecure."

"And what of this business of the silver mine? Have you heard of this inheritance before?"

"That I have no knowledge of it. Rechtabra, as tanist, keeps his eye on the silver mines of the Airthir Chliach and that is his duty to the Prince Gilcach. It could well be that the lady Scoth has a prior claim. But I thought that the matter was now in hand and that we were to wait for the return of Gilcach and his Brehon?"

The warrior was suddenly suspicious that Fidelma was pumping him for information about the tanist.

"You are quite right, Máen," she agreed quickly. "I cannot help being curious, that is all. Let us forget this matter."

***

On the morning of the third day, the winds had dropped and the skies cleared. Fidelma and Eadulf left the settlement soon after first light, having bid farewell to Scoth. They learnt that, even as early as they had risen, Rechtabra and his companion Máen had already departed. Fidelma was silent and dissatisfied as they began to head for the pass through Sliabh an Airgid. The conditions became fair and sunny, although the pale winter sun had no effect on alleviating the coldness of the day. However, the riding conditions were good, the track was firm although covered by a layer of crisp snow. Their intention had been to cross the ford over the river Maoilchearn, south of the Silver Mountains, then keep south-east, to join the main track south to Cashel beyond Cnoc Thaidhg, a small peak rising only 400 metres. It did not take them too long to pass through the four-kilometre stretch that constituted the pass through the Silver Mountains, and to come to the river crossing. It was here that Fidelma halted and frowned in sudden decision.

"Ahead of us is Sliabh Coimeálta," she announced, indicating the height. Then pointing, "Along the south bank of the river is a stone circle. If we turn directly south from there we will be able to climb into the high pass."

Eadulf groaned. "So you want to go back to see if those hill-farming folk were rescued?"

"It should only be a few hours detour, for it's a fair day. We can rejoin the main road south of Motharshliabh and there are several hostels along the route where we can stay if we are unduly delayed."

Eadulf glanced at her speculatively. "You are really intrigued by what happened to you the other night." He made it a statement, not a question.

She nodded slowly. "Let us say that I do not like mysteries that have no solution. There are certain things I want to rest my mind about."

It was midday when Fidelma called a halt again. The twisting valley was still covered in snow and it was hard for her to locate their position. She knew from the outline of Sliabh Coimeálta, across the valley to her right that she was on the right track but she could not locate the spot where the hill-farm stood. That she found curious. The two dark buildings should have been obvious on the hillside. Eadulf looked on as she tried to take a bearing from the peaks around her. She was certain, snow or no snow, she would have been able to see the buildings on her left, a little way up the hill. She compressed her lips in vexation.

"You did come here in a snowstorm," Eadulf pointed out, trying to reason with her. "Things might have seemed entirely different."

She shook her head. "But I did not leave in a snowstorm. I took bearings from the peaks. The farmstead should be somewhere up the hill in front of us."

Eadulf looked carefully over the slopes. Suddenly he uttered a sharp exclamation. "You are right. There *were* some buildings. There, look . . ."

Following his outstretched hand, Fidelma could see some dark patches a little way up the hill. Patches that were not part of the natural hillside. The snow had fallen and covered whatever it had been. Fidelma slid from her horse and looked about her, seeking to find a stone or object to secure the reins of her horse. Then she began to scramble up the hillside. After a moment's hesitation, Eadulf followed her example.

For Fidelma, there was something very familiar about the flat space she paused on. She breathed out long and hard. Beside her, Eadulf was puzzled. "It looks like a demolished cabin," he muttered, as his eyes drifted over the stones and pieces of wood that were strewn around.

"That was the cabin I spent the night in," she replied softly.

Eadulf shivered slightly at the tone in her voice.

"But you said . . ." he began.

"I know what I said. I know what happened," her voice was now confident.

Eadulf moved forward and began to brush the coating of snow from the stones and wood. Then he turned to her with a serious expression.

"Where did you say the barn was?"

Fidelma pointed without saying anything further. Eadulf went to explore, scraping the snow away here and there. Then he looked up with a shake of his head.

"One thing is for certain, a cabin and a barn stood here until a short while ago."

Fidelma turned quickly. "You mean that it was knocked down recently?"

"That I do," replied Eadulf. "And that must have taken several men, working hard, for some hours. Where they have left bits of wood, it has been smashed and obviously one can see that the breaks are not weathered. This was done very recently. But who did it and why? If there had been no snowfall during the last few days then we might have seen the remains of the buildings earlier."

"Maybe we were meant to ride past without noticing them. But did they drive off the cow, the goats and the chickens?"

"That would be logical," agreed Eadulf. "Also, you will have noticed that most of the timbers and a lot of the domestic materials are not here. Only the bits of rough-hewn stone that could not be removed have been left, knocked down and spread about. But why?"

"There must be some evidence of where the remains of this cabin and barn have been taken."

"With the snows of the last two days and nights, I doubt we could find a trail," murmured Eadulf, glancing around. He crossed back to the ruins of the cabin and stared at it thoughtfully. Then he suddenly bent down and rubbed snow away from some objects on the ground. He rose, holding them in his hand. "Maybe they were in a hurry, for these seem valuable, too valuable to leave behind."

Fidelma moved forward and peered at them closely.

"Not the usual tools of a hill-farmer," she muttered. "That is a *fonsura*, a chisel of the type used by miners, and that we call a lightning mallet, a *forcha-teinnighe*." She suddenly smiled and nodded her head. "I think that I am beginning to understand."

Eadulf gazed at her blankly. "Understand?"

"The voices I heard in the night. The thuds. What might have happened to the couple who lived here. Above all, why a man could leave no tracks in the snow. Why a so-called hill-farmer could have a colloquial knowledge of Latin. And why he would call himself Fáelur. It all begins to fit together."

"I wish I could follow this," sighed Eadulf. "Anyway, what do we do now?"

Fidelma was regarding the piles of stone which had marked the walls of the *bóthan*, and looked hard along the rocky slope that rose behind it and which bore towards the shoulder of the immediate hill.

"Come with me but watch where you are walking. It is very dangerous terrain here, I think. And, perhaps, we should be quiet."

Eadulf regarded her in amazement but he shrugged and did as he was told.

Keeping her eyes close to the ground, Fidelma walked slowly up from what had been the back of the cabin towards the distant shoulder of the hill. The way led past large boulder-like rocks that were as tall as a man. She had not gone far when she paused by the side of one such boulder. She bent down. Peering over her shoulder, Eadulf could see a place where it seemed twigs and fronds had been laid, but which the fallen snow had almost covered. Fidelma removed one or two of these and revealed an opening into the ground.

Eadulf was about to say something when a sound caught his attention. A distant thudding and he was sure he heard a voice calling.

Fidelma turned quickly, a finger to her lips, and motioned him to back away, returning to the cabin.

"We must get away from here immediately," she whispered.

Eadulf found the intensity in her voice frightening.

"Monsters? Dwellers underground? What is it?" he demanded.

She smiled thinly. "More dangerous than that. Come, let's get our horses. We have a long ride ahead of us."

"To Cashel?" Eadulf queried. "I thought we were going to stay at a *bruden* overnight?"

"We do not go to Cashel but to the fortress of Caol, the commander of my brother's bodyguard. We should be able to reach it before nightfall. Caol will be able to raise warriors so that we can return and put an end to this evil business."

★★★

It was two days later that a party of warriors, most of them wearing the golden torc collars of the élite warriors of the Nasc Niadh, bodyguards to the King of Muman, rode into the settlement of Béal Átha Gabhann. Fidelma and Eadulf were among them but it was Caol, their commander, who rode at their head. Swiftly he brushed aside the challenge of the guards, two warriors of Rechtabra, the tanist of the Airthir Chliach, by asserting the authority of the King. They stood uncertainly at the gates of the hunting lodge as Caol swept by them into the main hall. His men swiftly deployed to secure the place. Even as they did so, Rechtabra emerged from one of the rooms with Máen at his side. The tanist was red-faced in fury and demanded to know what was meant, while Scoth, with a female attendant, had emerged from another chamber. Scoth was looking frightened.

Caol had confronted them both. "We are on the business of your King."

He then stood aside and signalled one of his men to allow Fidelma and Eadulf to make their entrance into the hall.

"Fidelma!" cried Scoth. "'What on earth does this mean?"

"I have come to talk about silver mines," she said quietly.

Rechtabra's brows drew together and made a dismissive gesture with one hand. "What nonsense is this?" he demanded. "Do you think I would break my word? I have told you, that I am prepared to answer Scoth's allegations before my prince and his Brehon. What more do you want?"

"I want, cousin, to resolve a matter of illicit mining, of the kidnapping of workers to excavate the mine, and of the kidnapping of hill-farmers to prevent them revealing news of the whereabouts of the mine."

"I have told you that there is nothing illegal about the mines I run," snapped Rechtabra. "As for kidnapping . . ."

Scoth had turned to her cousin.

"Nothing illegal? You know full well that the mine is—"

"It is not of that particular matter I have come," asserted Fidelma. "I speak of the silver mine in the high pass opposite Sliabh Coimeálta."

Rechtabra stared at her for a moment and then laughed shortly. "There is no such mine there, let alone a silver mine."

Fidelma regarded him for a moment as if trying to peer beyond his bland expression, and then she turned to examine Scoth in the same way. Then she shook her head sadly before she began to speak.

"The main entrance to the silver mine was hidden on the far side of the mountain. But the seams that the miners followed ran deep. One of the seams came through the hillside – underneath, or close enough, to the cabin of Cuilind and his wife, Ciarnat. Apparently, they heard the thudding and the voices of the miners at work under their cabin. Cuilind, roused from his sleep, went to investigate. He found one of the air tunnels and was trying to find where it led when the warriors, who were guarding the miners, caught him. Ciarnat heard his call but was caught also. Their guard-dog must have set up a barking and, the poor beast, for adhering to its duty, was bludgeoned to death.

"The warriors made Cuilind and Ciarnat prisoners but were unsure of what to do next. They left the hill-farm alone until they could send for orders. That was when I arrived and spent a curious night there. I tended to the animals and, in the cabin, during the night, I also heard the miners at work as Cuilind must have done. Thankfully, so it seems, I did not go to investigate as he had done. However, the next morning I was confronted by a man calling himself Fáelur, wolfman. A nice touch of the dramatic. He was the overseer of the mine, who had come through the air tunnel to check on the hill-farm.

"I was perturbed that there were no trace of his footprints on a path leading from the main track up to the cabin. How had he arrived there in the snow without leaving footprints? It almost gave confirmation to the story of mystic forces. But, of course, there were no footprints because Fáelur had not come to the cabin by that route, He had emerged from the air tunnel at the back of the cabin. He was as surprised to see me as I was to see him. Once he knew who I was, he did not want the problem of kidnapping the sister of the King of Muman and bringing down the wrath of Cashel on his head. So he tried to persuade me that the couple were lost on the mountain and that he was a relative and would organize a search. I have met with very few hill-farmers who spoke Latin to the extent of knowing some of its complicated axioms. That alerted me that he was not who he said he was.

"When I rode off, he believed I was satisfied that there was no mystery there. However, he sent someone to report the matter to the person who was in charge of the illicit mining. They ordered the destruction of the hill-farm so that any future travellers would not notice it. The miners were told to destroy the buildings and remove the livestock to the other side of the mountains on the east. A lot of the materials, the wood that constituted the barn and things from the cabin, were taken into the mine because it would be useful for shoring it up and helping the work. The kidnapped miners were forced to do this work. Thankfully, one of them purposely left his mining tools on the chance they might be spotted by someone who would ask questions.

"Indeed, there was one problem. My suspicion. When I mentioned that I was going back through the high pass to see how the search for Ciarnat and Cuilind progressed, a means had to be devised to ensure that I did not travel back that morning – so as to give the miners a chance to do their work of destruction. As it turned out, such subterfuge was superfluous. The snowstorm ensured that we were snowbound for several days before Eadulf and I could begin our journey to Cashel. We went with stories of the Fáelur ringing in our ears in an attempt to persuade us not to return through the high pass."

She paused looking sadly from Scoth to Rechtabra.

"This is madness," the tanist responded angrily. "There is no mine where you say it is. You will have to prove it."

Fidelma sighed. "That I can do. Before we came here, Caol and his men raided the mine. We found Cuilind and Ciarnat and released them. The miners who had been kidnapped from local mines were also released. They were forced to work under armed guards, and the supervision of the person who called himself Fáelur. Fáelur was a professional miner and a specialist on silver mining. His motivation for the illicit mining was for a share of the profits. So there is proof enough for you, Rechtabra."

The tanist was staring at her unable to speak. He stood, shaking his head.

Scoth glanced angrily at him. "I knew something strange was happening. I thought it was odd when those miners began to disappear. Was the mine very rich in silver, Fidelma?"

"I am told it is one of the richest mines that the men have ever worked in."

"But how could Rechtabra hope to get away with the silver?"

"When I asked what motivation Rechtabra would have in trying to obtain the silver from a mine that you could prove belonged to you, you told me the motivation. With such riches, you said, one could go and live anywhere, for riches create power. Anywhere in the world, it is the same." Fidelma paused and added quietly, "Where did you mean to go, Scoth?"

The girl started uncertainly.

"I do not understand . . ." she began hesitantly.

"You did not think that you had bought the silence of the guards who dealt with you?" Fidelma asked. "Nor, in the circumstances facing him, do you think that Fáelur would shoulder in silence the retribution that must come? Even love has its limitations. While he still refuses to give his real name, his Bréifne origin betrays him."

Rechtabra was wide eyed, trying to understand what was being said.

"You mean this illicit mining was Scoth's idea?" he demanded. "But why? She is the daughter of Cilcach, Prince of Airithir Chliach. What need has she of more wealth and position?"

"Some people are never satisfied with what they have," Fidelma replied quietly. At her nod, two of Caol's warriors had taken up positions behind Scoth. But she had no defiance left in her. "Take her to her room while we consider how to deal with the matter. Her father and his Brehon must certainly be sent for now."

"I think you should explain," Rechtabra pressed, when Scoth had been removed. He was clearly still confused.

"It seems that she met Fáelur – I have no other name for him – who was from Bréifne. She is in love with him. You told me about this yourself. But he was not from a chiefly family so her father disapproved. He made his wish that Scoth and you should marry. She grew afraid that her refusal would eventually lead to her losing her wealth and position. We don't know who discovered the silver lode, but Fáelur opened it up with some hired mercenaries. However, to fully exploit the mine, he needed skilled miners; those who disappeared had been kidnapped and were pressed into service. Scoth and Fáelur probably thought that, once they had gathered enough silver from the mine, they would go somewhere where no one knew them and, with identities changed, would establish themselves with their wealth."

"How did you come to suspect Scoth?" asked Rechtabra.

"It was shortly after I arrived here that a man came to tell her what had taken place in the high pass. She immediately sent him back to Fáelur to tell him to destroy the hill-farm. Easier to say than to accomplish. I told her the story of my encounter at the farm and she took the lead from her lover. It was Scoth who raised the legend of Fáelur, of wolf creatures in the Silver Mountains, in an attempt to put me off travelling back that way.

"When she saw that I cared little for superstition and that I was intent on leaving the next morning, she had to come up with another excuse to keep me out of the high pass for a day or two. In that she was very stupid. Her accusation against you was very lame. But she thought that would delay me some time while I, as a *dálaigh*, tried to sort it out. It was silly because it was a matter that would soon be shown to be false. It was also, as I said, superfluous, because the snowstorm stopped Eadulf and I from travelling anyway. Had she remained silent, she might probably have escaped detection.

"So, when we were able to travel, my suspicions had been heightened to the point that I went through the high pass again and found the air tunnel to the mine. The rest followed."

As she paused there came the distant but distinct howling of a wolf, shortly joined by others and rising to a crescendo. In the quiet that followed, Fidelma smiled sadly. "The night of the snow wolf? Wolves are social creatures. I think we could learn much from them."

Jettisoned

Deirdre Counihan

This story has the most ancient setting in the anthology and takes us back to the Bronze Age around the year 2300 BC. It's easy to imagine that people back then were unsophisticated, unimaginative and crude. But this was the time that the Pyramids were built in Egypt, and Stonehenge in Britain. There is increasing archaeological evidence to show that those who lived in Bronze Age Britain led very sophisticated lives, and that their ability to understand and resolve problems was no different to ours today. The author brings out some of these points in a note at the end of the story.

Deirdre Counihan was born at the ancestral home of the gunpowder plotter Guy Fawkes – Farnley Hall – a link to a later story in this anthology. She trained as a book illustrator and also has an MA in Gender Studies. She has had a busy art career, specializing in archaeology and fantasy, and was co-editor of the magazine Scheherazade.

A great gull, lit white against the hectic slate grey sky, soared screaming in horror up past the sharp green of the eastern headland and then arched smoothly out across the dark expanse of the swollen river down below them. The bird headed majestically back again, still screaming in terror, over the western cliff where Grizzel stood hunched and shivering in her shawl, clutching the baby Niav against her shoulder.

She could not take in what had just happened.

One minute they had been there, her brother Diarma and his dear Befind, happily trying out Artin's new masterpiece, the next minute there was nothing but the lonely speck of their apple basket still swirling in a grey sea circle where the boat had been sucked down. No mast, no sail, no Diarma, no Befind, no Artin – all three of them gone, in an instant!

The fool, the fool. What had he done? She had hoped that it had simply been more clowning around. There had clearly been much mirth earlier, with Artin demonstrating how to work a sail, but the frantic scramble amidships that she had just witnessed could only have been a real fight. Poor Diarma must have guessed and lost his temper – their family failing – and now they had capsized. He had killed them all. Poor Artin would never find his young wife and little Niav had lost her parents.

Grizzel teetered as near the edge of the cliff as she dared, gingerly following the tidal surge inwards round the curve of the cliff, all the time holding tight on to the baby as much for reassurance as for safety. She felt the soft breathing against her neck. Surely, surely, there must be something?

It took slow steps to negotiate the hummocked grass of the steeply sloping clifftop. One missed footing and they could both be hurled into the sea, so far below them – but she tried to watch the swirling grey waters for even the tiniest scrap of hope.

Once she was safely on the bouncing turf of the path that led down to the river's edge, she started to run. The smudge of a dark head could be seen, bobbing through the current's swirl, in along the river – could they still be breathing? Would they whirl in on the tide or would the river catch hold and swirl them out to sea again? Grizzel knew the way the river could run.

Faster and faster over the grassy hillside, hoping against hope that she wouldn't trip and let fly the baby too, her whole family gone in one fell swoop. She could see a body – whichever one it was – still being tossed along the western side, trapped by the current. A sudden glimpse of yellow and she knew it was Befind – might she wash in where other people sometimes had – and yet survive?

Now Grizzel was speeding over the well-trodden route along the river bank. She almost slipped on a patch of slime, and baby Niav let out a yowl of protest which turned into a full-blown spate of yelling. Grizzel's breath was agony and there was a taste like dried blood in her mouth. "Please be alive, Befind, please be alive!" Surely someone from the village would still be around? There had been so many people there to see them off.

And Befind *did* wash in where the others had. Among the dark green reeds, Grizzel saw the crumpled shape, still recognizably Befind by the tatters of her yellow tunic. She was slumped half-in, half-out of the great, grey bowl of the headless snake-stone.

Leaving the yelling Niav firmly wrapped in her shawl between two rocks and well above the waterline, Grizzel waded over to the huge stone bowl. Befind's beautiful face was almost under the blood-stained water – her long auburn hair floating in tendrils around her. What irony to drown in her own blood, if somehow she had managed to survive the onslaught of the waves.

Standing with feet wide apart to get some purchase among the squelching mud and the reed stalks, Grizzel yanked Befind out of the hollowed stone in a promising trail of bubbles and dragged her up the bank. To the background clamour of the baby's yelling, Grizzel worked hard to force some life back into its mother. "Can't you hear her? You can't leave her, Befind, what would she do!"

A great blood-soaked cough – and Befind's eyes flickered open, only to close again. Grizzel wouldn't let her go. "What were they doing? Had Diarma seen?" She sat Befind roughly against a flat-faced rock and placed baby Niav firmly at her mother's breast. The yelling ceased.

Befind's eyes flickered again. "This is where Seyth . . ." she murmured, letting the baby nuzzle.

"Yes, yes – we are where we found Seyth washed in," Grizzel almost screamed in exhaustion and grief – she could see that she was losing her.

Befind was stroking the baby's tiny hand. She raised her head and looked across the river as though trying to focus for one last time on the image of the eastern headland and the mound of the Sacred Howe that she had betrayed for love. "I told them the bung . . ." she whispered through the blood, and with a final racking sigh, her head dropped forward on her breast.

Beating back the tears, Grizzel bent over them, knowing she would discover the worst, that Befind was dead. She found that baby Niav had her hand curled firmly round the shaft of her mother's sacred barra which, miraculously, was still held secure by its snakeskin strapping to the blood-soaked belt at Befind's waist.

"So much for its sacred power!" thought Grizzel contemptuously. "What good has it done Befind to make it worth her spiriting it away? What good would it do this poor infant either!"

And then the villagers arrived.

***

Niav picked her way to the top of the cliff-path, wiping away angry tears. A single pure white gull swooped and soared against the leaden clouds as she surveyed the familiar skyline from where the dark beast-like headland jutted out over the northern sea on her left, across the deep grey expanse of swollen river-mouth down below her, and on to the stately beauty of the sacred headland far to her right, with the wedge-shaped Sacred Howe in silhouette.

Maybe it should have been her sacred howe by now; who was she to say? Lower down the ridge, the ancient house that had been home to her mother and grandmother – and the countless grandmothers before that – stood out among the patch of smaller huts that clustered around it like so many limpets. Niav felt cheated, her Aunty Grizzel had *lied* to her – suddenly this was an unlovely world. The soaring gull did not impress her. She stood hunched and shivering in her shawl at the clifftop, gazing sourly up at it.

The replying scut of bird lime, which just missed, was somehow not a coincidence.

"I am *not* going to blame her for not telling me," she told herself as she glowered out over the grey sea, trying to fight her anger. "It must be terrible to have your brother scraped off a rock and then brought home by his greatest enemy, particularly if he could then look smug about it."

Was she fooling herself? Hadn't she a right to have been told a long time ago? She wasn't a baby, and, if there was some mystery about it all, it was a mystery that belonged to her. She was just so used to Aunty Grizzel's moods – but maybe there should be limits. She couldn't just throw those eggs away. It would be wicked to let them go to waste on a whim. And it was just a whim. Gloom, doom. People listened to Aunt Grizzel quite enough as it was. Being expected to act as fledgling to the local wise-woman really could be depressing if they treated you like a baby the next minute.

It had been a beautiful, sun-kissed morning and the rain, so far, was holding off. Niav had come down to her special spot by the river in search of bull-rush roots. Aunty Grizzel seemed in real need of sweetening up, and the roots, after a short spell shoved among the hot ashes, were the sweetest thing she knew.

They had told her it was meant to be a bad place, an unlucky place where unfortunate things were washed in, but there, amid the gentle rustle of the reeds, at the very centre of the great, headless snake-stone bowl, Niav had discovered an impeccable nest, exactly placed, holding six perfect eggs, and not a guarding parent in sight – almost a miracle.

But then cousin Kyle, that *vermin*, had ruined everything. He hadn't just burst through the rushes and spoiled the perfect moment, he had told her something utterly unforgivable – that this, her favourite place of all places, was where the body of her mother, Befind, had been found washed in "all bloated like so much bladderwrack!" And she had never, never known. No one had even so much as hinted.

Of course she threw an egg at him – and it did not miss.

She had held herself firm, while he crashed his way back through the rushes trying to wipe the egg yolk from his eyes. She didn't cry. Not only had she collected up the remaining eggs and packed them neatly in the basket, all carefully bounced out with moss as she had been taught, she had even gone grubbing for a respectable bundle of roots as well.

Unsurprisingly, the last thing Niav got when she reached home laden with her unexpected goodies was gratitude or congratulations.

"They will be bound to have gone rotten. Why else would they be left for you to find so easy?" Aunt Grizzel said sourly, after one glance at Niav's basket.

She had tossed her long wavy hair from around her shoulders and swept back towards the weaving-hut. The beads of her many-rowed jet necklace all flashed in a shaft of sunlight – she was a good-looking woman and everyone acknowledged it.

"Perhaps something got the parents – a fox or something. I don't know!" said Niav, trailing behind her in exasperation.

"Can't have been anything with any sense, or it would have eaten the eggs as well. No, they are bound to be bad. Get rid of them, I'd say."

"The egg I chucked at Kyle was just fine! I had a good sniff at what was left of it."

"What a waste, then," growled Aunty Grizzel. "Is that what you'd prefer me to say instead? And how did poor little Kyle offend you this time, Madam?"

Niav bit her lip. There had to have been a reason for her Aunt not having told her something about the snake rock. "Is it true my mum was washed in down by my snake rock?"

"Yes, she was. And—"

"Was she all bloated – like a blown up bladder – and blue and green?"

"No she was *not*. Befind was as beautiful as she always was. I wonder whose lively imagination that was? Pity you didn't chuck two eggs."

"And my dad?"

"No, he came in up by the Beast's Paw"

"Was he all bloated?"

But Aunty Grizzel just looked away. "Diarma floated in quite a while later . . ."

Niav had stood outside the weaving-hut as Grizzel started to pick through the basket of wools. "It's all going wrong," she growled, standing back from the loom to check the colour match of her new skein of wool. "And this one's wrong too. It's dyed a much deeper colour than last time – nothing's going right today – something's in the wind for sure."

"A bit of deeper tone will just make the pattern more interesting," said Niav, trying to maintain a cheerful front in spite of how she felt. She could see little difference in the shade this time, but Aunt Grizzel was much more aware of colour subtleties than she was, than anyone was – a real artist. "I think maybe I will just go for a walk on the clifftop – don't worry, I will be back before dark. I will leave the eggs on the cool-shelf, and there are some sweeties in the basket too. We can roast them before we eat – that'll be nice."

"Don't go too far then. I think there is rain brewing . . ." Aunt Grizzel was clearly not for a moment taken in by Niav's attempted nonchalance. "Like I said, the sea threw your Pa back on to the rock by the Beast's Paw. Lurgan went out in his coracle and brought him home – such a dutiful man, your Uncle Lurgan."

★★★

Now Niav looked down at the dark swirling river. Was there truly something in the wind? She wouldn't have cared to say.

But, suddenly, picked out by a moment's hectic beam of sunlight, something was scudding in fast ahead of the dark storm clouds that swirled around the eastern headland.

A smallish craft, desperate to make landing before the skies broke – Niav caught her breath in a sort of wondering ecstasy as she made out the symbol clearly painted in brown and yellow, wings picked out in white, right across the square leather sail. A bee. It must be Artin. It had to be Artin. Why did he always swirl in on the bow of a storm? Artin the Smith, maker of dreams, who had returned from the dead. People said that he had defeated the mighty Sea God in an epic battle, and some folk even went so far as to say he was somehow the Sea God himself; but he would only smile and say that he served a power far, far greater than that of the waves, or any other force of nature.

No wonder Aunt Grizzel was acting up. In her few years of conscious observation, Niav had noticed that her aunt was particularly prone to her nonsense when Artin was in the offing – almost like some people's dogs sensing that their owners were coming before they walked up over the horizon – uncanny! Perhaps this was the time when she might pluck up the courage to try to discover why.

Originally when she had seen her aunt so twitchy, she had thought that it might just be a general dislike of strangers. However, she had soon come to realize that that would be completely ridiculous. Though the strangers always made a reverent visit to the Sacred Howe on the east bank, the chief reason that brought them from far and wide to their river mouth was the trade with the artisans on the western bank. The strangers understood the quality of their weaving and pottery and in particular the value and beauty of their magic black stones – jet.

Jet wasn't merely something for making jewellery, it had very peculiar magical properties too. It was very rare – a stone, but as light as wood and as warm as wood to touch – even though it came out of the ground. When you polished it against sandstone it would show you reflections of a sunless, secret magic world. If you rubbed jet with woollen cloth, it could be made to pick things up. The fumes from burning jet could be used to test virginity, and they could even be used to drive out snakes. All the headless stone snakes which could be found dotted everywhere about the valley – though few of them were quite as large as the special one where Niav had found the eggs – were often pointed out as proof of this. But why such things were so was really still a mystery, even to the people from the river mouth, though of course they would be the last people to admit it.

Jet could be quite dangerous as well. Though you could collect jet along the sea and river shores, the best jet was mined – often dangling, from an exposed cliff face. This had to be done with caution; if you were not careful, you might awake the hidden spirits that lurked in the rock faces. If they were treated wrong they would get angry and the ground around the mines might burst into fire – to show the spirits' power and spite – and be of no use to anyone, unless, of course, you were trying to dispose of an unwanted serpent.

People like Uncle Lurgan (and her long chain of grannies stretching back into the past) on the eastern bank inherited the job of taking care of the right ceremonies for this sort of thing. It was time someone explained to Niav how and why she had lost this right when she ended up on the west side of the river.

No, Niav appreciated that her people were very special, and had been chosen by the gods because of their artistic talents and shrewd business sense, and not only for their wisdom and piety – so why this strange divide?

Aunty Grizzel summed the dilemma up. Of all the people who lived on the west bank, she was the most talented, on top of which she could look really beautiful. She might be shockingly failing in piety but she was also amazingly and universally accepted to be wise. For her, not liking strangers just for the sake of it would be particularly unlikely.

But it wasn't *all* strangers, she had eventually realized; it was the group of strangers led by Artin.

Looking down at the small, blunt-prowed boat, with its steering oarsman making purposefully towards the eastern shore, Niav remembered another thing said about jet: it could keep away dogs. Aunt Grizzel disliked dogs almost as much as she seemed to dislike Artin – and there was another bit of nonsense.

Kyle had a big half-sister called Estra (she was Uncle Lurgan's daughter but not with Kyle's mother, Aunty Helygen. Estra's mother had died when she was a baby). Estra could tell the most gripping stories – particularly ghost stories. There was one peculiar tale about the very first time that the people of the river-mouth had been visited by Artin. Niav didn't know how long ago this was supposed to have been. On the few times Niav had seen Artin, he always seemed to her to be quite young.

"It was a really wild evening," Estra said. "All the boys were up on the west cliff watching the sunset and then the sky opened and the rain came lashing down. Everyone started dashing down the pathway to get home but suddenly they saw this slip of a boat leaping from wave to wave, driven in by the storm. But it never made the harbour and crashed in under the east cliff – as boats do – and it was sucked clean under, all in a second." Then Estra put on her creepy story voice. "Everyone was stunned. There in front of them, something horrible and dark was fighting its way in through the surge and it leapt ashore – a great black dog – and they all watched it limp out of the water and clamber, really slow, up the path by the east cliff. It seemed to have injured its back left leg.

"But the next day, they found Artin (just a boy) lying out on the hillside with a horribly mangled left knee. The bodies of the other strangers floated in all white and bloated after that."

Niav was so taken with the story that she had told Aunty Grizzel.

"Now that must be a very old version of Artin's first arrival – I wonder where Estra got that from?" she laughed.

"But it's so weird – almost as though Artin's something evil. Estra's an idiot – she talks rubbish."

"You're happy enough to listen to her. She's just got a vivid imagination. Poor child, with her mother being drowned like that – you of all people should be a bit more understanding."

"But I'm not creepy and try to stand too close to people, or say I have got magical powers because my mother was some wise-woman!"

"Well, you could if you wanted; besides, Estra's poor mother, Seyth, was a wise-woman – where she came from."

"But Artin's not like that. And Uncle Lurgan almost worships at his feet . . ."

"Yes, nauseating, I know. But in the early days, everyone over there thought he was the spawn of Evil – couldn't ship him over to this side quick enough, forget hospitality! Your Uncle Lurgan decided that the nursing might be better done by your mother and father and me rather than him and Aunty Helygen – a delightfully backhanded bit of recognition."

Niav knew she had a lot to learn about the feud there had been between Uncle Lurgan and her father Diarma – even after he was dead. Things she had a right to know. But what a story! There must have been something in it, because Artin still walked with a limp to this day. And her parents really had nursed Artin the Smith – amazing!

But how strange, too, that story of the black dog. She knew there were tales of living black were-beasts – but more like cats than dogs – out there on the northern headland, but certainly not the east cliff. Imagine that though – Artin lying there in their hut, possibly even where Aunty Grizzel slept now.

Artin had hair the colour of honey and eyes the shade of new-dug peat. His smile was like dark sunlight and when he spoke to you, they said, he made a special moment for you all your own – a special place in time where you would understand, and know the way to go. But Niav herself had only seen him from afar.

"Artin took a long time to recover from the knee injury. Your father designed the first of those famous decorated wooden leg guards Artin always wears – we padded it out with moss to protect the shattered knee.

"He insisted on giving your mum and dad something for their kindness, though of course as healers we made a point of never asking for payment. So we were the first family that Artin showed how to tame bees, since we were fellow magical practitioners, so to speak.

"I think it started to restore your mum's good name; Shamanistic integrity, as it were, after eloping with a smelly weaver-dyer – from the west bank, like your dad – who had unsuitable ambitions of being a wise man and healer, too."

It was difficult for Niav to take in exactly what this must have meant, such a long time ago, when Artin was only an injured boy and not almost a demi-god. These days Uncle Lurgan seemed to see himself, somehow, as Artin's representative when he was not there (which was most of the time). She couldn't understand why Aunty Grizzel found the whole thing so ridiculous.

"What else can one do?" Aunty Grizzel smiled. "Yes, times do change, Artin had lost everything, but wanted to show his gratitude. He persuaded your mum to let him join me in learning how to make jet beads. He was a stranger and it is meant to be a secret but they let him. That's Artin for you. We would sit polishing them for hours on those flat shards of sandstone. You know what it's like, all the dust and oil getting up your fingernails. He was very good at it."

It was around this time too, apparently, that Artin had made the decorated sandstone plaque that was kept propped high up on the weaving-hut wall, tucked in among all the rugs and shawls that hung there for traders to haggle and bargain for. It showed the mountains and his home valley far away across the world. These days quite a lot of people, both local and visitors who had reached the river mouth by sea – and sometimes even overland – looked on it as a sacred object, and offered Aunty Grizzel the most amazing trade goods for it, but she simply laughed and said it should stay where he had left it.

"It was just a way of him practising decoration before we let him loose on the jet," she told Niav. "But it's a nice design – I've used it for I don't know how many rugs since then.

"But he wanted to return to his own family – poor boy. He had at least six brothers and as many sisters and he was the youngest of the lot, so he missed them terribly. He had a mysterious young wife, too, called Orchil. She was somewhere else, he said, and she was in danger. He was desperate to get to her.

"Everyone, on both banks, rallied round and helped him build a new boat – to his design of wood, of course; not a skin coracle like we were used to, or even a dug-out tree trunk like the people from the north – poor Estra's mother included – will insist on travelling in.

"We were not at all impressed with her and her boat. While our little community was graced with her presence, she tried hard to convince us that it was much the superior water-craft – and look where it got her, poor woman.

"Do you know the very first thing that you do when you are making one of those dug-outs? You wouldn't believe it," Aunty Grizzel scoffed. "You bore a big hole in the bottom to the thickness that you think your boat should be. Then you start hollowing the whole thing out from the top – it takes forever – and when you finally reach the original hole you made, you know it's finished."

"But won't it sink if it has a hole right through it?"

"Exactly. However, you bung the hole up. But when you need to beach the boat, where we, of course, would be able to turn our coracles over to dry, a dug-out is too heavy – that is when you pull out the bung to drain it.

"So, you can imagine that no one round here had any intention of trying their hand at one of those, but they did their best to help Artin to make the sort of craft that he was used to. They are obviously excellent boats, you have no idea of the distances they voyage or the weather they battle through. You never know if the strangers are lying, of course, but I don't think they often are – they all say much the same things.

"Anyway, *you* try stitching planks together with osiers and caulking it all with moss and resin – that's how they make their boats – I expect you have worked that one out. It's very tricky. But that's Artin and his folk all over, isn't it? Everyone was very eager to help, but it took months of experiment."

But when it had finally been tested, Niav knew that that had been a tragedy. Father and Mother she had been told, were out in the boat with Artin, and everyone was watching from the river's edge (with only young Aunty Grizzel minding new baby Niav back at home) and the boat had gone down at the river-mouth; only Artin's decorated knee protector that her dad, Diarma, had made had been washed in on the sands.

What happened after that? Niav was unsure. She now felt she might have been told a pack of lies. Little details started to add up. Memories of hearing people mention that it was when Artin came back about three years later, with a new boat, a new band of brothers, a new knee-guard and a welter of new magical ideas, that many people had started to feel that maybe Artin really must be some sort of miracle-worker or even a god.

Niav couldn't help feeling, from spending so much time with *dear* cousin Estra, that this was how the myths began. At the moment, what she wanted was the truth.

So what had it been? Time and time again, through all the years that Niav could remember, he had come whirling in, always on the brink of a storm; Artin the Smith – smoke and magic, golden metal and golden honey. They said he gave so much and had taken so very little in return, but now she wasn't sure.

Suddenly the skies opened and Niav dashed headlong down the ridge to tell the world.

***

"And how many did he have with him this time?" Aunty Grizzel was trying her best not to sound interested, as the rain pelted down on the turf of the roof and filled the drip-gully to overflowing.

"I think there were at least four of them, maybe five. One may have been a woman. I'm not sure. The light wasn't good."

"Five, that's handy, five eggs. You could give those eggs as a guest-greeting."

"I am sure those eggs are not bad," said Niav firmly.

"Then that's all right, isn't it? Anyway, they are beautifully packed."

***

Artin the Smith and his companions anchored their boat at the deep part by the eastern shore where the boys used to jump in from the rocks at sunset if no strangers were visiting. Next day the new arrivals were rowed over to the settlement on the opposing shore in a shoal of coracles reverently manned by a respectful escort of eastbankers – so that Artin could set up his furnace for the duration among the smells and grime of his fellow artisans on the western bank as he always did.

Artin smiled when Niav, standing at the gate of their compound, handed him the basket of eggs. It was the closest she had ever been to him. He passed it back on to one of his brothers directly behind him, who was collecting up all the gifts from the people of the west bank as they made their progress, and putting them into a hamper.

Uncle Lurgan was there in the crowded background, but trying to look in charge – as if you could with such a stupid beard and sandals, not to mention the hat (surely he didn't imagine that it made him look intelligent and wise). Aunty Helygen stood, drooping on his arm like some scrawny willow. They had even brought cousins Estra, Kyle and the youngest, Canya. They all looked very clean. Niav supposed there hadn't been room in the family coracle for the hound as well – a pity, since apart from Canya it was quite the nicest member of the family.

Canya was exactly what a cousin ought to be. Niav felt really cheered by the sight of her and they grinned at each other. People often told Niav that if she wanted to know what her mother, Befind, had looked like, she only needed to take a glance at Canya – and that was a strangely comforting thing to know.

Suddenly Niav's spirits lifted. The tension of all the frantic preparation that Aunty Grizzel had pretended wasn't happening was over. Things would be fine. Surely Artin would somehow know if the eggs were bad or not? He'd just know?

Aunty Grizzel was beside her, simply radiating beauty, and with a smug smile on her face. She had on her jet necklace and a woollen shawl so subtly woven and dyed that it looked like something that had burgeoned in the forest – not made by human hands at all. Needless to say, there was a woman in Artin's party and Grizzel had heard as much, instantly, from her contacts on the east bank.

"Did you tell my bees that I was here too, Grizzel?" Artin laughed into her eyes.

"Of course," she smiled sweetly. "I tell the bees everything."

"Well now you will be able to tell them that this time I have brought Orchil, my wife, to meet them too."

The new woman wore a long blue cloak and her hair was shining, jet black, but her skin was very pale, like new-chipped quartz. She stood behind him, between the two other men. She had great dark eyes, but she scarcely looked up at Grizzel at all, only down at her child, a raven-haired toddler, who slept quietly in a side-sling at her hip, his thin white legs dangling against her.

"And this is our son, Fearn."

★★★

So Artin and his brothers (for it turned out the second man was another brother) set up their bothy where Artin's people always did, and soon Niav could hear the bellows of his furnace working like the breathing of a giant beast, and smell the woodsmoke curling from his fire of alder-logs, drifting down towards them.

People from the local countryside sped to and fro across the river to visit Artin on their western bank. They brought him their broken tools and broken lives and went home smiling.

On the third day Artin himself came limping down to the weaving-hut. His wooden knee greave was decorated with swirling pokerwork patterns like the rising sun. He made a polite visit to the beehive, smiled sweetly at Niav and then turned his attention to Aunt Grizzel.

"Orchil, my wife, is unhappy. I would like to give a gift to her."

"A nice rug might remind her of home," said Grizzel sourly.

"No, not one of those. That was never her home. What I had in mind were those beads I fashioned."

Grizzel's hand leapt to her necklace. "No!" she said.

"They were not made for you."

"I strung them."

"But they were not made for you."

"Because of you we lost my brother and my brother's wife. If we gave the beads to anyone, it should be to my niece here, Niav."

Artin and Niav exchanged a glance and he raised one perfect eyebrow.

"Are you sure you wouldn't like a rug after all? They come from your design, you know," said Niav shyly "This blue one is lovely," she added, pulling one out from the pile laid ready for trading.

But he settled instead for a saffron-coloured belt with an arrow-shaped jet fastening like the one on Grizzel's necklace. Niav had woven it and she dimpled in pleasure.

She watched Aunty Grizzel holding Artin in animated conversation as they walked past the friendly, long-nosed pig that snuffled at the water-trough, and wove their way through the browsing flock of small-horned, dark-coated sheep till they reached the thorny compound hedge; then she slammed the gate after him. What on earth had all that been about?

★★★

Niav was troubled in her sleep; she kept waking to hear murmurings as Aunty Grizzel moved about the hut and finally went out on some night emergency – though she was back in her bed in the morning.

The next day the news spread that Artin's wife had died in the night. She must have been a bit more than unhappy. Had she even seen her new belt?

"Three rough men can't care for an infant!" declared Grizzel to everyone's astonishment except Niav's. The two of them walked up to Artin's bothy through the dry grass.

The little boy Fearn was not exactly an infant – a grave child, with his thumb in his mouth. He had his mother's hair and his father's eyes. He knew what was going on all right – not the first death he had seen, Niav felt sure.

She and Grizzel stood by him while the three men dug the grave beneath the alder tree, brothers in looks, brothers in action. All three of them, shirts laid aside as they navvied, had a white mark on their brown backs, in between the shoulder-blades, where the sun had refused to tan them. Artin's mark was the clearest and most symmetrically defined, like the wings of a great bee, or a double-headed axe.

No wonder people thought of him as one of the chosen.

"Under the alder," remarked Grizzel to no one in particular. "It was alderwood he used for his confounded boat that stole my family away." Niav winced at the pain in her voice. Weren't things bad enough?

"Of course he would, alder doesn't rot. It's just a tree. You use it yourself for your dyeing: most of the greens, and the gold – and the red too. Is that somehow an insult to my dad and mum as well? I never heard anything so daft." Symbols were all very well, but Niav felt her aunt could get a bit carried away sometimes.

"But never blue," Grizzel went on as though Niav hadn't said a word. She was watching the three of them bundle poor Orchil, wrapped in her cloak, into the readied grave. "I wonder what caused such unfairness? Bastard!"

Surely Aunty Grizzel must have meant that last word for fate – never for someone like Artin?

★★★

The people of the river-mouth were amazed, and deeply honoured, that when Artin The Smith and his brothers sailed away to the south, Fearn came to stay with Grizzel and Niav.

Uncle Lurgan took great exception to this and came storming up to their compound. He stood there, seething in his sandals, his wisp of a beard jutting in thwarted dignity while poor Aunt Helygen stood wringing her hands tearfully behind him.

"What that child is entitled to is a solid family life with us. He needs the proper preparation for his future. I am sure it would never have occurred to Artin that we would arrange for anything else!"

Aunty Grizzel stood there as majestic as a cedar, and as impervious. "He didn't mention it."

"Poor soul, he would be so grief-stricken. It must have slipped his mind," ventured Helygen. "There needs to be a responsible man in his life, like an uncle, for support."

"He isn't short of real uncles," Grizzel replied. "I can't remember that sort of offer ever being made by you for your real niece, Niav here."

Niav's heart almost stopped beating at the horror of the suggestion.

But it was eventually settled that Uncle Lurgan would take on the role and duties of Fearn's foster father. The only consequence as far as Niav was concerned was that Estra, Kyle and Canya ended up with more frequent crossings of the river in order to allow all the children "plenty of time together", and Fearn and Niav would often go over to the big family hut on the east side of the river.

"You have a perfect right to go there," Aunty Grizzel said cheerfully. "Rather more right than they have, if you want to be old-fashioned about your inheritance."

It wasn't too bad. What Uncle Lurgan felt he would gain by all this was unclear to Niav, though Aunty Grizzel seemed to have a pretty shrewd idea.

"He and Helygen probably hope that Fearn will end up with one of their girls," she said. "It's probably Estra, she is the eldest. Besides, Lurgan has developed the notion that Estra has inherited huge magical ability from both him and her mother, that wretched Seyth. I can't say I've noticed." Then she ruffled Niav's bright hair. "If we have an extra mouth to feed, I can do with any help I am offered. Besides," she laughed, "Fearn can always refuse. He is not daft".

That didn't help explain Aunt Grizzel's sudden sense of friendship – even duty – to Artin, when only a few days earlier she had seemed to be suggesting that he might have had something to do with the deaths of both of Niav's parents, not to mention that of his own poor wife, Orchil.

Kyle and Estra had to be endured, but Fearn seemed a tolerant child, if self-contained. However, spending more time with her younger cousin Canya was a real joy. Canya was pretty and clever and kind, and her voice was clear as a blackbird and smack on the note and you could suddenly find yourself singing in harmony with her without having planned it at all.

But cousin Estra was a problem. She could be so obsessive about things. All the river-mouth children liked to go beachcombing together in search of bits of jet, and the tiny snake stones that were small enough to turn into saleable jewellery, but Estra was always contriving ways of isolating Niav from the rest of the group because she wanted to be "special friends" with her. Niav found this most annoying, but frantic complaints to Aunty Grizzel fell on deaf ears.

"Nothing very special about poor Estra," was all she would say.

This seemed a bit harsh on Estra, who was the best of the three girls when it came to learning things from the two aunties. Helygen was not only a superb herbalist, she was incredibly house-proud and a consumate cook. Niav found she had a lot of catching up to do to be level with her cousins. Her aunt was also very conscientious, strict about care and safety with her herbs and potions with five children around, and a very good teacher too; extremely patient – not as erratic as Aunty Grizzel.

Uncle Lurgan would be out with the boys and the great dog, caring for the flocks, but was also responsible for their instruction in the skills of hunting and tracking. Niav and Canya would have loved to do this too, until Fearn told them how Lurgan managed to surround even that with endless ritual.

With Aunty Grizzel all three girls now learned the skills of spinning and weaving. Lurgan would probably have disapproved had he known that Grizzel also tried to hand on everything that she had learned from Niav's parents, even letting them take a try at scrying in the smooth stone water-bowl that was kept in pride of place on the dresser beside her little drum and the ritual rattle.

But Estra continued to be a real trial for Niav. She was convinced that there must be some sinister magical connection in the way that both their mothers, Seyth and Befind, had died in the clutches of the river and so, equally, this should make an important bond between the two of them. Niav found all this very upsetting. She wondered if her own nagging worries about her parents' deaths would seem equally crazy if she were to talk about it in public. She certainly didn't feel ready to haul everything out in the open for a loud-mouthed idiot like Estra to pull to bits and put together again, almost certainly all wrong.

In the end she decided to try to see if anyone besides Estra felt poor Seyth's death was anything other than a dreadful accident. It was the least she could do before dismissing Estra as annoyingly cracked in the skull. Since Estra, whether she liked it or not, was her cousin, she thought it only fair to ask people on both sides of the river what they thought.

She spoke to women rather than men because she didn't think it was the sort of thing men would feel they should be concerned about. Everyone seemed sincerely touched that young Niav was taking such a charming concern in her cousin Estra's tragic past. Niav felt almost ashamed.

The house-proud ladies on the eastern bank saw Estra's mother, the Lady Seyth, as an amazingly beautiful wise-woman, and they had almost woven her tragic ending into a romantic legend. As they saw it, Master Lurgan, the son of their wise-woman (Niav's grandmother) had gone off into the West on an "axe-quest" – something that devout young men did not do enough these days. He had returned to his mother's deathbed to bring a polished axe of superb quality, to everyone's universal approval. To all of them, it made some recompense (with respect) for the distress that they had all felt when his sister, Mistress Befind (Niav's poor mother), had chosen to disregard her birthright and throw in her lot with a weaver on the other side of the river.

Shortly after this – and even better – Lady Seyth, who had encountered Lurgan while on his questing, had fallen so deeply in love with him that she had deserted her own people and gone in search of him, bearing their new-born child. Such a beautiful thing – and they had all had every hope that she would be their new Lady.

This failed so completely to fit in with Niav's vision of Uncle Lurgan that she could barely keep a straight face. Besides, what about poor Aunt Helygen – where did she fit in? But for the eastbankers, Helygen was not part of the story – everyone moved on to the terrible tragedy of the drowning. They were all sure that poor Lady Seyth, a stranger to their river, had simply misread the currents on a stormy day – and nothing more.

Attitudes on the west bank were very different. There, it seemed to be generally felt that her uncle, Lurgan – who, if she didn't mind them saying so, was somewhat given to religious extremes – had taken it into his head to go off on the weirdly outdated custom of an "axe-quest", leaving his intended bride, poor Aunt Helygen and his terminally ill mother to wait for his return.

He had no sooner arrived home, to bore them all to death with the stories of questing, than a most unattractive and self-opinionated young woman calling herself Lady Seyth had arrived, in one of those unwieldy dug-out canoes with a baby girl that she claimed to be Lurgan's (though it looked nothing like him or any other members of his family). Lurgan had actually seemed on the verge of setting Helygen aside, when one torrential afternoon, the fool of a wise-woman refused to listen to everyone's advice not to attempt a crossing, misjudged the river currents, and, very sadly, drowned.

Bemused, Niav finally sought Aunty Grizzel's casting view on the matter; she was particularly condemnatory. "Dreadful woman! She would spout esoteric moonshine at you by the hour, but Lurgan was convinced she was a 'great mind'. Your granny would have died laughing if she hadn't already been dead. Poor Helygen, to be subjected to all that; she is such a brilliant herbalist and a really caring soul – not that I need to tell you."

"But where was Estra? Why wasn't she drowned too?"

"That is the appalling thing! That bitch, Seyth, had left Estra for Helygen to look after, as though she was her minion, while she swanned over here to get some unnecessary fiddle-faddle for her "work'. Poor young Estra, I am afraid, shows every sign of becoming another exhibitionist like her mother. Clear your mind of it. Nothing or nobody murdered Seyth – it was just an accident."

Totally deflated, after all her busy questionings, Niav wondered if, equally, maybe, nobody had murdered her parents either.

But then how was it that Artin the Magician had re-emerged, and such a long time later, when you would think that a cripple like him should have been sucked into the stormy seas beside them? No wonder people wondered if he wasn't some sort of godling. And why had Fearn's mother died suddenly like that? And, particularly ... why was it that Grizzel did not seem, any longer, concerned to know?

So, in spite of her own worried imaginings, Niav concentrated on trying not to lose her temper with Estra. She tried to feel sorry for her, because Aunty Grizzel clearly did, and Aunty Grizzel was not a one to suffer fools gladly. But she couldn't come to terms with the way that Estra obsessed so about what she seemed to consider were their exclusive rights to magical power.

To Niav, if, as a result of her family background, she ended up more able to help other people stay lucky and well, that was a gift she was happy and honoured to share. But if it came to some inbred right to dominate people and the forces of nature, just because you could, that was where Niav, very firmly, drew her line in the sand.

But Estra's next, worrying, foray into the worlds of imagination concerned the sacred "barra" or wand of power. Obviously every self-respecting wise woman would be expected to have one.

"We have to have barras!" Estra solemnly announced one afternoon as the three girls were busily engaged in collecting the latest harvest of wool that the sheep regularly rid themselves of in the thorny field hedges. "We have a great heritage, you and I, Niav, a mystic bond, I sense it! This river – it's malevolent. It wants to steal our powers! We have to join forces to face the river out. I know we can do it!"

"I think you have to wait for your barra to find you," countered Niav nervously, plucking out of the air a vague memory of something Aunt Grizzel had once mentioned. She had the greatest respect for the raging majesty of their river, but she doubted that it would waste its time on the rantings of two little girls.

Where on earth had this latest notion come from? Some puzzled questioning finally made Niav suspect that someone had mentioned to Estra that both her own mother, Seyth, and Niav's mother, Befind, would have had their barra with them when they died.

Somehow Estra had turned this obvious fact into a cosmic conspiracy, and Niav noted to herself that their mothers' barras hadn't proved much good against the power of the river. But still, she began to wonder what had happened to her mother's barra.

Had it been in their family a long time? Could Lurgan have told Estra as much, and made her feel that it should really have come down to her, his eldest daughter, because Befind had abandoned her birthright and should never have taken it away?

Aunty Grizzel, for once, seemed to think this was perfectly probable "Poor child, nobody likes her. She simply wants to feel special in some way. She will grow out of it, I expect."

"Did Mother's barra belong to Granny as well? Would I have had it?"

"I dare say it did – and possibly a whole string of grannies before that. It would have come down to you, in due course; certainly not to Estra, anyway – things like that would go down female relatives, and her mother was a complete stranger. Besides, it sounds as though she had also thrown away whatever birthright it was she *claimed* to have had – from wherever it was she came! It's just Estra's nonsense. Try to distract her on to something else. If either of you two is meant to have a barra, it will emerge when the time is right."

But it was her mother's death, not her mother's mislaid barra, that most concerned Niav. However, month followed month, and year followed year, with Artin showing not the slightest sign of reappearing at the river's mouth. There could be no chance of Niav (even if she had managed to approach him at all) questioning him successfully about her parents' tragedy. Artin seemed to be the most elusive of men – if he was just a man.

However, for all the other people who awaited him in the valley, the legend of what Artin was and the things he'd said and done seemed to simplify and became easier to understand – mainly because Uncle Lurgan was so assiduous in keeping his interpretation of Artin's teachings alive in people's minds.

"You know," Aunty Grizzel observed, "there are times when I doubt that Artin would recognize a word of what he is supposed to have said at all."

As for Artin's boy, by now everyone loved Fearn for himself as much as for the memory of whose son he was. He was found to be astonishingly creative even by local standards and determined to try his hand at mastering any skill that the people on the western bank would let him learn – besides what Lurgan tried to teach him over on the eastern side.

The bees liked him too and he helped to take over the care of the hives – as might be expected of someone who has been used to the mysteries of smoke and magic – and the honey yield prospered.

He missed his own family, of course, but he did not seem unduly surprised that he had been left behind. He could wait. He had seemed a silent boy, but Grizzel and Niav gradually came to appreciate that it was more the case of him knowing how to be silent in many different tongues.

His mother had not come from the same homeland as his father, and they had lived in another place entirely – and then there was the mixture of languages that the sailors spoke which was almost a language in itself. That was why understanding the people of the river-mouth had presented no problem to him at all. He could cope with Kyle's insipid attempts at bullying him and Estra's flurries of melodrama, and he really appeared to like Canya just as much as Niav did – he particularly seemed to delight in music just as they did.

Once he had been shown how to cut a set of pipes from his mother's alder, and saw the sap run as red as blood, he told Niav that he felt that Orchil was still alive, waiting for Artin too, and smiling down on him as he played.

Niav and Canya would sit enthralled, watching the dappled sunlight fall across Fearn's bare brown back – clearly marked with his father's white protective wings – as he sat, poised on the great rock that his father and uncles had placed beneath the shadow of the alder branches before they left. It seemed so magical a place that the girls were sometimes too in awe to sing.

Occasionally the visitors to the river-mouth included Artin's kin. They always made a point of giving small gifts to many of the children, not only Fearn.

Once, Niav was smilingly given a lovely greenstone bead, on a soft white leather thong, that looked almost as special as Uncle Lurgan's quested axe. But when Niav ran home with it to show Aunty Grizzel, she looked quite bemused. "That's a very valuable thing to give a little girl – mind you, don't flash it about when there are traders around."

"But why give it to me?"

"Don't forget your mum and dad saved Artin's life – maybe it's time it was remembered." She went off to look for Artin's brother and came back very quiet.

However, if Fearn begged him (or whichever other brother sailed in to the river-mouth) for news of his father, they would only smile and say that he was an amazingly busy man these days.

Every time they came, Niav felt that she would like to sail away with them and search for him too. Every girl would. How tragic it had been, everyone said, that such a beautiful man should have been reduced to limping his way around like that.

"Oh, it doesn't notice when he is lying down," Aunty Grizzel scoffed. "That's the way they wish they could have seen him; besides, time passes and he won't be looking quite so beautiful now."

Niav would try not to be put out by such sacrilegious observations. Aunty Grizzel was endearingly eager to shock, and Niav was determined to try and seem grown-up enough to be treated as her assistant and not just her niece. She tried to show an educated interest in Artin's injuries, and remarked how wonderful it was that he was able to give so much time and careful advice to people, when he must, surely, be in such acute pain. Had Aunty Grizzel any notion of what drug he might be taking to manage it?

"The same thing that gives him all his visions, I should imagine!" was all that Aunt Grizzel would reply – why couldn't she try to be serious sometimes?

But that was the trouble – she was. Aunt Grizzel always saw right through her, however hard she tried. The memory of Artin represented her masculine ideal, in spite of all her mixed suspicions about him otherwise. Even though she knew that most young girls of her age were already expected to be looking around, no one else that she met, even visiting young traders, ever seemed to come up to his standard. Her aunt was tolerant and did not pressure her, but she was obviously starting to get concerned about Niav's future happiness.

"You will become a broken-hearted wise-woman like me, if you don't watch your step, child," she chided her, not unkindly. "There are six lads at least that I can think of who are trying to run after you. Don't you notice? Don't you care? Do you want to spend your best years with a sarcastic bitch like me?"

"Oh, I'm quite fond of you really," smiled Niav, unmoved. "And, besides, Fearn can be fun to be with too."

She loved being with Fearn – something about the way their minds seemed to set one another's off, always something to make, something to do; why give that up to be with the spotty youths of her own age?

One day, not long after a visitation of a couple of uncles, Fearn was sitting pensively on his rock. "You know," he said, "I think that, this time, my uncles were trying to tell me that maybe I'm old enough to look under my rock."

"Why, what's under your rock?" said an astonished Niav; it was a vast thing and had taken both of his uncles and his father to get it set in place there, she remembered.

"Oh, he buried something for me underneath, to dig out when I was older. It needn't be difficult. There are ways of moving big rocks that would simply stun you. People round here probably know, but they don't seem to feel the need to do it. I doubt if there will be many future changes, either, with your uncle Lurgan smothering any new idea that tries to raise its head.

"Where we lived when I was little, they hefted rocks all over the place when they were feeling religious – it was quite exciting. Still, there is a lot to be said for the way you have things here. You let the children make themselves useful, beachcombing.

"Where we were, they'd have had me down a mine at the first opportunity – Orchil insisted on taking me away at the first mention of it; I prefer sunshine – so did she. But I can remember the amazing things they used to do and my uncles explained to me how they could be done. Maybe we should give it a go."

"*We?* What have *I* got to do with it? Surely it's meant to be your stone to prove your stupid manhood or something."

"Look, it took the three of them ages, they were sweating away all night to shift it by brute force. Wouldn't a couple of kids managing to do it – using my brain and organizational skills – prove my manhood?"

"Prove your bloody-mindedness possibly – I don't know; it isn't exactly my problem."

"Well, I'd like to give it a try."

Fearn demonstrated the method of using a lever, supported by a second stone, to prize up a smallish boulder. Though Niav had used slats of wood to loosen the odd flagstone in her time, she had never realized about using the smaller stone to help. She was impressed to discover quite how large a rock it was possible for two youngsters to move on their own with a proper-sized lever. However, in the end they called in the aid of Kyle, Estra and Canya who turned up unexpectedly.

All five of them were flung, laughing, on their backs as the mighty block was finally shifted to one side to reveal an intriguing cavity, lined with what looked like river-pebbles packed round a long, well-preserved leather sack.

Fearn knelt down and pulled it out.

With a muffled clang of metal on the stones, Fearn dragged it over to the others and squatted down to loosen the draw string and peel the bag open.

There was a long soft leather case, with a strap almost like a quiver for arrows, and about the same size, but heavy – a solid strip of metal. A bone handle protruded from the top, wound round with a tight string of what might be human hair – raven black, with gold plaited in. Gently, Fearn slid it out of the casing. It was coated with grease and came out easily.

"That's got to be the biggest knife I have ever seen!"

"But it's not flint . . ."

"No, it's *bronze*!" breathed Fearn incredulously.

It was the biggest blade of bronze any of them had ever encountered, slender as the finest arrowhead or dagger, but longer than any piece of flint that they could imagine in their wildest dreams. It was ridged down the centre, widening where it plunged into the bone handle. The blade shone, softly golden in the bright sunlight.

Gingerly, Fearn touched the leading edge with the tip of his finger.

"Youch, that's sharp."

"You could whistle through a patch of reeds with that one!"

"Reeds, my eye – that's for killing people!" observed Kyle with relish.

★★★

Fearn, Niav and Canya were busy displaying the new discovery to Aunty Grizzel in the sunshine outside the weaving-hut. She was looking down the blade with obvious admiration – after Fearn had demonstrated what damage he could do to a discarded mat – when Kyle, Estra and a sweating Uncle Lurgan came puffing up the path.

"What in the world are you thinking of – letting him loose with that *thing*, Grizzel!" he remonstrated. "Surely you don't imagine that his father will have intended him to retrieve it in such a haphazard, unorganized way. It's for a man to win in manly ceremony – not for children to play with. If I had known of its existence – and I cannot imagine why I was not informed of its potential discovery by one of his uncles; at least, if Artin understandably would not yet be expecting the time to be ripe – I would have put Fearn into training, composed a suitable ritual . . . Really, it's unforgivable!"

With quite astonishing speed, Lurgan had retrieved the scabbard from its resting place across a wool basket, plucked the dagger from Grizzell's unsuspecting grasp, and belted off back down the path to the river.

To Niav's surprise, it was Kyle who dashed fiercely after him, followed by Fearn, and they attempted a tackle half way down the steep road. Lurgan broke free from them with unexpected speed and skill and Fearn fell heavily on his back. Kyle made a grab at Lurgan's kilt and almost had him down, but only got smacked severely in the lip for his pains. Lurgan was away in the coracle as fast as lightning.

The three girls came tearing down the hill to find the two bewildered boys stranded on the bank.

Kyle was not allowed to cross the river the next day and Estra and Canya ruefully told Niav and Fearn that their parents had had the bronze blade securely hidden away by the time they reached home.

The five children – who so nearly bordered on not being children – were completely bereft. Aunty Grizzel was quietly furious. For once, Niav and Canya agreed with Estra in hoping that Aunty Grizzel would have decided to pour a few appropriate libations to deities who might take an active interest.

***

It was a pivotal moment, the point at which childhood dreams came to an end. In respect of Estra and Canya, in particular,

Helygen decided it was time for them to concentrate on adult occupations – they must knuckle down and think of the future. Kyle and Fearn were kept apart for almost a week.

Estra, like Niav, was perfectly content, in fact most enthusiastic, to take up an adult role in helping with the family's responsibilities for care and healing, but they both had trouble with trying to pretend that any of the local male talent raised the faintest flutter in their breasts. One would not have known what Canya felt about any of her young admirers; she was incapable of being unkind to anyone, so never voiced her feelings to anyone on the subject.

Kyle and Fearn were a different matter. Niav felt that Fearn was quietly seething – she did not know when he would break out, but she knew it would be well-planned when he did. In due course, Fearn built his own, small hut, further up the ridge, but still had a way of turning up at meal times, or bringing his washing along to be dealt with alongside theirs. However, his bed – on the right-hand side of the fire – that had been Diarma's before him, remained empty.

Kyle was a mystery. He stayed at home, but he seemed bewildered that he had attacked his father. He didn't come over to the west bank so often. Maybe he had never expected Lurgan to take the action he did. Maybe he feared that Fearn might feel betrayed by him and take appropriate vengeance – in other words, maybe he remained the suspicious, if slightly larger, stoat that he always had been.

★★★

No one could have suggested that, down by the river, there was any lack of opportunity within the seasons of the year for young persons to show their interest in members of the opposite sex.

Winter and summer, there was a whole succession of ceremonies to celebrate life, death, and, with special reference to the young, fertility. Even in the heart of winter, two hazelnuts, representing a would-be pairing, could be placed side by side in the embers. If they burned together slowly, it was said to bode well, but if one was seen to pop away across the ashes from the other – things were not held to be so good, and much laughter would result. Niav never had a nut which would stand still, while a Canya nut would smoulder away next to any suggested candidate. Niav never heard of anyone placing an Estra nut in the embers at all – maybe they would have been too nervous.

As spring arrived and the catkins on Fearn's alder tree sprang into life, the boys and girls put strips of bark with their own signs on into adjoining bags. All the girls dreamed of drawing Fearn, all the boys dreamed of drawing Canya. No one ever gained any sign that they were likely to get satisfaction.

Eventually, even Niav had to acknowledge the fact that she had followers. She found it difficult to separate the image of these young suitors from the little boys that she used to watch silhouetted against the sunset as they dived off the flat rock by the traders' landing point. She agreed to be courted by the least offensive of her suitors, but was very unsure about it. She had sincerely never realized that she was so sought-after. Aunt Grizzel started piling things up as bride-gifts.

***

So, one fragrant bee-hummingly radiant afternoon while Aunt Grizzel was busy, dealing with a difficult birth along in the settlement, Fearn came to find Niav in the weaving-hut.

"Are you going to get betrothed?" he asked.

"I expect so; don't you like him?" said Niav.

"No, he's fine. It's just that I think I should be going to find my father. But I would like to know that you are settled before I do."

"How could you find him? He could be anywhere."

"Oh no! I know where we came from. I don't forget things."

"But you came in a boat. You don't have a boat. Are you going to build one?"

"No, I don't need to. Mother came from a headland in the west. It's called 'The Place of the Great Worm' all the smiths get their copper there. I will just wait for him to arrive. Anyone could go there on foot if they wanted to, but ore and suchlike are heavy stuff, so metalworkers go by boat – you must have realized that. I only need to follow the setting sun; it's perfectly simple."

"You are going – just like that?" Niav stared at him wide-eyed.

"Well, I came to say goodbye. It's more than he did."

"But we always expected him to come back."

"Did you now?" said Fearn. "How little you knew him."

"You were only a toddler – how could you have appreciated subtle nuances like that?"

"But I was not stupid. Small children are not always stupid. Besides I get much more information out of my uncles than they think I do. Or maybe they are just testing me to sort out how much I can work out for myself. Anyway, I aim to leave tomorrow."

"What about your blade?"

"Oh, I plan to be getting my blade."

Niav could just imagine the scene – oh to be an insect on the Lurgan family wall! "And what about Canya?"

"What about Canya? She could have anyone she wants, why would she want me? Besides, Estra would take it very badly. You know as well as I do that that's who Lurgan proposes to pair me off with. I do not propose to come in the way of anything that Estra feels she is entitled to – it could ruin your life. Best to be elsewhere, I feel."

"How perceptive of you. Well if you are so sure, what can I say?" Then she paused for a moment – if she didn't ask him now she never would." I need to know something about Artin that you might be able to help me with."

Fearn raised a perfect eyebrow.

"It's about the death of my parents. You seem to be able to remember a whole lot more than a toddler might be expected to, so it's worth a try. I am told it was a good three years after my parents were drowned that your father reappeared like magic and people started to suspect he could be a demi-god. He never seems to have told anyone how he got away, or, if he did, there is some reason why no one one will tell me. Did you ever hear him talk of an escape, or maybe he said someone tried to kill him . . . ?"

Fearn pondered for a minute. "Maybe – but I don't remember details. Someone did try to kill him – but he went back and faced them out. In other words, yes, but I don't know if it was here. He can make himself unpopular all over the place I am told."

"Surely he wouldn't have brought both of you back here if it was dangerous?"

"My mother is dead, my father is gone – end of story!"

Niav was stunned – all these years and he could have been harbouring doubts and terrors just the same as hers. "We are probably both being as daft as Estra," she said, almost crying. "So that is that then. Is there anything I can give you to remember me by? I take it you won't be back either." Niav felt blank inside.

Fearn smiled, a smile like dark sunlight, and for her alone. "Now just imagine me," he said. "With my hair the colour of honey, and, if you wish it, a crippled leg – though, as Aunty Grizzel pointed out, that wouldn't notice if we were lying down. Or maybe think of me as him, reflected deep in jet – just to say goodbye to him, you understand – because, quite honestly, I don't think he is going to come back this way, and I would like you to be happy for once, if only at second best."

★★★

When Aunty Grizzel found them hard at work in her bed, she laughed till she wept. "Children, children, I do hope I am interrupting you before a truly delicate moment. Oh, but if you could see yourselves!" she cried. "A beast with two backs – and four wings! Really Niav, didn't you think – couldn't you guess? I hope nothing irretrievable has happened yet?"

"When would I get to see my back? Why did you never tell me?" screamed Niav in unbelieving shock.

"I'm going tomorrow," laughed Fearn, who undoubtedly had been aware of the hidden interest of Niav's back. "I don't suppose there is anything that I can do for you, too, before I go?" He paused as he did up his belt.

"Arrogant bastard, like father like son!" yelled Grizzel. "We didn't want my poor brother to know. So many years of marriage and no child – what else was your poor mother expected to do, Niav? Taunts of infertility get anyone down – men and women alike – and particularly when you are meant to be a healer."

"Exactly – I'm sure that my father was merely trying to repay the hospitality that he had received – I'm told that it's his way," countered Fearn, still laughing as he laced up his right moccasin.

"Viper!" retorted Aunty Grizzel, flinging the nearest thing to hand – a wooden milk dipper, which Fearn avoided with a backward leap that took him smacking into the dresser and nearly dislodging Aunty Grizzel's heavy scrying bowl. The drum and rattle bounced noisily across the earthen floor.

"Well, Niav," Grizzel sighed, suddenly looking her age, "When I delivered you and saw that birthmark, your mother and I thanked our stars for you being a girl. For the normal reasons of decency, it would probably remain well hid, if we could only steer you past the baby stage. I know your mother had reassured Artin as much. I don't

know which one of them had had the bright idea in the first place –
mutual lust is my suspicion, but then I'm over-suspicious by nature.

"Anyway, between us we were coping very well till one morning
my brother Diarma popped his head into the hut just as we were
bathing you. We didn't think that he had noticed anything.

"That was the same day they had planned to go out testing that
wretched boat. The whole village was there to see them off. At the
last minute your mother decided to go too, and handed you to
me to take home. But I went up to the west cliff so that we could
watch. Even with them that far out, I noticed a tussle of some
sort. Then the whole boat capsized and I thought them all gone
forever. Who could have blamed my poor brother if he had seized
a chance to push Artin in – but some people lead a charmed life.
Abusing hospitality seems a family failing round here."

"But it doesn't make me the bastard!" hissed Fearn, now
silhouetted in the doorway. "My mother loved him, you know,
and she loved me, and once upon a time my father loved her!
She was his wife! But you wouldn't give up the beads he had
made for her when he still pined for her and his distant home.
Even after you had to thrust his love-child in her face! Eggs – she
threw them at him, all of them – and they were rotten too! I forget
nothing!" said Fearn with a terrible matter-of-factness.

Grizzel had seized the broom. Niav had finished scrabbling
around for her scattered clothes. "Get out, you bastard's bastard.
You leave now, not tomorrow!"

"Yes, perfect timing, into the setting sun!"

They harried him down the cluttered compound, tripping
up on hay-rakes and buckets and panicked livestock, past
the weaving-hut and the herb garden and stumbling through
the clutch of hives. The last they saw of him, he was running,
screaming, towards the river, followed by a cloud of bees.

Grizzel dusted off her palms and walked sedately back towards
the well. She undid her jet necklace, held it for a moment catching
the sunlight and then, pushing the well cover aside, she dropped
it clattering down the shaft.

***

Aunty Grizzel sat down on the bed and put her head in her
hands. Niav suddenly remembered how tired she must be – she
had been called out at crack of dawn on a blisteringly hot day.

"Was the birth all right in the end?"

"Yes, she should be fine – but she has lost a lot of blood."

"And the baby?"

"Two boys!"

"Well, you thought it might be twins. Now you lie down. I will get you a nice camomile tea and then start the meal – at least I will know how many to cook for this time!"

At this, astonishingly, Aunty Grizzel burst into tears. Niav had never known her to cry real gulping tears, not in her whole life – she was more used to Grizzel comforting hers.

"I should not have done that," said Aunty Grizzel shakily. "That was a beautiful thing and I should have given it to you long since – my stupid temper, why must I do these things!"

"Your necklace? Why on earth to me? Maybe it should have been buried with Fearn's mum, and anyway, didn't you help to make it?"

"I only helped Artin to string it and, we were making it for Orchil, Artin's much-loved wife – he planned to take it to her when he sailed away, but of course that never happened. I have never had any right to it. It should have been yours because poor Orchil wanted you to have it. Don't you have any memories of my going out the night she was dying? Artin came back to fetch me.

"When Artin came down to see us at the weaving-hut, it was to get medicine for her as much as the necklace, but most importantly she had wanted him to bring the pair of us back with him to the bothy.

"But the fool failed to handle it right. For all his magic, Artin can be bad at asking for favours that he really cares about – he ended up picking a quarrel with me. That is why the poor woman threw the eggs at him in desperation (and they were fine, by the way Fearn remembered that wrong). She knew that she was dying. She was afraid Fearn would be put to work in the copper mines and she wanted him taken somewhere where that wouldn't happen to a child, and he could be safe till he was old enough to travel round with Artin."

"Couldn't they take him to all those relatives up in the mountains Artin carved?"

"That is a very long journey – she didn't think there was time, and she was right. Believe me Niav, Orchil was every bit as wonderful as Artin had always told me that she was, and she could not have been kinder. She said Artin trusted me, and neither of them mentioned my brother Diarma at all. Being asked by her to care for Fearn was an honour. She didn't begrudge your existence in the least. She felt you could be the daughter she would never be able to have, and she wanted the necklace to go down to you."

"Then why all the wretched secrecy?"said Niav in a tired voice.

Grizzel studied her for a moment. "Didn't I explain clear enough just now? Your parents were respected as healers. My brother Diarma was a great man – your mother and I would not have had him shamed, even after death. I could not bear the thought of Lurgan's gloating if he had known of my brother's betrayal. What angered me most was your mother's stupidity choosing a partner to make her baby with who came from a family that carried such distinctive features. It isn't as though she didn't know. Artin's brothers had been very busy for years round here – why do you think they doled out so many presents? But that green bead is special – and Artin's intentions were clear. I should have told you then."

Niav was wide-eyed, remembering some of the other children who had received gifts.

"Quite," Grizzel said drily, seeing her face. "But I think cousins would have been all right. Let's face it, everyone is a cousin of someone else round here. We didn't know you might meet any actual brothers then. But I was very angry with your mother Befind – not to her face, but angry." She recounted her finding of Befind on the beach. "I couldn't tell anyone what I thought I had seen my brother do – could I? I could only get nonsense out of Befind. I told everyone she had been dead, but she wasn't."

"But she did say goodbye to me?" Niav was crying too. "What was the nonsense?"

"Yes, she said goodbye, and she was still beautiful. She said something inconsequential about Seyth's death. You see, her corpse had washed in by your snake stone too, and it was she and I that found her. Your Mother was blaming the bung of her stupid dug-out boat again, still living in the past – ridiculous last words for a woman like her to go out on – better to say nothing."

By the time Niav made the tea Aunty Grizzel had fallen asleep.

It seemed a bit pointless to do any cooking. Niav went out into the sun-kissed evening and walked on past the well to see if the bees had settled down.

Niav hadn't heard the necklace hit the water and she knew how long it should have taken; they regularly registered the depth of water with her dad's – no, Diarma's – knotted string which still hung by the door. She knew the level was way down and that the roots could snag things.

"Well, should I?" she asked them.

The bees didn't say "No."

She shifted the lid right over as far as possible and gave the bucket rope a couple of extra twists round the hitching post for strength. With a last look at the darkening sky, she let the bucket drop right down to the water level and swung herself over the edge.

Once she got past the stone lipping, encroaching roots glimmered through the wattle that lined the earthen walls, and the air smelled cool and moist like leaf-mould. Down she swung and down, and still no luck. She was just giving up hope in the semi-darkness when she spotted something that spun and glittered just near the waterline. It was terrifying reaching down that far but with a frantic grab that almost made her lose her hold on the rope, she got it. The jet necklace.

As she tried to regain her breath for the long haul up, the unearthly stillness of the well was shattered by a furious Aunt Grizzel, who, having guessed what she was doing, was yelling at her down the shaft. Niav almost let the precious necklace slip, but just in time she grabbed it back and knotted it firmly in her belt. The climb up was going to be hard and she started to feel the first drops of much needed rain. Up above, Aunty Grizzel continued shouting at her in a most unhelpful way.

"Why, you could have died down there and never been found till the water went rotten ... and where would that have got anyone?"

Niav had succeeded in getting herself almost walking up the well wall, finding her footing in the wattle, when, unnervingly, her foot snagged itself through some slimy loop of root. It was exhausting trying to pull herself out, as the rain pelted harder and stung her eyes. She leaned down and managed to haul the root loose from the well wall, but it stayed clinging to her foot. She simply couldn't shake it off. As she swung there in the semi-darkness, it seemed not to want to let her go. It was not a root at all, but a longish, flexible wand of wood – partly snapped, but encased in what seemed to be plaited strips of snakeskin that had twisted themselves most successfully round her ankle.

"Would this be what I think it is?" challenged Niav, as she finally hauled herself over the lip of the well and waved her unexpected trophy in the face of an equally furious Aunty Grizzel. "Something else you should have saved for me?" It had to be her mother's missing sacred barra.

★★★

The rain beat down on the roof-turf during a long night of recriminations, but the next day, as Niav and her aunt were enjoying their bread and honey in the freshness of reconciliation and a sun-and-birdsong morning, a raging Kyle came crashing his way up from the river.

"Where is that arsehole Fearn?" he roared at his bewildered relatives. "He has killed Father!"

★★★

Grizzel and Niav were still completely bewildered as they fought to row their coracle across the swollen river, Niav with her newly mended barra at her belt.

"It must have been an accident. That thing is sharp and Uncle Lurgan had no right to have taken it."

"Calm down. We will see exactly what has happened when we get there," panted Aunt Grizzel, looking at the new patch of dark cloud moving in from the north. "That could be another downpour – I don't fancy getting trapped on the east side if we turn out to be unpopular."

"They might not even let us in – there isn't much reason why they should."

"Interesting that it was hidden in Helygen's 'Dangerous Herbs' basket all this time. I wonder how Fearn found out?"

"I told you – when he came to say his goodbyes yesterday, he seemed to know where the blade was, and he intended to get it. But I just don't see how it would have been hidden in there. I know the basket was kept well out of our reach in the roof beams

– but it's not as though she didn't winch it down often when she was teaching us; all those neat little jars securely sealed. We have used it lots of times. I never got a hint of anything concealed in it."

"Poor Kyle – he is shattered. He may have got that bit wrong. They have had a long night."

"I hope he doesn't find him."

They beached the coracle and headed up the hillside. Lurgan's hut – the ancient home of Niav's family – was a large, thatched, almost square building with the significant feature these days of having more than one room. It stood slightly set apart from the other buildings – a venerable place. Today it was in turmoil, or as near to turmoil as the east side ever got. Several of the assembled lady mourners gave a slight gasp as Grizzel and Niav arrived in the doorway.

Estra seemed to be the one in charge. After a moment's hesitation, she hurried over to greet them, gliding effortlessly through the milling crowd of well-wishers in an impressively dignified way. She ushered them over to where her mother was sitting, placed formally before the dresser, hunched among a huddle of her cooing and sobbing neighbours next to the wattle bier, suitably draped in his second best cloak, where a very clean Uncle Lurgan had been laid out in his finest kilt and cape in the light from the door. His dead fingers had been bent around his hard-won greenstone axe, and they had even given him his hat. Niav had always seen Uncle Lurgan's hat as the symbol of his pomposity; now it somehow seemed fitting and almost stately. His hound lay sleeping, slumped beside the bier, as if he knew his master would never wake.

Poor Aunty Helygen looked up at them as they came in. Niav could have sworn she saw her eyes flicker at the sight of the barra at her waist, but she didn't say a word. Grizzel didn't seem to register this at all and ran over and folded her in a warm embrace. Helygen clung to her, sobbing fiercely.

Estra left them to it and drew Niav over to the comparative privacy of the woman's section of the hut. "I am so glad you've got here," she whispered. "However did you find out? The river seems to be running very high – who managed to tell you?"

"Kyle came storming over to us – whatever happened?"

"You haven't seen Fearn?"

"Not since late yesterday afternoon. If someone stabbed your dad, Fearn hadn't got the blade then – so when on earth did this happen? Kyle was pretty difficult to get any sense out of."

"Kyle wasn't here. He came home just as Father breathed his last. The rest of us were, though. We heard them shouting outside and then Dad came staggering in. It was definitely Fearn, I'm afraid. Whatever came over him?"

Niav gave Estra a brief account of yesterday's revelations.

"Fearn's your *brother!*" Estra almost shouted, her mask of composure cracking for a moment. "And your barra – it seems it's found you too," she observed with unconvincing brightness, resuming the whisper.

Niav felt a distinct chill at the odd, widening sparkle in her cousin's eyes – just as she used to look when she put on her creepy voice and told them all some fearful story. "Oh, *your* barra will be making itself known to you any day now, I am sure," said Niav hurriedly. She had no intention of divulging anything about her journey down the well to Estra, who would no doubt construct some completely unwelcome significance from it. Niav did not want yesterday's simple recovery of two misplaced items to become some esoteric legend of questing for her heritage in the deep.

"Fearn's your *brother!*" This time it was Canya, who had stumbled in from the curtained room at the back.

"Oh do go back and lie down, Canya," said Estra, all concern. "She really isn't well at all," she whispered, turning to Niav. "You know the way traumas always go right to her stomach."

At this point, one of the east-bank ladies came hovering, for Estra's guidance over something. Probably Grizzel wanted to look more closely at Lurgan's body. "Your mother says it's all right dear but . . ."

Estra swept off with her without a second's hesitation.

★★★

Canya was very pale, and she had clearly been crying her eyes out. Niav suspected it wasn't simply her father's death that had brought her to this state. Niav had no recollection of traumas going to Canya's stomach at all. She was the most equable person she had ever met, and she had been amazed not to find her there bustling about and looking after everyone.

"Whatever's the matter Canya?" she said, holding back the curtain to the inner room and settling her down on the nearest stool in there, while she drew up another. "Now tell me all about it."

She could not help noticing that Aunt Helygen's herb basket stood open at the table's end – the long pulley-rope leading up towards the gloomy ceiling.

At first, Canya simply cried, holding her head in her hands. Then at last she looked up at Niav. "I do keep being sick," she said, ruefully.

Niav made a huge leap of reasoning. "Did you tell Fearn?" she asked.

Canya burst into tears again. "No," she said quietly.

"Well?"

"I didn't think Fearn would want to know. He could have anyone. I decided to try giving myself something to help things along a bit. So I winched down Mother's herb basket."

"What? The Penny Royal?"

Canya nodded, "It's what Mother always seems to recommend."

"For heaven's sake! How often have you been doing this sort of thing?"

"Only ever Fearn."

"How long has that been going on?"

"No, no, you don't understand. It was only the once!"

Well that explained a lot – it could be that she, personally, had had a lucky escape the day before if he was that fertile! "And?"

"Everyone was out. I winched the basket down; Mother is always so careful, but I am afraid I was so nervous, I let it down in such a rush that it hit the table with a huge crash. I was sure I must have broken something, but it was all all right – only the matting she uses to pad the bottom had come dislodged . . ."

"And you found Fearn's blade."

"That made me change my mind; I thought that when I told Fearn about the sword, we ought to have a proper discussion about what to do. It wasn't just my baby after all. He had a right to know. So I tidied everything in the basket, and winched it back to the roof.

"I was just trying to decide where to hide the blade, when I heard Father and the boys coming home down the hill. I rammed the blade up into the reed roof-lining – near the door as a temporary hiding place – just as they came in with the hound bounding all over the place. But I managed to whisper to Fearn about finding his blade. He wasn't able to pull it out of the thatch again with Father and Kyle there, so he said he would come round and collect it yesterday evening – I had thought there might be a quiet moment then."

"And it all went wrong?"

Canya started crying again. "I keep being sick. Obviously Mother and Estra started asking me questions – well, they are professionals and needed to check I hadn't eaten something bad. But you can't hide much from them. I didn't expect them to be quite so angry when I told them it was Fearn's. I really had no idea they intended Estra to marry him – did you?"

"Aunty Grizzel did."

"But Estra doesn't like boys – I didn't think she felt like that about Fearn."

Niav laughed. "She doesn't understand what 'like that' means. No, it's all about her mystic power being fused with his."

"I am starting to see that now. I had no idea she was so serious about it, or that Father and even Mother were too. It seems completely mad. Mother was determined that I get rid of the baby, she didn't want me to tell Fearn, and she particularly didn't want Father to know.

"At that point someone else called at the door and Mother had to go and see to them. She told Estra to winch down the herb basket and mix up the dose. She was horribly firm, not like she was my mother at all.

"Then things got even worse, because Fearn arrived. He had some bee stings – I see why he hadn't come to you and Aunty Grizzel about that now! He wasn't like my Fearn at all either.

"I treated the stings for him and then he told us, by way of thanks, that he was going. Just going! I couldn't say anything to him about our baby, and Estra was standing there, calmly mixing the Penny Royal to kill it."

"But how did your dad get stabbed in all this?"

Canya put her head in her hands again as she tried to get it straight. "Mother came through from talking to her visitor and, while she had her back to the door, I tried to make sure she and

Estra were looking my way – I said something about bee stings; Fearn took the moment to slip past Mother and grab his blade from by the door – it was the least I could do.

"But Father came in through the door and saw what Fearn had in his hand. It was just terrible – Father tried to grab the blade, but there was a scuffle and Fearn got away. There seemed to be a deal of blood, but the wounds did not seem much to me – it was mainly his hands. Mother and Estra rushed about trying to see to it all. You know the way Dad liked to be fussed over. In the end they had him lying back. He said all the stress had gone to his stomach and then spotted the drink standing on the table.

"'What's that for?' he said.

"'It's mint tea, dearest,' Mother said. 'Poor Canya has been feeling a trifle bilious.' Then he said that that was just what he needed, and poor Mother reached over and gave it to him to drink down."

Niav was starting to get even more frightened and confused. "Well I suppose Penny Royal could be called that – it is a sort of mint, after all."

"There is no way it should have killed him. I don't think those wounds should have killed him either. I don't understand anything any more."

The two girls sat in the back room listening to all the ritual moanings and comings and goings in the rest of the hut.

"I think Aunty Grizzel will be trying to get a look at the wounds," said Niav quietly. "We don't want to believe Fearn killed him any more than you do. Let's try and go through exactly how he died – as though we were in one of Aunty's lessons, shall we?"

"He complained of the bitter taste – well, Penny Royal *would* taste bitter. But then he said there was a burning in his mouth, and a numbness; that's when Mother wrapped him in a blanket – she thought it was the loss of blood, but it got worse, it was spreading all over. He said he couldn't see. Then he started to have terrible stomach pain and he vomited everywhere."

"That would be when Kyle came in."

"Yes, and Mother started screaming about the blade having been in the herb basket. She thought that Fearn must have spotted it while his bee stings were being seen to. I could see Estra was furious – she looked at me as though she would like me to turn to ash. She must have realized that it was probably me that gave Fearn the blade."

"But that doesn't sound like Penny Royal poisoning. We both know what that sounds like – both Aunties have described it often enough – Wolfsbane! Oh Canya!" cried Niav leaping up to hold her. "You must be terrified. It must have been in the drink Estra mixed for *you!*"

"That, or on the blade – could it have come into contact with it in the herb basket? Maybe it even got into the Penny Royal somehow when I let the basket crash down like that, but I did check everything very carefully. I have been sitting here trying to sort things out in my head."

"We will have to get you out of here, whatever happened. Is there anything small you feel you have to take away with you? Be quick – they mustn't suspect you of anything odd."

"Just my beads and my best shawl."

"I think they'd wonder about that shawl – it's so big. Promise we will give you another three times as nice."

While Canya went to the back of the room to rescue what items of jewellery she couldn't live without and secreted them away, Niav took a judicious glance into the contents of the herb basket. All Aunty Helygen's careful little herb jars were correctly sealed – whoever had doctored the Penny Royal with Wolfsbane must have done it deliberately.

Niav delved gently down to the matting at the basket's base and pulled the rest of the matting up from what was left of its stitching. No root of Wolfsbane snuggling anywhere. But there were two smallish things, neatly wrapped in fine white leather. She unfurled them to reveal some water-stained bits of wood, not unlike large stoppers from a jar. One of them had a bit of string threaded through a piercing near the top.

She held them in her hand for a minute, puzzling over exactly what they might be. Then her heart almost stopped at the realization.

"Ready!" whispered Canya, and Niav frantically pushed the two bits of wood into her scrip.

"I am escorting you out to the midden because I'm a bit worried about you and we will insist that Aunty Grizzel comes too."

Their obvious urgency convinced Aunty Grizzel that she had to do what they asked. Once outside the hut, Niav took one glance at the sky and she was even surer that what she was doing was right.

They dashed down the hillside to the river, launched the coracle and paddled desperately for the western shore. The sky opened over them as they headed up the bank. Glancing back through the downpour, they could see no sign that anyone from the other bank was looking for them yet.

***

"Would you like to explain?" asked Aunty Grizzel politely as she stoked up the fire and the rain thundered down out in the compound. "Shall we make a nice cup of tea whist we are drying?"

"Not mint tea for Canya, I'm afraid," said Niav. "Any kind but that!"

"Oh poor Helygen! Let's hope she never guesses that it must have been her hand that gave Lurgan what killed him," gasped Grizzel, once the two girls had explained to her what must have happened. "You are right, those wounds that Fearn gave Lurgan should never have endangered his life – I simply could not understand it."

"How terrible if she were to realize that Estra meant to kill me – Estra is mad and we have left poor Mother with her," said Canya, starting to cry all over again.

"Yes, Fearn got it right when he said that it could ruin your life if you came in the way of anything that Estra felt she was entitled to," Niav said. "I wish I knew if he was talking about his life or yours. He didn't know that you were pregnant no one knew what had happened between you. He may have felt that it was safest for you if he removed himself from endangering your life before things got really serious.

"But I'm sorry – when it comes to Aunty Helygen, I don't think it's quite as simple as that." Niav delved into her scrip and produced the two mysterious bits of wood. "You might recognize one of these at least," she said, holding them out to Aunty Grizzel.

When she saw the piece with the leather cord through it, she started to shake. "I bored that hole and threaded it through," she whispered.

"What is it?" said Canya, mystified.

"I think you will find they are the bungs from boats. The one Aunty Grizzel is looking at is the bung from the boat that my parents made with Artin."

"I remember now, Lurgan and Helygen putting the apple basket and the rug over where the bung-hole would have been," said Grizzel. "Maybe the rug was shoved so firmly into the hole that it took a while for the water to start coming through – they were quite far out. There was I assuming that she dwelt somewhere in the past, but what your poor Mother was trying to say to me made solid sense . . . I wonder if Artin realized that all along? He would take a huge delight in their fear that he might have known. I wonder if it was just Helygen that time or if it was both of them and that's why Lurgan changed his tune? So your father Diarma and Artin were not fighting – they were struggling to try to block the hole. Maybe my poor brother never realized he had been betrayed – I do hope so."

Now it was Canya's turn to shudder. "And the other bung? Whose boat was that from?"

"Why, that would be the bung from the dug-out boat that Estra's mother thought so highly of. I can't honestly say that I don't understand Aunty Helygen's feelings there. But how is she going to feel about Estra now that your dad is gone? He was her reason for doing everything. Helygen's a brilliant herbalist. If we have been able to work out that the drink that Estra mixed for you was something stronger than Penny Royal, once she is over the shock, Aunty is bound to realize it too. She knows the symptoms of Wolfsbane better than we do. Estra tried to kill you – the last thing your mother intended, I'm sure. Then the potion killed your dad, and it was poor Helygen who handed it to him. If she is the sort of person who likes to keep reminders of previous times – when perhaps, she meted out 'justice' as she saw it – I wouldn't want to be in Estra's shoes for anything!"

"And what about Kyle and Fearn?"

"Well," said Aunty Grizzel. "If they haven't killed each other yet – and before they do – I think we should try to reach them. I think you need to find them, don't you. How good a tracker is Kyle, would you say, in all honesty?"

"Not amazing, but how will that help us?" said Canya.

"Oh, Kyle has no idea where Fearn is heading, but I think Niav knows where he will have gone, don't you Niav?"

"He said he would head into the setting sun."

"Well then, first light tomorrow, you both head West and let's hope that you reach them in time."

"But what about you?"

"What about me? What have I got to lose?" Aunty Grizzel smiled. "At least this time I won't get left holding the baby."

Author's Note

Artin and his brothers are metal smiths. In the early Bronze Age, metal smiths were itinerant – as in the Greek story of Icarus (a Bronze Age legend), who tried to escape the Labyrinth and flew too near the sun. Metal-working was new and considered to be magical, and it was much in demand. Smiths with magical powers appear in many legends.

One such legend is that of Wayland, a metal smith who is traditionally held to have had his smithy in the megalithic chamber-tomb on the Ridgeway, not far from the Uffington White Horse in Oxfordshire (formerly Berkshire).

The metal smiths seem to have been family groups, travelling by sea rather than overland, as bronze is so heavy. To make bronze you need copper, and the most important copper mines were at the Great Orm ('worm') in North Wales. However, known metal smiths, whose graves have been found (like the Amesbury Archer), seem to come from abroad (as identified by their tooth enamel) and from as far away as Switzerland! At about the same time, bee-keeping seems to have started – and, as metal working in bronze and gold uses the lost wax method, there is thought to be a connection between the two activities (as, again, there is in the story of Icarus and Daedalus).

The story is set on the coast of north-east Britain, where Whitby now stands. The Sacred Howe and the headland mentioned at the start of the story would long since have fallen into the sea, but there are good reasons to suggest that it was near where St Hilda's monastery at Whitby also once stood – sacred sites tend to stay sacred sites, and there is a surviving late Neolithic Howe slightly further along the coast towards Hartlepool. Aunt Grizzel's hut would have been where Pannet Park is now located, under the Whitby museum and art gallery. In that excellent museum they have a very early bronze sword – or dagger – of the right sort of date, found out on the moors, that would have originated in Cyprus, but no one has any explanation of how it got to Whitby. The museum also has a facsimile of the sandstone picture panel that I refer to.

A Fiery Death

Ian Morson

Ian Morson became well known as the author of a series of novels featuring William Falconer, a Regent Master at Oxford University in the thirteenth century. The series began with Falconer's Crusade *(1994) and has currently reached eight books. Morson is also one of the group of writers known as the Medieval Murderers, who not only give talks on medieval mysteries but have collaborated on several books, such as* The Tainted Relic *(2005) and* King Arthur's Bones *(2009). Recently, with* City of the Dead *(2009), Morson began a new series featuring Venetian "wheeler-dealer" Niccolo Zuliani who, having to leave Venice, serves as bodyguard to Friar Alberoni and finds himself at the court of the Mongol emperor Kublai Khan. The following story, however, takes place much later in Zuliani's life, when he has eventually returned to Venice, but doesn't find the peace and quiet he might have hoped for.*

The conspirators slipped out of the house one by one. The moon was up, and it cast a silvery light across the canals of Venice. But the men leaving the house exited by the rear entrance, giving out on to a narrow alley between the house and the Church of San Giuliano. They dispersed silently into the night like fleeting shadows, some south towards the great Piazza San Marco, and some north towards the Rialto Bridge. The old man left behind in the big, damp house pulled his fur-trimmed cloak around him, and toiled up the stone staircase to the attic rooms at the top of the building. Here, he was furthest from the damp that crept inexorably up the walls of the old house from the basement, so the attic rooms were relatively dry. But it still felt cold, and the old man shivered, longing for the flames of a fire, and some heat. His bones ached terribly, and he longed for the warm sun of the East. Once, almost in another life, he had travelled to the ends of the Earth. But now his world was reduced to a few cold rooms in a crumbling palazzo squeezed between a church and a canal that bore the same names. In the Venetian dialect, they were both called San Zulian.

The old man had been born in the house, and had played in these very attic rooms as a child with his English mother. He sighed as he remembered her features – the dark hair hanging glossily around her pale face, and her blue-green eyes that he had inherited. His eyes were a little cloudier now, and his once red hair was less glossy. He tugged at his salt-and-pepper beard, wishing he could pull out the grey hairs and leave the burnished gold. He was approaching seventy. Disconsolately, he reached out for the Tartar bow that he had been fiddling with before the Tiepolo and Querini family members had arrived for their council of war. He had been trying to tension it, using the elastic properties of the horn and sinew strips fixed either side of the wooden core. But it had not been strung for more than thirty years, and he had been afraid the horn would crack if he tested it too far. He now dropped the bow on the floor, and pulled an arrow from the quiver at his side. It was a three-foot long arrow with a tip that had been plunged in salt water when red-hot, to render it armour-piercing. He twirled it in his fingers, and thought of the words that had been exchanged in the great hall below.

Francesco Tiepolo had lost his temper first.

"God damn Piero Gradenigo. He has got us all into this mess."

Giovanni Querini had patted his arm to cool him off.

"Francesco, have patience. We will rid ourselves of this nuisance of a Doge, and consign him to Hell soon enough."

The old man stroked his beard, and offered a wry comment from where he sat in the shadows.

"I think you will find the Pope has already ensured Doge Gradenigo will go there. Hasn't he pronounced an excommunication and interdict on the whole of Venice?"

Francesco Tiepolo had been called on to lead the conspiracy against the Doge. But he was a poor stand-in for the main man, his cousin Bajamonte, who had not yet arrived from exile on the mainland. Francesco had a loud mouth and a fiery temper all the same.

"Shut up, Zuliani. This is a serious matter, and not a time for jests."

Niccolo Zuliani, the old man in question, leaned back in his chair, and held his hands up in mock submission. The truth of the matter was that he agreed with Ticpolo. The papal interdict was very serious for trade. It had been invoked because Venice had tried to take control of Ferrara when Marquis Azzo had died two years earlier in 1308. The Pope was determined to prevent the takeover, and had declared all Venetian goods and possessions confiscate, all commercial treaties annulled, and all trade and traffic suspended. Anyone could grab Venetian goods and ships with impunity, and the Serene Republic's enemies had done so with relish. Venice and its commercial lifelines were being stifled, and Zuliani stood to lose as much anyone. But, in his opinion, if you couldn't see the funny side of a desperate situation, you might as well slit your own throat.

Still Ticpolo had ranted on, with Querini and one or two of the other once-rich merchants trying to pour oil on the waters to no effect. In disarray, they had all slipped away like ghosts, fearful of discovery. The heavy hand of the Signori di Notte – a bunch of nobles and their henchmen who ensured the safety of Venice's six districts, but who chiefly worked for the benefit of the older-established families – were a sinister mob and to be avoided

The old man dropped the arrow on the floor, and looked around him at the accumulation of years spent thousands of miles away from his family home. Hanging on a frame was a full suit of armour made of boiled leather. Its looming presence in the dark corner of the room struck fear into any visitor who had not seen it before, lurking like some monster on the edge of their vision. To the old man it was a comfortable friend, ageing along with him. He only hoped he would not get as mouldy as the leather was now. A large black stone lay on the rickety table. Sharp and angular, the old man had seen others like it being set fire to and burning with a fierce flame. He could not remember which part of Cathay he had got it from, and had always refrained from setting light to it himself. It was too precious a memento to him. However, now that the cold struck through him so, he was mightily tempted. Next to the rock on the table lay a large bound book. He had thumbed its pages regularly over the years, checking it against his view of the heavens. The Chinese almanack had always told the truth about the sky, and he marvelled at the magical, predictive skills of the sages who had written it. Thinking of the far distant place where he had acquired the tome, he rose from his chair, and hobbled over to the window.

He stared for an age at the dark, starry sky, wondering why he had embroiled himself in the plot to overthrow the Doge. He knew the conspiracy would fail, and that he would have to extricate himself somehow, even if, by doing so, he blew the whole plot. But as yet he didn't know how. He sighed, and cast his gaze down to the canal. On the opposite bank he saw a figure standing boldly in the starlight staring back at him. It was the same slender youth whom he had seen the previous night and the night before. In fact, he had had the feeling the youth had been following him for days. He wondered if his part in the conspiracy was already known, and this youth was stalking him on behalf of the Signori di Notte. If so, his goose was cooked. Irritated, and not a little frightened, he called down to the figure on the canal-side.

"You, boy. Who are you? What are you up to?'

For a fleeting moment, the youth ignored his challenge. And then, only after he had shown he did not care whether Zuliani saw him or not, he pulled his cloak around him and slipped away into the darkness.

★

Zuliani spent a restless night, listening to the wind blowing a storm across the lagoon. He could hear the sea fret crashing against the quays along the edges of the man-made island that was Venice. He even fancied he could hear the creaking of the thousands of wooden posts that had been hammered into the mud banks to create the land on which his and hundreds of other houses stood. It was the very nature of the crazy enterprise that was Venice – a city built on pilings in mud flats in the middle of nowhere – that stirred his and other Venetians' blood to madcap projects. But sometimes its precarious nature was driven home by foul weather. The chill air of an easterly wind blew through his sleeping chamber, and he could feel the salty spray on its gusts. He huddled beneath the warming lion skin that he had purchased in Kuiju. He had never seen the animal alive, but had grown fond of the skin and its gaping jaws. The head now lay somewhere round his feet, and the tail tickled his icy cheeks until he pushed it away.

The stormy weather would at least have driven the boy who stalked him back to his own home. Zuliani resolved to slip out early in the morning and take action to sever his connection with the plot to bring down the Doge. Why he had aligned himself with the Tiepolos and Querinis he was not sure. They were part of the *case vecchie* – the Venetian aristocracy, who had always done the likes of the lower class Zulianis down. On the other hand, their enemy, Gradenigo, had over the last few years effectively closed the doors of the Great Council to those whose fathers and other paternal ancestors had not been members in the past. It was a closed society that ran Venice, and Zuliani, the last of his family, stood outside it. So he had been flattered a few days earlier when Francesco Tiepolo, one of the old school, had called on him, ostensibly to view Zuliani's collection of Eastern treasures. He had taken the overweight, red-faced Tiepolo up to his attic rooms, and brought out part of his collection. Tiepolo had at once picked up a heavy golden bar with swirling patterns on it, hefting it in his hand.

"What is this worth, Zuliani? It must weigh three hundred saggi at least."

Niccolo smiled politely, seeing that the man only saw the surface value of the item he held.

"To those who possessed it, it was priceless. It was not just a bar of gold, it was a permit that gave the owner access to all corners of the Great Khan's empire – and power over anyone in that empire. It is called a *paizah*, and the inscription reads 'By the might of the Great God and the great grace he has given to our Emperor, blessed be the name of the Khan, and death and destruction to all who do not obey him.' "

Zuliani ran his fingers fondly over the curly writing.

"There were ones wrought in base-metal or silver, but the gold paizah carried the highest authority. It was given to me by Kubilai Khan himself."

Tiepolo grunted, unimpressed by the old man's story. He could only see the value of the gold. A Venetian saggio was about one sixth of an ounce, and that made the bar at least fifty ounces of gold. He laid the bar down reluctantly and peered at a pile of fancy clothes. Pushing aside a plain grey cloak of coarse material that lay atop the Chinese garb, his eyes once more lighted on the golden embroidery that covered the robes underneath.

"Who would wear those? The emperor?"

"Oh not these. They are the court dress of his Chinese subjects, and would be considered quite ordinary. That cloak is more interesting."

Tiepolo listened politely as the old man explained the history of the cloak, though he hardly absorbed what he was being told. And then he even let Zuliani drone on about his collection a little more before broaching the subject of the conspiracy to overthrow the Doge. This was the subject he had really come here to discuss, because he knew that, if he could lure men like Zuliani into the plot, he could bring the ordinary *cittadini* – citizens, to his side. When he left, he fancied he had been completely successful, later even flattering Zuliani by holding one of his meetings in the man's home.

Now Zuliani was left tossing in his bed thinking of a way of escaping the coils of the conspiracy. Restlessly, he rose from under the lion skin, and dragged his heavy fur-trimmed robe around him. The only thing to do was to go to the Doge and make it look as though he had only joined the plot in the first place to act as Gradenigo's spy. Even so, such a betrayal stuck in his craw. Not that he had any worries about offending some sense of honour. God knows, he had served his own ends often enough in the past. No, he merely worried that Gradenigo and his cronies might only see him as untrustworthy in the future, and not give him the preferred status his betrayal should provide. He struck his brow with the flat of his hand, angered by his own indecision.

"Come on, Nick, boy, you would have not hesitated like this twenty years ago. Get it done, and worry about the consequences later."

He quickly dressed, and descended the winding staircase down to his street door. He avoided the water door because he didn't want his servant and boatman Vettor knowing of his purpose. Outside, the wind still howled, as he pulled his cloak close around him and hurried down the Calle Specchieri. At the far end of the narrow alley, he should have carried straight on but something told him to turn left. The Doge's palace was straight ahead, but he again had the feeling he was being followed. It would be better if it was not known where he was bound. Walking swiftly on, he turned left again and crossed the bottom end of the Rio di San Zulian. He knew this maze like the back of his hand, and darted under the porch of a house almost opposite his own, but on the other side of the canal. Soon, a slight figure dashed past his hiding place, and he made a grab at the youth who had been dogging him for days. He shouted out in triumph.

"Got you, you little bastard."

The boy tried to wriggle out of his grasp almost breaking away, but Zuliani was having none of it. He swung his arm around the lad's chest, grabbing at his tunic. He was shocked to feel a soft bosom under his hand, and almost let his stalker go. But he had the presence of mind to hold on to an arm as the figure whirled round and slapped his face. Zuliani laughed out loud, as he looked into the soft face not of a youth but a pretty girl. She was furious at being manhandled.

"Keep your hands off my tits, you old lecher."

"By all means, mistress. But I wonder if a grope is not what you wanted all along. After all, you have been following my every move so slavishly."

The girl blushed, and pulled her cloak around her, hiding the immodesty of her boyish garb.

"Let me explain."

*

"You wanted to know about what it was like to live in the East?"

He was seated opposite the girl in his attic room, and, though she had kept her cloak drawn around her, she had removed the sugarloaf hat she wore. Her hair had tumbled down, and Zuliani could now see it was blonde but with traces of red that turned it into gold. Her face had the roundness of a young girl – she could be no more than fifteen but her angular cheek bones and aquiline nose told of a beauty emerging from a chrysalis. He found her looks disconcertingly familiar, but he put that down to his knowing her family well. She had given her name as Katie Valier, and Zuliani recalled an old adversary of his from that family. Pasquale Valier had been a rat-faced little squirt though, and now long dead. This pretty girl could not be one of his brood. He realized he was drifting, and tried to concentrate his wandering thoughts.

"If you wanted to know about the East, why didn't you just come and talk to me. God knows, I have a tale or two to tell."

In fact, when he had returned to Venice after a long time serving Kubilai and his sons, people were disinclined to believe his stories. Some had laughed at him behind his back, accusing him of weaving fanciful travellers' tales. But he knew they all were the God's honest truth. By and large.

The girl shrugged at his question, and pouted.

"You are so great a man, and I'm just a child. You wouldn't have paid me any attention."

Zuliani grinned.

"Now I know you are lying. Someone your age thinks they know everything, and is full of bombast." He peered closely at Katie.

"Are you spying on me for the Doge?"

It was the girl's turn to laugh.

"Do you really think the Doge would employ a child to check on you? Besides, you're not so important that you would worry so great a man."

Zuliani was taken aback by the girl's poise. It reminded him of someone from his distant past, at a time when he had to flee Venice under a cloud. He recovered himself quickly.

"So you are of the Gradenigo faction. The Valiers always rolled over for those in power."

The girl's face reddened at this scornful criticism of her family, but she was not thrown as much as Zuliani had hoped. She merely returned his gaze, and tossed a question back at him.

"Where were you going this morning? To the Doge's palace to split on the Tiepolos?"

Zuliani knew he would not like to have this child as a business opponent. She was too canny for her own good. If she – a mere child – knew about his involvement in the conspiracy, who else did? She saw the wary look in his eyes, and reassured him.

"Don't worry, no one else knows. Though it was easy enough to get your servant drunk and have him tell me who had been visiting you."

Zuliani cursed Vettor under his breath, and resolved to fire the man. Or slit his throat. He felt as if he was trapped in a vice, neither knowing if he should betray the plot or ride it out and pray no one would link him to it. The girl smiled at his discomfiture.

"I can help you, if you like. You don't want the Doge to know you were even linked with the Tiepolos' plot, do you? So you can't tell him about it without implicating yourself."

Zuliani shook his head in bewilderment. Was this a girl or a demon?

"What do you suggest I do, Katie Valier?"

The girl settled back in her chair, letting her cloak fall open. It revealed the short, boyish tunic she had worn to fool Zuliani in the first place. A little ashamed of himself, he admired the long legs that were encased in tight leggings. She was enjoying her triumph, and didn't notice his lascivious look.

"I have a cousin – Marco Donato – who is close to the Gradenigos. He can warn the Doge, and even put in a good word for you as his source of information."

"That sounds like an excellent idea, mistress. But why would you do this for me? What is your reward?"

The girl sighed with pleasure.

"In return, you can tell me all about your sexual exploits at the court of Kubilai Khan."

*

It was Monday the 15th of June, the Feast of St Vitus, and the conspiracy was in motion. Two groups, led by Bajamonte Tiepolo and Marco Querini, made their move at first light, crossing the Rialto Bridge and advancing towards the Piazza and the Doge's Palace. They were supposed to have been supported by a third group led by Badoero Badoer from the mainland. Unfortunately, on the night before, there had been a violent summer storm, which whipped up the waters of the lagoon. Badoer and his party were unable to cross to the city. Not knowing this, and unaware that the Doge had been informed of their intentions by a certain Marco Donato, the others galloped through the narrow streets in driving rain to shouts of "Liberta, e Morte al Doge Gradenigo".

Bajamonte Tiepolo might have pulled it off, but his arrival in the Piazza had been delayed slightly. Zuliani had received a message from Marco Donato by the agency of his new friend

Katie, who was at his door at some unearthly hour of the morning. She had merely said that the Doge wanted Tiepolo held up – minutes would suffice. A reluctant Zuliani had pulled his heavy, fur-trimmed cloak around him and braved the rain. He suspected the ruse was a way of the Doge showing the conspirators that Zuliani was a turncoat. He didn't like it, but the die was cast. He hovered by the great elder tree outside the front of San Zulian Church until Tiepolo and his men approached. He held up his hand, and the impatient Bajamonte reined in his steed.

"Zuliani, what now? Not having second thoughts, I hope."

Zuliani grimaced.

"Indeed no, Tiepolo. I just wanted to wish you success."

Impatiently, the leader of the conspiracy pulled on the reins of his dancing horse, eager to be off. What was this old fool playing at?

"Thank you. Liberty, citizen."

"Liberty, Tiepolo." Zuliani now had his own hand on the horse's reins, preventing Tiepolo from proceeding. "This is a necessary deed . . . isn't it?"

Tiepolo let out a cry of rage at the old man's prevarication. Thank God they had not involved the dodderer any more deeply into the conspiracy. Age had robbed him of his former clear thinking, and he could not come down from off the fence. He wrenched his reins free, and rode off. Zuliani's eyes lost their vacant stare, put on for the dumb show, and he grinned at Tiepolo's disappearing back. His task was done.

Even as Bajamonte imperiously threatened the Piazza, the local populace failed to rise in support. Instead they hurled insults and imprecations. One old lady even resorted to tipping a heavy piece of stone parapet out of an upper window. It missed Tiepolo, but struck down his standard-bearer. The banner, emblazoned with the word Libertas, lay in the mud. The insurrection was over almost as soon as it began, and the conspirators scattered throughout Venice.

★

The *Avogadori* – the representatives of the justice system of La Serenissima – had a field day following on from the disaster that was the Tiepolo/Querini uprising. Or, more properly, a number of field days. Over the next week, many of the Querinis were summarily murdered, whereas the lucky Bajamonte negotiated his banishment from Venice. Francesco Tiepolo and his closest lieutenant, however, disappeared entirely, even though all the Querini and Tiepolo family houses were ransacked in the search for the two men. Doge Gradenigo became increasingly irritated by the fact that one of the primary conspirators had escaped his net. The following week, the search spread wider, and the Signori di Notte examined every nook and cranny in every *calle*, and every refuge on every rio. No alley, canal, bridge or cellar was left out of the trawl for the great traitor. Slowly it was moving towards San Zulian, but Nick was unperturbed by all this disturbance. He had had the daily pleasure of the company of Katie Valier well away from Venice.

On the day of the insurrection, she had delivered her message and he had acted on it. Then he had convinced her that it was prudent not to be on the streets for a while. He had shown her his collection of artefacts from the Mongol Empire of Kubilai Khan – the Greatest Khan of them all.

She had politely sat through his well-rehearsed speech, and his tales of derring-do, then suggested they leave Venice and all the disturbance. They crossed the lagoon to Torcello, and hid away for a few days. There, Katie had got him talking again, only on a different tack.

"They say the girls at Kubilai's court were the prettiest in the world."

Zuliani had laughed, and touched Katie's rosy cheek.

"But not as pretty as you."

Which was true. Abandoning her boyish garb with which she had stalked Zuliani, Katie now had emerged as a true beauty. Her golden hair was set off perfectly by her blue gown that clung to her shapely thighs and bosom. Zuliani recalled clutching her breast when he had thought her a boy. He could almost feel the firmness of it still. He had avoided talking of the women he had known in the East on that first occasion. But on the next day, and the one after that, Katie had skilfully turned the conversation round to the same topic.

Finally Zuliani reckoned it was safe to return. The day was sunny, and they had stopped outside the dark and damp confines of Zuliani's house under the great elder tree next to the church.

It was the scene of Zuliani's Judas kiss with Bajamonte Tiepolo, but, just now, he didn't care about that betrayal. He had a pretty girl by his side. He knew Katie was young enough to be his granddaughter – or even his great-granddaughter – but he liked the feel of her warm thigh against his own. The sun shone on his face, and he gave in to her persistent demands for salacious gossip about his conquests in the East. He closed his eyes, leaned back against the smooth trunk of the tree, and smiled.

"There was one girl, actually. Well, there was more than one, but this one was special. Gurbesu had long, black hair, a dark complexion, and curves in all the right places." He sketched the shape of her body in the air with both hands. "She had brains to go with her body too, and helped me with my duties as Kubilai's chief crime investigator."

Katie laughed out loud. It was like the tinkling of a small bell.

"You were an *avogador*?"

"Yes. What's so funny about that?"

"My grandmother said you were the biggest rogue in Venice."

"Well, your granny was wrong." He paused for effect. "The biggest rogue in Venice is the Doge. But I ran him second best."

They laughed together, their treble and bass blending like a peal of bells in a tower.

"Anyway, you know what they say. Set a thief to catch a thief."

Katie leaned against his shoulder, her long tresses draping over his arm.

"About this Gurbesu. Did you love her?"

Zuliani waved his hand dismissively.

"Love? What's that? She was beautiful, mind you. All Kungurat girls are – the Khan gets a hundred of them every year for his harem. Virgins all. That's why Gurbesu had to be smuggled away. You see, before she got to the Khan, she had lain with me. But as for loving her . . ." He shook his head. "There's only one woman I loved."

"Really? Who was that?"

Zuliani stared off into the distance, and pictured the woman he had been forced to abandon almost forty years earlier. His crooked deals and an untimely death had caused him to leave Venice abruptly. Leaving behind the incomparable Cat, love of his life. Her true name was Caterina Dolfin – she of the peach complexion and pale blonde hair – but he called her his Cat. Her slender but muscular body moved like a cat too when they made love. There were tales of her giving birth to a child while he had been in the East. But her family had spirited her away to the mainland and, when he had returned many years later, he had been unable to trace her. He sighed.

Katie prodded his ribs with a slender finger.

"Who was she, this love of your life?"

Zuliani was looking at her eager, young face, and about to tell all, when he heard a piercing cry. He looked up and saw his neighbour, old Justinia, waddling across the square. He had never seen her move so fast. She was waving her hands and screaming. And he could hardly believe what she was saying.

"Signor Niccolo, your house is on fire."

Stunned, Zuliani remained seated under the elder tree, until Katie took a firm hold of his hand and hauled him to his feet. Together, they ran down the west side of the church, and towards his house. They could both hear the crackle of the flames before they could even see the house. Reaching the canal, they looked up. Flames were shooting out of all the lower windows, the shutters merely shards of burnt timber already. Zuliani gasped.

"I don't believe it. The place is so damp. How could it have gone up like this?"

Katie just gazed in horror at the sight.

"Nick. All your precious things from the East."

Zuliani knew what she meant. It was a lifetime – his lifetime – going up in smoke. Even as they watched, the flames found their way up to the next floor, only one below his attic rooms. And all his memories. Tongues of fire burst from the shuttered windows, and smoke billowed out across the canal. Suddenly, Katie pointed upwards.

"Look!"

Zuliani followed where she was pointing, and saw a face at an upper window. Someone was inside – but who? Zuliani had left the house bolted and barred. Vettor, his servant, had been sent off to visit his family at Malamocco. Surely he could not have returned yet? If he had, he was in dire trouble now. The figure at the window leaned out, waving his arms. Zuliani's eyesight wasn't so good, but Katie recognized him.

"It's Francesco Tiepolo."

"Tiepolo? What's he doing in my house?"

Even as Zuliani spoke, the terrible cries of the traitorous conspirator carried over the roar of the flames.

"For pity's sake, help me. I am roasting to death."

Zuliani called up to him.

"Is there anyone else trapped with you?"

For a moment, Tiepolo seemed to look fearfully back into the room, and Zuliani thought there was someone. But Tiepolo must have just been looking at the encroaching flames. He now turned back to the horrified onlookers, terror in his eyes.

"No one. Please, help me. The stairs are on fire."

Zuliani thought of the beautifully carved oak handrail he had slid down as a boy, only to be faced with wrath of his father, Agostino, at the bottom. He had slid off before encountering the iron escutcheon on the newel post, cast in the shape of a lizard. That would have been painful. But his father's beating had been just as painful. Now the staircase was in the middle of a raging fire. Zuliani felt infinitely sad, but called up to Tiepolo all the same.

"I will try and open the door. Can you reach it?"

"I will try."

By now, two or three enterprising neighbours had arrived with wooden buckets, and were ferrying water from the canal to the site of the fire. Zuliani could see their efforts were useless. Each bucketful turned into steam even as it was thrown in the ground floor windows. Somehow, the fire must have taken a strong hold in the accumulated junk he had stored on the lower floors of Ca' Zuliani. His childhood home was burning down before his eyes. Zuliani edged closer to the doorway, holding his cloak up as a shield against the heat. He leaned against the iron-bound door. The wood was hot and the metal straps even hotter. It was no use. The lower floors were already an inferno.

As he scuttled back from the heat and flames, a horrible scream pierced his heart. He looked up to Tiepolo, and saw the man's face disappear from the upper window. It was replaced with a sheet of flame. Francesco Tiepolo was gone.

★

The representative of the Avogadori de Comun was a fat, ponderous man who lifted his long, fur-trimmed robe to keep it clear of the blackened, water-damaged debris in the shell that once had been Nick Zuliani's home. His name was Matteo Mocco, and he would have preferred to have avoided entering the house. Especially as he could still feel the heat of the fire through the soles of his fine leather shoes. But it was necessary for him to see in situ the charred lump of flesh that was all that remained of Francesco Tiepolo, traitor to the Serene Republic. Zuliani had found it on the second floor, one level below the top rooms where Tiepolo had last been seen alive. It had been a while before he could get back into his home, and he had cautiously tested the stairs and each floor level before venturing into the recesses of each room to find out what had happened to Tiepolo. On the top floor, he had found that most of his collection had been destroyed. The lion skin was merely a burnt jawbone, and the wonderful almanac a pile of papery ash. Even his old companion, the suit of armour, was unrecognizable. He had hung his head, and descended to the next floor down. There, he had found the body.

Now Mocco was poking the husk cautiously with the toe of his shoe. It stirred in a way that suggested it was as light as the ashen remains of a burnt log. The avogador shuddered and wiped the black smear on the tip of his shoe on the back of his leggings. He snorted.

"Good riddance."

"What am I to do with the body?"

Mocco shrugged at Zuliani's question.

"If it was me, I would throw him out with the rest of your fire-damaged rubbish. But I suppose he warrants a Christian burial. If there are any of his family left after recent events, tell them to come and collect him."

Mocco departed, leaving Zuliani staring at the blackened remains.

"Is that him? Tiepolo?"

The question had come from Katie Valier, who now stood in the doorway of the room that was Tiepolo's last resting place for the time being. As ever, she did not take much care of her fine clothes. Zuliani could see a layer of soot and ash on the dress's hem. There were dark marks on the front of her gown too. She must have got soot on her hands, and had wiped them clean on the sumptuous material. Zuliani wondered if her grandmother, of whom Katie spoke a great deal and with adoration, would approve of her granddaughter's careless attitude. Even as he looked at her, he saw her move her hand from the door frame, where it had come to rest, down to the side of her dress. Another black smear ensued. Endearingly she also had a sooty mark across her brow.

"You should not be up here. It is not safe."

He strode over to her and, whilst still reprimanding her, wiped the smear from her face with his thumb. She laughed.

"Nonsense. If the floor can stand the weight of Matteo Mocco, it can bear three of me."

"Yes, but there are not three of you, Katie Valier. There is only one, and I am sure your mother holds you to be precious."

The girl pulled a face.

"My mother and father are dead. Of the plague."

Zuliani apologized for his blunder.

"I am sorry for that. Then it is that blessed grandmother of yours of whom you should think." Hearing a creak, he cast a fearful glance up at the ceiling. "Let's get downstairs before this all falls in on us."

Despite his best efforts, Katie still managed to get a good look at Tiepolo's body before Zuliani could grab her arm and steer her down the ruined staircase. They stayed close to the wall as the wooden handrail had almost gone, but, at the bottom, the newel post and metal strap still remained. Katie pointed at the lizard shape that adorned the metal, and smiled.

"Look. It must be a salamander to have survived the fire. They do say that the creature can put out fires with milk from its skin."

Zuliani gave her a sceptical look.

"Then this one failed miserably, didn't it. Besides, it's all a legend, and . . . oh, never mind."

Zuliani was thinking again of all he had lost in the fire, and he couldn't bear to contemplate it. Better to forget than get morbid. Besides, he needed to find somewhere to stay. As of now, he was homeless. The same thought must have occurred to Katie.

"I think it is time you met my grandmother. We have a spare room, and you could stay until you sort out your own house."

Zuliani gratefully accepted the offer. To tell the truth, he didn't know what else he would have done. His last few years had been spent more or less as a hermit, inhabiting the upper reaches of his now ruined house. His few forays into trading had been with partners who were young enough to be his grandsons, and with whom he had nothing in common, other than the love of a good deal. Most of his old friends and adversaries were long dead. Loneliness was the penalty of longevity. Until Katie had appeared, he had not thought much of his situation. Now he longed for company again, and her company in particular. The idea of staying in the same house as her appealed greatly. But he was not so sure of the grandmother. Would she be some whiskery old lady who harboured suspicions about his motives in relation to Katie? As they made their way on to the Rialto Bridge, Zuliani clutched the girl's arm.

"Will your grandmother approve of this? It is quite something to foist an old, cantankerous bastard like me on a frail old lady, at a moment's notice."

Katie's tinkling laughter rang out, dispelling any doubts Zuliani had.

"I shall tell her you said that . . . frail old lady indeed." She released her arm from his grip, and sped off, lifting her skirts up to help her to run. "Come on, last one over the bridge must pay a forfeit."

He groaned.

"I am too old for this. Wait for me."

When she faltered, he laughed and sped past her. Elbowing the crowds of people that thronged the bridge out of the way, he reaching the other side of the Grand Canal first. He cheered his victory, but his heart was pounding in his chest. He leaned forwards with his hands on his knees, gasping for breath.

"Are you alright?"

Zuliani waved away Katie's anxious enquiry with his hand.

"Let me get my breath, and I will tell you. In the meantime, lead me to your house."

He was shocked to be taken to a palazzo he had once been very familiar with in another life. He stood before the heavy oaken doors and frowned. He turned to Katie, who had a broad grin on her face. He could barely speak.

"What is this? This is the old Dolfin palace. But there's none of the family left."

The girl made a moue with her lips.

"Except for me. And grandmother. Come and meet her."

It was a strange feeling for Zuliani to cross the portal he had never been able to as a young man. He had been the lover of Caterina Dolfin, but her father had disapproved of the daredevil trader whose family was not recorded in the *Libro d'Oro* – the Golden Book of ancient families of Venice. Now, he half-expected the old man to rise from his grave and peremptorily demand he leave. Instead, another voice from the past did quite the opposite.

"Welcome to Ca' Dolfin, Nick. It's about time you saw inside those doors."

Suddenly, his breath was taken away in a far more exhilarating way than when he had raced Katie. He was so disconcerted he managed only one syllable.

"Cat?"

Down the other end of the long-pillared hallway stood a woman, slender and erect. She was in semi-darkness, and for a moment Zuliani thought he had been thrown back in time. It was the Caterina Dolfin of forty years ago – slim, but curvy in all the right places, her exquisitely carved features framed by thick blonde hair that tumbled over her shoulders. He moved towards this vision, hardly believing it as real, and she stepped into the light of three candles set atop a tall stand. Then he saw that his vision was real after all. Of course it was his lover Cat, and of course she was older, just as he was. Closer to her, he saw the wrinkles round the corners of her eyes, but they were the same clear, blue eyes, full of mischief. The blonde hair had strands of silver, but was just as thick and alive. She smiled at Zuliani, and her face lit up just as it used to when he stroked her naked body.

"What do you think of Katie's old grandma, then?"

Zuliani pulled a face.

"You've aged somewhat better than I have, Caterina."

She reached out a hand, and stroked his weather-beaten, wrinkled face.

"Ah yes, but I like older men."

Before either of them could say another word, Katie broke into their colloquy.

"Granny Cat, can Nick stay here? Only, his house has burned down."

A look of alarm crossed Caterina's aquiline features.

"Burnt down? My God, how did that happen?" She squeezed Zuliani's arm. "You weren't inside, were you?"

Zuliani waved her concerns aside, still unable to tear his gaze from her face.

"No, no. I am fine."

Katie couldn't contain herself, though, and had to take over the conversation.

"But Francesco Tiepolo isn't. He burned to a crisp. I saw him."

Cat turned a stern gaze on Zuliani.

"When I asked my granddaughter to talk to you, I didn't expect you to show her dead bodies. God, you haven't changed, have you?"

She turned her back on him and took a few steps away into the semi-darkness. Katie was about to speak, but Zuliani quieted her with a raised finger. He walked over to Cat and, from behind her, whispered in her ear

"So you sent Katie to spy on me. I thought it was all her idea. Of course, I didn't know then that she was your granddaughter. I was flattered enough to imagine that anyone of her generation had even heard of Niccolo Zuliani. All my celebrity is in the past, after all." Then he recalled the fire. "And what was left of it has just gone up in smoke."

Cat's face, when she looked at him again, showed her deep feelings. She looked distraught.

"I am so sorry about that. But surely there are friends who can help you? You were always such a . . ."

"Schemer? I was, but that is the problem. People you get to know only want you for your expertise, or else you con them out of money and don't want to cross their paths again." He squinted at Cat as another thought crossed his mind. "Was it your idea that Katie asked about my love-life?"

Cat Dolfin had the good grace to blush at this stage and look away from Zuliani. He laughed uproariously.

"It was, wasn't it?"

She stamped her foot, and bunched her hands into fists.

"Don't you laugh at me. It was you who dumped me forty years ago when I was carrying your child."

That stopped Zuliani in his tracks.

"My child? So Gurbesu was right all along."

Cat wagged a finger at him.

"Gurbesu, eh? That was your Eastern . . . trollop, I suppose."

Zuliani gave her a wry smile.

"One of many, actually. But none so . . . exotic as Gurbesu." He leaned forward, and whispered in her ear again. "She reminded me of you."

Cat pushed him away, but she couldn't wipe a smile off her lips. This old man with grey hair shot through his red locks was as roguish as he had been all those years ago. She couldn't help loving him all over again.

"You couldn't keep your hands off me, could you?"

"Not then, not now."

He grasped her round the waist, and felt his manhood hardening. That hadn't happened in a long time. He realized Cat was gazing over his shoulder and coughing. He turned his head to see what had distracted her. Katie stood in the centre of the hallway, a big grin pasted on her face. He had completely forgotten about her. Gently the two lovers pulled themselves apart, and Zuliani apologized.

"Not in front of your grandchild, I suppose."

Cat shook her head in dismay.

"Has it not entered your thick skull yet? I just said I was pregnant when you left forty years ago."

Zuliani frowned.

"Yes. I am sure you and your family did well for the child. But it's too late for me to play the father now."

Cat grimaced.

"It is. Agostino died five years ago of the plague."

Zuliani was touched that she had chosen his father's name for the child he never knew. But that was the point. He had never known the boy – or even the man. So how could he mourn? He reiterated his point about not being a father. Cat prodded his stomach.

"Yes, but not too late to be a grandfather, you ninny."

Zuliani gaped at Katie, who stepped up to him and hugged her new granddad.

★

After the three members of the newly united family had eaten their fill, they sat back with some of that famous Dolfin wine that Zuliani had long envied. Over protests from Katie, Zuliani had insisted on watering the girl's wine judiciously. He was taking his role as grandfather seriously. He was also revelling in the sight of his long-ago lover, who sat curled up in an armchair in a way that brought to mind the creature he had named her after. Cat may be a grandmother, but her body was still as lithe as any feline. He wondered if she might let him bed her later. But there was still one question that nagged at him, and he couldn't resist asking it of Cat.

"Why have you hidden away from me for so long? And why did you have Katie hunt me out now?"

Cat eased back in the chair, considering her answer. She decided the truth was the best way forward.

"When I sat in this very house, pregnant with Agostino, and my father told me you had murdered someone and fled Venice, I was angry more than sad. I didn't entirely believe him, but I was angry at you for leaving me in his clutches. I had to endure the 'I-told-you-so's' for months. Then I was even angrier at you for forcing me to marry Pasquale Valier."

Zuliani sat bolt upright.

"I forced you to marry rat-face Valier?"

"Well, what else could I do? He accepted your child as his own and gave him a name. You weren't there to do that. You were enjoying yourself living the high life at the fabled court of Kubilai Khan."

Zuliani thought to intervene and tell her just how hard life had been for him then. But he knew better than to set her straight just now. Uninterrupted, she went on.

"Pasquale was a good husband, and father. And our life in Verona was . . . settled.'

She stared pointedly at Zuliani at this statement, challenging him to protest. He bowed his head, and took the cheap shot.

"And now? Why now?"

"Because Pasquale died last year."

"I'm sorry to hear it."

She ignored his comment, as if she had rehearsed her story for a long time, and now nothing would stop her telling it.

"And because I yearned all those years to be back in Venice, but I couldn't bear to come and see you, and not get to know you again."

Zuliani stirred with excitement in his seat, but Cat held up her hand.

"Let me finish. That is why *now*, and also because Katie told me you had got embroiled in the conspiracy to overthrow the Doge. I could not bear the thought that I was free to see you again and you were once more risking being expelled. I persuaded my great-nephew Mario to pass on the news of the conspiracy to Gradenigo. And get you off the hook."

Zuliani should have felt euphoria about his old lover caring so much for him that she had extricated him from the mad enterprise that had been the Tiepolo family's conspiracy. But a very nasty thought was burgeoning in his head. He had been aware of Matteo Mocco's look, when the avogador had inspected Francesco's body. It had been one of sour displeasure. Until this moment Zuliani had imagined it was occasioned by the nasty nature of the fire-crisped corpse. Now, he was fearful that the displeasure had been reserved for himself. Mocco had been wondering why the sought-after Tiepolo renegade had been in his house in the first place. Was he guilty of harbouring a criminal. He groaned, and Cat leaned forward, touching his arm.

"What's wrong, Nick? Did I do the wrong thing?"

Zuliani waved aside her concern, and was about to keep his worries to himself. But then, looking from the older woman to the younger and back again, it dawned on him he had a family. And what else were families for if not to share your concerns with? He took a gulp of that good Dolfin wine, and explained his quandary.

★

In order to pull Zuliani's irons out of the fire – almost literally, bearing in mind what had happened to his home – the three of them agreed to divide up their resources. Cat had suggested she would be in the best position to talk to other members of the *case vecchie* – the old aristocracy of Venice. After all, she was a Dolfin, and one of the *case vecchie* herself.

"I will see what the gossip says about Francesco, and if there are still perceived to be any links to you, Nick."

Zuliani had agreed with this strategy, only briefly wondering what their lives would have been like if they had joined forces forty years ago. With Cat's connections and his gift for underhand dealing, they would have been unstoppable. He only hoped they would be so now, or he would have to flee Venice for the second time.

"And Katie and I will revisit the scene of the crime, and see what we can dig up."

Cat started to protest, concerned about her young granddaughter seeing the no doubt ugly corpse again. But Zuliani calmed her worries.

"Have no fears, the body will have gone by now. I sent a message to the family to come and collect it. I said that, if they didn't, it would be dumped in the lagoon along with all my other burnt rubbish."

Now, he stood outside the door of his shell of a house with Katie at his side. She prodded him.

"You didn't send a message, did you? I was with you all the time from when Mocco left to when we got to granny's house. There was no time for you to send a message."

Zuliani grinned conspiratorially at his granddaughter.

"I won't tell, if you won't. Now, do you want to examine this body or not?"

Katie clapped her hands with delight.

"Yes, please."

The interior of the house looked even gloomier as the day was drawing to a close. But Zuliani had anticipated this and provided them with a lantern from the Dolfin palace. The wind was getting up, and the candle had almost blown out as they crossed the Grand Canal. Even now, inside his empty house, the yellow flame flickered, casting strange shadows on the walls. They ascended the perilous staircase in order to examine Tiepolo's body once again before the light gave out altogether. It still lay where Zuliani had left it, and he crouched down, holding the lamp close to the gruesome sight. Tiepolo was nothing more than a blackened shell, his knees drawn up to his chest. Any facial features had been destroyed by the fire. His clothes had largely burned away, though Zuliani could see a belt-buckle adhering to the remains, at the point that would have been Tiepolo's stomach. What was left of his hands were clenched like the talons of a falcon about to grasp its prey. Zuliani glanced at Katie, who was crouched at his side, holding her skirt in a bunch to keep it from the worst of the mess on the floor.

"What do you think?"

The girl grimaced.

"I think he died a bad death."

"Whoever he was."

Katie frowned at this statement from Zuliani.

"What do you mean? It's Francesco Tiepolo – we saw him at the window."

"Look at the body again. Then bring to mind what you know of Tiepolo, and what you saw when he was standing at the window waving his arms around."

Katie pouted, but did as she was told. For a while she didn't understand, then she smiled broadly.

"Move the lantern over here." She pointed at the claw-shaped hands. "Closer."

Zuliani held the lantern so that the candlelight shone where Katie had commanded. She clapped her hands again.

"There are no rings on this man's hands, and yet when I saw Tiepolo waving his arms out of the window, there were rings on many of his fingers. I saw the light sparkling on them." She liked this clever deduction, but she still had a doubt. "Might not the fire have melted the gold?"

Zuliani nodded.

"It might. But even if that were so, where are the gems? They would not have been destroyed. The other thing that worried me was when I saw the belt-buckle stuck to this man's stomach. Despite him being burned to a crisp, there is no sign of Tiepolo's fat belly. This was a slim man in life."

Having made this deduction, Zuliani had crouched over the body for too long, and tried to stand. His knees protested, and he would have stumbled if Katie had not taken his arm and steadied him. Grouchily, he thanked her, not relishing showing his infirmities to a woman, even though she was his granddaughter. Katie made as if she was unaware of his annoyance, and eagerly pursued him concerning the riddle of Tiepolo's demise. She pushed her errant locks from off her face, once again smearing soot on her brow.

"If this is not Tiepolo, then where is his body?" She glanced down at the dead man. "And who is this?"

"That's what I would like to know – where Tiepolo is, I mean. As for this body, I would say it's Girolamo Lando, Tiepolo's lieutenant. He went missing at the same time as Tiepolo."

"But then why didn't Tiepolo say Lando was trapped by the blaze too? Why didn't he call out 'Save us'?"

Zuliani pointed a finger at Katie.

"Exactly." He stepped towards the door. "Perhaps it had something to do with Lando being already dead before the fire took hold."

Katie was stunned.

"How do you know that?"

Zuliani carelessly waved the lantern at the body, almost extinguishing the guttering candle.

"Because there is a crack in the man's skull that was made by something heavy striking it, not the fire. So, either Tiepolo dragged a dead man into my house or he himself killed his lieutenant on this spot."

Katie turned back to look at the head of the corpse to see what she had missed. But Zuliani had already left the room, plunging her and the dead man into darkness. She had a momentary sense that the body was moving towards her. Maybe it was only the movement of the shadows as Zuliani left with the lantern in his hand, but she didn't want to wait and see. Shuddering, she rapidly followed her grandfather upstairs.

When she entered the upper room, she recalled those happier times when Zuliani had shown her the little treasures he had brought back from his travels. The window shutters where they had last seen Tiepolo standing were still wide open, but it was now dark outside and a wind whistled eerily through the opening. Zuliani was picking disconsolately through what remained of his collection. He groaned.

"Even the gold *paizah* has gone. Melted away in the heat, I suppose."

Katie looked around.

"And Tiepolo's body is not up here, either." She took Zuliani's hand, dragging him away from the horror of his loss. "Let's go downstairs. The fire must have started down there in the first place. Perhaps Tiepolo managed to get down the stairs before he died."

"Yes. Let us look there for him. I told him to try and get to the front door. Maybe he almost made it."

But there was no hope of finding a body on the ground floor. It was a blackened, wet mess of burned wood. The fire had obviously started here, but Zuliani could not tell how. Katie looked around.

"What is all this?"

"Old furniture from when my parents lived here. I could not use it, but I couldn't bear to part with it either. So I just piled it up here. What I don't understand is how it could have caught fire. It was so damp from the closeness of the canal. What is sure is that we will not find Tiepolo in a hurry in this mess."

Katie stood at the bottom of the staircase rubbing her hand on the cast-iron image of the lizard on the newel post which was all that had survived the holocaust. Thoughts of the salamander emerging from the flames came to her again. Nick might have told her that it was all a myth, but she liked the idea. He wiped the smudges from her face.

"Come. Let us go and see what your grandmother has discovered. When my manservant, Vettor, returns from visiting his family in Malomocco, I will set him to cleaning this up. Maybe he will find the body."

★

At the end of Nick Zuliani's first full day as a grandfather, he sat with his one-time lover, Caterina Dolfin now called Valier, and Katie, the offspring of his unknown son, Agostino. He pondered broaching the possibility of the girl changing her name to Zuliani, but decided first they had more pressing matters to discuss. He told Cat what they had found at his house – omitting the small matter of the body being still there. He made out to her that they had seen the ringless fingers earlier, but had not realized the importance of it until now. The corpse therefore was not Tiepolo's. Cat was shocked about the identity of the body, and pointed out to Zuliani a matter he would have to deal with urgently.

"As the Tiepolos have already taken the body you say is that of his lieutenant, Lando, you must tell them before they bury it thinking it is one of their own."

Zuliani and Katie exchanged glances, then he spoke up.

"I don't think they have had time to do anything yet. It is too late. I will tell them tomorrow. First, tell us what you have learned."

Cat shrugged her ivory-skinned, bare shoulders, causing a little flutter of Zuliani's heart.

"I am not sure what I have found out is very helpful. It is mainly gossip. Apparently, Francesco Tiepolo was engaged on a colleganza which aimed to try and break the Pope's interdict on trade."

"What's that, granny? A colleganza."

Zuliani puffed out his cheeks in astonishment at Katie's question.

"Call yourself a Venetian, and you don't know what that is? It means Tiepolo had funded a trading enterprise along with others. He must have had a ship ready to sail just before the rebellion kicked off. In the situation we are in at the moment, that was a very risky thing to have done. He must have been pretty desperate." He turned to Cat again. "Anything else of use?"

Cat paused for a moment, and then looked Zuliani in the eyes.

"There was something else, but it sounds foolish. Don't laugh when I tell you."

"Carry on. Anything, no matter how small or insignificant, could be important."

Cat looked away, and took a deep breath.

"It is something your neighbour, Justinia Erizzo, said to me. Now, I know she is scatterbrained, and has been a little inclined to get emotional about death since her husband died."

"Spit it out, Cat."

"She said she saw Tiepolo's soul flying away from the fire just at the end when the flames had reached him in the topmost room."

"What? Out of the window?"

Cat frowned, and swirled the dregs of her wine in the bottom of her goblet. The sediment rose and with a grimace she put the goblet down.

"No. That was the oddest thing. She said she saw his soul fly out of the back door. You know her house faces that alley between your house and San Giuliano Church."

Katie laughed at the idea of a soul using a door, but Zuliani had a serious look on his face. This wasn't just a foolish woman's whimsy. He felt sure there was something of substance about the vision. He waved his hand in the air, trying to urge his tumbling thoughts into some sort of order.

"This vision of a soul. How was it made up? Did she say?"

"Well no. A soul is . . . a soul. What should it look like?"

Katie stared at her grandfather. She was beginning to understand what he looked like when he was on to something. His body tensed, and he scowled.

"What is it, grandpa?"

Zuliani groaned.

"I hate it when you call me that. Call me Nick like you did before all this family stuff came up."

Cat hid a smile behind her slender fingers. Zuliani was clearly discomfited by all this personal closeness. He had always preferred to be a free agent. But Katie would soon cure him of that – he couldn't resist her charms – and Cat herself fancied getting as close as they had been all those years ago. The truth was she yearned to bed him. For now, she concentrated on the mystery of Tiepolo's death.

"I too know when something is bothering you, Nick. So get it off your chest."

Zuliani squinted at the two women, and shook his head decisively.

"Not yet. Not until I have verified a few more facts."

Cat rose from her chair and stamped her foot.

"I swear, Niccolo Zuliani, you are even more exasperating now than you were forty years ago. I am not going to let you out of my sight until I get the truth out of you."

Zuliani pushed himself out of his chair too, his bones creaking alarmingly.

"Then you must both come back with me to Ca' Zuliani. But it is too dark now, and Justinia will be abed."

"You intend to ask her about this nonsense about Tiepolo's soul?"

Zuliani nodded.

"If it is nonsense, then I will have lost nothing by asking. But if it is not . . . I will have solved the whole mystery. But first, I need some sleep."

Katie led him to where he would sleep that night, and then tripped down the passage to her own room. He stepped wearily into the room and was about to close the door, when Cat's face appeared in the gap. She smiled knowingly.

"Do you need your sleep, old man? Or can you put it off for an hour or two?"

Zuliani grinned wolfishly.

"Only an hour or two? Your appetites must have diminished, granny."

Cat growled, grabbed his arm and dragged him to her bed-chamber.

★

Zuliani arose early the next morning and tiptoed to his own room. He had no wish for Katie to know of the carnal nature of her grandparents. But it seemed his circumspection was all in vain. When he descended the stairs having splashed his face with cold water and dragged his fingers through his unruly hair, there she was in the main hall grinning from ear to ear.

"You look tired out, grand . . . Nick. Up all night, were you?"

Zuliani had no doubts about her meaning, and even blushed a little.

"You should be more respectful to your elders, Katie Valier. I am refreshed and ready to go. Are you?"

Cat entered the room, and yawned.

"So early? It is such a cold morning, why do we have to go now?"

Zuliani grinned at the two mystified women.

"I have a reason, but I can't tell you now."

Katie turned to her grandmother with a questioning look.

"Did you get nothing out of him last night?"

Cat withered the girl with a stern look.

"That is not how I brought you up, young lady." She then paused, and laughed. "But you are correct. I got nothing out of him – from an informational point of view. He always did play his cards close to his chest. That was because, if he told no one his opinions, when he turned out to have got it wrong, no one could tell him so."

Zuliani was beginning to wonder if he wanted to be bossed around by two women. But then he looked at the two of them and knew, for different reasons, it was worth it. Still, he decided he would string them along a little longer.

"If you ladies are ready, we should get moving."

"Where are we going?"

It was Cat's question, and he took delight in answering it in his own way.

"To my house first to look for something that is probably not there. And then to the docks to find something that we thought was no more."

Before they could ask what he meant, he was out of the door and into the chilly morning where a thick mist swirled around the streets. The two women had to hurry to keep up with him as he crossed the Rialto Bridge and made for his own house in the Castello district. The morning mist made them seem like three wraiths flying through the *calles* of La Serenissima. Katie giggled, and thought too of Tiepolo's soul fleeing the fire. There was something about Venice that resonated with death and life. She laughed out loud, and Cat gave her a curious look. But there was no time to stop, as Zuliani suddenly snapped his fingers and turned away from where his house stood. Cat called after him.

"Where are you going?"

His voice carried over his shoulder as he almost disappeared in the mist.

"An urgent errand. You go on to Ca' Zuliani and I'll meet you there."

"Yes, but what are we looking for?"

It was too late. Zuliani was gone. Grumbling at his erratic behaviour, Cat stalked through the streets with Katie at her heels. When they got to the blackened shell that was Zuliani's home, she turned to her granddaughter

"What the hell are we looking for, Katie?"

The girl shrugged her pretty shoulders.

"Something that won't be there, he said."

"Then how are we going to find it?"

"I don't know for sure, but let's go up to the top floor. That's where Nick kept his treasures. If anything is missing, it is likely to be one of them. He showed me everything, so I may be able to recall if one of them is not there."

At the bottom of the stairs, Cat touched the metal lizard on the newel post. She had the same thought as Katie had a few days ago.

"A salamander, perhaps? It didn't help put out the fire though, did it?"

Katie gasped.

"Grandmother, you are a genius."

She ran up the staircase, leaving a puzzled Cat at the bottom.

"Me, a genius? What did I say?"

She followed Katie up the stairs at a more sedate pace. When she got to the top room, she was appalled by the mess. She could now understand why Nick was so devastated by the fire. All his possessions were ruined – blackened lumps in a fire-seared room. But Katie, already covered in soot, was exultant as she bounced around the room.

"It's not here."

Cat took in a deep breath, holding in her exasperation. She calmed Katie down with a downward wave of her hands.

"For God's sake, don't you start. Just tell me what it is that isn't here."

Her answer came from the doorway, where Zuliani now stood.

"The salamander cloak. I should have realized sooner, but I wasn't thinking then of anyone having escaped the fire."

Cat was shocked.

"Escaped? How could anyone have escaped the fire? If it was as bad as you described ..." She waved her hand around the room. "... as bad as it looks, no one could have escaped. It started on the ground floor and, from what you have said, Tiepolo was driven up the stairs. How could he escape from there? Unless he flew."

Katie clapped her hands with pleasure.

"Tell her about the cloak, Nick." She turned to Cat. "It's made of salamander hair, you know."

Zuliani laughed at the monstrous idea.

"Where did you hear that? All that is just part of the myth that no one really believes. The reality is that a fire-proof material does exist, and it's made of material dug from the ground. I have seen it produced, and it is grey when woven. Throw it in a fire and it emerges undamaged, though by then it is white. There is a Greek

word used for it – ασβεστος. Asbestos means unquenchable. I
had a cloak of this material, and it should be in this upper room.
Even the fire should not have damaged it. So, if it is not here, then
someone wore it to flee the fire."

Cat was catching on quickly.

"Then Tiepolo could be alive. But it doesn't explain why he
was in your house in the first place. Though he should thank his
lucky stars that, as he was, he could use this miraculous cloak."

Zuliani shook his head.

"No. It was not chance that led him here. You see, it was only
days before the failed conspiracy that I showed Tiepolo my whole
collection in this very room. He was one of a very few who knew
about the salamander cloak."

Katie was bursting to speak, so Zuliani allowed her to complete
the curious sequence of events.

"He planned it from the beginning, gran. Once he was
on the run, he knew he would be safe if he could fake his
own death. Recalling seeing the cloak, he broke into Nick's
house—"

"When I was conveniently away."

Katie acknowledged this with a little bow of the head.

"Tiepolo was in luck there – though perhaps not, thinking
about it. Perhaps you, Nick, were going to be the body found
after the fire. Then no one would have worked out his means of
escape."

Zuliani went pale at the thought that had not occurred to him.
Katie was right. Tiepolo would not have left anything to chance.
He was to have been Tiepolo's stand-in body and, when he was
found not to be at home, Tiepolo's lieutenant, Girolamo Lando,
had been killed instead.

"It is I who was the lucky one, then."

Cat rounded off the story.

"Tiepolo's other stroke of bad luck was his escape. He had
thought no one would see him leaving by the secret back door,
used only by the conspirators. But he had not bargained on
the nosiness of your neighbour, Justinia. What she thought was
Tiepolo's soul flying to Heaven was a very corporeal Tiepolo
wrapped in . . . asbestos." She sighed. "So he has escaped justice,
after all."

Zuliani raised a finger, and winked.

"Don't be so quick to despair. Remember, there is one more place for us to call this morning."

Cat was puzzled.

"You said the docks, didn't you? What can be there?"

Zuliani grin wolfishly.

"Come and see."

★

The morning mist was clearing, though some stray strands of it weaved around the only ship at the dockside. Since the pope's proclamations on Venice, hardly anyone dared trade – and stand to lose everything to marauders sanctioned by the Church. But one solitary ship was ready to sail, and a group of men huddled on the quay ready to board. Each had his cloak pulled around him and the hood up against the cold wind blowing off the lagoon.

"Whose ship is that?"

Zuliani answered Cat's question.

"It is Tiepolo's colleganza, and I see those seeking passage on it are ready to board."

Cat made a move to walk down to the ship, but Zuliani stayed her with his arm.

"Just watch. My little errand this morning was to ask the captain the time of his sailing. And to ask him a favour – to shake the hand of everyone as they boarded."

"Why?"

"You will see, Katie."

They watched as each man was welcomed aboard in the way Zuliani had prescribed. Each man took the captain's preferred hand and shook it. The last man, well wrapped up from the weather, winced as the captain squeezed his hand heartily. Zuliani whooped in delight, and ran down the quay, his fur-trimmed robe flying out behind him. He grabbed the final passenger by the arm firmly, pulling him back on to the quay.

"Francesco, I think you have a case to face here in Venice."

As the big man turned round, his hood fell away. His features were reddened by fire, and his eyebrows had been singed off. But it was unmistakeably Francesco Tiepolo. He snarled at Zuliani, and would have aimed a blow at him, had not the captain held him back. Something heavy fell from his cloak on to the quay. Zuliani scooped it up with a whoop of delight. It was the gold *paizah* that gave him the authority of the Great Khan. Not everything had been lost in the fire after all, thanks to Tiepolo's greed. Tiepolo cursed Zuliani roundly.

"Damn you. You should have burned in that fire, then no one would have known anything. A perfect crime that could never have taken place before now, as no one knew of the salamander cloak but you."

"And which can never happen again, now the cat is out the bag. Trade with the East means that more and more will know about the magical properties of asbestos."

Zuliani snapped his fingers in Tiepolo's face as the burly figure of one of the Signore di Notte appeared out of the mists. Zuliani had requested their presence earlier. As he and Cat and Katie watched Tiepolo being led away, the girl asked a question that had been burning to be asked.

"Why did you ask the captain to shake the men's hands?"

Zuliani's face broke out in a superior smile.

"I wanted to be sure which man was Tiepolo. Tell me something, Katie, what was your natural movement every time you descended the stairs in my house?"

The girl paused for a moment, then grinned.

"I always put my hand on the bottom newel post, where the cast iron lizard sits."

"Exactly. I always did it, even as a child. I reckoned Tiepolo would have done it too, especially as he was groping through the flames with the asbestos hood over his eyes. He would have reached out for the bottom newel, and the metal would have been very hot. I am sure that, if you looked at his hand, you would see, burned into the flesh, the image of a salamander."

Hide and Seek

Tony Pollard

Dr Tony Pollard is one of the world's leading battlefield archaeologists and is Director of the Centre for Battlefield Archaeology at the University of Glasgow. He also works as a forensic archaeologist and led the team that discovered the graves of hundreds of First World War British and Australian troops at Fromelles in France. He regularly appears on television and radio and was co-presenter, along with Neil Oliver, of the popular BBC TV series Two Men in a Trench *(2002). He has written widely on archaeology and history for popular and academic audiences and is co-editor of* The Journal of Conflict Archaeology. *His first novel,* The Secrets of the Lazarus Club *(2009) is a thriller based around the life of the famous Victorian engineer Isambard Kingdom Brunel.*

For the following story, however, we go back to the months following the discovery of the Gunpowder Plot of 1605, and the search for the conspirators.

Nicholas Owen had been in tight spots before, most of them of his own making. But it is one thing to build a priest hole, quite another to hide in it. If they did not find him, he promised himself, then the next would be made with an eye to comfort. Owen had lost count of the number of these secret chambers he had constructed over the years, but that was not to say that they were all alike. Every hidey-hole, just like the houses in which they were concealed, had its own character, its advantages and disadvantages. Whether inside a fireplace, beneath the stairs, under floorboards, within the hollow core of a wall or behind a tapestry, they differed in size, shape, airiness, level of illumination, ease of escape and method of entry. While each of these factors was always a consideration during conception and execution it was perhaps in rendering the last of them that Owen had proven himself the absolute master. Every commission required him to approach the challenge of concealment afresh, to impart a unique flourish and avoid the tricks and traps of his last. In repetition were sown the seeds of capture, torture and death.

No matter how well designed, there was always the risk of discovery, either through betrayal or thanks to the talents of one of the small number of priest hunters who turned a hefty profit from seeking out these hiding places and bagging their occupants. Every time the secrets of a hole were exposed, so the task of creating a new one became all the more difficult. With every discovery, the hunters learned something more about the habits of their prey. Like dogs pursuing a fox's scent, they knew where best to look inside a house and how to recognize the tell-tale signs that a priest was hiding behind what to the uninitiated appeared to be a wall devoid of aperture, or a fireplace with nothing more than a fire in the grate.

An architect will always strive for perfection, but, however cramped his present conditions, Owen knew better than anyone that, when lives of his brethren were at risk, comfort was not a priority. What was there to be gained if, in creating it by making the chamber larger or diverting light from a nearby window, locating the entrance became easier for the hunters? A chink of light here or too wide a wall there was all that was needed to give the place away to a practised eye. In any case, a little cramp in the legs or a crook in the neck was nothing to a man born with a twisted back and known as Little John, thanks to his permanent stoop. But it was just this peculiarity, which God had chosen to bestow on him, which marked him out as ideal for the task. This was, after all, more than a mere profession; it was a calling, as strong as that which drove the many priests – who at times had cause to make use of these sanctuaries – to keep the Roman Catholic faith alive. It was his absolute belief that God had chosen him, just as he had chosen Noah to build the Ark, to serve as the architect of these hidden places. No one was better suited to spend days on end working in confined spaces. There were times, however, when he had to remember that not everyone was as small as he, and it was true that one or two of his creations were a little cosier than they could have been.

For the whole of Owen's lifetime, and longer, it had been a crime to be a practising Catholic in England. It hadn't always been so; during her brief reign, Mary Tudor had put fire and sword to bloody use in her determination to return the nation to the bosom of a mother church so cruelly defaced by her father, Henry VIII. But things changed again when her Protestant sister and rival Elizabeth came to the throne in the year of our lord fifteen hundred and fifty eight. Thus it was, that under Queen Bess Catholicism was outlawed; priests and Jesuit missionaries were regarded as enemies of the state and those who refused to deny their faith could be put to death. As a result, Catholicism was not only driven underground but also into the walls and under the stairs. But, just as the Romans had realized so many centuries before, it took more than persecution to kill a faith. And now there was James, the king from north of the border, of whom there were, at first, hopes of a more enlightened rule. His mother, Mary Queen of Scots, had after all been a devout Catholic. But within just a year the persecutions returned and it was the recent ill-fated attempt to put a stop to this reign of terror that caused Owen to be here now – a fugitive in a hide of his own handiwork.

It was the twenty-first day of January in the year of Our Lord sixteen hundred and six. Two months earlier, on a cold November night in London, Guido Fawkes had been discovered lurking within the cellars of the House of Lords in the company of dozens of barrels of gunpowder and a lighted lantern. The taking of Fawkes brought an end to what they were now calling the powder treason – a plot by disheartened Catholics to kill the king and as many members of parliament as were present in the house during the state opening. Other plotters, including their ringleader, Sir Robert Catesby, had been taken since, while others still were already dead. Owen was one of the few remaining at large and, despite his lowly ranking within the scheme, he had been tasked by its leaders with a heavy responsibility, and it was that which sat between his feet, confined within a leather sack – just as he was, between walls of timber and stone.

If failing anatomy and hard labour caused him some discomfort, this was nothing when compared to the agonies of torture. He knew all too well what the rack could do to a man, having before now been tied to the state's favoured instrument of torture. His crime then had been to speak out against the arrest of a neighbour for attending a mass; but even under torture he refused to speak out against his fellow Catholics. In truth though, he had been on the verge of breaking when his freedom was purchased by a wealthy local family for whom he had built several holes in the past. This time though, if taken as a traitor and failed regicide, torture would merely be the first of many horrors to be faced.

As yet there had been only a little discomfort, though he was grateful for the blanket helping to shield him from the chilled air blowing in through a fissure in the exterior wall. But only half a day had passed since the hammering on the door. Now he would see how good his work had been.

*

"We have them," said the first of the two horsemen to arrive in front of the red brick house. Tired but still restless, Noyce's mount shifted on the carriage-way just inside the ornate gate posts. Removing his broad-brimmed hat he bent forward across his horse's flank, studying the ground. The heavy wooden gates were slightly ajar and the gravel was scuffed and mounded – the legacy of a half-hearted attempt to drag them closed, but, with the house still a good distance away and their pursuers closing in behind them, their quarry had given it up as a bad job.

Hindlip Hall was a rambling pile with ivy-covered walls and towers, projecting wings, too many windows to count and spiralled chimney pots stacked high above the roof. Gathered behind the riders were foot soldiers, armed with half-pikes and muskets. Their easy posture and the patches of rust on their helmets and breastplates marked them out as something less than the king's élite.

"Hiding like rats in the walls," said Sir Henry Bromley, the well-dressed and even better fed local Justice, as he drew up alongside Noyce on a sweat-flecked bay.

Noyce's horse threw back its head, stamped a hoof and through flared nostrils pushed smoky breath into the cold air. The sudden movement prompted the man standing closest to them to take a step back and almost drop the partizan he was carrying. He was the captain of militia, a gangly fellow with a thick grey beard in need of a trim and men in want of orders. "What a peculiar breed of coward they are, these Catholics. They dare try their hand at killing our king but then hide behind the wainscoting. You are correct Sir 'enry, vermin all of 'em."

"That may be, captain, but they are clever vermin," replied Noyce. "I have been hunting these people and their like for years. It will be a job of work to pull them from their holes, have no doubt of that." He turned to look doubtfully at the slouching soldiers behind him. "We must hope that your men are up to the task at hand."

"They will be, sir, once they've got their wind back. It is not an easy thing for infantry to keep up with cavalry."

"Well, now you have arrived," interjected Sir Henry. "You can instruct your men, winded or not, to surround the house. It would not do for our rats to leave the trap before we have closed it. There are outbuildings to the rear. Billet your men there. One of them is a smithy. When the house is secure I will require the services of the blacksmith." He patted the side of the horse's neck. "He has shaken loose a shoe on that damned forest track. Now, sir, be good enough to deploy your men."

The captain strode towards his charges, bellowing orders. He was eager for his men to prove themselves to the intimidating outsider. Although he had never had cause to visit these parts before, the reputation of Mr Jonathan Noyce – the most successful priest hunter in all of England – preceded him and, among other things, it was well known that he did not suffer fools gladly. "Half of you spread out across the front of the house," yelled the captain. "The rest of you close the circle from the rear. If anyone tries to leave the house stop them, but hold your fire for god's sake. The king requires these people alive."

He was pleased with his closing remark; it sounded professional. But his orders brought only disorder. Where there had been a suggested lack of military precision there was now chaos, as some of the men collided with their neighbours, while others seemed uncertain whether they were to move or not. Only the intervention of the sergeant and his bill-staff, which was applied liberally to shoulders and backsides, brought the mêlée to order.

As the soldiers moved off at a trot, Noyce reached into a saddlebag and pulled out a parchment, which he unrolled and began to study. "Now, tell me Sir Henry, who is the woman of the house?"

Sir Henry let out a laugh. "Perhaps, sir, we should postpone such niceties until we have completed the business at hand."

"You mistake my intent Sir Henry," replied the priest hunter, clearly irritated at the remark. "The house may have a master, but I'll wager it is ruled by the mistress. Experience has taught that the women are oft times more devout than their spouses, and protective of priests as they are of their own children. Now who is she?"

"Why, she is . . . she is Habington's wife of course. I think her name is Mary," said a cowed Sir Henry. Then, eager to make amends for his gaff, he added, "My sources tell me that her husband is away from the house."

"Then by God, she has full reign. Mark me sir, she is harbouring our prey. The woman is as much an enemy of the king and the Protestant faith as any of those men sheltered within her walls."

"True, it is well known to be a Catholic household, but they have never given me any cause to interfere in their affairs. Unlike some, they have not been foolish enough to flaunt their beliefs."

"What say you to harbouring failed assassins of the king? Cause enough for a little interference, would you not say?"

Sir Henry, let out a snort of indignation. "We should save our trouble and put the place to the torch. Smoke them out or let them roast. The fires of hell will be familiar to them soon enough."

Noyce rolled up the parchment and slapped it against the palm of a gloved hand. "Do you know what this is?"

"I have no idea of its contents sir, though I would be pleased enough to read them if you felt it would advantage our cause."

"That will not be required," said Noyce as he repacked the document. "It is a king's warrant for the arrest of all of those known or suspected to have taken part in the gunpowder plot, or to have given the traitors aid or succour. It states that the greatest care is to be taken, in servicing said warrant, and is most specific about the importance of collecting any evidence which may prove guilt or innocence."

"*Evidence*," scoffed Sir Henry. "There will be enough of that spilling from their treacherous tongues once they are strapped to the rack."

"You wish to question the *king's* warrant sir? I should not need to explain to a King's Justice that hard evidence is much preferred to testimony gathered under torture. And we are hardly likely to pull much of worth from the charred ashes of the house, are we?"

Sir Henry was watching his soldiers amble across the lawn, their armour clinking as they surrounded the house. He was growing tired of being patronized by a mere commoner. But he was also mindful that the man held the king's commission. "We will do the king's bidding, sir, rest assured of that."

"Follow my lead, Sir Henry, and you can rest assured the king will reward you, but fail and you will be exchanging your grand house for a cell in the Tower of London."

Sir Henry looked as though he was about to explode but, just like those barrels of powder beneath parliament, the conflagration failed to ignite. "The king shall not find me wanting, sir, and I trust nor will you," he thundered. "And now, sir, if we have finished our debate, might I suggest we set to *work*." Without waiting for a reply, the knight spurred his horse and cantered off towards the house, his dander flying like a banner.

The other rider sat for a moment, pondering the impact of his words. It was going better than he could have hoped and his earlier fears melted away. More confident now, but determined to remain alert, he urged his own horse forward.

*

The place was like a castle under siege. There were sentinels at the gates preventing free passage to and from the house; meanwhile, troops patrolled the gardens and clattered about inside, overturning furniture and prying away panels in the search for hiding places. They had been at work for almost two days now and, with no sign of their prey, Noyce was becoming frustrated at the haphazard nature of the search.

"Your men charge about the house like so many children playing games," he complained to Sir Henry. "A search like this requires care and, most of all, quiet. I need to hear the house."

Sir Henry, who was eating, as he always seemed to be, slapped his fork down on to the table. Since morning he had been suffering from a stiff neck and it was doing little for his mood. "Gads, sir, you suggest that I remove my men from the house? Perhaps you would like me to withdraw them from the grounds also, in order that you might *listen* to the house?"

"The first of those things would greatly assist my work, though I think some of your men should be sent away." He cast an eye over the dismembered chicken carcass sitting in front of Sir Henry. "We have emptied the pantry three times over and your men are now scouring the locality for victuals. If the looting continues, sir, you risk stirring unrest, and that will assist neither your personal standing nor our present task."

Sir Henry knew all too well that, as the local Justice, failure to capture the fugitives would reflect badly on him, as would complaints about the misbehaviour of his men. Food could be paid for of course, but the coin would have to come from his own purse. He turned back to his fowl but seemed to have lost his appetite. "Very well, Mister Noyce, I will speak to the captain. I shall give you the house and send away some of the men. I trust though, that, with the fulfilment of your request, we can look forward to a satisfactory end to this affair. Find me the traitors, and find them soon."

"I will find them, Sir Henry, but it shall be for the king that duty will be served, not for your own gratification." With that, Noyce turned on his heels and left. Sir Henry looked as though he was about to shout after the impudent fellow but, instead, picked up the fork and thrust it angrily into the chicken's breast.

Leaving Sir Henry fuming at the dining table, Noyce went to the kitchen where he found the mistress of the house in the company of her servants. A scullery-maid was reporting on the condition of the house. "There is a great tear in the tapestry in the upper gallery and this morning they have ripped up boards from the floor in the great hall."

Mary Habingdon listened as the list of desecrations grew: panels removed, doors unhinged, stairs lifted. The maid was clearly anxious, her voice quivering as she continued her litany. Mary on the other hand was the very picture of calm, and she seemed more concerned with re-adjusting her bonnet than fretting about the damage done to her beloved house. It was typical of her behaviour since the arrival of her uninvited guests, thought Noyce. She had treated them with haughty contempt, done nothing to assist or provoke them and had remained adamant that she had nothing to hide.

"The wainscoting can be replaced and the floorboards polished but the tapestry is another matter," she said. "Repairing it will certainly be beyond my skills with needle and thread. May God forgive those foolish oafs." Unaware that Noyce was watching, she crossed herself.

Noyce coughed, announcing his presence. One of the servants let out a surprised gasp on turning and seeing him loitering in the door. The group dispersed, returning to the tasks which had busied them prior to their mistress's arrival and leaving her standing alone.

"Mr Noyce, have you tired of destroying my house?"

"Such is the price for hiding priests and traitors both, Mrs Habingdon. Now I think it is time that you and I had a talk."

The woman strode towards Noyce, her annoyance only now showing. "I thought you and your kind preferred conversation over the rack. Is that what you have in mind for me Mr Priest Hunter? Torture, until I tell you where these supposed priests are hidden?"

It was indeed a pretty bonnet, thought Noyce; it was just a shame that the face it framed was now exuding barely disguised contempt. "Let us hope that it will not come to that. Perhaps we could proceed in private? I am sure you would not want to expose your servants to any more unpleasantness than is truly necessary. Let us not forget that I have still to question them about what goes on here."

This veiled threat to her servants was enough to encourage a change of attitude. "Very well, Mr Noyce, come with me." She gestured to the door and Noyce followed her from the room.

"Will he torture her?" asked a young girl with a scrubbing brush in her hand and fear in her voice.

"I would like to see him try," said one of the cooks with a reassuring smile. "He will pay dear for the torn tapestry. Her father brought that back from the wars in Flanders."

Noyce was standing by a glowing fire and had taken care to adjust his sword so as to keep its tip away from the flames. At his insistence, Mrs Habingdon had taken to a chair, beside which a needlework frame stood idle, coloured threads dangling to the floor. She eyed her own handiwork critically and once again her thoughts turned to the damaged tapestry, which she had yet to examine for herself.

Noyce pre-empted her. "The damage is most unfortunate, Mrs Habingdon. The soldiers are incompetent. They do not know how to search a house. I may however be in a position to rid you of them."

"And what have I done to deserve such treatment, Mr Noyce? To you I am nothing more than another pestilent Catholic. Why would you wish to ease my discomfort?"

The man took a step forward from the fire and drew his sword, causing the woman to shrink back in her chair. To demonstrate that no threat was intended he placed the blade on a nearby table and took a seat in the chair opposite her, on the other side of the fire.

"Because, my dear lady, easing your discomfort might just have the same effect on my own, shall we say, rather unenviable predicament?"

Mrs Habingdon was studying him, trying to gauge his measure. There was something about him, a charm which she would not before have associated with a man who chose to hunt priests for a living. "In my husband's absence you might think me obliged to act as he would in such circumstances as these. But in the world of domestic affairs I am the mistress of my own destiny. Now, sir, you have my attention so, pray continue with your exposition."

*

With the house cleared of soldiers and more than half of them now marching away, Noyce was left at peace to advance the search. But, when Sir Henry found him, he was sitting idle in the great hall. "Well, Noyce, what do you hear? I can assume that you are listening and not just resting your backside?"

"Quiet as the grave I am afraid. They are not hiding in here. Of that I am confident."

"Then where in the blazes are they? There are dozens of apartments in this pile. Is it your intention to sit in each of them until it becomes apparent to you that Jesuits in hiding know better than to create a din?"

"No, I intend to search the long gallery. You might care to join me."

"Anything to hasten an end to all of this. If only Habingdon would return. *Then* we would make some progress."

"And how is that, sir?"

"Why, we can rack him of course. I refuse to torture a woman but, when he gets back, I will know the location of each and every one of the hiding places soon enough."

"Now that would be a shame," said Noyce, jumping to his feet. "I have always taken pride in winning my prize without recourse to torture. It is such a noisy, messy business and it entirely takes the sport out of the chase. And, in any case, there is a flaw in your proposition."

"And what is that sir?"

"I have not noticed you with a rack about your person. Nor have I observed your men setting one up in the gardens. I can only suppose they are too busily engaged in ripping up the roses and pissing on the lawn."

Sir Henry was quick with his response. "I am sure a rope thrown over a rafter in the barn will provide more than one way of producing the requisite agonies."

Noyce had never marked Sir Henry out as a man of initiative. "In the meantime, might I suggest we continue the search? Perhaps now I can prove to you the nature of my talent."

Sir Henry was already pondering what sort of knot might best secure a man suspended by his hands, preferably while they were tied behind his back. But he saw no harm in going along with the priest hunter, at least for now. "The long gallery I believe you said?"

Owen had finished taking stock of his victuals and did not like the result of his accounting; the biscuits and quince jelly would last no more than another day, the beer perhaps another two. There was a fortune in the bag at his feet but a man could not live by silver coins alone. There were far better holes in the house, but, being only a lay brother, he had shown favour to the priests. The previous day, the sound of soldier's boots stomping across the floor and the crash of furniture had died down, almost to the point that he thought they may have abandoned the search. But then, with his ears straining, he picked up quieter stirrings, the pad of stockinged feet and the gentle teasing of the woodwork. These were not sounds to sooth the soul. Oh Lord, he prayed, I would prefer a company of clumsy soldiers – who are no better than the blind leading the blind – over a single priest hunter.

Equipped with the tools for the job, he could work on improving his surroundings, for, even with the great risk of the searchers hearing the sound of his labours, doing something seemed a better option than doing nothing. But, in the absence of tools, he had no option but to wait – either to be discovered in hiding or for his enemies to give up their search. But, as time slipped slowly by, another option came to mind. And so it was that he determined to leave his hiding place, and then the house, if it were possible; if it were not, then he would make for one of the better appointed priest holes.

Once again, with his best ear to the wall he listened to the house and what she had to tell him about the hunter. At first, all was silent; but then he heard it, the sound of someone upstairs, walking down the long gallery from where the floorboards were creaking. The timbers there were badly seasoned and it had long been Mrs Habingdon's desire to have them replaced; but, whenever he arrived at the house for a period of employment, he was tasked with creating a further hiding place. There were now so many, he was afraid that the house, thus honeycombed, would collapse on to its foundations. Until then, the number and precise location of all of the holes would be known only to him and the lady of house.

He always worked alone and at night, reciting prayers as he carved his way into the fabric of the house. Then, when the work was done he would unveil his latest creation to his mistress and teach her its secrets. There were regularly priests and lay brothers in the house, but never so many as to require the use of more than two or three of the hiding places. Nevertheless, the mere knowledge of their presence seemed to gift Mrs Habingdon with a peace of mind which only the attendance of a mass in her hidden chapel could improve upon. This time though it was different. These were not priests making one of their regular clandestine visits but a group of desperate men, traitors caught up in a plot which had gone terribly wrong. There would be no giving up on the search for them as had been the case on many a previous occasion. This time they would be hunted to the ends of the earth.

*

Noyce was running a lighted candle across the surface of the wood panelling. He was crouching now, holding it close to the junction of the floor and the wall. At first Sir Henry thought the flame was merely providing illumination, shedding light into the nooks and crannies. But then, as it continued to move along the flame flickered, leaping away from the wall for just an instant before steadying again as it resumed its passage across the skirting. When drawn back and held steady the flame guttered almost to the point of expiration.

It was obvious even to Sir Henry that the draught was coming from a void behind the panel and he watched, fascinated, as the priest hunter stood up and began to feel along its edge. Unable to get a purchase with his fingertips, he pulled a knife from his belt and began to prize away at the beading. The blade disappeared behind the wood and then, after a little agitation, there was a click and the wood popped away from the wall.

Stepping back, Sir Henry unsheathed his sword and pointed its tip towards the widening gap. "I should call for the men, they might be armed."

"Indeed they might," said Noyce as he held the dagger above the loosened panel. "But I think we still hold the advantage over those within."

"Very well," replied Sir Henry, who was now speaking in a whisper. With his free hand he too drew a dagger and with both blades poised, he motioned with his chin for Noyce to pull open the panel.

With a jerk the hidden door opened and Sir Henry cleared his throat before bellowing into the dark. "Come out from there." There was no reply. "It will go better for you if we do not have to come in and take you." Nothing stirred. "There is nowhere left to run. Come out!" Still nothing. There seemed little option but to enter. Sir Henry eyed the narrow gap and then looked down at his prodigious, sash-bound frontage.

"Perhaps you will allow me?" said Noyce.

The Justice did not need to hear the offer made twice. "Yes, yes of course. You are the priest hunter and I am sure you have seen more of these niches than many a Jesuit."

Noyce could barely mask a smile as he ushered his companion out of the way and followed the candle and point of dagger into the void. Once inside, the candle flickered wildly. But there was light enough to illuminate a small box-like space just large enough to accommodate a crouching man of no more than medium stature. But there was no crouching man. The priest hole was empty.

Noyce took a moment to study the interior, noting the vent in the back wall through which the draught entered. At least, he thought, the occupant would not suffocate, but even with the door open he was beginning to find the atmosphere oppressive.

"Empty?" asked a disappointed Sir Henry as Noyce backed out into the hall.

"This has not seen an occupant for some time."

"You are certain of that?"

"A man would leave behind some trace. We would smell him."

Sir Henry sheathed his sword and dropping to his knees, peered into the hole. There was nothing in there, neither seat nor commode. "Zounds, there can be few torture devices in the Tower as bad."

"It is strange is it not," offered Noyce, "the lengths to which a man will go to avoid being disembowelled alive?"

Sir Henry closed the door and frowned. "There are times sir, when your sympathies would appear misdirected."

Noyce was already walking away. "My work has made me a student of the human animal, that is all. Now, sir, shall we begin our search again? A house this size may have a dozen such places concealed within it."

Sir Henry paused before following, taking the time to run his fingers across the edge of the secret door. He could not help but admire the skill required to conceal the join so well. To all but the most experienced eyes there was nothing out of the ordinary to be seen here. Noyce may be insolent, he thought, but the man clearly knew his business.

★

By noon the next day two more holes had been breached, and each was empty. The first was concealed beneath the floorboards of the vestibule, cleverly placed so close to the front door that it was almost outside rather than being buried within the heart of the house as might be expected. The second was in the pantry, concealed behind the heavy stone walls of the under-croft and with access provided by a hatch cut into the back of a high shelf. The priest hiding there would require the dexterity only to be found in a young man, and, from the size of the hiding place itself, Noyce could only assume the architect intended it for the concealment of a boy.

Despite the cupboards being bare, Sir Henry continued to be impressed with the priest hunter's abilities, at one point comparing him to a terrier let loose in a rabbit warren, albeit a warren which lacked rabbits. By the time the third of the day's discoveries was made – the largest of them all – inside a fireplace, the Justice began to worry that the birds had flown. Noyce paused only to enquire whether Sir Henry would prefer him to find birds or rabbits before continuing with his search.

*

"I want no more than twelve men remaining," insisted Sir Henry, as he rode along the ragged line of men. It had been three full days since he first arrived here, at the gates to the house. Although Noyce had succeeded in sniffing out four hiding places, not one of them had produced a fugitive. He did not doubt that, given enough time, the man would find every secret space in the house. But further delay would not impress his superiors in London, and with every passing day so his own costs mounted. Noyce was right; it was an expensive business to keep soldiers in the field. He contented himself with the thought that if the fugitives were still bottled up, and pray God they were, then there was nothing that a dozen of them couldn't do as well as a hundred.

The priest hunter was watching the activity at the gate from a window in the long gallery. He was pleased to see yet more men being sent away and, having won the confidence of the Justice, was looking forward to making his move before the evening was out.

The captain yelled orders to the men, who, with no great hurry, organized themselves into marching order and began to move off. Progress along the track was halted almost immediately by a party of riders approaching at speed. The men on foot stood aside as the horsemen cantered along the centre of the track without so much as a sideways glance.

"Who in God's name is this?" asked Sir Henry, to no one in particular.

"I have no inkling sir," said the captain, "but they look to be carrying enough armour to equip a small army."

"I fear that is exactly what they are captain," said Sir Henry, who had a dreadful sense of foreboding about the new arrivals. Could it be that news of his lack of success had already reached his superiors? Whatever the motive behind this unexpected development, the grim expression on the face of the lead rider did not bode well.

There were half a dozen of them on tall military mounts, all breastplates and thigh-covering tassets, though the man in front was marked out not by his armour, of which he wore none, but by the austerity of his dress, which lacked both collar and cuff. He pulled up his horse in front of Sir Henry's mount and gave an eye to the house before speaking.

"You will be Sir Henry Bromely?"

"I am sir, and those are my men you just forced off the road."

The newcomer cast a glance over his shoulder. "On their way home are they? Can we presume then that your task is complete?"

The colour was rising in Sir Henry's cheeks; he had suffered enough impertinence over these past days. "Whatever my task might be I am hardly likely to report its results to persons unknown. Now who in blazes are you and what is your business here?"

The stranger did not even have the decency to look at him when he answered, for his eyes were fixed on the house again. "I am Jonathan Noyce, sir, officer of the king tasked with bringing his Catholic enemies to justice."

Like bolted claret, the colour immediately drained from Sir Henry's cheeks. "Jonathan *Noyce*? That cannot be. You are an *impostor*, sir."

The man pulled a parchment from his satchel. "This is a Royal warrant, bearing my name and the king's signature." He held it out to Sir Henry.

"But you cannot be Mr Noyce."

"Will you take the blasted warrant and examine it, sir. I am here to take over the search of the house. And your obstruction will go badly for you."

Sir Henry took the parchment and unrolled both it and the uncomfortable memory of the time when Mr Noyce – the other Mr Noyce – had refused to let him examine his warrant. Unfortunately, *this* document appeared to be genuine, but it was difficult to keep it from rolling up again while he used one hand to rub his aching neck.

"It looks, sir, as though your endeavours are taking their toll," observed the new arrival.

"There is many a draught in that old house," replied Sir Henry, "and they are not good for the bones." He looked up from the warrant and let out a curse at his own stupidity. "Hell's teeth, the draught!" He tossed the rolled parchment back to Noyce and, without a "by your leave", put spur to horse. He had not gone far before Noyce followed, beckoning his men to do the same.

*

Noyce's arrival might have caused Sir Henry considerable discomfort, but his appearance was having an equally dramatic effect on the watcher at the window. From there, he could only guess at the nature of the conversation which had just taken place. No doubt the luckless Sir Henry had explained how the man known to him as Jonathan Noyce had fallen into his company two weeks previously, not long after learning from a local informant that refugee plotters might be hiding in his county. In turn, Noyce would have explained that, after spending weeks searching Holbeach and nearby houses, he too had received word that the notorious Nicholas Owen and two priests, all of whom were suspected plotters, had been run to ground at Hindlip Hall.

With the men fast approaching, the watcher turned and began to run along the gallery, glancing through the windows as he passed them. Armed with Mrs Habingdon's information, which had already guided him to the four empty priest holes, his course was pre-determined. As though on ice, his boots skated across the boards and he turned into a smaller hallway before bursting through a door.

*

The pounding of feet, booted now, grew louder, striding across the floor in a fashion so determined that there could be little doubt about the final destination: his hiding place. All of a sudden, the ends of the earth seemed closer than Owen had imagined. With no weapon at hand he uttered a final prayer. But even now, as the light began to break in through the gap in the shifting timbers, it came to him that a locking device on the interior could prevent such an uninvited entry. But it was too late. There would be no more building projects. The enemy had breached his defences and he was about to be taken. He pressed himself against the back wall, determined to make his extrication as difficult as possible, and watched as the man who would be claiming bounty on him showed his face in the entrance.

"Mr Quick!" exclaimed Owen, scarcely able to believe his eyes. "Gads sir! I thought . . . I thought you were a priest hunter."

"There hangs a tale," said the breathless man in the aperture. "This is far too small," he said, shaking his head in disappointment at the sight of the crouching man on the other side. "There is barely room for one in there, let alone the two of us."

Owen had been holed up for so long, that the implication of this observation appeared to pass him by. "What of our friends?"

Quick tried to ignore the miasmic stench emanating from the freshly exposed hiding place. "Never mind them. We have enemies a plenty about to enter the house. We need another hiding place. As the house seems riddled with them I trust you can oblige?"

Owen nodded. "I was not far from trying to remove myself from here to there, when you made your entrance."

"Then we must move quickly," said the man, who for days had been known as Mr Noyce but was now answering to Mr Quick. After checking that the coast was still clear, he reached in a hand and pulled the hunchback from his refuge. "The silver, you have the silver?"

In response, Owen produced a bag, which he had some difficulty lifting. Quick took it from him and closed the hole behind them. As they moved off with Owen in the lead, it was obvious that days of confinement and immobility had taken their toll. He was limping along on stiff limbs, when a sprint was required. Quick, perhaps eager to live up to his true name, did what he could to help him along and speed their progress.

Quick served as crutch to his companion and struggled to keep a grip on the bag as they hobbled down the hall. At the top of the stairs they halted, the sound of raised voices giving away the presence of men in the vestibule below. But there was also a woman's voice. It was Mrs Habingdon delivering a tongue-lashing. "Mr Noyce has been in my house for these three days past, prying into crack and crevice and now you tell me that *this* is Mr Noyce? Have you lost your senses Sir Henry, or are you incapable of telling one man from another? It bodes poorly sir for the execution of justice in this county, indeed it does!"

They did not wait to hear Sir Henry's reply, and thanks to the ever resourceful lady of the house and her raised voice, knew better than to descend the stairs. "This way," whispered Owen, gesturing along the landing. With the movement returning to his legs he guided them to the rear of the house to a more modest set of stairs. "For the use of the servants," he said as they made their way down. Quick glanced out of a window and was perturbed to see any chance of slipping out through a back door denied them, as soldiers took up fresh positions in the rear court. On reaching the ground floor they disappeared down another flight of stairs and entered into the under-croft.

*

Sir Henry was the first to enter the room but Noyce, still unaware of the reason for the Justice's agitation, was not far behind. Although in disarray, the bed-chamber was an elegant room, which was why Sir Henry had commandeered it on his arrival at the house. Garments lay scattered throughout, but in the absence of his man-servant and dresser – and Mrs Habingdon's unwillingness to provide such – how could he be expected to keep the place in order? The drapes hanging from the beams of the four-poster were billowing like sails in the wind. Sir Henry drew his sword and approached the bed. He pulled back one of the drapes and let out a gasp.

Noyce lifted an edge of the thin wooden panel before letting it fall back on to the bed. With sword drawn Sir Henry climbed up on to the bed, cracking the panel in two as he set his feet upon it. At the head of the bed there was a hole in the wall, which had been exposed by the removal of the panel. Sitting a small distance back from the panel's frame were sturdier timbers, sitting one on top of the other like the planks in the hull of a boat. These had been pulled aside to reveal a dark chasm through which a draught of cold air was blowing.

"Your room I presume?" said Noyce, as he kicked aside a large night-shirt while securing a view into the exposed hiding place.

Sir Henry was standing on his own pillows and peering into the darkness. He said nothing.

Noyce could barely disguise the contempt in his voice. "Then one of them was hiding less than an arm's length away from where you have been resting your head at night."

Sir Henry put a hand to his neck and replied bitterly, "That would appear to be the case. And thanks to this damned draught I can now barely move my head on my shoulders."

If Noyce was wondering how Sir Henry could have failed to notice the draught previously, the sound of an empty bottle falling from under one of the pillows was enough to provide an answer. "Let us hope, sir, that your head stays on your shoulders. The king will not look kindly on failure in this matter."

*

Owen and Quick tip-toed past the busy kitchen, where a soldier could be heard working his charm on one of the serving girls. They approached the pantry, where the day before Mrs Habingdon had directed Quick to an unoccupied hiding place. Small it may have been, but his "discovery" of that cubby-hole – along with several others, in the company of Sir Henry – had done much to impress the Justice of his reliability. The scheme had almost worked: he had succeeded in passing himself off as the country's most celebrated priest hunter, had all but convinced Mrs Habingdon of his allegiance to her own cause and, with the soldiers out of the way, stood every chance of getting the silver off the premises. But all that had been spoiled by the appearance of Noyce.

Gratifying as it was that their destination was not the dreadfully tight space in the pantry, this more accommodating space in the scullery next door was still considerably smaller and more uncomfortable then even the rudest cell in the Tower. While incarcerated here, his devout companion had his rosary beads and prayers to keep his mind occupied, but Quick needed more than incantations and baubles to distract him from the closeness of the walls. When what he had always considered to be a long line of female conquests proved only long enough to provide a pitifully brief distraction, his thoughts turned to the events of the past few weeks.

*

The taking of Guido Fawkes and his powder, sitting unburned within the confines of hoop and stave, had been only the beginning. The plot involved a dozen or more conspirators at its heart, and many more with knowledge of it. Under instruction from the Spanish Ambassador in London, Quick arrived at Huddington Court, where, with his impeccable references he was accepted into the company of thirty or more conspirators and supporters; despite being grateful for that, he couldn't help look down on them for their naive lack of suspicion. In the event of the plot's success, which required king and parliament by then to be blown to the high heavens, this meeting would have seen the formation of an army. At that moment their numbers were small, but spurred on by success there would have been determination and money enough to expand their ranks a thousandfold.

But king and parliament, being alive to do so, went to great lengths to broadcast their survival and to expose the plot as a failure. It was a state of affairs which made these thirty or more – not first recruits, but a gang of desperados – hell-bent on saving their own skins. It would have been good to complete his business there at a time when, at least for a man who knew his business, escape was still a straightforward matter. But the opportunity did not arise, for it was panic not planning which now dictated the course of events. Some of the conspirators had already been taken, while those with weaker resolve had given themselves up only to find their pleas for mercy falling on deaf ears.

If it were not bad enough that the king's men were casting their nets, the Catholics too, through the mouthpiece of the Archpriest Father Blackwell, were falling over themselves to damn the conspirators as traitors, while professing their unswerving loyalty to the king. Fearful that their rendezvous was compromised, Sir Robert Catesby, the chief conspirator, gave the order for departure. Some went their own way, melting into the night, but Quick had no option but to join the leaders. Their next destination was to be Holbeach House on the border with Staffordshire, and so, early in the morning of November the seventh, the party, in sombre mood, stepped out into heavy rain. Weapons previously intended for use in the uprising were now carried for personal protection, and as much powder as could be carried was transported along with the muskets in an open wagon. Though he kept a watchful eye out for their pursuers, Quick took time to study his companions carefully, looking for any sign of the documents which were the subject of his mission. But with cloaks tightly wrapped against the rain it was difficult to see who might be carrying what.

On arriving at Holbeach the following evening, the men, who were by now much reduced in numbers, heard mass said by one of the two priests in their company, made confession and set about fortifying the place. The priests and one other, the crook-backed Nicholas Owen, left soon after. Their horses were laden with the saddlebags containing the silver coins which, with a fairer wind, would have financed the uprising. It was obvious to Quick that those of his companions who remained had no intention of being taken as, in preparation for what must surely be their last stand, the wagon was unloaded and the weapons distributed. Jesuits and plotters may have it in them to be martyrs but their cause was not his. Though a clean death in battle was always preferable to the lingering agonies of torture, neither particularly appealed to Quick and so, without drawing attention to his actions, he spent what little time there was left working out a way of escape. The courtyard to the front of the house was a death trap and the back gave on to open fields, easily covered by well-deployed musketeers. The best hope lay to the side of the house where the woods were closest, and a loosened window would provide an exit. Offering to check the approaches to the house, he used the opportunity to conceal his horse among the trees.

He returned as dawn rose, to be rewarded with a glimpse of the leather-bound bundle being examined by Catesby, in the company of fellow conspirators Digby and Rockwood. Now unfastened, the package revealed a series of parchments, which Quick was certain represented the coded agreement between the plotters and those among the Spanish court who wished to cause mischief between the Royal houses of Spain and England.

"These shall be of little help to us now," said Catesby as he spread the half dozen or so documents across the table, rubbing his fingertips over the ornate seals and reading the contents as nothing but lost opportunities.

"Perhaps they may serve as passports," said Digby, a man whom Quick had previously observed to be armed with an optimistic demeanour. "The king would have an interest in their contents and so we might trade them for our lives."

Catesby rolled up the parchments and tied off the bundle. "You shall require no passport to enter through the gates of heaven, Mr Digby. Now, gentlemen, shall we break our fast and see what the day holds?"

"Two hundred men is what the day holds," said Quick, as he stepped out of the shadows at the edge of the room. "They are no more than an hour away and, from their line of march, know well their destination."

Catesby stepped back from the table, leaving the bundle where it lay. "I for one intend to be here to greet them." He strode towards the door, but paused before leaving. "From your continued presence I can only assume that each of you intends to do the same." Digby and Rookwood nodded but Quick had taken care to step back into the shadows. "Then so be it. Make sure the men know their places."

There was a flurry of activity as the doors were bolted and the part-finished barricades of furniture completed. Quick joined the others in the main hall to find the Wright brothers breaking open casks of gunpowder. While Kit Wright took an axe to the barrels Jack Wright distributed the piles of dark powder across a sheet laid out in front of the fireplace.

Quick was horrified to see a healthy fire blazing in the grate not half a pace away from the carpet of powder. "What in god's name are you doing?" he asked, being careful to remain at a distance.

Kit took a pause from his labours and propped himself on the handle of the axe. "The rain has soaked the powder. We should have transported it in a covered wagon."

"And by this do you intend to dry it or blow us all to hell?"

"What choice do we have?" said Kit, who was pushing the powder around with all the nonchalance of a baker working flour. "The enemy are upon us and we have not a usable grain."

"Perhaps we should have sent you rather than Fawkes to blow up the Houses of Parliament? If this exercise is anything to go by, I doubt whether a single stone would have been left standing."

With their task complete, the brothers turned their attention to a large chest which Catesby instructed them to move to a window. Meanwhile, Rookwood, who was cutting fresh matches for the muskets, wandered over to check the condition of that powder which had been lying for the longest time. Quick had seen enough madness for one day and, with everyone occupied, he returned to the parlour, where the bundle was lying unattended. He had no sooner picked it up when there was an almighty roar and the shock of an explosion powerful enough to rattle the glass in the window panes.

Quick hurried back into the hall, where through a cloud of acrid smoke he could only vaguely make out the scene of devastation. After a few moments the grey veil rolled back to reveal a gaping hole in the floor where the powder had been. Flames licked over the charred boards at the crater's edge and several pieces of furniture were on fire. Writhing bodies littered the room and the cries of men provided a high-pitched echo to the explosion. Those unharmed in the blast, which thankfully had been limited in scale by the diffuse spread of the powder on the floor, attended their injured colleagues.

Rookwood was among the casualties; his clothes were torn to rags and his flesh blackened, but with help he was able to stand. A man called John Grant had not been so fortunate; his face was badly burned and it would be a while longer before it was realized that his eyes has been scorched out of their sockets. Catesby too was burned about the face, though after the application of a water-soaked rag it became apparent that his eyes were unaffected. Quick assisted with the injured but only after pulling the parchments from the bundle and tossing each of them into the heart of a fire which, if not quickly attended to, would engulf the entire house. The Wright brothers went for water but Quick was satisfied that the incriminating parchments were burned to ashes well before they returned to quench the flames.

"It must have been a spark from the fire," said a sheepish Jack as he emptied a pail, and stamped at the smouldering rug beneath his feet.

"Well who could have predicted such a thing?" replied Quick, who had decided it was time to leave.

With the fire under control and those of the wounded still capable of fighting back on their feet, the final preparations were made. The muskets were loaded with the small amount of dry powder removed from the pile before the explosion, and the men took up their positions behind doors and windows. All of them, that is, apart from Quick, who took the opportunity to climb through the window at the side of the house and made good his escape. There was just enough time for him to make it to his horse and retire a little further into the woods before the first of the troops arrived. Making for higher ground, he took up a position which allowed him a view of the scene below.

He watched as the soldiers encircled the house, leaving their horses picketed at a safe distance, before moving forward to engage. One of their number – their commander, he supposed – entered the courtyard at the front of the house and yelled something. The men were too far away to make out the words, but he guessed that they were an order to the occupants to give themselves up. An answer was shouted back but again he couldn't make it out, though he didn't need to. On hearing it, the officer left the courtyard just in time for his men to open a withering fire on the façade of the house.

The crack of musketry echoed from all quarters, even from those where there were no opponents to return it. But, at the front of the house, puffs of smoke were emitted from the barricaded windows as the defenders began to use up the powder for which they had paid such a heavy price. In the ensuing minutes, one or two of the attackers fell, but with their overwhelming numbers there could be only one outcome. Then, perhaps in their determination to take as many of their foes with them as possible, the defenders opened the front door and three of them dashed into the courtyard, discharging muskets and pistols as they headed for the gate. He thought he recognized Tom Wintour out in the lead, with the Wright brothers close behind. It was a suicidal enterprise and Wintour was the first to fall, clutching his shoulder as he went down. Both of the brothers fell soon after; the last to fall – Kit, he thought – made a desperate attempt to crawl to his brother before being struck by another ball.

Quick watched as soldiers entered into the yard and cautiously made their way to the door, some of them checking on the condition of their fallen foes as they did so. The Wright brothers must have been dead, as they were left where they lay, but Wintour was pulled to his feet and dragged back through the gate. Wintour would live to regret his survival, thought Quick, as he finally spurred his horse away from the house and its doomed inhabitants.

He rode away from the sound of muffled gunshots coming from inside the house, content at a job well done. But he should have known better than to let his guard down, for he had travelled no further than a half mile from the house when his path was crossed by a party of horsemen, who seemed determined not to let him proceed. He laid a hand on the woollen blanket lying across the front of his saddle and took comfort from the two holstered pistols concealed beneath.

"Sir, you come from the direction of Holbeach," said one of the men, though whether this were intended as a statement of fact or a question, Quick was not quite sure. He decided on the latter, as the fellow had an interrogative manner about him – his eyes roving inquisitively, and his thin lips framing a tongue untainted by any flavour of sympathy. In short, he looked accustomed to asking questions of his fellow man and receiving answers.

"Indeed I do," answered Quick. "But it is not a place I would recommend to the casual visitor at this time."

"There are times when a man needs to travel towards the sound of guns," came the response, the man briefly standing on his stirrups so as better to hear the crack of musketry still coming from the direction of the house. "And I would say from the look of you that you have soldiered yourself. Flanders perhaps?"

"Aye, I have seen service. But a man is always wise to put such excitements behind him while he still can."

"There are many who would agree with you sir. Might I ask your name?"

"Indeed you might but I would expect yours in return."

"A fair bargain, and as a show of good faith why don't I offer mine first. I am Jonathan Noyce, a servant of King James, whose royal person was so rudely endangered not two days past."

Quick knew of the man – his reputation as the country's most successful priest taker was second to none – the mere mention of his name was enough to put the fear into any Catholic. "In which case Holbeach is most likely to be your destination. From what I have just heard, there are enough Papists hiding there to keep you in business for some time to come."

"You are well informed sir, but alas you remain a well-informed stranger, for your side of the bargain has yet to be met."

"I am Peter Quick, one time soldier, as you so correctly surmised, but now making ends meet in the wool trade."

"You had cause to be at Holbeach?"

Quick shook his head. "I had hoped to discuss this year's fleeces but found the house besieged and was informed by a soldier that the traitors responsible for the attempt on the king's life were holed up within. In the circumstances it did not strike me as the most profitable port of call for a man in my trade."

"And I trust you are no friend of the Catholic?"

"I care not which religion a man chooses to secure his entry into heaven but when it comes to assassination and treachery in the name of God, then that is a different matter."

Noyce had spent the whole time studying Quick. "You certainly do not meet the description of the men we are seeking. In which case we shall let you pass. We shall not rest until we have brought each and every one of the plotters to justice. No matter where they hide, I shall find them. But be warned, sir, this is no time to be seen expressing sympathy towards Papists."

"Your words shall be heeded, sir. As for your searches, I wish you well and would now be pleased to be let by. I have lost business already today and can ill afford losing any more."

As Quick rode away the relief of evading capture quickly evaporated, and to his alarm there remained an ominous sense of entrapment. It took him only a little time more to realize that his involvement in the affair was far from over. With the tenacious Noyce now on the plotter's trail, it could only be a matter of time before those not killed or captured at Holbeach were taken, and any incriminating materials in their possession recovered. Paramount among these concerns were those blasted priests and the plotter's treasury. If Noyce and his men reached them before he did, then all his efforts thus far would be in vain. He had no option but to ignore his own advice and ride towards where the sound of their guns might soon be heard.

*

"All of this is your handiwork?" asked Quick of their new surroundings. The move had been as sudden as it had been unexpected. Once satisfied that the way was clear, Owen had led them in an early dawn dash from their hiding place to the nearby kitchen, where the removal of the stone slab beneath the cooking hearth revealed the entrance to a tunnel.

Owen's shake of the head was barely perceptible in the lamplight. "I cannot claim credit. This is an old drain, built to carry water from the moat which once surrounded the house. They filled in the ditch long ago but this was left behind."

Out of sight, out of mind, thought Quick; if only the same rule applied to them. The moat may have long gone but the tunnel was still damp, and in places water trickled through the green slime covering the walls.

Owen knew full well that if they were to stand any chance of escaping the house, then the tunnel was their only hope. With Noyce on the job it would be only a matter of time before their hiding place was discovered and, with or without him on their scent, Quick was only too happy to leave the confines of those dreadful walls. They continued their passage for what seemed an age, before the closely bonded bricks gave way to timber walls. "I dug this part," said Owen. "Surfacing at the end of the original drain would place you in open ground, so I extended it."

They had not been in the wooden portion of the tunnel long when progress came to a halt. Owen climbed a short distance up a ladder and opened a trapdoor just wide enough to let in a chink of light and to allow him to check the way out was clear.

The trapdoor was concealed within the earth floor of a smithy. The blacksmith was absent, but the coals in his forge were content enough to give off a gentle glow without him. Owen closed the hatch while Quick took in his surroundings. Dozens of horseshoes, great and small, were hanging from nails in the beams above their heads; the middle of the floor was occupied by an anvil resting its heavy weight on a block of wood, and the many tools of the blacksmith's trade were scattered about.

Placing the bag of coins on the anvil Quick crossed to a window and, peering out, was relieved to see nothing more than an empty yard, overlooked by a few ramshackle sheds. The tunnel had put a good musket shot between them and the house, but he would have been even happier to see a pair of horses tethered close by. The best hope seemed to rest with the long building on the other side of the yard, which from the halved doors looked to be a stable.

"There are still two men in the house," said Owen.

"I think there will be a good few more than two in there now."

"I mean the priests, Mr Quick. The men who accompanied me in the flight from Holbeach House."

Quick let the sacking drop back across the window. "Do they have coin, or any other materials of importance with them?"

"They have nothing but food and drink with them, and precious little of that. All of the money was left in my charge. Its presence seemed to make them uncomfortable."

"They would learn to feel more at home with it as bishops," said Quick, trying not to let his relief at the answer show. "But there will be no chance of promotion now. You know as well as I that they will be taken before long. We must look to our own salvation, which I fear is far from assured."

Owen was standing beside the anvil and casually brushing his fingers across the crescentic ridges created by the coins in the bag. "Could we not buy their liberty? This was intended to finance a rebellion, to pay for the taking of lives. Could it not be put to a better use and pay for their lives?"

In what appeared to be an almost involuntary action Quick pressed down on the bellows and momentarily excited the coals in the forge. "Silver might help a man remain at liberty," he said, watching the flames die away before pressing down again. "It will fix safe passage at sea or secure victuals enough for the voyage, but it will not buy back liberty once lost, at least not when the shackles have been fastened around the limbs of a failed assassin of the king." He pressed the bellows once more before stepping towards the anvil. "But I am afraid there is another reason why your friend's captors will not be receiving their thirty pieces of silver." With that he removed the bag from Owen's caress. "The coins are coming with me."

Owen took a step back as though offended. "But my instructions were to ensure that the money be put to the service of our cause."

"That cause is lost."

Owen looked confused. "We do not know that. Others may have made good their escape. We should decide together to what use the money could be put."

"Believe me, Mr Owen, the cause is lost. I saw some killed and others taken at Holbeach House, and today the same is going to happen here. As you said, this money was to finance a rebellion. With the survival of the king there will be no rebellion, and so the money will go along with me."

"Without authority such an act would be thievery. Is that what you are, Mr Quick, a common thief? You arrived in our company late and seemed to be a stranger to all. Did you join us merely so that you might profit from the failure of the exercise? There is money enough there to make you a very rich man, Mr Quick."

"If I was a thief, I would have killed you before now."

"I do not believe you would have, sir, not while you needed me to get you out of the house."

Quick recalled the lengths to which he had gone to keep the searchers away from Owen. "Let us not debate who got who out of the house. I have been tasked with the recovery of those coins. They are to be returned to the donor unspent, that is all."

"So you are an agent of the Spanish?"

"Yes, but not those of whom you are thinking."

"I do not understand. The Spanish provided the funds for the rising. Those are silver reales in that bag. How can you talk of—"

There was a noise from the yard. Quick guessed it to be the scrape of a spur against a cobblestone. He put his forefinger to his lips and gestured for Owen to conceal himself beside the brick chimney. Dashing to the window he looked out to see two soldiers, muskets canted over their shoulders, wandering in a casual fashion across the yard. They were checking the buildings for fugitives; one would wait by the door while the other entered briefly, before returning with a shake of the head. A glance at Quick's face as he moved away from the window was all Owen needed to know that their prospects had taken a down-turn. Any uncertainty about how bad things were was immediately dispelled when he was ordered to reopen the trapdoor.

"We are to return to the house?"

"We can hide in the tunnel while they search this place."

"But we won't be able to properly conceal the lid from below," said Owen, as ever the perfectionist.

"It is a risk we must take, now get the cursed thing open."

With his feet on the ladder Owen began his short descent, but his head had barely disappeared from view when, like a

Jack-in-a-box, it popped back up into the room. "There are men in the tunnel!" he gasped, as he cleared the hole.

"Noyce," spat Quick. "He has found the entrance. The man lives up to his reputation, damn him."

There could be no doubting it. Quick, who was now lying on the floor and peering into the tunnel, could see a lantern moving towards them, perhaps half way along the tunnel. His head was barely clear of the void when a shot rang out. With the trapdoor slammed shut he dashed to the anvil. Owen saw his intent and, without bidding, joined him to lift the heavy lump of iron. With the anvil lowered on to the closed trap door both men, anticipating the arrival of men below them, stood back. The move was a wise one, for, moments later, a ball exploded through the timber and embedded itself in the roof.

"One door closes," said Quick, as he returned to the window.

"And another door opens; isn't that how the proverb goes? I see only one other door. Are you really intending to go out there?"

"We have no choice. There are still very few men nearby. But we have to move quickly; news will be on its way out from the tunnel." Quick checked his weapons – the pair of horse pistols he had been careful to carry from the house. As he prepared them for firing, the door bowed inwards, the impact pushing out clouds of dust from between the boards. But it didn't give.

"Break it down," barked a voice from the outside.

There was a flash and a crack from Quick's pistol and a cry of pain from the man in front of the door, followed by the receding clatter of boots on cobbles. The return of fire was not long in coming. Musket-balls thudded into the outside wall, some of them punching narrow shafts of light into the building before bouncing off the back wall.

It was clear from the volume of incoming fire that more men had arrived in the yard. Quick let go another shot and made to reload his pistols, only to discover that there were just two more lead balls in his pouch. If their chances of escape were poor before, they were almost non-existent now. He returned his attention to the contents of the smithy.

"There is a crucible over there, which means there must be a shot-mould also."

Owen began to search a bench and its attendant shelves, rooting through tools and all manner of smithing paraphernalia. "Here it is, and also some lead," he said, handing over a fist-sized ingot.

With one hand working the bellows – forcefully this time – Quick continued to observe the movements of the men in the yard. There were many more of them now, some of them probably from the tunnel, from which there was little sign of activity. His next instruction came as a shock to Owen, even in their extraordinary circumstances. "Empty the coins into the crucible and put it on the coals."

"But you mean the lead sir, surely?"

Quick threw him a determined glance. "No, the coins, put the coins in the crucible. Do it now!"

"You have seen the devil out there, is that it. You need a silver bullet to kill him?"

"Something like that, now do it." Whether the unflappable Owen had spoken in jest or not, the reality wasn't that far from the truth, for Quick had just seen Noyce arrive with his men.

Owen reluctantly righted the upturned crucible and commenced to empty the coins into it, there was just a trickle at first, as though someone had cut a hole in a purse.

"All of them," yelled Quick.

The choke on the bag was released and a shower of silver fell into the bowl. Using a pair of tongs, Owen manoeuvred the heavily laden vessel into the coals, which were now glowing like the interior of a volcano thanks to Quick's continued effort with the bellows.

A second shot was delivered from the window, leaving Quick no option but to abandon the bellows while he reloaded with his last remaining shot.

"You said you were an agent of the Spanish," said Owen, picking up on their interrupted conversation.

"I am an agent in the service of his Catholic Majesty King Phillip of Spain," he said, dropping in a ball and ramming it down on to the powder. "His Majesty has no connection to those financing your rebellion."

"But surely they were members of the Royal court? I heard Sir Robert say as much."

Quick shook his head. "The men with whom your friends had dealings are a rebel group acting outside of the court." He took another shot with the pistol and grimaced as a ball passed through thin timber close to his head. "They are nobles who lost riches and influence when England and Spain signed a peace treaty not two years past. Their intention was to implicate the Spanish court in the plot and, in so doing, bring about another war."

Owen was stirring the half-melted coins with a knife, pushing the mass around the crucible as though it were thick gruel in a cooking pot. "And what then is your role in all of this?"

An hour ago Quick had no intention of explaining his mission, but the prospect of shared death draws men closer together than even the smallest of priest holes. "I have orders to remove all physical evidence of the plotters' dealings with the Spanish. At Holbeach House I destroyed the documents, and here," he waved a pistol towards the crucible, "you have just destroyed the last of that evidence."

Owen stared into the crucible, where the silver was now fully liquefied. "Of course, the coins. They are Spanish!"

"And they are not just any Spanish coins. They are fifty reale pieces, a coin minted only at the order of the king, for special use. Each of them carries the royal crest and is as incriminating as any document seal. But now they are reduced to anonymous silver and my work is done."

Owen was using a ladle to transfer some of the silver into the bullet mould. "Not quite I think, until . . . until you kill me. Should I be put to torture I am sure to mention the Spanish."

Another bullet came crashing into the room, ricocheted off the brick chimney and smashed an earthenware jug. "At the moment, it seems unlikely that we will live long enough to be captured. But, in any case, there would be no advantage in killing you, though you might thank me for doing so rather than let them drag it out. There are those who know as much as you who have allowed themselves to be taken. They will no doubt speak of the Spanish when they are tied to the rack, but James will not go to war over testimony given under torture, not without physical evidence to bolster it." He gave out a bitter laugh. "Indeed, should you recite all of this while on the rack, then it may do more good than harm. At least someone will be testifying in King Phillip's favour."

The men outside were getting closer, using the buildings to cover their approach around the sides of the yard. Quick let go another couple of shots, one of which brought down a man, but he knew there was to be no holding them back.

Owen had returned to stirring the silver. Indeed he seemed transfixed by it, staring with fixed eyes into the sluggish vortex, entirely oblivious to the ever increasing number of bullets flying around his head.

With his pistols loaded with silver, Quick pulled the door part-way open and looked back at his companion. "I am going to take the air, Mr Owen. Would you care to join me?"

"No thank you sir. I too have work to finish before this day is done."

There was no time to ask what he meant. "Very well then, I wish you godspeed, Mr Owen."

"And god bless you, sir."

Quick pulled the door fully open with his foot and stepped out into the yard. He fired one of the pistols, took a step forwards and fired the other, before falling back dead with two balls in his chest.

As Quick's body hit the ground, Owen was using the tip of an old scythe blade to scrape away at the hard packed dirt on the floor, scoring first one line and then another. The liquid silver spat and smoked as he poured it into the grooves. With the crucible empty, he smoothed the cooling metal with the flat of the blade. A quenching pale of water raised clouds of hissing steam, scorching the architect's naked hands. Although still warm, he was able to lift out the casting, brushing away dirt from the underside before holding it out in front of him. The edges were rough and ready, reflecting the makeshift nature of the mould, but then he was no silversmith. Approaching the door but remaining behind cover, he looked out to see Quick's body sprawled across the cobbles.

"I am unarmed' he called out to the musketeers, now leaving the protection of the buildings.

"Then yield!" came the shouted reply. "Stand where you can be seen."

Stepping outside, Owen stood over the body and for a moment watched the crimson channels of blood creeping between the cobbles. Then, reciting a prayer, he straightened Quick's legs and arms, kissed the middle of the large silver cross and laid it across the dead man's chest. He took a last look at his companion's face, which now wore the peaceful mask of a death nobly earned. Guilty of the sin of envy for the first time in his life, he crossed himself and turned to confront his advancing captors.

Historical note

Nicholas Owen and the powder-plot priests captured with him, were taken to the Tower of London where, like the rest of the conspirators, they were tortured. Owen's suffering was enhanced by his disability, and he was kept alive only through the application of a military breast plate, which prevented his intestines from spilling out of his body. With no confessions extracted, all of them were dragged to their place of execution, and there hanged until almost dead, before being disembowelled and cut into quarters. In 1970, Owen was canonized by the Catholic Church, and today is regarded by magicians and escapologists as their patron saint. On his death, in the grounds of Hindslip Hall, Peter Quick, agent to his Catholic Majesty Philip III of Spain, disappeared from the pages of history, as did what came to be known as the Quicksilver Crucifix. Thanks to Quick's efforts, England and Spain were to remain at peace with one another for over a hundred years.

The Fourth Quadrant

Dorothy Lumley

When not occupied as a literary agent with her Dorian Literary Agency, Dorothy Lumley writes romance novels and stories, usually under the name of Jean Davidson. Her latest historical romance is House of Secrets *(2010), and she also contributed the crime novel* Lost and Found *(2009) to the Black Star list, as Vivian Roberts. The following story marks her first appearance under her own name.*

For this anthology, Dorothy was fascinated with the life of Ada Lovelace, who was a mathematical genius, and daughter of Lord Byron. Ada became involved with Charles Babbage, the creator of the Difference Engine – regarded as the world's first computer – and assisted him in the creation of his new Analytical Engine. Although this was not completed, Ada's notes include what experts have called the first computer program. The following story takes place early in Ada's involvement with Babbage, in 1834, before she married William King, later the Earl of Lovelace.

Robert hefted the truncheon in his hand, feeling the warmth of the wood under his fingers. It was heavy, but then it needed to be to do this evening's work. Inwardly he sighed. It was not work that he enjoyed, and it was not why he had joined the newly formed Metropolitan Police. But, judging from the expressions of some of the men around him, they *were* looking forward to this night's work.

He cast his eyes over the police unit surrounding him. Some refused to meet his gaze. They were the nervous ones, often the youngest. Others, like him, had a set look that said: Come on, let's get started, get it over with, then we can go home to our wives and sweethearts. But some met his gaze with a wink and a smirk. They and their sticks and cudgels would get pleasure from this night's outing.

"All right Bob?" his friend Will, standing next to him, murmured.

"It still doesn't seem right, breaking up a peaceable meeting, just because they're talking about unions."

"You're in the Police now. Can't take sides. Anyway, Sergeant says this 'un's illegal."

"Right boys, time to move forward." Sergeant Cummings at last gave the order. Robert felt his pulse quicken. Gaslight flickered and hissed overhead — the lamplighters had already been abroad along Holborn and the Gray's Inn Road on this damp October evening. The usual hubbub of carriages and carts and hansom cabs all fighting it out in the London street carried on. But he and the rest of his unit were about to enter a dark and unlit alley, right on the edge of a notorious Rookery. *The* notorious Rookery, in fact, where most of the poor Irish lived. Fortunately, the White Hart public house they were heading for, where the meeting was being held in a back room, or so they'd been informed, was nearby.

"You six go into the yard in the back, lay into anyone who sneaks out that way." Sergeant Cummings picked the most eager-looking men. "Rest of you, follow me. Two short blasts on the whistle and we're in. Right, boys?"

A flicker of white caught Robert's eye as he moved into the alley behind Will. "Feargus O'Connor of the Northern Star and Robert Owen to speak concerning the Conditions and Plight of the Working Man . . . The Iniquity of the New Poor Law . . ." – he had to move on before he could read more of the poster. That would be a legitimate meeting, one they would not be called on to break up as had been happening so many times this past year all over the country. He hoped he might be sent on that detail, he'd like to hear the two great orators speak and, as he was expected to wear his police uniform at all times, he could hardly attend in his own right.

The two short blasts on the whistle reverberated down the dark alley. Already passers-by were jostling them and jeering and trying to knock their tall hats off. Any further into the Rookery and they would be in too much danger from the lawless folk who lived there, but here he could look back and see the safety of the well-lit London street – now, though, he was running forward, and found himself yelling, along with the others, as they charged into the meeting room at the back of the White Hart.

In the lamplight Robert had a glimpse of startled faces turned towards him, mouths open in shock and anger. Then the gathered men launched themselves forward. Robert staggered, but managed to keep his balance. It was every man for himself. He pushed and shoved, shouting all the while, "Outside, outside with you!", while dodging fists and blocking painful kicks.

Above the noise he could hear Sergeant Cummings blowing his whistle and commanding, "This illegal gathering is over. Go home or we'll have you in front of the magistrates in the morning."

"We're 'aving an educational meeting," came one gibe.

"Yeah, *you're* the ones breaking the law – the laws of justice and brotherhood!" came another.

The sergeant's reply was lost in the general mêlée. Robert felt a blow on the back of his head, his reinforced hat saving him from the worst of it. He settled the hat more firmly on his head and looked round for the culprit. At the far end of the room he saw a tall bearded man standing on a makeshift podium made of boxes and planks. He wore a black suit and top hat, his stock was fresh and white at his neck, while two men in working attire stood at his side. He was continuing to declaim, one hand raised above his head, to the struggling mass below. "Stand up, stand up against our oppressors . . . are we not free men . . . the right to order our own destiny . . . we should have the right to vote, not just those with money and power . . . This is an outrage against justice and natural law . . ."

Sergeant Cummings had managed to force his way through to the front and was reaching for the ankles of the speaker. The two men beside the speaker sprang into action, hustling him from the makeshift stage and through a door at the back of the room. Cummings did not follow them. His orders were to break up the meeting, with force, and he'd go no further.

Robert began to lay about him again, more in self-defence than attack. He felt rather than heard his truncheon crack here on a shoulder, there on a man's back. He didn't put all his strength in it, just enough to send a message. He, Robert, was still in control, unlike some of the others on both sides around him, their faces red and contorted, spittle flying.

But, with the speaker gone, those who had been listening to him were losing their steam and there was a mass exodus for the door. Robert tried to stand back, but, unprepared, received an elbow in his stomach which took his breath away. He doubled over, coughing and retching. It was in that moment that he felt a hand shoved hard inside his tunic then as quickly withdrawn, but when he looked up all he could see were men's backs and the heels of their boots.

"Will, Will," Robert called out, catching sight of his friend. He instinctively pushed his own hand into his tunic. "I think I've been stabbed!"

Through both of their minds ran the memory of Calthorpe, the policeman killed only a year ago during a similar confrontation. Will hurried to his side; he had lost his hat in the affray, his hair was dishevelled and there was a smear of blood on his cheek. "All right, Rob, my friend, where's he cut you?" he asked as he supported him.

"In my chest I think. He stuck his hand right in." With trembling fingers he undid the remaining brass buttons that had not been wrenched off in the fight "Funny thing is, it doesn't hurt at all."

As the last button came undone, a piece of crumpled and folded paper fell to the floor.

"What's that?" Will asked, bending to pick it up and handing it to Robert.

Robert shook his head. "I don't know." He ran his hand over his shirt, then couldn't help laughing. "I'm not hurt at all. Must've been pushing that bit of paper in. I've got the wind up me right and proper."

"You and me both, mate." Will squeezed his shoulder. "Reckon we deserve some ale after this. Maybe a visit to a chop house. Coming?"

"Good idea." Robert automatically began unfolding the piece of paper. Why would someone have gone to the trouble of pushing this on him? The same person who elbowed him in the stomach so he couldn't see their face?

"What the heck's that?" Will asked, looking over his shoulder. "Looks like a lot of nonsense to me."

They gazed at a jumble of letters, numbers and pictures. "This here's Egyptian writing." Robert pointed to hieroglyphs. "I've seen them in the British Museum. I can't make any sense of it."

"Did he have mad staring eyes, the man who shoved it on you?"

"Go on." Robert poked his friend in the ribs. "No more than you do! All the same, I think I'll pass this on to the Sergeant. It might mean something, though I don't know what."

"Another one of your hunches. All right, and then we're off duty and can go for our supper."

Robert nodded. Once he'd handed the paper over, it was no longer his responsibility and Sergeant Cummings could decide what to do with it.

★

Ada stared at her breakfast plate. Half a slice of toast was left. If she cut it in tiny squares and chewed each one as long and as slowly as she could, she would be able to complete the task she'd set herself at the same time as finishing her toast. Why was the 47 times-table such a tricky one? She continued reciting it in her mind. Although she tried to stop them, her lips kept trying to form the numbers, but chewing the toast helped hide that.

Across the table, her mother rustled *The Times* newspaper and gave a noise of disgust. Ada tried to shut out the sound, and speeded up her mental exercise. With her mother's three friends all taking their breakfasts in bed, claiming they'd come down with autumnal colds, she'd seized advantage of her freedom from having to respond to their remarks about the weather, or the minutiae of the life lived by their Mortlake neighbours, to allow her mind to continue to play with numbers. She enjoyed not having their eyes constantly watching her, checking her behaviour and how much she ate. Her mother's watchdogs – whom to herself she called the Three Furies.

Her mother gave another snort of rage, folded the newspaper and tossed it down. It was no good, she'd only reached 47 times 23, and her mother was about to launch into a tirade.

"Yet another one of these meetings by those uncouth ruffians usurping the name of Robert Owen for their own ends. When are the government going to put a stop to it? That's what I want to know. The Police Force had to go in and break it up when they should have been out on the streets catching thieves and murderers. And it's my taxes that pay for that. It will give the Co-operative movement a bad name, and set back all the good work of Owen, and Feargus O'Connor with his Northern Star newspaper." She thumped the pink tablecloth for emphasis, making the silver spoons rattle in their delicate Crown Derby porcelain saucers. Ada sensed the footman wincing as he feared for the whole breakfast service.

"Their meeting place, some tavern or other, was set fire to; only the quick thinking of the Metropolitan Police managed to put it out. Irish malcontents or extreme radicals, that's what they were. You'd think that the example set by what happened to those farm-workers in Dorset would have been enough to deter them, whether you think their fate was the right thing or not, but, oh no—"

"Tolpuddle. They were from Tolpuddle, Dorset. Twenty men sentenced to transportation to Australia for seven years' apiece. In March this year," Ada said.

"Yes, yes, I know all that. Don't interrupt me." Her mother settled her lace cap more firmly on her dark hair, then fixed her fierce eyes on Ada. "The point I'm making, Ada dear, is that some unscrupulous men, pretending to be allied to O'Connor and Owen and Cobbett, with their talk of combining into unions, are instead using the common man for their own ends, not for his good. Their purpose is to destabilize the government and bring down the monarchy. They want to incite the mobs into a rabble running through the streets of London, burning and pillaging. Why, they're nothing but . . . but Republicans!"

The word hung dangerously in the air. This was the spectre her mother hated and feared the most. Would England become infected by the Revolutions of 1830?

"I believe they only talk of rights and wages and conditions, Mama, not of – of that," Ada said. "Especially as the Reform Act has not extended suffrage very much."

"And what right do they have to question the natural order of things? The men who run the factories and mines bring prosperity, jobs and advance for everyone. They should be praised, not attacked."

Ada pushed her plate away, abandoning the last two small squares of toast. She would not complete her task now. "They create wealth through their knowledge and daring, and invention. They carry the risk with their own money. Without them there would be no jobs, and starving families. A logical equation, it seems." This was what her tutors taught her, even though the words sometimes had a hollow ring. Her mother espoused the Co-operative Movement, yet still feared what she called the "ungoverned elements".

"And another thing." As usual her mother didn't listen to her, and her tirade was not yet over. "Here we are, spending money building workhouses for the poor to give them shelter and food – again out of my taxes – and yet they've done nothing but complain about them for the past two years."

Ada looked around their comfortable breakfast room. The walls were a delicate shade of *eau de nil* and white, with mouldings of fruit and flowers. A coal fire burned in the grate, and they sat at a walnut table. Everything in this room spoke of good taste and good quality – and money. Money her mother had inherited. Servants stood, unmoving, by the wall, ready to fulfil any order their mistress might have.

Ada had seen, by contrast, illustrations of workhouses, with their bare stone walls and high windows, and had read how men and women were separated and that families were not allowed to live together. But she must not think about those things. For that way madness lay, and her mother did everything she could, for her daughter's own good, to keep her from the possibility of that downward spiral . . .

"Lady Byron, a message for Miss Ada." The footman, John, had entered carrying a silver tray on which lay a small white envelope.

Ada knotted her fingers together under the table and squeezed them, starting to count backwards from one hundred, to stop herself from feeling faint. She was not angry that her mother now read all her invitations first – "It really is for your own good." She felt herself flush at the memory of last year's folly. She felt again William's caresses, his kisses – the adventurous thrill as they planned their elopement. Quickly, having counted back to one, she focused on *The Times*'s headlines, reading upside-down:

"October 1834", she read, then made out the words "King William and the Royal Party . . . Wellington . . ."

"It's from our friend Charles Babbage." Her mother's pursed lips had broken into a smile. "He requests your company today to stimulate his mind in the discussion of logarithms and calculus."

Ada held her breath and squeezed her fingers even tighter.

"I suppose I can let you go today. It is Saturday, and you are far enough ahead in your studies, your tutors tell me. But tonight is Lady Conway's Ball, a fancy dress masque, so be sure you're back in plenty of time to prepare for it."

Ada managed to hold in her shriek of pleasure, but couldn't stop herself clapping her hands. "Shall I wear my new red dress, Mama?"

"It goes well with your dark hair, and you might be seen while in the carriage, so, yes."

What have I done to deserve such a day, Ada wondered as she left the breakfast room, giving a skip as she crossed the threshold. She was wanted, she was needed, and by the one man in whose company she could release all her passion for mathematics and know she would be understood. They could share their love for the arithmetical world. Furthermore, she would wear her new dress, and tonight there was her favourite – a fancy dress ball.

As she passed through the drawing room, her eyes slid over the painting above the fireplace which was covered by a green curtain. It was a portrait of her father, but she had never defied her mother's wishes and looked at it. She did not want to gaze into the face of that wicked darkness . . .

*

"Welcome, welcome, my dear Ada." Charles Babbage held out his hands in greeting and she felt their warmth coursing through her. His black wavy hair framed an attractive face with a fresh complexion. He was of medium build, with strong shoulders. "Is that a new dress? Most becoming."

Ada smoothed down the folds of red silk decorated with yellow flowers. The sleeves were fashionably widely puffed at the shoulder and the skirt flared from the high waist, finishing just above her ankles. It had not creased in the journey from Mortlake to Marylebone.

"Let me ring for refreshments – hot chocolate? – and then I'll show you the equations I've been working on, which only my mathematical muse will be able to fully appreciate."

Ada took a chair beside the glowing mahogany table which was strewn with Charles's papers. One wall of the room was lined with books covering all the sciences. There was a miniature cosmology on a side table, given to him by his friend the astronomer Herschal, showing the position of the planets around the sun. Around the room were various inventions both abandoned and in progress, such as the shoes for walking on water, and instruments for examining eyes. But towering above them all was the Difference Engine, awaiting its move into the new building next door, created especially for it and paid for by public funds. Solid and foursquare, with its brass columns and cogs, its ivory numbers and black plates, it seemed to Ada to be a machine in waiting, longing to have its mechanisms clicking and slotting into place and providing answers at astonishing speed to those mathematical sums it took the human brain so long to work out. If only Charles could persuade the government to release more money for its development.

As soon as she'd heard about it – the machine that was the talk of London society – she'd longed to see it, but her mother had at first refused. Then, finally, when she'd gone to see it on one of Charles's Open Days, she had understood it instantly, and she and Charles had recognized each others' passion for the world of numbers. And now she had another dream. She was eighteen, soon to be nineteen, but when she was twenty-one – surely, then, he would hire her as his official assistant.

As they bent their heads over pages of diagrams and figures, forgotten chocolate congealing in its cup, Ada sensed that this was as much an escape for Charles as it was for her. He grieved still for the loss of three of his sons – following that of his wife – and very recently her namesake, his daughter Georgiana. But in the pure precision, the light and air of mathematics, they were given respite from worldly emotions. Charles Babbage, inventor, mathematician, astronomer, and – yes, surely – his able assistant, Ada.

The knock on the door made them both jump.

"Mr Clark, Under Secretary to the Home Secretary, wishes to see you." Barely had Charles's manservant spoken, than a tall thin man was pushing his way past him, followed by a young stocky man in the dark blue uniform of the Metropolitan Police. When he saw Ada, the young man removed his tall hat and placed it under his arm, and then took up a position standing at ease beside the door.

"I apologize for intruding Mr Babbage," Clark said. There was a gleam of excitement in his pale blue eyes and this, with an agitation in his manner, gave a sense of urgency. "We met at dinner at the Prime Minister's house."

"I do recall it, yes. Some Madeira wine perhaps?" Charles nodded to his manservant, who withdrew. "Sit down, sit down." Charles waved a hand towards a chair, but Clark continued striding about the room, casting glances at the Difference Engine.

"I need to consult with you over a Government matter," Clark said. "Can it be now?" He looked at Ada.

"May I introduce Miss Ada Byron, my assistant in all things?"

"Miss Byron!" Clark took her hand and bowed his head. "I am sure I can speak freely in front of you," he said, then rushed on. "I remember well how you talked about ciphers and codes, Mr Babbage, and how you are amassing notes to write a book on them."

Charles exchanged glances with Ada, his face lighting up. "Indeed. I have a short paper in preparation already, and I exercise my mind regularly by attempting to decipher the codes used in *The Times* personal column. Some messages are easily solved, but others prove wonderfully challenging."

"I knew you were the right man to see this, and to tell us – is it some kind of code, or is it gibberish? And if it is indeed a code or cipher, can you break it to reveal its secrets? I thought perhaps the Engine could help us."

Ada held her breath. Charles could be very touchy on the matter of the Difference Engine. But he laughed. "The purpose of my machine is to help us with speed and accuracy in reaching mathematical answers. It cannot make those leaps of judgement that the human mind can. And at the moment, it cannot even make those mathematical sums. I am thinking of a new Analyser but without the money that—"

"What codes are you talking about, Mr Clark?" Ada interrupted him, to distract Charles from the subject of research funding.

"Ah yes. Constable Duckett, step forward and give your account of last night's events at the White Hart tavern near Holborn, and give Mr Babbage the piece of paper."

Ada noticed that the young policeman was not intimidated by his surroundings. He was clean-shaven, and he'd made an attempt to slick down his springy brown hair. His eyes were a darker blue than Clark's.

"That was the Union meeting where there was a fire," Ada said. "Mama was reading about it in the paper this morning."

"A lamp was dropped, but the flames were quickly put out, Miss," the constable told her, then continued. "But just before then, towards the end of the fracas, when the men attending the meeting was dispersing, I received a blow to the stomach and then this here paper was pushed inside my tunic. At first I thought I was stabbed, but then I found this piece of paper. Because I was bent over I did not see who put it there. I decided to give it to the Sergeant in case it was important."

"Bravo," Charles said, and took the piece of paper. "Did you see anything of the man who gave this to you?"

Constable Duckett hesitated. "Not really, I was bent double. He may've had a missing finger. Something like that."

Constable Duckett then returned to his place by the door, as the Madeira wine arrived. As Ada sipped hers, the young constable met her glance equably, then looked away awkwardly. He'd not been offered refreshments; was that because he was only a constable?

"Look here, Ada, what do you make of this?" Charles said. He spread the paper on his work table and together they bent over it. Immediately she saw a pattern. There were four quadrants, each with its own distinct features. The upper left was composed of hieroglyphs, the upper right and lower left were what seemed to her random groups of letters. The lower right was some sort of equation with complex polyhedrons on one side, symbols and a rhyme on the other. Underneath were two shapes.

"It's four—"

"Yes indeed, those hieroglyphs will be quickly read. I have a book—"

"The letters will need application of the code-breaking—'

"Indeed, we can begin with the simple frequency system and go on from there—"

"But those equations—"

"Yes, Ada, they will prove troublesome, but I'm sure we can do it."

Clark had stopped his nervous prowling and had been excitedly listening to their interplay. "Then you think it does mean something?" he interrupted.

"We won't know till we've cracked some of it, but, yes, I think this is a coded message."

As the two men talked, Ada stared down at the paper, allowing the pictures, letters and symbols to flow, reform, break up, so that her mind could explore and absorb without direction. On another level, she was aware that Constable Duckett was saying, "I don't know why I was chosen, or whether I was mistook for someone else." And Clark replying, "It feels as if we are being played with." Charles countered with, "We have no certainties until we uncover the true meaning of the codes or ciphers."

"Wanstead Abbey," Ada heard herself saying.

All three men stopped speaking and stared at her. She pointed to the three lone symbols at the bottom. "Surely that's a gryphon, and, beside it, what could be a lake, and the sign of a cross."

"It could be any ecclesiastical building," Charles said gently. "And those three symbols may be related to the context of the other codes—"

But Clark had seized on her words. "Wanstead Abbey? But that's where—"

"I know, my ... Lord Byron lived there." She sounded as indifferent as she could. "It's all I know about him." She turned away and drank some more of the rich wine. It was William who'd described to her – in the most romantic terms – the now ruined Abbey where her father had once lived, and near which he was buried.

"It all falls into place!" Clark was saying. "This must be the focus for Republicanism, the hidden face behind the philosophical unionists and their talk of Charters and Rights. Is it Irish Home Rule, or some more sinister form of Radicalism? We must find out. I was right to take this seriously. It is either a warning to us, or we've intercepted a message destined for another conspirator.

Mr Babbage, will you bend all your powers to unravelling these codes, and put everything else aside? We must know what it says. For the safety of the realm."

On the carriage ride back home to Fordhook, Ada studied the copy she'd made of the coded message, with the Under Secretary's permission. She knew Charles was right. They should not necessarily interpret those three symbols as meaning Wanstead Abbey. There had been no rumours, no whispers, of a movement using that name as their rallying cry. And the composer of the message could not have known that she, or anyone of her family, would see it. Until the answer was found, they must be open-minded. At home she had her own pamphlets and notes on hieroglyphs – it would be a race between her and Charles how quickly these could be translated. But she did not have the key to the rest. She hoped to learn from Charles.

Was Under Secretary Clark over-reacting when he feared a threatening conspiracy to overthrow the government and establish a republic? She sighed. Her mother was not the only one to worry about such things. Would a republic be such a bad thing, she brooded? No Englishman could feel proud of their recent monarchs, though William IV was not as embarrassing in his excesses as George IV. Lady Byron often remarked that the Court set a terrible example and did not command respect. But then she said the same thing about Members of Parliament too. Only the Duke of Wellington, now their Prime Minister, escaped her criticism, but those who hated the way he'd let the Reform Act go through were not republicans!

I must listen carefully at Lady Conway's Ball tonight, she thought, and pay attention to what is being said about politics and the matters of the day, instead of just enjoying myself showing off my costume and dancing. At least I have the advantage in that my mind is trained to notice such things.

She put the paper away in her purse – made of matching red silk and decorated with a black transfer-printed motif of the Tower of London – and found herself thinking of Constable Robert Duckett. There had been an honesty about him, and his manner was neither subservient nor insolent. Why did he make her think of William? She managed to hide it from her mother and the Furies, but she still felt pain at the thought of the young man who would have been her husband for the past eighteen months, if their elopement had not been thwarted. They'd barely managed to make it down the driveway that night. Where was he now? She hoped he'd managed to obtain another post as tutor, and was comfortable somewhere. But, a tiny part of her acknowledged, it had been a lucky escape. His energy and ardour had not matched her own.

Not that she thought of Robert in the same way. He was only a constable, albeit good-looking and someone with initiative. A girl would be happy to be seen on his arm.

*

Robert pulled his coat closer around him against a squally burst of rain. What a dreary night to be out without my snug uniform, he thought. It was strange to be out without it. When he'd first joined the Metropolitan Police, freshly recruited from Bristol, he'd felt very conspicuous wearing it at all times, as he was pledged to do. Now he felt vulnerable without it.

He paused. Looking up and to his right he could make out, through the foggy gloom, the dome of St Paul's in the distance. He was headed, though, for somewhere godless – or so people said – towards St Giles and the Rookery. One of those warrens of alleys and courts, with ancient houses that jutted out above till they almost touched, tottering and in danger of collapse. Not a week went by, it seemed, than one old house or another collapsed in a cloud of choking dust, killing anyone unfortunate enough to be asleep inside. The Old Mint, Turnmill Street, Saffron Hall, whatever the warren was called it was always the same, as densely packed with humanity as a sewer with rats. Sometimes two families occupied just one room, sleeping space on stairways was hotly contested, and spots in hallways rented out.

These people might scratch some kind of living in an honest job, but the vast majority were engaged in some form of criminal activity or another – from as young as an orphan boy who could pick pockets, to the ancient ones, bent-backed and grey. Whole courts were devoted to such trades as pick-pocketry, swindling, or confidence-trickstering. And nowhere could you escape the smell of unwashed bodies and clothes, of open drains and sewers and the dankness of regular flooding in the cellars from the River Thames, kindly returning the sewage that had been dumped in her earlier. He took an experimental sniff now, and nearly choked, his stomach churning.

What a contrast he thought, turning up his collar, from his visit to Mr Babbage's house in Marylebone. The new houses in the West End were built of smart stone, the streets were wide and well paved and lit with the new gas-lighting at regular intervals. Not only there but all over London was the feel of a town making goods, selling goods, importing and exporting them, inventing them and advertising them. As well as sewers, there was a smell of money. The chasm between those with money and the huge number who lived in worse conditions than a pig in its sty seemed to grow bigger every day, especially as the numbers of poor were swelled continuously by those arriving from a failing countryside, their rural lives even harder than those in the towns.

Robert was one of the lucky ones though, even if his job might be dangerous at times, like tonight. "Duckett," Sergeant Cummings had said five days after the meeting at Babbage's house, his little sandy moustache bristling, "That government man has sent for you again. A special job he says. Mind you do your best."

"I will Sarge," Robert had promised.

He'd arrived at an address not far from the new General Post Office building near the church of St Martin-in-the-Fields. From not far off came the sounds of hammering and construction, as the fire-blackened ruin of the old Houses of Parliament was removed, to make way for the new grand building designed by Barry.

He was shown into a small, cold windowless antechamber painted cream, one wall being devoted to leatherbound volumes of law. Under Secretary Clark joined him in there, and began his usual agitated walking as he spoke in a breathless way.

"I could've called upon one of the old Runners – most've them have gone into private investigations, and it really is no good that we have no detecting force now, though I intend to put forward ideas to change that – but I decided the fewer who know the better. You've not been talking?"

"No, only me and the Sergeant know and we don't even talk to each other."

"Good man, good man. I have news. Mr Babbage has made some progress, in fact he sounded almost disappointed that the first quadrant of code was so easy to crack."

Robert was still. "What does it say?"

Clark stopped in front of him. "It's not good. It says: 'You have looked on my works, and ignored them, the cleansing fire, the falling rocks. Beware my next eruption.' "

"You were right sir, it looks like a warning. What of Miss Byron's reading of the signature?"

"It still seems possible, but we can only wait as they work on the rest. Babbage mentioned something about frequencies and transpositions which I don't understand. I leave all that to him. Meanwhile, I have used my own official channels and have found that the mastermind of last Friday's meeting lives and works in the Rookery, very near the White Hart Inn itself. I'm asking you to go there – not in uniform of course – and strike up a conversation, see what you can find out."

"You don't think our coder is the same person who organized the meeting then?"

"That's Connor O'Brien, a hothead, with links to protection rackets, but this is not his style."

Robert nodded. "The man who penned this message, though, he must be an educated man, maybe someone who's fallen on hard times."

"Or deliberately turned his talents to criminal activity. There are plenty of clever minds in these rookeries, the ones that organize the faking and the swindling."

"But why choose such a random way of passing on his message?"

Clark's face darkened as he paced up and down. "He thinks he's a clever man, much cleverer than us. This is part of his cat-and-mouse game. If we don't respond, he scores, then he tries again. Thank you, Constable Duckett, report back direct to me." Then as Robert did not leave he said, "You have a question?"

"He says his previous messages have been ignored. What did he mean?"

"I was afraid you'd ask that. This is to go no further, understand?" Clark leaned closer and spoke in a low voice. "There have been two earlier messages, both dismissed as nonsense.

One was pushed through Wellington's letterbox and was written in children's doggerel verse. It spoke of houses tumbling down – and there was that terrible collapse in Borough when many died and were injured. The second, we worked out, was Biblical References, and, when we found the verses, fire and brimstone were mentioned—"

"The Houses of Parliament burned down earlier this year." Robert was ahead of him.

"Exactly. There has never been any suggestion the fire was anything but an accident but . . . we can't take any chances."

Now, Robert looked up at the sign of the Inn. Outside was a board advertising an Ordinary Fish Supper. He was the bait, he thought, being sent in in the hope that their fish would reveal something of himself. Even though he would revert to his full Bristolian accent, and mention Dorset enough he'd be associated with the Tolpuddle martyrs, he was sure the people here could sniff out a policeman a mile away, however much he tried to disguise himself.

Four tankards of watered down ale, with an "aftertaste of the Thames" later, he'd made four new "brothers", who promised to let him know when the next political meeting was being held – "Legal or otherwise" – and they'd make them all illegal if they could. "Combined, we can make a difference, ain't that right?" one had said.

He staggered across the threshold, the sound of Irish singing in his ears, and began to thread his way along the alley towards the bigger, safer street ahead. He tried to marshal the few facts he'd gleaned into some sort of order before they floated away in a beer haze. Names of speakers, the principles of combining into unions; was there any fact or name that stood out? Someone who was a bit different, whether in speech or beliefs? He thought there was something that had been said, but what was it? He tripped on something sludgy and nameless in the dark and automatically put out a hand to steady himself when . . .

Pain exploded across his left shoulder, he lost his balance completely and collapsed on the ground, hitting his forehead. All the breath seemed to have left his body and he struggled to breathe. As he blinked to clear the cloudiness from his eyes, he felt the hard cap of a boot connect with his ribs, then another. He tried to curl into a ball but could not make his body obey. The shock of the attack had robbed him of control over his limbs as well as his senses.

Then he heard a shout, "Here, you! Leave that man! Get off him!" He heard footsteps running off, and then felt the blissful end to the well-aimed kicks.

Robert managed to pry his eyes open. A face swam into view.

"What took you so long?" he managed to croak. "Nearly had him, though, didn't I?"

"Sure," came Will's cheery voice. "You had him against the ropes. Think you can stand?"

With Will's arm supporting him Robert managed to clamber upright on to wobbly legs.

"Ouch. He must've had steel caps on those boots. I thought you were never coming. You know I bruise easily!"

"Had to finish my ale didn't I, keep up appearances. Besides, I'd bought the round."

"Nothing . . . to do . . . with the pretty barmaid then?" Robert panted, then groaned as he took a step.

"What an idea! Good thing you asked me to shadow you and watch your back. What've you done to rile that man? Owe him some money do you? But isn't this the place we came the other night."

Robert nodded, and instantly felt sick. "Thought I'd try and spot the one who shoved that paper on me, find out why me . . . ooh, I feel dizzy."

"Here, I think you need proper attention." There were voices ahead on the high road and Robert heard Will saying, "This feller's been attacked, robbed most like – stop a cab can you, he needs a doctor," before he lost consciousness.

*

Ada walked swiftly along the corridor of Westminster Hospital behind the orderly. The hospital still smelled new and fresh, not yet overlaid with the stench of sickness and medicines. She felt a tingling sensation between her shoulder-blades, as if her mother was watching her, or at the very least knew exactly what she was doing, and was planning a severe punishment as well as a lecture. But she would be only ten minutes here, no more; and who could object to her spontaneous gesture of giving – bringing a basket of food to the sick and needy in this brand new building, just opened on Broad Sanctuary, Westminster, on her way home from a shopping trip in the Strand? The waiting driver in their carriage would not know she had actually spoken to one of those needy patients.

"Constable Robert Duckett, Miss," the orderly said, opening the door to a private room and, leaving the door open, positioned himself on a chair outside.

Robert was sitting up in bed, several pillows behind him. His forehead had a bruised swelling on it and he was pale, but otherwise well – and surprised to see her.

"Why, whatever are you doing here—"

Ada held up a finger before he could say her name. "And why shouldn't your cousin visit? Were you hurt badly? What happened?"

He quickly understood. "Thank you, cousin, I was set upon from behind near the White Hart Public House. I hurt my head when I fell." He touched his forehead then winced, "But it's my ribs he gave a good workout, and they're all bandaged up. Nothing broken though."

"Do you have everything you need?" Ada asked. "I've spent so many long hours in the sick-room at home, struck down by debilitating conditions – *erm*, as you of course know – the hours can hang heavy. I could send you a book."

"Thank you. And my friend Will's sending in pies for me to eat."

Ada glanced over her shoulder. The orderly was standing in the middle of the corridor gossiping with a passing laundrymaid. She dropped her voice. "Did you learn anything? We've been working night and day on the ciphers. I expect you heard we broke the second quadrant."

"I learned nothing; but, the second quadrant ..." Robert leaned forward, eyes bright.

" 'Where many are gathered together, and the light is bright, there shall I strike,' " she repeated the words carefully. "It was the simple frequency method that worked in the end; we found that every third—" She broke off, as Robert leaned back, eyes closed, frowning. "Are you all right? Some water?" She reached clumsily for the glass at his bedside, accidentally brushing his bare arm, but he didn't seem to notice, or was too polite to react.

"Very Biblical sounding," Robert said. "There's something there but, no, I can't recall." He opened his eyes, their blueness startling her as she leaned close. "That knock on the head has affected my memory. I was sure there was something said – a name, maybe a place, in the White Hart, but it's gone now." He looked at her. "I call him the Prankster, this code-maker. It's all about proving how clever he is, making us run round in circles. He knows he's hooked us, with me going in that pub."

Ada gasped. "You mean it was him who attacked you? Not one of the Radicals or a robber from the Rookery?"

"Not him in person, I suspect, but word got back to him the police were sniffing around, and he sent us another message of a different kind. How did you know I was in here anyway?"

"When Mr Babbage was telling Mr Clark our progress with the code, Mr Clark said we were on the right track, and that he'd sent you to the public house 'with no results but a cracked head' was how he put it."

"Huh!" Robert said.

Ada heard the orderly returning to his chair, and straightened up. "I have to go now. God speed your recovery. You are a brave man," she added, cheeks flushing, before marching out.

Robert lay back on his pillows. Brave? He didn't think so, but, if a young lady wanted to think it, he didn't object. And now Miss Ada Byron would return to her world of dances and supper parties, and he to his lodgings – his family far away in Bristol.

He imagined himself at a supper party – and what a botch he would make of it – when he had a sudden thought: November the Fifth. That was a night when there would be crowds and bright lights, and a man with a political statement to make could set the largest number of tongues wagging. And perhaps even explosions of his own to make. He'd pass that on to the Sergeant for what it was worth.

But just for now he was feeling very uncomfortable and very tired. Time to have another sleep.

★

"Miss Byron! I did not send for you." Charles Babbage fiddled irritably with the small microscope in front of him, not meeting her eyes.

So, he was in one of his moods, and she was Miss Byron today, not "my dear Ada". The maid who'd announced her still hovered in the doorway, in case she had to show her out again. Ada stepped forward, taking off her bonnet and gloves and handing them to her. She would not be deterred by his grumpiness. The maid shrugged and left the room.

"I saw Constable Duckett two days ago," she said sharply, noting that he wore his oldest smoking jacket, its elbows rubbed, and his stock was all askew. "In hospital."

"What?" He sat up and looked at her, but not with his usual sociable warmth. "Oh yes, Clark said something to me, I don't know what—"

"That's right," Ada said, sitting on the low Ottoman that now stood where the Difference Engine had been. The Engine had at last been moved to the building next door. "Mr Clark sent him there to find out more information. The Constable was very brave . . ."

Charles muttered something under his breath that sounded like, "Spare me another one of your heroes," but she ignored him. A black mood was not to be indulged. Lady Byron had taught her that lesson well.

"I have not heard from you in three days. We must redouble our efforts on the cipher. The Prankster knows we have it, or he would not have set upon the Constable. We must—"

"It's all folly. What can I do about it?" He stared gloomily at the blank wall above her head, where the Engine had stood.

She sat bolt upright. "You can do everything! Supposing Mr Clark is right and the code is warning of some terrible event to come. We can save lives, preserve the stability of this Government—"

"Why should I care what happens to this Government? Short-sighted fools that they are." Charles jumped up. "None of them has any understanding of what I can do, of what I can achieve. My ideas – the new ideas of any inventor – are like pearls before swine to them. I've told Wellington I must start again, build a newer and better Engine; maybe *he* understands, but those around him are dolts and dullards."

He must have had his latest request for funding rejected, Ada thought, and that coupled with his long running dispute with the engineer who built the Engine and who now refused to return the plans, would explain the black cloud over him.

"You will prevail eventually, Mr Babbage," she told him. "With me at your side, we can achieve everything."

He stared at her. The flush left his cheeks. He was about to speak when there was a knock at the door.

"Miss Byron, good morning." Charles's mother-in-law stood in the doorway with Dugald and Henry, Charles's youngest sons. They wore warm coats. "Charles, I'm taking the boys out for fresh air and exercise. Say goodbye to Papa, now."

Ada watched as he spoke fondly to his sons, patted their shoulders, and then went to the window to watch and wave as they crossed the street. His eldest son was visiting relatives in Devon.

Now can we get back to the code, she thought. It was like an itch in her brain, the longing to fill her mind with puzzles and patterns, calculations and calculus. She'd lain awake for most of the night yet again, with figures and numbers whirling and cascading through her mind – as if she was the Difference Engine herself – and till her heart was hammering, and she'd broken out in a sweat. Only here could she find some relief from the pressure of – she did believe it sometimes – her genius.

Charles was ringing the bell to the kitchen. "I'll order some coffee to be brought to the dining room and we can use the table there. I want to be away from this room with its aura of doomed projects."

At last Ada could slide into that other world, the one of symbols and of certainties, of patterns that sounded in her mind like music. She passionately believed that if she followed the logical steps, the truth would be revealed. Nothing would be hidden from her any more. She'd find an absolute truth, without questions or evasions; no hidden meanings or obscurities. In this world her mind could soar, her heart and body be left behind. If only she could stay and lose herself in this world forever.

Coffee cups drained and pushed aside, they worked on the lower left quadrant. Having exhausted the possibilities of the frequency method, Charles suggested they now move on to transposition. "As you know, Ada, this is how science works. We work our way through each of the postulations till, at last, one of them matches all the parameters and we can fit the key. Although," he added, with the twinkle returning to his eye, "A leap of the imagination often helps too."

Ada gave an internal shudder. Imagination. That's what her father had had, in abundance. It had led to terrible things. What exactly they were, she had not been told. Sometimes, when she languished in her room in one of her ill periods, all sorts of weird images came into her mind and made her feel worse. They were not to be spoken about, her mother had made plain. *He* was not to be spoken about, but she must never forget that he was a ruiner of lives – his own as well as others'.

The letters swam before her eyes and she did her best to focus, and to banish these thoughts before they dragged her down again. Apply the method, following Charles's instructions, and she would be in control again.

After a while she became aware that Charles had put down his pen and was staring into the distance. She became as still and quiet as possible. This was what he was like when new ideas were coming to him. He got up and went to the window, staring up at the cloudy sky then down at the autumnal leaves that had collected on the pavement. He turned back.

"That's it," he said. "While we are still working on the cipher to uncover what message our man is sending, I will send him one of my own. You said that Constable Duckett was ordered to that public house in the hope of drawing out – what did you call him? – the Prankster. It may not work, but my guess is that this man will also enjoy the challenge of *The Times* Personals. I shall place a message for him."

"What will you say?"

"That's what concerns me. How about something like 'The net is getting tighter. You cannot succeed. We are very close.' Or something like that," he waved a hand airily, seeing Ada's frown.

"But how will he know it's for him, that could be for anyone."

"True, and that's why, Ada, I have a special request." He sat down again beside her and took her hands in his. "I would like to use the symbols that you interpreted as Wanstead Abbey, along with the name of Byron, perhaps a line from *Childe Harold*. Would you allow that? It's all I can think of using – we could mention bright lights, being ignored – but again that's open to interpretation."

Ada lifted her chin. Robert had not been afraid, neither would she. And she knew none of her father's poetry, so it would not matter to her. "You must use it. Why not ask him to meet you? Or ask what it is he wants!"

"I'll work on it. Thank you, Ada."

"But – don't you think we should ask Mr Clark first?"

"Hah – if we wait for government departments to make up their minds, we'll still be waiting for an answer at the next Millennium!"

★

"Is the syllabub to your liking, Ada?"

"May I fetch you some wine, Miss Byron?"

"You are looking a little pale, are you chilled? Shall I fetch your shawl?"

Ada smiled. It was certainly flattering to have the attention of these young men, to be surrounded, when other young women looked on in envy. And she never lacked for partners when the dancing started, which was good because she enjoyed it so much. Yes, it might be because of her name and her fame but, if they didn't like her, surely they wouldn't stay?

"Yes, and yes please, and no thank you, I'm not cold," she answered. As one swain went to fetch her some wine she said to the other two, "Have you seen Mr Babbage's Difference Engine? I've had the pleasure of working with him on—"

"A most fantastical machine, I've heard," interrupted the first young man hastily. "But I wanted to ask you, Ada, if there was perhaps something fantastical at the theatre you would like to see? Perhaps your Mama would allow—"

"Nonsense, not the theatre. Miss Byron, I could arrange a day at the races, would that be more to your liking?"

"It would indeed. I was at Doncaster not long ago, and the thrill of it! I want to learn about horses, and, of course, the arithmetical calculations on the betting odds are intriguing – oh!"

Her wine was being handed to her, but not by one of her swains. Instead, it was Mr Clark.

"Good evening Miss Byron. May I compliment you on your yellow outfit? A most striking and vivid combination. A beacon in this room." He indicated the rest of the soirée in the candle-lit room. Small baize-topped card tables at one side were fully occupied. In the far corner a small group sat listening to the gentle tones of a guitar played by an Italian maestro. Still others, like her own coterie, sat gossiping together on chaise longues and low padded chairs in the French style. The cold buffet supper was over, the last of the desserts now spooned up and the plates and bowls cleared away by the servants.

Ada felt her spirits lift further, having previously resigned herself to an evening of pointless small-talk.

"May I?" He sat down, and the two younger men melted away.

"Have there been any developments?" Ada asked, managing to lower her voice. "I have not heard from Mr Babbage for two days. And how is Constable Duckett?"

"Mr Babbage has broken the third quadrant. 'I have many masks. I am the Destroyer.' Strong words. They are the Prankster's, not mine."

She noted he was using Robert's name for the code-maker now. "Did Mr Babbage say anything else?"

Clark shook his head. Candlelight reflecting from his spectacles made his eyes seem to glitter. "Only that the solution to the final quadrant would take longer. As you know, it contains geometrical figures and a nonsense rhyme. Mr Babbage says there are no equivalences for these, so the key could be anything. Does he threaten to destroy Wanstead Abbey? What reason would he have for doing that?"

"I think of nothing else," Ada said. "Some nights I hardly sleep, my mind cannot let this puzzle go."

"I'm sorry to hear that your rest is disturbed. Perhaps we should talk no further."

Ada shook her head. "It would make no difference. I want to know – I dearly want to meet the challenge the Prankster has set us. And when I look around a gathering like this I wonder, is he here? Could he be in this room right now?"

Clark was observing her closely. "Especially as he tells us he has many masks. Does this mean that he can mix with any part of society he chooses? I am beginning to think that he is no radical, he is not trying to change a political system, he is simply after notoriety."

At last he stepped on to the narrow wharf constructed of large blocks of stone, from which a flight of steps led down to the muddy shore below. A few wooden boats, one with a mast, were pulled up on the mud, and a few brave souls were picking through the smelly ooze to see what treasures the murky waters might have washed up. Anything that could be sold for a farthing or more was worth keeping.

Robert eyed the several derelict buildings that lined this small wharf. Wide wooden eaves jutted out over upper storeys, which in turn jutted out over the lower ones. There wasn't a straight line to be seen; all the timbers, windows and bricks seemed to be at odds with one another. As he wandered slowly by, he glanced inside. One building appeared to be some kind of offices, with clerks scribbling over piles of dusty papers. Another, a sort of chandlery. The third seemed to be unoccupied.

Robert slouched on past. He'd find himself a hidden corner out of the wind and get himself comfortable. He had a couple of pies he'd bought from a passing pieman, and a stone bottle of ginger beer, as well as an old blanket rolled up in his pack. There were worse ways to pass a sunny day than watch all the craft going by on the river, and the mudlarks at work below.

*

Ada felt the warmth of the late October sunshine on her back as she strolled her favourite walk between the market gardens that ran down to the Thames. It was a circular walk from Fordhook to the river and back. Winter vegetables grew in ordered rows, and a few late butterflies and bees foraged in the hedges. Behind her she could hear her tutors Dr King and Miss Noel deep in discussion on a philosophical point.

She quickened her pace. Ahead lay the grove of willows that she loved, and beyond that the small wooden jetty where she could stand and watch the flowing water, see the boats plying and find a moment's peace. Particularly, she wanted to forget her mother's pronouncement on Mr Clark. She'd researched his background and found it severely wanting on his mother's side two generations back. "Barely more than a seamstress," her mother had announced. "You'd better not be planning a secret romance." She'd watched Ada even more closely, and she was still forbidden reading *The Times*.

"As Mr Babbage says, he has set a challenge. Do you truly think he set fire to the Houses of Parliament? And what about the 'collapsing houses' he mentions?"

"We have no way of knowing on the former. As for the latter, these old buildings in poorer areas from times gone by are not looked after, and do collapse from time to time anyway."

"I have tried to think where he means to strike next. Could it be an assassination attempt on the King? There have been several already."

"My choice is the railways. Perhaps a bridge. I am confident it will be in London. I have every policeman and special agent on full alert – including Constable Duckett, yes." He smiled. "That young man is out of hospital and taking some days off to recover, unpaid of course. But now, I think I'd better leave you, before tongues start to wag." He stood up and bent over her hand.

Ada was suddenly aware of her mother's close scrutiny from the group around the musician. She sighed inwardly. Her mother would not rest till she had tracked down every last detail of Clark's family and background to find out if he was grand enough for her daughter. Her mother was suspicious enough of her already. She'd caught Ada scrutinising the Personals, looking of course for Babbage's message to the Prankster. Now her mother had forbidden her to read the paper. "I shall be most annoyed if I find you are conducting correspondence with a young man through that column," she had said, despite Ada's protestations that she was exercising her code-breaking skills, as suggested by Mr Babbage.

So now it was a race to solve the fourth quadrant. She would put everything aside and think of nothing else.

*

Robert put his head down and literally pushed his way through the throng that was shoving and jostling its way between the carriages and carts that had come to a standstill at Charing Cross. There was a "lock" on. The numbers of wheeled traffic had built and built till no one could move, though this was not one of the most notorious places for it to happen – they were towards the City.

Carters and drivers yelled and shook their fists, horses snorted and struggled in vain in their harnesses and shafts. Robert battled his way through this tumult to the south side of the Strand, where he breathed easier and began to walk eastwards.

It was a crisp bright autumn morning with a chill in the air. Sunlight slanted on the advertising in shop windows, and on tin plates fastened to the walls above. A myriad of manufactories, shops and cafes shouted their wares at him. If Charing Cross was the centre of London, then the Strand was its beating heart. It was the new London, brash, confident, a centre for all the forms of commerce, industry and entrepreneurship. Even the pavements were lined with women and children selling flowers and fruit, from baskets on the ground.

After a while he turned to his right into an alley and began the descent down to another world, to an older London that still lined the river. He was in deep shade now – cast by the brick walls and timbers of tall buildings. The noise, colour and life were left behind. He was entering a world of scuttling shadows, of figures that hid in doorways, of glimpses of pale faces behind grimy windows hunched over soulless tasks. He pulled up the collar of the patched coat he wore, and pulled down the lip of his shapeless greasy cap. Both had been bought for a few pennies at a rag-pickers, the boots on his feet with worn heels and holes in the toes from Seven Dials.

As far as Sergeant Cummings was concerned, Robert was resting in his lodgings – he had enough savings left after what he sent home to his mother in Bristol to tide him over. Not even his good friend Will knew what he was doing.

A whiff from the Thames carried on a rising breeze caught his throat, and he coughed till he retched; and that made him clasp his side which still ached from the kicking he'd received. He still had flashes of pain in his head, too. This was one of the reasons that had made him decide to investigate by himself. He wanted to make the man who'd ordered his beating pay.

The other reason was the bloodless face, blue about the lips, of the body of a young man that he'd witnessed in the morgue yesterday afternoon. Will had been off-duty, so had come to meet him at Westminster Hospital and share a licensed cab home with him. As they'd waited at the kerbside, Will had said casually, "Remember you told me, when that paper was shoved on you, you thought the man was missing a little finger? A lad with a

missing finger showed up on the morgue reports, fished up at the side of the Thames. Thought you'd like to know, seeing as how you went back to the White Hart on account of that business, and ended up here for your pains."

Robert gripped his arm. "Can we go to the morgue now? I'd like to see him."

"What, reckon you're well enough to be looking at dead bodies? Will they let us in?"

"I'll tell them the Sarge sent us and square it with him later."

Will sighed. "Well, you're his blue-eyed boy at the moment. Can't say it's much of a substitute for a quiet pint of ale, but, all right then!"

They'd talked themselves into the morgue, but Will decide to wait in the office, while Robert was taken through to view th body. When the cloth was pulled back he'd stared down into t face of a young man he recognized. Not from the night the broken up the political meeting, but from the White Hart. been one of the group of men he'd struck up conversation A quiet, nervous lad who'd laughed in the right places b said much. And now that elusive memory that had been kr from his head when he fell, returned.

A newcomer had sidled up to the lad, face obscure felt hat so that all that could be seen were the brown s his teeth and a chin disfigured by a deep scar. A few w muttered, the young man had gone pale. He'd quickl his drink then got up and left.

Robert recalled now the name he'd managed to cat the hubbub of the public house: "Chapterhouse knew these stairs, or steps, down to the riverbank, between Temple and Puddle Dock.

"Where was the body found?" he'd asked, surprised to be told, "Near Puddle Dock Stairs."

He'd not said anything to Will beyond "Yes, I lad. Tell the Sergeant for me will you? I think I lie down now." Will had understood and gone f own, while Robert had devised his plan and his disguise. And now here he was the next through the maze of lanes that went beyond t towards Blackfriars and Chapterhouse Stairs

In her purse she carried her notes on the fourth and last quadrant of the secret cipher. She'd hardly slept the past two nights for trying to puzzle it out, not caring if her mother thought she was pining romantically. But to no avail. "10S, 15C, what is the rest of me?" Ten times S and fifteen times C? That was the correct mathematical notation. Then last night she'd wondered if it was proportions. Ten plus fifteen was twenty-five, so 75 of what, to make one hundred? It made no sense to her. As for those polyhedrons, she'd found herself idly redrawing them, separating out each individual shape, and turning them into a necklace. Could some of them represent jewels? Then, annoyed at her inability to penetrate the Prankster's cipher, she'd put a big cross through it all.

Quickening her pace again, she glanced round. Good. They'd stopped, deep in argument. She lifted the willow fronds and hurried through the grove to the jetty. There she intended on tearing up the paper into a hundred tiny pieces and flinging it into the river. From henceforth she was going to renounce all codes and ciphers!

A small skiff was moored to the end of the jetty with one man sitting at the oars and another standing beside it on the jetty. She turned her back on them and was reaching for her purse when she felt a strong arm about her waist. "If you want to see your friend Babbage alive, you'll come with me and quiet about it."

In shock, heart thundering, she gasped for breath as the man on the jetty hurried her into the waiting skiff, and the oarsman – a big bearded fellow – pulled fast into the river, heading for a larger boat. The man who'd taken hold of her now draped a hooded cloak over her. "Keep silent," he hissed. "Or Babbage don't live to see another day."

Ada heard herself whimper. She closed her eyes in terror. Could it be true? Was Charles's life under threat? What had been done to him? The boat rocked wildly and she felt nauseous, putting a hand to her mouth, as she was quickly bundled on to the large boat.

"Lie down!" came the order, and she felt a foot placed on her back as she obeyed. Now she thought she could hear a faint cry of distress, like a marsh bird, from Miss Noel at finding her gone.

As the boat wallowed in the water and her stomach heaved, she kept her mind fixed on one thing. Charles is in danger. For some reason I am part of this – perhaps I can help him.

★

Robert jerked his eyes open. Dammit, he'd fallen asleep. What had awoken him, apart from the uncomfortable stone that was pressing into his back? Voices, he thought he'd heard voices. Stiffly, he forced himself to sit upright so that he could see over the weather-beaten boards behind which he'd found his pitch. A new boat was being pulled up on the mud, by a large man with a lot of woolly grey hair and a beard. Two other figures stood inside: a man and a woman in a rough woollen cloak.

Robert looked around. All the mudlarks had scattered and were determinedly looking the other way. They knew who these people were, Robert thought, and apparently they were people it was best one didn't know anything about.

The man on the boat said something, but he couldn't make out what, and then the bigger man lifted down the woman and they all went up the stairs and headed for the building he'd thought was unoccupied. The big man was glancing around, as if to make sure no one was watching them. Robert kept very still.

Then, as clearly as St Paul's bell, he heard the woman say "Is he in here? Will I see him now?" For answer, she was escorted in, and the door closed behind them.

He frowned. It couldn't be. He must be imagining it. Were his brains still scrambled? But that voice – it sounded like Miss Byron. What could she be doing here? He began to struggle to his feet. He had to find a way to get inside – or at least see inside – that dilapidated building.

★

"Are you telling me the truth, Mr Babbage? She has not come here to your house? And you know nothing of any romantic liaison?"

"Believe me, Lady Byron, I'm as worried as you are. She has not come here, and I've not seen her since she was last here several days ago. As for romance – we confine our discussions strictly to science and mathematics, and matters of the higher mind."

Lady Byron bit at her knuckle as she wandered to and fro in Babbage's drawing-room. "Then where can she be?"

"How long since she disappeared?"

"Four full hours. She's never been a robust child, and without proper care she might easily fall ill. Where has she gone? I hope the foolish girl did not have romantic notions. I've seen her reading *The Times* Personal columns, but she assured me—"

"Ah, that would be because of me. We were – testing out a new code."

"So she *was* telling the truth." Lady Byron sank into a chair and put her head in her hands. "She can't have . . . it's too much to think . . . it can't be in her blood . . . the water—"

"I'm sure she has not taken her own life," Charles declared bluntly. "She was too engaged in our mathematical studies. There is only one answer. She must have departed by boat. Yet no one saw her?"

"Her tutors did not see her on any of the boats passing by. Only her purse was lying on the ground."

"Do you have it with you?" It was clear now to Charles that Ada has been abducted and hidden on one of the passing boats. If she'd gone by choice, she would not have dropped her purse. Had she left it on purpose? Might there be some clue about it?

Lady Byron opened her own bag and handed the purse to him. "I showed it to the police, but they did not need to keep it."

Charles also sat down, and opened the clasp of the yellow satin bag then emptied the contents on the mahogany occasional table in front of him. He stirred them with his forefinger. A handkerchief with the initials AB entwined in red embroidery in the corner. A tortoiseshell comb. A small mirror. For some reason he thought of his beloved daughter Georgiana, so much missed, and his eyes misted over. Ada could not be a substitute for her, but he felt the same fatherly protective instincts for her as he had for his daughter.

He blinked. There was also some paper. He opened it up and recognized the elements from the fourth quadrant, whose solution had so far eluded him. Her busy mind had been working hard on them. He scanned her notes and suggestions, and the back of his neck suddenly prickled with excitement. She'd written "Proportions?" and what was this, a decorative necklace?

Of course! His mind leapt ahead and reached the conclusions she had not. But then he'd been blinkered by following the normal code-breaking routes, whereas she had made a sideways leap of the imagination.

"Lady Byron, may I take this? I have a contact who may be able to help us."

"Anything – but hurry. Her reputation! Poor girl." She gave a sob.

"Please wait here. I'll send a messenger as soon as I can."

Hatless and shrugging into his coat as he ran downstairs and out into the street to hail a hansom cab, his mind worked feverishly. Even though Ada had crossed through her workings and written "hopeless", he was sure she'd made the right connection. The other 75 was saltpetre – combined with 10 parts of sulphur and 15 of carbon, it formed gunpowder. If so, then could the jewels on the other side of the equation be a ransom? Pay me a King's ransom in jewels, or Wanstead Abbey would suffer the same fate as Parliament! Was that what the Prankster was threatening? No, why bother to blow up Wanstead Abbey? It had to be some other ecclesiastical building – and where else to make a bigger mark than St Paul's Cathedral!

★

Robert crouched on the outhouse roof to regain his breath before testing the stability of the drainpipe above him. He'd first tried knocking at the door of the building, and, when the big fellow with wild woolly hair had opened it, he'd said, "Any knives need sharpening? Any rags you want got rid of?"

"Piss off or you'll be buried so deep, even the mudlarks won't find yer." And the door was slammed in his face.

As he cast about the row of ancient buildings looking for another way in, by luck he saw a messenger-boy emerge from the door where he'd seen the clerks scribbling away. He gave him the Under Secretary's address, his own name and that of the Stairs, plus a silver coin. He could only hope he was an honest boy.

A short while later he'd come across the entrance to a very narrow gunnel that ran behind the buildings, and now he was attempting to reach a first floor window to force his way in. He shivered. It was cold and dank here and he felt sick and sore. But he had to find out if Ada was inside, and why. Bracing himself, he took hold of the drainpipe.

★

It was getting dark, Ada noticed. The room she'd been forced into was getting gloomier by the minute. She'd been standing upright in the middle of the room for most of the time since being locked in. The floor was bare boards and there was no furniture, only a pile of musty sacks in one corner.

Her first action had been to look out of the one small window but all she could see was a brick wall opposite and a tiny glimpse of sky above. And then she heard them. Rats – mice – scuttling in the walls and above her head. There would be silence and then they'd be running by again. She visualized thousands swirling through the building. She tried not to think of the Plague, of rat bites – she stared down at her hands and saw to her disgust how they trembled.

She longed to sit down but could not bring herself to use the sacks. Supposing they were infested with fleas? Once or twice she sat down on the hard floorboards in the centre of the room, the only place she felt safe. She could imagine hundreds of beady eyes peering at her through cracks . . . horrible!

She'd tried banging on the door and shouting, but it had had no effect. She had then pressed her ear to it and heard the two men who'd brought her here laughing and cursing. It sounded as if they were playing cards. They ignored her.

She was cold, hungry and afraid, but as time passed her strongest emotion was anger – at herself. How could she, clever Ada, have been fooled so easily? Charles Babbage wasn't here. She'd been tricked. But why? They knew of her association with Charles. Did that mean she'd been watched? And what did they want of her?

She heard the door being unlocked and drew herself up straight, assuming one of her mother's sternest expressions. She would meet her fate with dignity.

In the glow of a lamp, a new man stood framed in the doorway. He gave a slight bow of the head. "Miss Byron, come and join us."

Hesitantly she followed him into the outer room, which she'd only glimpsed before. A fire burned in the grate with hall chairs either side, while her two abductors sat at a small card table on the other side of the room. They glanced at her then resumed their game.

"Sit," said the newcomer, indicating the chairs by the fire. She managed to make herself walk over and sit down. She watched as he poured some wine from a beautifully engraved decanter into equally exquisite glasses, and handed her one. There were other items of quality in the room too, she noticed. A French clock on the mantelpiece, and the rug at her feet was Chinese silk.

The man sat opposite her. His trousers and jacket were very well cut, and there was a diamond-tipped pin in his expertly tied stock. His blond hair was straight, and just brushed the collar of his jacket. Finally she looked into his eyes. They were a cold, cold green. Was this the Prankster?

"Your health, Miss Byron." He raised his glass and drank. "I have sent for some supper. I intend to look after you. You're far too valuable to me to be neglected."

Valuable? For a moment she wondered if he wanted to employ her mathematical skills, but his next words disabused her.

"I can see you are your father's daughter. You are brave, if not as beautiful as he was." He smiled, but she did not sense any warmth. His speech and manners marked him as one of the gentry, but she'd never seen him before. He went on, "How much, I wonder, is Miss Byron worth? What do you say, my friends-in-evil?" Now he laughed and the other two joined in.

"A tasty piece," the bearded man said. "Five hundred gold sovereigns."

"At the very least. Add that to our pay-off for not blowing up St Paul's and I reckon we might live comfortably – for a little while."

"They were jewels. A ransom," Ada said, finding her voice.

"I knew you'd solved it when I saw your coded message in the Personals." The cold green eyes glittered. He stood up and leaned on the mantelshelf. "The poetic quotation was not as apt as I would have expected, but confirmed your identity. You decoded my message with help from Mr Babbage – my men have told me how you visit him. Now all that needs to be done is give the location where our ransom should be placed. I'm sure Mr Babbage can manage that alone."

"I still don't see why we need her." The younger man who'd grabbed her on the jetty jerked his thumb at her. "I say she's a liability. The ransom for the cathedral is enough."

"Enough!" The blond man spoke quietly but with such venom that the other two men shrank back. "Nothing is enough, I've told you that before. I can never be recompensed for what I've been denied." He looked at her, and she felt herself flinch. "I should have had the privileged life you've led – even more so. My father, the Duke, refused to acknowledge his by-blow, though. My mother told me everything. So I am making him and his kind pay – but on my terms." He tossed back the last of his wine and went to the decanter for a refill. "As for why Miss Byron is here – I've sent a strong message: 'Look at what I can do. "Look on my works, ye Mighty, and despair". Ozymandias should be my middle name.' "

"Where did you learn to cipher?" Ada asked.

"Oh, I had a good education, the best. But I was bored, and found other things to interest me."

"I have been tutored at home. And now," she declared standing up, "I demand that you return me there."

Her adversary flung his head back and laughed. "What if I decide to keep you? No one would be surprised. Mad George Byron's daughter run off with an adventurer – only to be expected."

Ada felt her throat grow tight. "My father," she began, when suddenly she heard a voice from behind.

"Miss Byron, are you all right?"

"Robert!" He stood, pale and swaying a little, in the doorway to the second room.

"Get him," the blond man ordered. As the other two men stood, Ada jumped up and ran to Robert.

"Leave him alone," she said, standing protectively in front of him. "Haven't you harmed him enough?"

"Not nearly enough," growled the bearded man "He should've died for his pains."

"But someone did die," Robert said. "That young man. You sent a message to the White Hart for him to come here. Why? Tell me that, before I follow him into the Thames."

"He disobeyed me. He was supposed to hand my coded message to the speaker that night, to send the police searching after Radicals. At first he said he'd done so, but then we found out he was too frightened so he'd planted it on a policeman – you – to get rid of it. He's learned his lesson now."

"So that paper was never meant for me," Robert said. "It was just chance. You chose that meeting to throw suspicion on the union men or the Irish."

"Or even a latter-day Guy Fawkes. Now, get rid of him." The blond man flicked his fingers and Ada braced herself, just as the sound of wood splintering, shouts and the blasts of whistles came from below.

"Quickly, out the back way. Bring her, kill him."

Ada felt Robert's arms take hold of her and together they struggled against the bearded man. She found a strength she didn't know she possessed as she kicked out. But in the next moment the police had stormed up the stairs to their rescue and the blond man had shoved past them to escape through the back window.

★

"I have ordered up some meat and potatoes, and here's some porter to drink." Clark was smiling. Ada had heard him say several times, "A very good outcome indeed. Very good indeed."

She sat beside Robert on one side of the grate, where the flames of a generous log fire gave as much light as the few candles around the room. Charles Babbage was on the other side, legs stretched out in front of him. They were in an upper floor private room of an eating house in the Strand. News had been sent to her mother that she was safe and would be home soon. She had been waiting for Clark's restless energy to subside, but her questions could no longer wait for him to settle. She swallowed some of the bitter drink, her first taste of porter, coughed, and said, "You found me because of the message Rob— Constable Duckett sent?"

"It arrived at the same time Babbage did, with his news of your abduction and the final solving of the cipher – as well as the part played by his coded message in *The Times*. I should reprimand you, Mr Babbage, for acting alone and without sanction, but it had the desired effect. It drew our man out."

"He thought Ada placed it. I'm sorry, Ada, for what happened," Charles said.

"You asked my permission and I gave it." She smiled at him.

Beside her, Robert stirred and coughed. He had a rug around his shoulders and the colour was returning to his face. "How did you know I was there?" she asked him.

Robert recounted his story of the young lad in the morgue and his returning memory. "The young man was punished all right. That villain, that Prankster, is a cruel man."

"If you hadn't posted extra men at the back of the building, Mr Clark, he might have escaped. Do you know his true name now?"

At last Clark sat down. "He has refused to give it, but in fact I recognized him from a State Assembly I attended in the summer. Henry de Bellfont. He was thrown out of the Assembly for making a fracas, and I learned his sorry history. No doubt he hatched his plot then. With apologies, Miss Byron, he is the bastard son of a Duke and, although his father did provide enough money for a good education, he has refused to acknowledge him publicly, for the sake of his legitimate children. Henry was sent down from Oxford University for underhand dealings and general misbehaviour, at which point the Duke stopped sending money altogether."

"He felt he wasn't getting what he was due – despite the rest of us having to earn our living, or our position in society," Robert observed.

"He was cold and calculating," Ada said, remembering his green eyes. "All he wanted was riches."

"Pure self-justification. But he is very clever," Charles said. "The codes were the work of a brilliant mind, only used for the wrong purpose."

"Now," Clark was suddenly serious. "I must ask each of you to keep all the details of this affair secret. As far as the police are concerned we have captured a thief and dealer in stolen goods. I have tried to protect Miss Byron's identity."

"Why a secret? Sir?" Robert asked. His tankard of porter was already drained.

"No good cause would be served by tarnishing those close to the king. We must preserve stability at all costs. And we don't want speculation and gossip about Henry de Bellfont's claims that he burned down Parliament and is capable of blowing up St Paul's Cathedral."

"They were empty threats?" Ada asked. "He didn't have a hand in that fire? Or the collapsing buildings?"

"With that mind, he could plan anything," Charles said, "but would he have been able to carry it through?"

"I shall make very discreet investigations, but I believe not. He seized on two events and pretended he caused them, so we would pay to save St Paul's. I doubt he had any intention of blowing it up. Abducting Miss Byron was to add strength to his claims."

"What about his trial? He might take the opportunity to boast of these deeds?" Robert said.

"We shall find another way of dealing with him," Clark said. Ada saw a glint of ruthlessness in his eyes that made her wonder if Henry de Bellfont would ever reach a courtroom. Perhaps he'd be encouraged to go to Tasmania, or America. She caught Robert's eye and saw he'd come to the same conclusion.

The door opened and two serving-women came in carrying trays of food. Once everything had been laid out, the porter topped up, and the women gone, Clark said, "I propose a toast. To Miss Ada Byron, without whose mathematical genius, ably assisted by Mr Charles Babbage, we would not have averted this crime."

As the three men raised their tankards, Ada laughed, and felt herself go pink. She wondered if she would ever be so content again.

Brodie and the
Regrettable Incident

Anne Perry

Anne Perry has written over fifty books including two long-running series set in Victorian England. The first features Thomas Pitt who, though he rises through the police ranks, finds it difficult to mix with members of society because of his lowly background. The series began with The Cater Street Hangman *(1979). The other main series, which began with* The Face of a Stranger *(1990), features William Monk, who manages to join the police force despite having lost his memory. He also has a rather chequered career, as he struggles to find his past. Both series have proved popular, though Perry has found time to dip into other periods, ranging from the French Revolution to the First World War. The following story fits into neither of these series, but clearly begs for one of its own. It features Miss Brodie, a highly inquisitive middle-aged lady's maid in 1890s society, and Mr Stockwell, the butler.*

"Really?" Colette raised her delicate eyebrows in an expression of surprise and implied contempt. "You allow the cook to do it for you? In France we always prefer to boil our own." She was referring to the rice, the water from which was used to stiffen linens and muslins. "One can get so much better a consistency," she continued, looking at Brodie with a very slight smile.

They were in the ironing room of Freddie Dagliesh's country home. Colette was the young and very pretty lady's maid of Mrs Violet Welch-Smith, house guest, and wife to General Bertrand

Welch-Smith. Brodie was considerably older, of a comfortable rather than handsome appearance, although she had possessed a considerable charm in her youth. Now the first thing one noticed about her was intelligence, an air of good sense and a sharp but suitably concealed humour. She was lady's maid to Pamela Selden, Freddie Dagliesh's widowed sister. Since he was unmarried, he always invited Pamela to act as hostess when he had a house party he felt of importance, or where he was concerned he would be out of his depth. Violet Welch-Smith was a woman to give any man such a feeling.

Colette was still regarding Brodie with an air of superiority, waiting for an answer.

"Yes I do," Brodie replied, referring to the cook and the rice-water. "Cooks, especially in other people's houses, prefer that visiting servants do not attempt to perform tasks in the kitchen. They invariably get in the way and disrupt the order of things, upset the scullery maids, boot boys and undercooks."

"Perhaps that is what happened at the last house where we stayed," Colette retorted, changing the flat iron she was using on her mistress's petticoat for a warmer one from the stove. "The food was certainly not of the quality we are accustomed to in France." She looked very directly at Brodie. "I had not realized that that was the cause."

Brodie was furious. Normally she was of a very equable temper, but Colette had been trumpeting the innate superiority of everything French, both in general and in particular, ever since she had arrived nearly two days ago. This was enough to try the patience of a saint . . . an English saint anyway, most particularly a north country one, used to plain ideas and plain speech. Unfortunately, she could not at the moment think of a crushing reply; she merely seethed inside, and kept a polite but somewhat chilly smile on her face.

Colette knew her advantage, but pushed it too far.

"Do you think your cook would be able to manage rice-water as well as preparing dinner for guests?" she said charmingly. "Would it be kinder not to ask it of her?"

Brodie opened her eyes very wide. "I had not realized you were attempting to be kind!" she said with exaggerated surprise. Then she smiled straight at Colette, this time quite naturally. "Perhaps a French cook would find it an embarrassment, but our cook is English – she is quite used to being helpful to the rest of the staff." And with that she picked up the enamel jug sitting on the bench, and swept out with it. "I shall ask her immediately," she called back, before Colette could think of a response.

She made her request in the kitchen, and was on her way towards the back stairs when she all but bumped into the imposing figure of Stockwell. He was the most dignified and correct person whose acquaintance she had ever made.

"Good afternoon, Mr Stockwell," she said somewhat startled. He was eight inches taller than she, and of magnificent stature. He had probably been a footman in his distant youth. Footmen were picked for their appearance. Height and good legs were especially required. A poor leg was most observable when a man was in livery.

"Good afternoon, Miss Brodie," Stockwell replied stiffly. She disconcerted him, and he had not yet worked out why, although he had spent some time thinking about the matter. She was really quite agreeable, even if a trifle over-confident, and opinionated above her station. It was not becoming in a woman. But she had been of great assistance to him in that terrible business of the murder of Lady Beech. A certain latitude was perhaps allowable. "A most pleasant day," he added. "I fancy the ladies will be enjoying the garden. Spring is one of the most attractive seasons, don't you think?"

"Most," she agreed.

He frowned. "Is something troubling you, Miss Brodie? Is it a matter with which I could assist?" He owed her a certain consideration, a protection, if you like. She was a woman, and a visiting servant, and this was his house. Her welfare was his concern.

"I doubt it, Mr Stockwell," she replied, her lips tight again at the thought of Colette. "I find Mrs Welch-Smith's maid very trying, that is all. She is convinced of the superiority of all things French, and she is at pains to say so."

"Ignorance," Stockwell said immediately. "She is a foreigner, after all. She may not know any better."

"Stuff and nonsense!" Brodie snapped. "She is not in the least bit ignorant. She is simply . . ." She stopped abruptly. What she had been going to say was unbecoming to her. She closed her mouth.

Further down the corridor a maid went by with a dustpan in her hand.

"Fortunately the General's man, Harrison, is as English as we are," Stockwell said, looking at her sympathetically. "In fact he seems to have very little liking for France or the French. Although naturally he is discreet about his remarks – merely an inflexion here or there which the sensitive ear may discern."

"I have barely seen him." Brodie thought about it for a moment. "Is he the rather portly young man with the brown eyes, or the fair-haired man with the absent-minded expression?"

"The fair-haired man," Stockwell answered. "The other is the coachman. But it is understandable you should be confused. Harrison spends at least as much time in the stable. I confess I don't think I have seen him in the laundry or the bootroom or the pantry. And the General looked rather as if he had dressed himself. I believe he shaves himself also."

"Then what is Harrison here for?" Brodie said curiously.

"That is a mystery which I have solved," Stockwell replied with satisfaction, a smile on his long nosed, rather round-eyed face. "The General is an inventor, of sorts, and has brought with him his latest contraption, which is intended, so I believe, to clean and polish boots by means of electricity."

"Land sakes!" Brodie exclaimed. "Whatever for?"

"For something to do, I imagine," Stockwell replied. "Gentlemen are largely at a loss for something to do."

"How does this concern Harrison?" Brodie asked.

"He is assembling the machine in the stables," Stockwell answered. "Or at least he is assisting the General to do so – although I fancy Harrison may be doing most of the work. However, he seems to enjoy it, in fact to take a certain pride in it." A look of puzzlement crossed his rather complacent features. "There is no accounting for the difference in people's tastes, Miss Brodie."

"Indeed not," she said with feeling, and proceeded up the stairs.

★

Dinner was an awkward meal, in spite of the unquestionable excellence of the food: a delicate consommé, fresh asparagus from the kitchen garden, picked at it's tenderest, fresh trout, grilled until it fell from the bone, a saddle of mutton, several kinds of vegetables, followed by apple pie and thick cream, or trifle or fruit sorbet of choice. The awkwardness was caused largely by Violet Welch-Smith. Pamela Selden could see very easily why her brother had wished assistance over the week. Violet was a difficult woman, and she believed in candour as a virtue, regardless of the discomfort it might cause. She was also an enthusiast.

"We had the most marvellous food on our recent trip to France." She looked at her husband who was sitting opposite her across the table. "Didn't we Bertrand?"

Bertie Welch-Smith was unhappy. He thought the remark, just as they were finishing a meal provided by their host, to be unfortunate.

"Didn't care for it a lot, myself," he said with a frankness his wife should have admired. "Too many sauces. Like apple sauce with pork, or mint with lamb, or a spot of horseradish now and again, that's about all. Oh, and a good custard to go with a pudding of course."

Pamela hid a smile. She liked Bertie Welch-Smith. He was in his middle fifties, retired from a career in the army which was brave rather than brilliant. He had reached the rank of General in the old system of his father having purchased a commission for him, and then his turn for promotion having come fortunately soon. A single escapade of extraordinary valour in the Ashanti wars had brought him to the favourable notice of his superiors. He was not a naturally belligerent man; in fact, he was not unlike Freddie Dagliesh himself – good natured, rather shy, something of a humbler except in his particular enthusiasms. For Freddie it was his garden, a thing of extraordinary beauty with flowers and trees from all over the world. For Bertie Welch-Smith it was mechanical inventions.

"You need to cultivate your taste more," Violet said earnestly.

"What?" Bertie was already thinking of something else.

"Cultivate your taste," she repeated slowly, as if he were foolish rather than merely inattentive. "The French are the most cultured nation on earth, you know." She turned to Pamela. "They really know how to live well. We have a great deal to learn from them."

Freddie stiffened and looked at Pamela in desperation.

"I think living well is rather a matter of personal preference," Pamela said, with a smile. "Fortunately we do not all like the same things."

"But we could learn to!" Violet urged, leaning forward across the table. The lights of the chandeliers winked in the crystal and the silver. The last of the dishes had been cleared away. Stockwell came in with the port. The ladies did not retire, since there were only four people present altogether. They took a little Madeira instead and remained.

"Do tell Freddie and Pamela about our stay in France, Bertie," Violet commanded. "I am sure they would be most interested."

Bertie frowned. "I had rather thought of going for a stroll. Take Freddie to see my new machine, what?"

"Later, if you must," she dismissed his plea. "It is a harmless enough occupation, I suppose, but there is absolutely no requirement for such a thing, you know. There are valets and bootboys to polish one's shoes, should they require it. Which brings something to mind." She barely paused for breath, her Madeira ignored. "Do tell Freddie how you found poor Harrison and employed him. A French valet is a wonderful thing to have, Pamela; and a French lady's maid is even better. I cannot tell you the number and variety of skills that girl has." And she proceeded to tell her, detail after detail.

Bertie attempted to interrupt but it was doubtful in Pamela's mind if Violet even heard him. Her enthusiasm waxed strong, and Bertie's eyes took on a faraway look, although Pamela guessed they were really no greater distance than the stable, and his beloved machine.

"So very modern," Violet gushed. "We really are old-fashioned here." Her hands gesticulated, describing some facet of French culture, her face intent.

"I say!" Freddie protested. "That's hardly fair. We are the best inventors in the world!"

She was not to be deterred. "Perhaps we used to be," she swept on. "But the French are now . . . endlessly inventive . . . and really useful things . . ."

Bertie opened his mouth, then closed it again. He looked vaguely crushed.

"You should tell them about finding Harrison," Violet glanced at him, then back to Freddie. "And French menservants are excellent too, not just capable of one skill, like ours, but of all manner of things. Bertie never ceases to sing Harrison's praises."

"Harrison is English!" Bertie said with umbrage. "Dammit Violet, he is as English as steak and kidney pudding!"

"But trained in France!" she retorted instantly. "That makes all the difference. His mind is French."

"Balderdash!" He was growing pink in the face. "He speaks the language, because he spent time there. That was where we found him. But he was more than happy to return home again with us . . . his home. He made that very plain, at least to me."

"I never heard him say that!"

Pamela hid a smile behind her napkin, pretending to sneeze.

"You don't listen" Bertie muttered.

"What did you say?" Violet looked at him sharply.

"He said you don't—" Freddie began.

Pamela kicked him under the table. He winced and opened his eyes very wide.

Pamela smiled charmingly. "He said he won't miss it," she lied without blinking. "I presume he meant that Harrison won't miss France, when he has been with you for a while. After all, you have adopted so many French ways, haven't you? And you have a French maid yourself, so he can always speak the language, if he chooses."

Violet looked confounded for a moment. She knew something had passed her by, but she was not quite sure what.

Pamela rose to her feet. "Shall we go for a stroll in the garden?" she suggested. "There is a clear sky and a full moon. I think it would be very beautiful."

Freddie sighed with relief. Bertie's face broke into a smile. Violet was obliged to agree, more so, civility demanded it.

*

The following morning Brodie woke Pamela with a hot cup of tea, and drew the curtains to a brilliant spring day, with light and shadow chasing each other across the land. A huge aspen, green with leaf, shivered in the breeze and the garden glistened from overnight rain. Pamela's clothes were ready, since she had decided the previous evening what she would wear. After a few exchanges of pleasantries Brodie left to run the bath, and came face to face with Colette on the landing, looking efficient and very pretty, and to Brodie's eyes, a trifle smug.

She looked even more pleased with herself two hours later when Brodie encountered her in the kitchen. She had just come in from the back door and, glancing towards it, Brodie saw a nice looking, if rather foreign, young man in the yard, somewhere between the coal chute and the rubbish bins. He seemed to hesitate for a moment, as though undecided whether to leave or return, but Colette did not look back, and indeed she flushed with colour as she caught Brodie's eye. But there was no way to know if it was annoyance or embarrassment. Brodie thought the former.

A junior housemaid, a girl of about twelve, passed by with a bucket full of damp tea leaves for cleaning the carpet. They were excellent for picking up the dust. She nodded to Brodie respectfully, and walked past Colette as if she had not seen her. Brodie assumed she was another victim of the superiority of all things French. What did the French clean their carpets with? She had heard they did not drink tea! Coffee grounds would hardly serve. The very thought of it was unpleasant.

The cook was giving orders for the day's menus. She was a buxom woman with a face which at first glance seemed benign. But Brodie knew her well enough to be aware that a fierce temper lurked behind the wide, blue eyes and generous mouth. At the moment it was drawn tight as she caught Colette's smirk at the mention of custard for the suet pudding. "Yes?" she said challengingly.

Colette shrugged. "In France we 'ave more of the fruit and less of the suet," she said distinctly, but without looking at anyone. "It is lighter, you understand? Better for the digestion, and of course for the form." She was petite herself, beautifully curved, and moved almost like a dancer on a stage. Brodie felt a little squat and clumsy beside her. "Although you could be right," Colette went in with a delicate little shiver. "After all, the climate, it is so damp! Maybe you need all the suet fat to keep you warm." And without allowing time for anyone to think of a retaliation, she swept out, giving her skirts a little flick as she turned the corner.

"Oh!" the cook let out a snort of exasperation. "That girl! I swear if she comes in here one more time and tells me how good French cooking is, I'll . . . I'll . . . I'll not be responsible!"

The kitchen maid muttered her agreement and heartfelt support.

Stockwell arrived looking portentous. It was his job to keep the entire household in order, and domestic difficulties were his to deal with. He had anticipated trouble in his address to the servants in general, in this morning's prayers before breakfast, but it appeared that might prove insufficient. He should have known the cook by now, but habit and duty were too strong. "I am sure you will always be responsible, Mrs Wimpole," he said smoothly. "You are the last person to let us down by behaving less than perfectly." He straightened his shoulders even further. "We must not allow other nationalities to think we do not know how to conduct ourselves . . . even if they do not."

Mrs Wimpole snorted again and banged her wooden spoon so hard on the kitchen table she all but broke it. The scullery-maid dropped a string of onions and gave a yelp.

"We all have our own difficulties to bear," Stockwell said sententiously.

"Leastways Mr 'Arrison in't French," the bootboy said venomously, looking at Stockwell as boldly as he dared. "And no visitin' General in't makin' a machine wot'il take away yer job from yer." He looked thoroughly unhappy and frightened, his blue eyes wide, his blond hair standing slightly on end where the housekeeper had cut it rather badly – when Stockwell had been absent, up in London with Freddie.

"It won't take your job, Willie," Brodie said comfortingly. "I don't suppose for a moment it works and, even if it did, do you imagine any gentleman would use it himself?"

"Mr Stockwell is all-fired keen on it, Miss," Willie said doubtfully, " 'im or Mr 'Arrison and the General is out there in the stables playin' wif it every chance they gets."

"They are assembling it, Willie," Stockwell broke in. "That is entirely different."

"I don't see no difference," Willie replied, but he did look rather more hopeful.

"Of course there is a difference," Brodie reassured him. "In fact there is no relation. Putting it together is invention – a very suitable occupation for a gentleman, keeping him out of the house and harmlessly busy. Operating it every day to clean shoes would be work, and entirely unsuitable. Whoever heard of a gentleman cleaning his own boots?"

Willie was almost mollified. There was only one last hurdle to clear.

"Wot if 'e 'specs Mr Stockwell ter use it, seein' as it's a machine, an invention, like, and Mr Stockwell's clever, an is 'is butler, an' 'e don't keep a separate valet?"

Stockwell stiffened.

"Butlers don't clean boots," Brodie pronounced without hesitation. "Regardless of how clever they are."

"Oh . . . well I s'pose it's alright then."

"Of course it's all right," Brodie said briskly. "There is no reason whatever for you to worry."

★

After a late and excellent breakfast of the sort Bertie Welch-Smith most enjoyed – eggs, bacon, sausages, kidneys, crisp-fried potatoes and tomatoes, followed by toast and sharp, dark Dundee marmalade and several cups of strong Ceylon tea, all of which he had sorely missed in France – he and Freddie went out to the stables to tinker with the machine.

"Ah!" Bertie said, with satisfaction, patting his stomach. "Can't tell you, old chap, how I missed a decent breakfast in France. Don't mistake me, food's very good, and all that, but I do like a proper cup of tea in the morning. Don't care for coffee much, what? And I like a little real marmalade, some of the stuff you can taste, not all these damn pastries that fall to bits in your hand."

"Quite," Freddie agreed. He had never been to France, but he did not approve in principle. There weren't many people he disliked. One had to be either dishonest or unkind to offend Freddie; but he did dislike Violet Welch-Smith, although he would not have dreamed of letting Bertie see that. Bertie was both his guest and his friend, and therefore sacred on both counts.

They strolled side by side in the sun towards the stables and the marvellous machine.

"And then you must come and see my magnolias," Freddie said hopefully. "I've got some purple ones which really are very fine, if I say so myself."

"Certainly, old boy," Bertie agreed. "Delighted!" He did not know what a magnolia was, but that was irrelevant. Freddie was a good fellow.

*

Brodie busied herself about her duties. There was delicate personal laundry to be done. There was a spot of candlewax on the gown Pamela had worn the previous evening, and she must take it to the ironing room and press it between blotting paper with a warm iron. She would have to remove the pink with a little colourless alcohol. Gin was best. It was a tedious job, but it was the only way. Then naturally there would be a great deal of other ironing to do. A lady's maid's accomplishments were many, but Pamela very seldom desired to be read to or otherwise entertained. She always found more than sufficient to occupy herself. Anyway, she was obliged to accompany Violet, and listen continuously to her endless account of her sojourn in France, and its sophisticated pleasures.

Just before midday, Brodie was walking through the hall towards the conservatory to deliver a message, when she saw a newspaper lying on the table near the umbrella stand. It was the local newspaper, and it had obviously been read and cast aside because it was open at the centre page. She glanced at it and her eye was caught by an advertisement for an exhibition of modern inventions, to be held in the town. Apparently it was most remarkable for the variety and ingeniousness of the machines. In fact, in two days' time the French Ambassador himself was going to open the exhibition formally. In the meantime, it was possible for local people to attend a preview on the following afternoon, if they should so wish.

Brodie was not interested in machines. On the whole, she considered them inferior to a mixture of industry and a little common sense. But perhaps she should keep abreast of ideas, even if only to know what they were, and ease the minds of poor souls like the bootboy.

Tomorrow was her afternoon off. There was really very little for her to do here. All but the most urgent of jobs could wait until she returned home. It would be a pleasant diversion from having to be civil to Colette. The matter was decided. She made a mental note of the time and the place, and continued to the conservatory on her errand.

Stockwell also saw the newspaper, but the copy that caught his eye was the one that Freddie had read and cast away, folded where he had finished it. Stockwell bent to tidy it quite automatically. Books and papers out of alignment, pictures crooked, odd socks, a smear on a glass, all scraped his sensibilities. As he folded the papers neatly, his eye fell on the advertisement for an exhibition of the latest inventions to be held in the town hall, preview possible tomorrow, for local persons with a scientific interest. Stockwell most certainly had a scientific interest. He was eager to acquaint himself with all things modern, and to keep up with the latest challenges and conquests of the intelligent man.

If Mr Dagliesh would permit it, he would make a brief sortie into the town and observe what was on display. The household would take care of itself quite adequately between, say, two o'clock and half-past four tomorrow afternoon. He would be home again in plenty of time, to make sure that everyone did their duty at dinner. There was no need to mention it to anyone except Mr Dagliesh. Mrs Wimpole would be about her own skills in the kitchen, the footmen did not need to know anything except when he would return, and it was not a suitable matter to discuss with Miss Brodie. After all, scientific inventions were hardly women's business.

*

The evening was long, and punctuated with moments of definite unease. Violet Welch-Smith kept repeating recipes for food that was supposed to be remarkably good for the health, which embarrassed her husband, though not greatly. He was too rapt in his satisfaction with his boot polishing machine, which Harrison had assured him was now perfect. Freddie endeavoured not to listen, simply to make agreeable noises every time Violet stopped talking long enough. Pamela kept the peace as well as she could – and her temper as well as she thought possible.

Brodie had the curious experience of seeing Colette's admirer again. It was just after ten in the evening and she was coming back from fetching a petticoat she had inadvertently left in the ironing room, when she saw Colette standing in the passageway with her back to the light, and not a foot away from her was the man Brodie had seen her with before. This time he was facing the light and she saw his features quite distinctly. He was very dark with fine brows and a slightly aquiline nose. She judged he would normally be a very pleasant looking man, but at this moment his expression was one of earnestness bordering upon anger, and he was whispering fiercely to Colette, something which seemed not to please her at all.

"Auguste, c'est impossible!" she said furiously.

Brodie did not speak French, but the meaning of that phrase was clear enough, as was Colette's defiant stance, hands on hips, chin raised, shoulders stiff.

Something must have distracted Auguste – perhaps the light reflecting on Brodie's face or the faintest of rustles as the fabric of her dress brushed against the wall. He turned and left so quickly, melting into the shadows of the passageway back to the door, that, had she not seen the look on Colette's face, she might have supposed he had been a figment of her imagination and not a real person at all.

Brodie disliked Colette profoundly, but to tell tales was a contemptible thing to do, something she had never stooped to since one dismal episode in her youth which she preferred not to think of now. She contented herself with looking at Colette meaningfully – to Colette's discomfort – and then, with a decided swing in her own step, she continued on her way.

*

The following afternoon Brodie, with Pamela's good wishes, dressed in her best afternoon skirt and jacket, a green which became her very well, and set out to walk briskly into the town. It was only a matter of some two miles or so, and she expected to accomplish it in half an hour. It was an extremely agreeable day, mild and bright with a steady breeze carrying the heady scents of hawthorn blossom. There were still primroses, pale on the dark banks of the ditches. Birds sang, and far away over the fields a dog barked. Other than that there was no sound but the wind in the trees and her own brisk footsteps on the road.

The exhibition was very well signposted and she found it immediately. There were few people attending, which was fortunate. It would give her time to look for the General's device without being hurried on.

The first machine which caught her attention was a travelling electric stairlamp, made by M. Armand Marat, obviously a

Frenchman with a name like that. In fact about everything she saw in the first room appeared to be invented, designed or made by a Frenchman.

She passed to the second room, but, before she could examine the machines in it, she saw the back of a very upright man of robust physique, his clothes immaculate, his hair greying and perfectly barbered, a completely unnecessary furled umbrella in his hand. What was Stockwell doing here? She considered retreating, then was furious with herself. Why on earth should she allow Stockwell's presence to dictate what she should do? She would not be driven out!

"Good afternoon, Mr Stockwell," she said decisively.

He turned around very slowly, his face almost comical with surprise. "Miss Brodie! What on earth are you doing here? Has something happened?" Now he looked alarmed.

"Yes, something has happened!" she said disgustedly. "It appears that the French have stolen a march on us. All the inventions in this miserable place are French! There is barely a single exhibit that is English that I have seen! It is most disconcerting."

"I agree," he said unhappily. "It is most regrettable. However, I can think of nothing whatever to do about it, except take defeat like gentlemen ... and ladies. To concede defeat with grace at least has dignity, and that we must never lose, Miss Brodie. Stiff upper lip in times of hardship."

Brodie disliked conceding defeat at all, even if she were rigid to her eyebrows.

"Is there nothing British here at all?" she asked.

"Only the General's boot polishing machine," Stockwell said grimly. "I fear it is hardly a great cultural step forward for mankind, nor will it be of particular benefit to anyone at all. As you quite reasonably pointed out to young William, it is merely a toy for gentlemen, until they tire of it and find a new one. Probably the best that can be said of it is that it is not dangerous. No one will cut off their fingers, or set fire to the house with it."

Brodie sighed. "I suppose we had better have a look at it, since we are here anyway." She gazed around her. "Where is it?"

"It is in the next room, where the curator is. Although what harm he imagines could come to any of these, I don't know. I suppose someone might try to use one of them?"

Brodie gave him a withering look.

He shrugged.

Side by side, but not touching, they made their way to the third room and its exhibits. The curator was standing in the centre. On the wall by the door as one would leave was a poster declaring proudly that the event would be opened officially by the French Ambassador to the Court of St James, on April 12th, which would be . . . the day after tomorrow.

"Well, which is it?" Brodie whispered, staring around her at the extraordinary array of machines and contraptions of every size and shape that were established against the wall. Not one of them looked obviously useful. Some resembled clothes mangles, others tin boxes with wires, yet others elaborate typewriters. One looked rather like a bicycle stood upside down on its saddle, with two rather small wheels. Stockwell pointed to it.

"That is it," he said very quietly, so the curator would not hear him.

Brodie's heart sank. It really did look extraordinarily cumbersome – more fun than a brush and cloth and a good jar of polish, but a great deal less convenient. She was now quite convinced that William's job was in no jeopardy.

"Oh dear," she murmured sadly.

They walked over with affected casualness and stared at the contraption. Viewed from only a yard away, it was even more like a bicycle. It was possible to see quite easily which were the moving parts, where the brushes were, and where one was intended to place one's foot in order to have one's boots very highly polished. There was a metal foot with many joints, and a ratchet to alter its size according to the boot in question, but it would still be an awkward and rather time-consuming task to place the boot accurately. It was so much easier simply to put one's hand into a boot or shoe, and polish with a brush in the other hand. Brodie refrained from comment.

"Ah . . ." Stockwell said thoughtfully. "I believe I see the principle upon which it works. Simple, yet clever. It would obtain a most excellent shine."

"Yes," Brodie agreed loyally. After all, it was a British invention and the General was one of the household. "It certainly would. Unparalleled." She continued to look at it in the hope she could see something she could admire more genuinely. The longer she looked at it, the less hope did she feel.

Stockwell must now have been feeling the same, judging by the despair in his face.

Brodie went over the mechanism in her mind once more, envisioning precisely how it would work, when switched on. There seemed to be a part whose function she could not see; in fact the more she considered it, the more convinced she was that it was not only redundant, but it would actually get in the way when the thing was set in motion. There were two parts of it, metal parts, which were bound to touch when they moved in the only way they could. She pointed it out to Stockwell.

"You must be mistaken, Miss Brodie," he said quite kindly. After all, how could she be expected to understand how a machine would work.

"No I'm not, Mr Stockwell," she replied. She was very good at judging the length of a thing with her eye. Good heavens, she had sewed from exact measurements for enough years. She knew the length of a skirt, the size of a waist or the width of a hem to an exactness. "It will strike that piece there!"

"Really!" he said with diminishing patience. "Do you imagine Mr Dagliesh and the General have not tried it out?"

Actually, Brodie thought that was very likely, since she was more than ever convinced that the rising bar would catch against the angled cross bar – not violently, but sufficient to graze it – and since they were both apparently metal, to strike a spark. It also looked long enough to touch the bar immediately above, but perhaps that did not matter. That might be where it was meant to rest. However, with the best will in the world, which she had, she could not admire it with any enthusiasm.

Stockwell was still regarding her crossly, waiting for an answer.

"I suppose they must have," she conceded reluctantly, and then with a parting shot. "I don't understand what that piece is for?" She pointed to the metal bar against which the moving part must rest when it had completed its cycle.

Stockwell's face took on a look of indulgent superiority.

"It is part of the structure, Miss Brodie, necessary for the strength of the machine when it is in motion."

"I don't see how." His tone troubled her. "Surely that piece above it is sufficient for that purpose? It is not going to bear either weight or stress." Her mouth compressed into a thinner line.

"It must do, or it would not be there!"

"What stress? Surely the piece above it serves that purpose?"

"Do not concern yourself, Miss Brodie," he said coldly. "Machinery is not the natural talent of women. It is hardly to be expected that you should understand the principles of engineering. It reflects no discredit upon you."

She had not for an instant considered it might. It was discredit to the machine she had in mind. But she could see from the set of his face that he did not understand it either, and therefore would brook no argument. However, he added one word too many. "I am sure you can appreciate that, Miss Brodie!"

"No," she said abruptly. "It is not myself I am questioning, it is the machine. I am afraid it is not quite right, and may let the General and Mr Dagliesh down when the French Ambassador comes to test it."

"Balderdash!" Stockwell retorted, pink in the face now and plainly discomfited. "I think, Miss Brodie, that we have looked at this exhibit long enough. I am going to have a cup of tea. I observed a very agreeable establishment a mere five minutes away. If you wish to join me, I do not mind."

It was an uncharacteristically ungracious invitation, made under duress, but Brodie accepted it, partly because she would not be dismissed like that, but mostly because she was extremely ready for a cup of tea. It had been a long, thirsty walk into town, and would be the same on the return, especially if she were to try to keep up with Stockwell's pace.

"Thank you," she said stiffly in reply.

He looked a little surprised, but after a moment's hesitation offered her his arm. He would never have dreamed of doing so in the house, but this was different. Here they were practically socially equal.

She accepted it as if it were her due.

They walked together across the street and along the pavement without speaking any further, but when the tea was ordered by Stockwell, and poured by Brodie, he broke the silence at last, tentatively to begin with.

"Miss Brodie . . ."

"Yes, Mr Stockwell?"

"I have observed a ... person ... around the house and grounds lately, a foreign-appearing person, who seems to be paying attention to Mrs Welch-Smith's maid. Have you noticed anything?"

"Yes I have," she said quickly – mention of Colette thawing her annoyance with Stockwell very rapidly. After all, it was a very secondary matter. "I have seen him twice now. I heard her address him as 'Auguste', and say what I believe was 'it is impossible'."

He leaned forward. "You believe? Did you not hear clearly?"

"What I think she actually said was 'c'est impossible'."

"I see. No doubt you are correct about the meaning, but it could refer to anything, even another meeting between them. But let us be diligent, Miss Brodie, and be warned. It is not unknown for servants of a certain character to open the way for accomplices to rob a house. We must be ever aware of the possibility. I shall have the footmen be extra alert where locks are concerned . . ."

"That will be no use if she lets him in," Brodie warned. "And . . ."

"And what?" he said urgently. "There is something else? Strive to remember, Miss Brodie. Crimes are solved by deductive reasoning, and prevented by acute observation beforehand." He blinked very slightly. "I am still reading the exploits of Mr Sherlock Holmes in the *Strand Magazine*. I find him most satisfying in his logic, and somewhat instructive as to the processes of detection. Please, inform me of all you recall of this person 'Auguste'."

Brodie thought very carefully before she began. It was most important that she did not allow her feelings to colour her memory, for the sake both of truth and most particularly of honour – in front of Stockwell of all people. "It is more a matter of impression," she said, guardedly. "He was a good looking man . . ."

"I have seen him," Stockwell interrupted. "I have no difficulty in accepting that Colette may be enamoured of him. I wish to know something of use . . . relevant to . . . to detection! Perhaps I have not made myself clear . . ."

"You do not need to!" she said politely. "If you had permitted me to finish it would have become apparent."

He flushed faintly pink, and stared back at her. He was not going to go further than that. An apology was out of the question. He waited.

She cleared her throat. "He was very neat about his person, well shaved, well barbered, his shirt collar clean and pressed, his tie straight ... that was as much of him as I observed. The shadows made it impossible to see the rest of his apparel clearly enough to describe. He gave me the impression of a service clerk in some form of business, or ..." she hesitated. "That is not quite right."

"Yes?" he prompted, curiosity getting the better of him.

"Yet he had rather more confidence than I would have expected in a man of such an occupation. He left very quickly upon seeing me, as if he did not wish me to look at him too closely, yet I detected in him no feeling of alarm, certainly not of guilt. When I look back on that, it is curious."

"It is indeed," he agreed, drinking his tea "Are you quite sure of that, Miss Brodie?"

"Yes, I believe so. And the oddest thing is that, rather than stop flirting with each other when they became aware of me, that was the moment they started. Before they saw me – or to be more accurate, before *she* saw me – they were talking earnestly, as if about some matter of importance. There is a good deal of difference between a woman's attitude when she is talking to a man simply to play, and the subject matter is irrelevant, and when she means what she says."

"I was aware of that." He pursed his lips. "I have dealt in my profession with a large number of young housemaids and footmen. This what you describe is most puzzling. We require to know a great deal more about Colette and her admirer, if that is what he was; although now I begin to believe he may be something else. The question is, is he deceiving her too, pretending to be enamoured of her, but, in truth, merely using her to gain access to the house, or is she a knowing accomplice. And what of the valet, Harrison? He is an unusual man." Stockwell frowned, puzzlement marked deeply in his normally smooth, even, and complacent face.

"In what way?" she asked, sipping her tea, but not taking her eyes from his. "I have barely seen him. He is never in the laundry or ironing rooms ... or the stillroom or bootroom either, for that matter."

"Quite," he agreed. "It seems to me that the General does the greater part of his own valeting, while Harrison is in the stables attending to that invention of theirs. Now it is safely installed, he is back in the house, but I still see little of him. However it was his remarks, his expression to which I refer."

"What remarks?" Tacitly, she offered him more tea, and he accepted. She poured it while he answered, after she had disposed of the now cold dregs in the slop basin.

"He says very little about France. Thank you," he said, referring to the tea. "But when anything French is mentioned, a look of distaste, almost of anger, crosses his face. I am not certain if it is his own personal feeling, or if he is merely embarrassed that Colette, and Mrs Welch-Smith, should be so eager to praise everything French while in the house of an Englishman. They do it to a degree which borders on offence."

"It is well across the border!" Brodie said tartly, helping herself to a fresh scone, butter, jam and clotted cream – a very English delicacy in which she would not normally indulge. She would have to abstain from pudding at supper.

"You are correct," Stockwell agreed graciously. "I am afraid several of the staff are beginning to be ruffled by it. There is some peacemaking to be done."

Brodie sat in silence, thinking. There was indeed a mystery. Perhaps something genuinely unpleasant threatened. She and Stockwell must join forces, as before.

"This time we must prevent any crime before it happens, Mr Stockwell," she said very sincerely.

"I have every intention that we shall do so, Miss Brodie," he agreed with feeling. "We must be equal to the task. As before, I shall find your assistance. You shall be my Watson!"

On the contrary, she thought to herself, *I shall be* your *Holmes!* But she had more tact than to say so.

The evening did not go smoothly. When Brodie returned to the house, more than a little footsore, Colette surveyed her tired face and wet feet with disdain, and made a remark about the glamour and excitement of Paris, and the charm of the French countryside, where of course the climate was kinder. Sunshine was so very good for the spirits.

Brodie glared at her, and went upstairs to change into dry

shoes and her uniform dress. Even in the days of her youth she had never had a figure like Colette's, or the art to tie a bow till it looked like a frill of lace for the occasions when an apron was required.

After dinner, quite by chance, as she was returning from the stillroom, Brodie again saw the mysterious Auguste. He was walking along the passage from Stockwell's pantry towards the back door. He had not seen her, and she had time to study him quite carefully, making mental notes to observe with skill, not mere curiosity. To begin with he was quite tall, and he walked with an elegance. Certainly he did not sneak or cower. His jacket was well cut, but, as he passed under the lamp on the wall, she could see that it also was not new. She glanced very quickly at his feet. One could sometimes tell much about a person's station in life from their boots. His were very well worn indeed, and now wet.

"Good evening, Monsieur," she said briskly.

He froze, then very slowly turned and stared at her. He was obviously abashed at having been seen, but he did not look guilty, rather annoyed at himself.

"Good evening, Madam," he replied courteously. His voice was pleasant enough, but heavily accented.

"I assume you are looking for Colette?" Brodie continued.

For a moment he was taken aback. She thought he was even going to deny it. Then he made an awkward little movement, half a bow. "No thank you, I was just about to go." He indicated the way to the door.

She looked him up and down closely. His suit fitted him too well for him to conceal anything of size in his pockets. At least on this occasion he had not robbed the household.

"Goodnight, then," she answered pleasantly, and resumed her way towards the kitchen. She was pleased to see Colette there, busy preparing a special egg-and-milk drink which Mrs Welch-Smith liked before retiring. She was looking for the nutmeg.

"Second drawer in the spice rack," Brodie said tartly.

"Oh!" Colette spun around. "How do you know what I wanted, Miss Brodie?"

"Well, that's black pepper you have in your hand! Or maybe you like pepper in your milk in France, even last thing at night?"

"Of course not!" Colette snapped. "Although, if you know anything about cuisine, you would not need to ask! Really, such an idea! All the delicacy would be lost. But then, English cooking is hardly an art – is it!"

"Well, it is obviously not one you know," Brodie returned. "Nor is a decent respect for the household of your host, or you could not make such an unseemly remark. But then French manners are hardly an art either!"

Colette drew in her breath to retaliate.

Brodie got there first. "And another thing, while we are discussing it, it is not done in England for a visiting maid to have her followers in the house without permission – which would not be granted. I dare say Monsieur Auguste is a perfectly respectable person, but it is a principle. Some maids can attract a very dubious class of followers . . ."

Colette was furious, but oddly she did not explode with outrage. She seemed on the verge of speech, and then to hesitate, as though undecided, even confused.

"Many houses have been robbed that way," Brodie added for good measure.

Extraordinarily, Colette started to laugh, a high pitched giggle rising towards hysteria.

Stockwell appeared at the door, his face dark with disapproval.

"What is going on here?" he demanded.

Brodie was annoyed at being caught in what was obviously a quarrel. It was undignified. And by Stockwell, of all people.

She was prevented from replying by the arrival of Harrison, General Welch-Smith's valet. He was a pleasant-featured man with fair hair and large, strong hands. At the moment there was a sneer on his lips.

"Saw that follower of yours going across the yard," he said to Colette. "You'd better make sure you don't get caught, my girl! French may have the morals of an alley-cat, but English don't like their servants having strange men in off the streets. Imagine what the mistress'd have to say if I brought some dolly-mop into the house! Get caught having a quick fumble in the cupboard under the stairs, and the mistress won't be able to protect you, no matter how well you can use a curling tong . . . the General'll have you out!"

Colette looked at him with utter loathing, but she seemed to have nothing to say. She turned on her heel, but, when she stopped at the door, the milk and nutmeg temporarily forgotten, the look in her face was not one of defeat, but of waiting malice, as if she knew she would triumph in the end.

*

Brodie went to bed unhappy and profoundly puzzled. There was too much that did not make sense, and yet when she examined each individual instance, there was nothing to grasp. Who was Auguste? He did not behave like a man in love. Why did Colette seem to think she had some peculiar victory waiting for her? Why had Harrison been living in France so long if he disliked the French as he seemed to? She realized in thinking about it that she had heard him make other disparaging remarks, and there had been a light in his eyes of far more than usual irritation or disapproval. There was some deep emotion involved.

How on earth was the General's machine going to work when one piece was going to strike another as soon as it was set in motion? And what about the extra cross bar? So far as she could see, it offered no additional strength, no purpose, and certainly no beauty.

She went to sleep with it all churning in her mind, and woke in the middle of the night with the answer sharp and horribly clear, as if she had already seen it happen: the two pieces striking would ignite a spark ... the extra piece had a hideous use ... it was not metal but dynamite! It would explode – a mechanical bomb – killing the French Ambassador, or at the very least seriously injuring him.

General Welch-Smith would be blamed, naturally. He designed the machine. He made it, with Harrison's help. He had just returned from a long sojourn in France.

And Freddie Dagliesh would also be blamed, by implication. The General was staying in his house, they had been friends for years; Freddie had assisted in the last minute touches to the machine. It was quite horrible.

Perhaps Colette knew of it? That could be why she had that look of secret triumph in her eyes. Then who was Auguste? An accomplice? He must be.

But an accomplice to whom? Surely the General had not really done this? Why? What had happened to him in France that he could even think of such an idea?

The reason hardly mattered. The thing now was to prevent it from happening. She must tell Stockwell. He was the only person who would believe her. Then together they would tell . . . who? Not the General, certainly. And would Freddie give a moment's credence to such a tale?

She and Stockwell must do it alone, and there would be no opportunity to speak in the morning. They would all be far too busy with their own duties. She needed time to persuade him of the inevitable logic of what she had deduced. He could be stubborn now and again. And he would be appalled at being woken in the middle of the night. It was conceivable there had never been a woman in his bedroom, in his adult life, except a housemaid to clean it. If he had ever had any personal relationships they would most assuredly have been conducted elsewhere, and with the utmost discretion.

She sat up and fumbled in the dark for matches to light the candle. There were gas lamps downstairs, of course, but on the servants' level – even the superior servants such as herself – it was candles. She succeeded, then reached for her shawl; there was no time to bother with the fuss of dressing, chemises and petticoats and stockings. Wrapped up with a shawl for decency more than warmth, she tip-toed along the corridor to the farther end where she knew Stockwell's room was situated. There was a connecting door between the male servants' quarters and those of the female servants, as decorum required, but it was not locked.

She was watching ahead of her so carefully, that she caught her toe against the leg of a side table where ewers of water were left. She almost cried out with pain, and there was a distinct rattle as china touched china.

Good heavens! What on earth would anyone think if she were found here? She was right outside Stockwell's door. How could she possibly explain herself? She couldn't! The General's invention was going to explode and kill the French Ambassador! She could hear the laughter now, and see the total contempt in their eyes. It was almost enough to make her turn back. She had a blameless reputation! It would be a lifetime's good character gone – and for what?

To save one man's life and another man's reputation, that was what.

Dare she knock?

What if someone else were awake and heard, and thought it was their own door?

They would answer it. They would see her standing here in her nightgown and shawl, her hair down her back and a candle in her hand, waiting at Stockwell's bedroom door. She would never be able to live it down! She could hear the young maids' comments now! Hear their laughter. They would never let her forget it! Silly old woman – absurd – at her age!

That was it. It was decided! She put her hand on the knob, turned it and went in. She closed it behind her very nearly without sound. Stockwell was lying curled over on his side in the middle of the bed, blankets tucked up to his chin, nightcap – a little askew – on his head. He looked very ordinary and very vulnerable. He would probably never ever forgive her for this.

"Mr Stockwell . . ." she whispered.

He did not move.

"Mr Stockwell . . ." she said a trifle more loudly.

He stirred and turned over.

Heavens alive. What if he saw her and cried out? That would be the worst of all possibilities. "Don't say anything!" She ordered desperately. "Please keep quiet!"

Stockwell opened his eyes and sat up slowly, his face transfixed with horror. His nightcap slipped over one ear.

She could feel her face burning.

"I had to come!" she said defensively.

"Miss Brodie!" The words were forced between his lips. He was aghast. He opened his mouth to continue, and could not.

"I know what is wrong!" she said urgently. "With the machine! With the General's machine! It is going to explode . . . and kill the French Ambassador . . . and General Welch-Smith will be blamed. I don't know . . . perhaps he should be. But Mr Dagliesh will be blamed also, and he shouldn't. We must do something about it before that can happen."

To do him justice, he did not ask her if she had been at the port, but his expression suggested it.

"Imagine it in your mind!" she urged. "Visualize how the contraption will work. The French Ambassador places his foot on the rest, presses the button and the polish cloth rubs his boot, then the second piece starts to move." She waved her hands to demonstrate. "It has to come down, in order to buff the leather. It strikes the cross bar, only very lightly, but sufficiently to cause a spark." She leaned forward a little. "Now – visualize the other piece . . . unnecessarily double, you recall . . . That is the dynamite, Mr Stockwell . . . it will ignite, and explode!" She jerked her hand and nearly threw the candle at him.

"Miss Brodie!" he cried.

"Be quiet!" she whispered in agony of embarrassment. "Think of where we are! I had to come, because there will be no time in the morning. We may not even see each other till half way through the day. We must do something to prevent this! No one else will. It lies with us."

"I . . . I shall speak to Mr Dagliesh," he offered. "In the morning!"

"To do what?" she said exasperatedly. Really, Stockwell was being very obtuse. Perhaps he was one of those people who woke only slowly?

"Well . . . to . . ." he looked uncomfortable. He could now see the pointlessness of expecting Freddie to do anything at all about it. He would only speak to the General, in his own innocence, believing Welch-Smith to be equally blameless.

"If the General knows about it, he will deny it," she pointed out. "And if he doesn't know about it, of course he will deny it. Mr Dagliesh will be immensely relieved, and tell us we do not need to worry. All is well."

He frowned. He was obviously feeling at an acute disadvantage sitting up in the bed, but he did not wish to rise with Brodie standing there. He felt very exposed in his striped nightshirt. There was something about being without trousers which was highly personal.

"Perhaps all *is* well?" he said with a thread of hope. "Surely it is more than possible the design is simply clumsy?"

The perfect answer was on her lips. "Do you imagine Mr Sherlock Holmes would be content with 'a possibility', Mr Stockwell?"

He straightened up visibly, forgetting his embarrassment and his doubts.

"I shall meet you at the stables at a quarter past eleven, Miss Brodie," he said with absolute decision. "We shall take the carriage, as if on an errand, and determine for ourselves the exact nature of this wretched machine. Be prompt. Whatever your duties, see they are completed by then. We must act."

She smiled back at him approvingly. "Assuredly, Mr Stockwell. We shall prevent disaster ... if indeed disaster is planned. Goodnight."

He clutched the sheet with both hands. "Goodnight, Miss Brodie."

★

It was a fine day and the ride to the town was swift and pleasant. Outside the exhibition hall were posters proclaiming the official visit of the French Ambassador the following morning. Inside, there were rather more people than there had been yesterday. Brodie and Stockwell were obliged to excuse themselves and pass several groups standing in front of various examples of French ingenuity and design. They heard exclamations of admiration and marvel at a people who could think of such things

Brodie gritted her teeth, remembering why they were here. The French might be the most inventive race in Europe, but it would be English courage and foresight, English nerve and integrity that saved the Ambassador.

They found the boot polisher, looking more than ever like a bicycle upside down. Brodie was both relieved and offended that there was no one else in front of it, admiring the ingenuity which had thought of such a thing. That was the trouble with the British ... they always admired something foreign!

She glanced at Stockwell, looking utterly different this morning: in his pin-striped trousers and dark jacket, his face immaculately shaved, if a little pink, his collar and tie crisp and exactly symmetrical. She thought she saw in his eye a reflection of the pride, and the conviction she herself felt. It was most satisfying.

She turned her attention to the machine. It would not move without the electrical power, and that was to be turned on tomorrow, by the Ambassador; but, the more she looked at it, the more certain she was that the parts would rub against each other with sufficient force to strike a spark. There was only one thing that remained to be done. She leaned forward to touch the redundant piece and feel its texture. Metal . . . or dynamite? She did not know what dynamite felt like, but she knew steel.

"Don't touch the exhibits, if you please, Madam!"

It was the voice of the curator, sharp and condescending, as if she had been a small child about to risk breaking some precious ornament. She flushed to the roots of her hair.

Stockwell leaped into the fray with a boldness which surprised even himself.

"Yes, my dear, better not," he said calmly. He turned away from Brodie as if the order would be sufficient, his word would be obeyed, and engaged the curator in conversation. "Please tell me, sir, something about this remarkable piece of equipment over here." He all but led the man across the room to the farther side, and a monstrous edifice of wires and pulleys. "I am sure you know how this works, the principle behind it, but I confess I fail to grasp it fully."

"Ah well, you see . . ." the curator was flattered by this upstanding gentleman's interest, and his perception in realizing that a curator was a man of knowledge himself, not merely a watchman who conducted people around. "It's like this . . ." He proceeded to explain at length.

"Well?" Stockwell demanded when he and Brodie were back together in a quiet corner.

"You were magnificent," she said generously, and quite sincerely.

He blushed with pleasure, but kept his face perfectly straight. "Thank you. But I was referring to the redundant piece. Is it metal?"

"No," she said without hesitation. "It is soft to the fingernail, a trifle waxy. I was able to take a flake of it off without difficulty. I believe it is dynamite."

"Oh . . . oh dear." He was caught between the deeper hope that it would not after all be necessary to do anything and the anticipation of being right, and with it the taste for adventure. "I see. Then I am afraid it falls upon us to foil the plan, Miss Brodie. We shall have to act, and I fear it must be immediate. There is no time to lose."

She agreed wholeheartedly, but how to act was another thing altogether.

"Let us take a dish of tea, and consider the matter," Stockwell said firmly, touching her elbow to guide her towards the doorway, and at least temporary escape.

As soon as tea was brought to them, and poured, they addressed the subject.

"We have already discussed the possibility of informing the authorities," Stockwell stated. He glanced at the tray of small savoury sandwiches on the table, but did not touch them. "The only course open to us is to disarm the machine. We shall have to do it so that no one observes either our work, or its result. Therefore we must replace the dynamite with something that looks exactly like it."

"I see," Brodie nodded and sipped her tea, which was delicious, but still rather hot. "Have you any ideas as to how we should accomplish that?"

"I have an excellent pocket knife!" he replied with a slight frown. "I think I should have relatively little trouble in removing the dynamite. I believe it will cut without too much difficulty. I could also use the blade as a screwdriver, should one be necessary. However, I have not yet hit upon any idea of what we should put in place of that which we remove."

Brodie thought hard for several moments. She took one of the sandwiches and bit into it. It was very fresh and really most pleasant. She took another sip of tea. Then the idea came to her.

"Bread!" she said rather more loudly than she intended.

"I beg your pardon?" Stockwell looked totally nonplussed.

"Bread," she replied more moderately. "Fresh bread, very fresh indeed, may be moulded into shapes and made hard, if you compress it. I have seen beads made of it. After all, it is in essence only flour and water paste. We still have to paint it black, of course, but that should not prove too difficult. Then we may put it in place of the dynamite, and we will have accomplished our task."

"Excellent, Miss Brodie!" Stockwell said enthusiastically "That will do most excellently well. But of course it is only a part of our task . . ."

"I realize making the exchange will not be easy," Brodie agreed. "In fact it may require all our ingenuity to succeed. The curator is not impressed with me as it is. He will not allow me near the machine again, I fear."

"Don't worry, I shall accomplish the exchange," he assured her. "If you will distract the curator's attention. But that is not what I meant. We cannot claim our task is completed until we know who placed the dynamite in the machine." He shook his head a little. "On considering the problem, it seems clear to me that it can only have been either the General himself or Harrison. I have weighed the issue in my mind since you brought it to my attention, and I believe that the General has no reason for such a thing, and would bring about his own ruin, since he will naturally be blamed. Whereas Harrison appears to dislike the French, and may have some deeper cause for his feelings than we know. He has far less to lose, socially and professionally speaking. And he would be able to disappear after the event, take the next train up to London, and never be seen again. We know nothing of him, whereas we know everything of the General. Mr Dagliesh has had his acquaintance on and off for thirty years."

"I am sure you are right," Brodie nodded. "But as you point out, it remains to prove it – after we have removed the dynamite. I shall purchase some fresh bread at the bakery across the street. Can you obtain some black paint and a brush without returning to the house?"

"I am sure I can. Where shall we meet to do the work? It must be discreet."

Brodie thought hard, and no answer came to her.

"I have it!" Stockwell said with pleasure. "There is a public bath-house on the corner of Bedford Street. It has private changing places for both ladies and gentlemen. If you use the rooms for ladies, you can make the bread the requisite size. Do you know what that is?"

"I do. It is two inches less than the distance from my wrist to my elbow, and as thick as my thumb."

"Bravo! Then we shall begin. I think I may say 'the game's afoot'. Come, Miss Brodie. Let us advance to battle."

*

But distracting the attention of the curator was less easy than they had supposed. They returned some considerable time later, the long, black stick of bread, paint just dry, concealed up Stockwell's sleeve. The curator regarded them with displeasure. Had it been anything but the utmost urgency, Brodie would have left and gone home. But that would be cowardice under fire, and Brodie had never been a coward. England's honour was at stake.

"Now, Miss Brodie," Stockwell said gently, and perhaps with a touch of new respect in his tone. "Charge!"

She gulped and sailed forward. There were only four other people in the room: a gentleman and two ladies, and of course the curator.

"How wonderful to see you again!" she said loudly, staring at one of the ladies, an elderly person in a shade of purple she should never have worn. "You look so well! I am delighted to see you so recovered."

The women stared at her in perplexity.

"And your great uncle," Brodie went on even more loudly. Now the others were staring at her also. "Is he recovered from that appalling affair in Devon? What a perfectly dreadful woman, and so much younger than he."

The woman now looked at her in considerable alarm, and clutched at the hand of the gentleman next to her.

"I don't know you!" she said in a high-pitched voice. "I don't have a great uncle in Devon, or anywhere else!"

"I'm not surprised you should disown him," Brodie said in a tone of great sympathy, but still as loudly as she could, as if she thought the woman in purple might be deaf, and shouting would make the meaning plainer. "But older men can be so easily beguiled, don't you think?"

Two more people had entered the room from one of the other halls, but they paid no attention to Stockwell or the exhibits. They focused entirely upon Brodie and the scene of acute embarrassment being played out in the centre of the floor. The curator dithered from one foot to the other in uncertainty as to what to do; whether to intervene in what was obviously a very private matter, or to pretend he had not even heard. Sometimes the latter was the only way to treat such a matter with kindness.

The woman in purple was still staring at Brodie as if she were an apparition risen out of the floor.

"Of course she was very attractive," Brodie resumed relentlessly. Stockwell could not be finished yet. She must buy him time. "In an extraordinary sort of way. I've never seen so much hair! Have you? And such a colour, my dear! Like tomato soup!"

"I don't know you!" the woman repeated desperately, waving her hands in the air. "I have no great uncles at all!"

"Really!" The man beside her came to her rescue at last. "I must protest, Mrs Er . . . I mean . . ." He glared at Brodie. "Lady Dora has already explained to you, as kindly as possible, that you have made a mistake. Please accept that and do not pursue the matter."

"Oh!" Brodie let out a shriek of dismay. "Lady Dora? Are you sure?" Lady Dora was very pink in the face, a most unbecoming colour.

"Of course I'm sure!" she shrieked.

"I do apologize," Brodie shouted back, still on the assumption Lady Dora was hard of hearing. "I mistook you for Mrs. Marshfield, who looks so like you, in a certain light, of course, when wearing just the right shade of . . . what would you say? Plum? Claret? I really should remember my spectacles. They make such a difference, don't you think? I am quite mortified. Whatever can I do?" She asked it not rhetorically, but as if she expected and required a reply.

Lady Dora looked not a whit comforted. She stared at Brodie with loathing. "Please don't distress yourself," she said icily. "Now that the issued is settled, there is no offence, I assure you."

"You are too generous," Brodie exclaimed. Where on earth was Stockwell. Had he finished yet? She dared not glance around in case she drew anyone else's attention to him. What on earth was there left for him to do? "I feel quite ill with confusion that I should have made such an error." She rolled her eyes as if she were about to faint.

"Water!" Lady Dora's companion said loudly.

The other woman moved forward to offer assistance, still looking sideways at Lady Dora as if she half-believed Brodie's tale of the uncle. There was something of a smile about her lips.

"For heaven's sake fetch some water, man!" Lady Dora's companion commanded the curator, who at last moved to obey. With much assistance, Brodie was led to a seat and plied with water, a fan, smelling salts, and good advice. It was a full five minutes before she could bring herself to leave. She staggered out into the fresh air and was overwhelmed with relief to see Stockwell looking triumphant, and pretending not to know her, as the curator let go of her arm, and suggested very forcefully that she did not return.

"The atmosphere is not good for you, Madam," he said, between thin lips. "I think for your health, you should refrain from such enclosed spaces. Good day."

★

The following morning Pamela and Freddie went with Bertie and Violet Welch-Smith to see the formal opening of the exhibition. Both men were very excited about it, and Pamela felt she had to balance Violet's disinterest by feigning an enthusiasm herself. They were accompanied by Harrison, a just reward for his many hours of work in helping to construct the General's machine, and for his care and maintenance of it.

When they got there, it was very difficult. Almost all the exhibits seemed to be French. There were electric jewels invented by Monsieur Trouve of Paris, largely for use on stage. Next to that was an optical theatre designed by a Monsieur Reynaud. There were other French inventions: a portable shower-bath, created by Monsieur Gaston Bozetian; a device to prevent snoring; a construction for reaching the North Pole by balloon; and an invention by Dr Varolt – again of Paris – for electroplating the bodies of the dead so that they were covered with a millimetre thick layer of metallic copper of a brilliant red colour, so that the remains of a beloved could be preserved indefinitely. Violet became even more appreciative, praising them vociferously, and making Pamela feel more and more irritated.

At eleven o'clock the French Ambassador arrived, a neat and elegant man immaculately dressed and carrying a furled umbrella as if he did not trust the mild and delightful spring day. He declared the exhibition open, made several remarks about the service that inventors performed for humanity, and then proceeded to walk around the various exhibits and examine each in turn. He was followed by a small crowd of people.

He reached the boot polishing machine at about a quarter to twelve.

"Oh! And this is the English invention!" he said with as much enthusiasm as he could muster. He looked at it carefully, and it was apparent he was highly dubious about its value, but it would be a national insult if he did not try to use it.

Pamela watched, as gingerly, he put his foot on the pedal and reached for the switch to turn it on. She saw Harrison, his face alight with jubilation, as if a great moment of triumph had at last arrived.

The Ambassador's finger was on the button.

"No! It is a bomb!" someone yelled wildly, and a dark-haired, dark-faced man leaped from the crowd, waving his arms, and hurled himself on the Ambassador, carrying him forward on to the machine, and the whole edifice collapsed beneath them in a pile of fractured metalwork and flailing arms and legs.

There was an indrawn breath of horror around the room. The women screamed. Someone had hysterics. One woman fainted and had to be dragged out – she was too big to carry.

"Send for the fire brigade!" the curator shouted. "Bring water!"

A quick-witted man fetched a fire bucket of sand and threw it at the Ambassador and the other man on the floor, knocking them back again and sending them sprawling.

"A bomb! A bomb!" the shouts were going around.

Pamela stared at Freddie, and saw the complete bewilderment in his face.

"What on earth is going on?" she demanded fiercely. Then she looked farther across and saw consternation in Harrison's face, and thought perhaps she glimpsed an understanding.

Someone else arrived with a pail of water from the tearooms opposite. Without asking anyone, he also threw it over the Ambassador and the man, who was even now attempting to rise to his feet. They were both drenched.

"I say, old fellow," Bertie moved forward in some concern. He put out his hand and hauled the Ambassador to his feet. He was sodden wet, covered with sand and mud, and purple in the face. "I say," Bertie repeated. "I can't imagine what this is all about, but it really won't do." He looked at the other man. "Who are you, sir, and what the devil are you playing at? This is a machine for polishing the boots of gentlemen, not dangerous in the least . . . and certainly not a bomb! You had better explain yourself, if you can!"

The man saluted smartly and addressed himself to the Ambassador, ignoring Bertie.

"Auguste Larrey, sir, of the French Sûreté. I had every reason to believe that this device would explode the moment you pressed the switch, and that you would be killed . . . sir . . ."

"Balderdash!" Freddie said loudly.

The Ambassador tried to straighten his coat, but it was hardly worth the effort, and he gave up. He looked like a scarecrow that had barely weathered a storm, and he knew it.

"Monsieur Larrey," he said with freezing politeness. "As you may observe, I have met with great mischance, and in front of our neighbours and friends, the English, but the machine, it has not exploded. It has imploded, under the combined weight of your body and mine. It is wrecked! We owe the English a profound. apology! You, sir, will offer it!"

"Yes, Monsieur," Auguste stammered wretchedly. "Indeed, Monsieur." He looked at the assembled company. "I am most deeply sorry, ladies and gentlemen – most deeply. I have made a terrible mistake. I regret it and beg your forgiveness."

⁂

"Really?" Brodie said with wide eyes when Pamela told her of the incident that evening, when they were alone in the withdrawing room, the others having retired. Stockwell was just leaving to see if the footmen had locked up. She looked at Stockwell and caught his answering glance. "How very regrettable" she said with quiet sobriety.

Pamela looked at her narrowly, but said nothing further.

Stockwell cleared his throat. "Indeed," he said with shining eyes and a rather pink face. "Most regrettable, Madam."

Forty Morgan Silver Dollars

Maan Meyers

Maan Meyers is the collaborative pen name of husband-and-wife writing team Annette and Martin Meyers. They have both written novels individually under their own names, but together have penned a series about the Tonneman family in New York, through the centuries. The series began with The Dutchman *(1992), set in 1664, and later novels depict descendants of that family, all with roles in the police or detective forces, up to the late nineteenth century. The latest novel,* The Organ Grinder, *is set in 1899. The following story takes place soon after the events in that novel and includes two surprising but well-known individuals. The authors impressed upon me that just about every person and almost every event in this story actually happened. Almost ...*

1

The idea arrived with the mashed potatoes, gravy, plantation stew and biscuits, that week's house lunch special at the Fred Harvey in Dearborn Station, Chicago, though it had been simmering for a while now.

South America.

They were two travellers, not much different from any of the others, except their hands were gnarled and calloused, their eyes a little more knowing than the travelling salesmen they sat among at the counter.

The one with heavy red side-whiskers had deep-set, wary eyes. The other's eyes were blue, his hair and handlebar moustache black. They spoke in short sentences, as if they'd been together a long time and knew what the other would say.

Harvey's food was good and gave value for the money, but Red Whiskers was getting fidgety. He had the itch to get moving. Damn, he couldn't keep track of all the stuff hopping around in his head. They were almost out of money, and his partner was sitting there shovelling stew and biscuits into his mouth like there was no tomorrow, his moustache full of gravy and crumbs, and him making goo-goo eyes at the waitress.

"Time to skedaddle."

"Why not." Handle-Bar gave his moustache a good wipe with his napkin and twirled the end of each point. He winked at the pretty Harvey Girl in her black dress and white apron, felt there was promise in her smile as she cleared away their plates and delivered their coffee. She bobbed and beamed, but she was only doing what Mr Harvey taught the pretty girls he hired to do.

"So?" Red Whiskers said.

"What?" Handle-Bar reckoned that the Harvey Girl was sweet on him.

"Good guess our mugs are all over the place."

"Better than good."

"You said something about South America." Red Whiskers set his cup down. The coffee was hot and bitter.

"Something."

"Ship out of New York."

"Right." His companion downed what was left of his coffee.

"Train stops in Philadelphia." Red Whiskers rolled a smoke and passed it along, rolled one for himself. "I'll go out to Mont Clare and see the folks."

That sparked a grin from Handle-Bar. "Should we just ride the train, or give it a rob?"

Red Whiskers grinned back. "Just riding's fine. This time."

"Eastward Ho it is, then." Handle-Bar smoothed his moustache. Neither man was used to being in one place for long. "So she's gone to New York?"

After a noisy slurp of coffee, Red Whiskers nodded.

"There's a train heading East in ten minutes on track five."

"You're a sneaky cuss, ain't you?

"Knew you'd follow her, one way or t'other."

A railroad man in a dark blue uniform and a Pennsylvania Railroad cap walked through the restaurant. "New York train departing. Five minutes, track five. Stopping Philadelphia . . ."

The two settled their tabs and hoisted their carpet bags. Handle-Bar called, "Another time, sweetheart," to their waitress, who was already busy setting up for the next patron.

The men ambled out on bowed legs to where they'd left the crates with their saddles in the care of a Negro porter. "Track Five," Handle-Bar told the porter, handing him two bits. "The eastbound Pennsylvania Railroad train."

2

Glass shattering. Shouting. Obscenities. Blasphemies.

The clamour broke as they grappled with their braces, half dressed, boots to come, bickering over who would boil the coffee.

Dutch Tonneman threw open the front door. Snow was piled high on the porch, covering the half dozen bottles of milk in their metal nest. Rooster Bullard stood on the street near his milk wagon swinging a ragged, dirty boy in mid-air, all the while screaming threats and curses.

Cold snow bit into Dutch's bare feet as he slipped and slid down the six icy steps to the street.

"Hold on there, Rooster!"

"The little rat's been after stealing my milk for weeks, Inspector. Today I got him." Rooster's beaky nose twitched. The milkman shook the wailing boy by the scruff of his raggedy collar. "The Inspector's gonna put you in the Tombs, where you belong."

"No! No!" the boy yelled, blubbering. "There's little ones hungry. Ain't fair."

Dutch clapped Rooster on the back and Rooster dropped the boy in the snow. "Okay, Rooster, we got him. You got your route."

Bo Clancy, boots on, stomped down the steps. "And this don't happen again, right, kid?"

Rooster adjusted his cap and climbed into his milk wagon. "I'll run the little snot down I see him 'round me again." The milkman flicked the horse, and the milk wagon groaned, spokes squeaking as it moved off down the street to the next group of houses.

"So what do we got here?" Bo looked down at the cowering boy. To Dutch, he said, "You like walking barefoot in the snow?"

"How many of you at home?" Dutch asked the boy.

"Four. Another on the way." Snivelling. "What'll happen to them if you put me in the Tombs?"

"Where's your da?"

"On the wharfs, daytimes, sir, Callahan's at night."

Dutch dusted off the snow from the metal container of six bottles resting on the stairs. "Here you, boy, take these, but I don't ever want to see you stealing like this again. Next time you feel it creeping on, you come to see Inspector Tonneman at the House on Mulberry Street."

He and Bo watched the boy grab the container and run off towards Second Avenue.

Bo said, "A fine howdy do, my tender-hearted Coz. You give a little thief the milk for our coffee, he'll be robbin' banks by the time he's fifteen."

The cousins were a study in contrasts.

Bo Clancy, a big, dark-haired Irishman, sported a substantial moustache. At thirty-five, he was the elder, by two years. His cousin John "Dutch" Tonneman was of equal height but trimmer, his ruddy complexion and thick yellow hair inherited from his ancestor Pieter Tonneman, a Dutchman who'd been the first sheriff of New York.

The cousins lived together in Dutch's shabby Grand Street home like overgrown boys: empty beer bottles, dirty plates, mice kept in check only by Finn the cantankerous orange tomcat who'd appeared one evening a month ago – like Meg Tonneman had sent him to keep her house clean, like she was coming back to the old neighbourhood. But all along Grand Street the neighbourhood was changing, filling with foreigners, and English was no longer the only language on the street.

What with Ma living in Jersey City to help Annie, now that his sister's weak heart had made her an invalid, and her with her brood of seven, Dutch had thought to sell the house. But Ma wouldn't hear of it. Still and all, he couldn't blame Ma for not wanting to give up her marriage home.

This snowy dawn was not an ordinary one for the two Inspectors. They'd been summoned to Police Commissioner

Murphy's office, their concern being that, with a new police commissioner about to put his arse down at 300 Mulberry Street in less than a month, their special positions with the New York Police Department were about to be eliminated.

★

In February of 1901, the Honourable Robert Van Wyck, of good Dutch ancestry, was the less than energetic Mayor of the Great City of New York. He didn't need energy or even a moral compass; he'd been elected with the strong support of Tammany, the powerful Democratic Machine, run by Boss Crocker.

It was under Tammany's guidance that Mayor Van Wyck appointed Colonel Michael C. Murphy as the first Police Commissioner of the New York Police Department, the now-combined departments of the five boroughs of greater New York.

Colonel Murphy, a sickly specimen, was unable to digest solid food. But he was lucky. Crocker's fine hand had guided the frail Murphy with his appointments of deputies throughout the police department, a department until now almost an adjunct to Tammany.

Then, wonder of wonders, came the election of November, 1901.

The Tammany slate went down in defeat. Reform was in the air.

Starting in January 1902, New York would have an independent new mayor, Seth Low. And a new independent police commissioner; Colonel John Partridge in his shiny top hat, would be sitting at Theodore Roosevelt's old desk at Police Headquarters.

Finally! There would be a police commissioner who would choose his own deputies, and run his precincts and borough commanders. Under the fresh rules he would serve a five-year term and could be thrown out only by the mayor or the governor.

Commissioner Murphy and Commissioner-to-be Colonel Partridge were both well aware of the special police unit known as the Commissioner's Squad, which one of their predecessors, Major York, had put in place to deal with special cases. There was no knowing if the new commissioner would cotton to the importance of the squad's existence.

A special case could be anything from murder to certain indiscretions that needed special attention lest embarrassment, or worse, fall on the police department and the City. The squad was a two-man affair run by Inspector Fingal Clancy, known as "Bo", and Deputy Inspector John "Dutch" Tonneman.

Bo and Dutch worked out of police headquarters, the grim building at 300 Mulberry Street, called by many the House on Mulberry Street. In order to aid the squad when dealing with its varied assignments, Bo Clancy had the power of the commissioner's office to requisition men from any other part of the force.

On this particular early morning in December of 1901, it was the retiring Commissioner Murphy who summoned his two-man squad to a confidential meeting.

The Commissioner's office was not genteel, but it was well laid out. Every commissioner since Roosevelt had used T.R.'s big desk because of the aura it had. Teddy Roosevelt had gone from being Police Commissioner to Governor of New York, to Vice President and, now, President of the United States.

A sputtering fire had been laid in the hearth but provided little heat, and the windows let in the thin morning sunlight, with a glimpse of the snow-coated tree branches. Bo and Dutch waited, tense, in the chairs in front of the famous desk, prepared for bad news.

The commissioner wore a sour expression as he lit his second cigar of the day. "You were summoned . . ." Murphy's weak chin trembled.

Bo shrugged at Dutch, mouthing, *here it comes.*

"There's at least one Pinkerton looking to make trouble here," Murphy said. "And one is one too many."

Christ! "Pinkertons!" Bo Clancy shot out of his chair, walked to the window, hiding a face-stretching smile. He searched the street below. They were not being fired. They were needed! And in a big way! It was clear Murphy had no idea what to do next. And, maybe because he had only another couple of weeks left on the job, he was going to dump whatever it was on Bo and Dutch and the new commissioner.

"If you don't mind, sir, how do you know? Did the Pinks send word?" Dutch gave Bo a warning look: take this serious.

Murphy grunted. "Hardly. I had a telegraph from a connection in Philadelphia. They're heading this way. And they're not known for respecting local law enforcement."

"Yeah," Dutch said. "What do they want?"

"The damned reward," Murphy said. "And there's nothing they won't do to get it."

"So there's a reward, is there?" Bo said, this time not bothering to hide his delight. "How much?"

"Ten thousand in gold for whoever . . ."

Bo broke in. "I'll be damned if I don't want a piece of that myself."

"Hold on, why here?" Dutch said.

"They think they've got Butch Cassidy and the Sundance Kid cornered in the City."

Bo looked dubious. "Jesus, Mary and Joseph. Sure as hell not their territory."

"Supposed to be passing through on their way to South America," Murphy said.

Now it was Dutch who laughed out loud. "Butch Cassidy and the Sundance Kid cornered? Here? Any fool could hide in plain sight in this city, unless of course they decided to rob a bank."

3

The building was a neoclassical, granite-faced temple, with a freestanding portico suppored on four huge Corinthian columns. Its majestic entrance-way stood well back of the columns, far enough from the street to deaden any sound from within. Indeed, when the first shots rang out inside, no one even heard the blasts on the busy streets surrounding Union Square.

In fact, not a soul was aware that there was a problem of any kind until the first robber barrelled down the icy, shallow steps and slammed into a young woman, sending her and the small leather case she carried flying.

The man hit the icy pavement, scattering the grey sacks he was carrying. His pistol skimmed along the sidewalk, stopped only by the left boot of the young woman he had knocked to the ground. She, not a damsel of faint heart, hid the weapon under her voluminous skirts.

When he raised his blood-scraped face, she had only a few seconds to make a mental photograph of his visage with its big red moustache and the strange beard that followed the line of his jaw, before a second man, sacks swinging from his shoulders, raced down the steps, pursued by a collection of men yelling, "Stop! Thieves! Police!"

The second man cursed his fallen companion with, "Stupid arse." Turning, he fired into the hollering crowd streaming down the steps after him. Howls of pain erupted. Fearing for their lives, people scattered, falling, scrambling away from the gunfire. Two victims lay bleeding near the entrance to the bank.

The first villain scrambled to his feet as police whistles piped. "Sorry, Butch."

"Sundance, you goddam clumsy fool." Butch sported a pencil-thin, black moustache and took in the situation with hard, black-button eyes.

The young woman sitting on the sidewalk stared, noted the drawling western accents.

"Seen enough?" Hard Button Eyes pointed his still smoking pistol at her, changed his mind, and swung one of his heavy sacks smack into her head, knocking her flat. "Come on, Sundance. Coppers." The miscreants calling each other Butch and Sundance took off, losing themselves in the bustle and traffic around Union Square.

The bells of an ambulance sounded, and, seeing that the robbers had escaped, people crouched on the steps of the bank, giving aid to the two wounded men.

"Here, ma'am, let me help you," A clean-shaven fellow with deep blue eyes squatted beside the fallen woman. The blow had knocked the wind out of her. He tilted his derby back and helped her sit up.

She reached under her skirts and pulled out the pistol.

The man held up his palms. "Hey, hold on there, Missy. Don't shoot. I'm no thief, just plain old Robbie Allen, good Samaritan."

"Is she okay, Robbie?" another man asked. This one was wiry built, tall, also clean-shaven.

The woman tried to clear her head. She looked again at this new pair. Two gentlemen. Had the first two returned? No. What was she thinking? This pair was very different from the first. Perhaps it was the fall that confused her.

"You okay, ma'am? Do you want me to take that firearm?" The man called Robbie made a quick survey of the area. Everyone seemed to be either clustered on the steps of the bank with the wounded, or running off towards Union Square in pursuit of the robbers.

"No, thank you, sir. The thief dropped it. I know someone of authority who'll be very interested in seeing it." As she tucked the gun into the leather pouch still attached to the shoulder of her coat, the small movement causing a stab of pain in her knee.

"Ma'am?" Both spoke at once.

Robbie said, "You're hurt."

"No!" The pain sharpened her mind. The robbers had called themselves Butch and Sundance. Was that possible here in New York?

At that moment the young woman remembered her Kodak camera. She'd been holding it before she was struck. Spying the Brownie among the refuse in the gutter, she said, "I'll be obliged if you'll help me to my feet so that I can retrieve my camera and see what damage has been done."

The man called Robbie stood behind the woman, holding her elbows. Once standing, the pressure on her injured knee caused more pain. The young woman flinched. Her knee wouldn't hold her and, as much as it troubled, even embarrassed her, she had to lean against the stranger, while his friend squatted near the gutter and dusted the refuse from the camera with the side of his sleeve.

"That's my friend Harry, ma'am. He'll bring your camera." Now that he had a better view, Robbie liked what he saw. "Pardon me." He reached down and straightened her hat.

She wished he'd stop fussing at her. She raised her right hand and readjusted her hat. Her dark hair had come loose from its roll and lay on her shoulders.

Though she had a bright red bruise on her chin, Robbie saw that she was a beauty. "Ma'am, I do believe you're having trouble standing. Not that I mind a pretty lady leaning on me."

Her face flushed. "I don't live far and I'm certain I'll be able to walk."

"I'm not as certain of that as you are, ma'am," Robbie said. "If you live nearby, me and Harry will help you home." He was watching the first police wagon arrive, the coppers heading straight into the bank.

"My name is Esther Breslau." She inspected her Kodak, a hardy little box unit. "You are both very kind. I live at No. 5 Gramercy Park West. It is not four blocks from here."

A mob had gathered in front of the Union Square Savings Bank. Another police wagon pulled up. The uniforms poured out, but could hardly get past the onlookers, doctors and victims.

"So here we were." Robbie squinted at the second police wagon, "New to the big city, ready to put our life savings in this solid-looking old bank, when it goes and gets robbed by two villains." He tucked Esther's arm in his.

"Yes, well." Esther started at his touch, stammered, "The two villains . . . they appear to be real bank robbers. I heard them call each other Butch and Sundance." She wondered which gave her more discomfort: this stranger clutching her arm or her aching knee.

"Did you hear that, Robbie?" Harry shaded his eyes from the sudden bright sunlight. He patted his slight paunch. "Butch Cassidy and the Sundance Kid. Here in New York. And we saw 'em in the flesh."

"Oh, yeah, we did, didn't we?"

"And with the local sheriffs now to the rescue, Miss Esther," Harry said. "We'll just see you home and carry on to our business appointment."

"I'm sorry to take you out of your way," Esther said, trying not to put too much pressure on her knee.

Robbie gave her hand a squeeze. "Not out of our way at all, Miss Esther. We have no hard and fast schedule, only that we need to find a rental carriage and driver to take us to meet an associate up north of the city."

"Oh, but I know just the man," Esther said as they approached Gramercy Park. "And since I'm so much in your debt perhaps you will join us for a small meal while Wong, our man, rings the very dependable Mister Jack West about hiring a carriage."

4

Early in the advent of the automobile, former prize-fighter Battling Jack West foresaw that sooner rather than later the carriage business would no longer be profitable. For this reason he had Little Jack Meyers paint a new legend on the red brick wall of his MacDougall Alley stable behind his townhouse on Washington Square North.

Right under the recessed sign for his carriage service, the newer sign, painted in block letters, black on a grey shingle, said simply:

CONFIDENTIAL INVESTIGATIONS: JACK WEST

A year before, Jack West had bought a small advertisement with the same tasteful inscription to run weekly in the *Herald* and the *Post*. Now, when he advertised, he added the name of his young and eager protégé, Jack Meyers. And, directly under his sign, he included in smaller block letters:

ASSOCIATE: JACK MEYERS

"Boss, wait'll you hear." Jack Meyers, panting, stormed up the stairs, almost colliding with a corpulent woman swathed in furs, dabbing at false tears as she descended: Missus Eugenia Walsh, a client. Her missing husband Ferdinand had been found by Jack West Confidential Investigations in the morgue, with no identification on him, a victim of a fatal attack. "My deepest sympathies, Missus," Little Jack Meyers said. "Can I escort you home?" He'd recognized the elegant horse-drawn carriage below, with the fashionably dressed young man inside.

"No, no, that's very kind of you, young man. I have a carriage waiting."

Meyers was smirking when he burst into Jack West's office. "Well, the ample Widow Walsh is already amply well escorted."

"Not our case anymore." Jack West shrugged. "She settled up, and the coppers don't have to look far for the murderer. But they won't bother. Just another street mugging." Jack West chose a cigar from the black leather case on his desk, licked it, bit the end off and lit the cigar. "Now what were you going on about when you came in?"

"The Pinkertons, boss. They're in town. I heard all about it at the scribblers' shack this morning. Someone in the telegraph office spilled to Beatty from the *World*, so now every scribbler in New York knows about the great big secret. Also, Murphy called

Bo and Dutch in this morning and put them on it. You won't believe this one . . ."

Jack West smiled around his cigar. "Try me."

"Now, who would you think are the most wanted pair of desperados in New York City?"

"I've got no patience for your tomfoolery, boy. Spit it out."

"The dumb-arse Pinkertons are in New York City looking for Butch Cassidy and the Sundance Kid."

"The Western bank robbers? What would they be doing here?" The news amused Jack West as much as it did Little Jack. "Not their line of country." Big Jack's cigar had gone out. He lit up again. "And the Pinks don't know this territory. At all."

"Same for Butch and Sundance," Little Jack said, "who are supposed to be heading for South America." The boy's eyes grew wide. "Guess what, there's a ten thousand dollar reward."

"Ah. That's my sharp lad."

"We're smarter'n they are, don't you think, Boss? You wouldn't believe what the Pinks done."

"Yes, I would."

"Got my ear to the ground, Boss. I already know something stinks like *goyisha* . . ."

"What?"

"Sorry, boss, something stinks like rotten fish when a clown comes along and don't know anyone and opens a beer hole down on Delancey near Essex."

"So?" Big Jack asked, going along with the game.

Little Jack grinned. "And calls it PINKYS."

5

Harry put his fingers to his derby. "Thank you, Wong."

Robbie made better use of his hands by holding one of Esther's between them. "So we'll say farewell to you, Miss Esther, and trust to meet you and your good father again under better circumstances. Let's hope the coppers catch up with those *notorious* robbers, Butch and Sundance."

Esther Breslau smiled at how Oz Cook would react at being called her father. He'd been proper to their guests during their meal, but Esther knew he was suspicious of how easily they'd entered her life. It was, after all, his home. She had been a poor immigrant hired to work as his assistant because she spoke Yiddish, so that he could photograph life on the Lower East Side. As her mentor, he had taught her the art of photography and invited her to share his studio and darkroom. She lived in her own flat on the top floor of his house.

Adroitly, she removed her hand from Robbie's. The sun dazzled, glancing off the crusty snow cover. She waited a moment, then, holding her Brownie camera at her waist, made photos of the smiling Robbie and Harry, tipping their derbies to her.

As he watched the delectable Esther enter the house, Robbie said, "The fucking nerve of them low-life imposters. Right in our faces."

Harry grinned. "What do we care?"

"What do we care? We have only one fucking Jackson to our names, that's all of it. And we have to pay the driver."

"We done a little better than that."

"What done? What the hell you talking about?"

Harry patted his paunch, and palmed a bank note from the grey canvas bag stuffed in between his belly and his trousers. He flashed the bill at Robbie. "Found money."

Robbie got pop-eyed, so much so that Harry thought they would fall out. "I'll be damned."

"Me, too," his partner said. "But now we can afford *the trip* to damnation."

★

Jack West made the turn on to Gramercy Park, reined-in his matched pair of greys and stopped in front of No. 5. He jumped down from his perch and tipped his shiny black top hat. "Jack West, misters."

Robbie came forward and shook Jack West's meaty hand. "Robbie Allen. This is my friend Harry Kidder." He was quick to size up the carriage-driver. Short but thick. Tough. Could take care of himself. "We're meeting a friend in a place called Inwood, up north of the city. You know it?"

"I do. Maybe two, three hours, or more, depending on the road and me avoiding the subway construction around Longacre Square. There is a train, you know, New York Central. Stops along the northern line near the Hudson at Dyckman Street. But you're better off with me if you don't know your way around up there. Mostly farms and summer estates. Deserted this time of year."

"We'd be obliged if you would make a stop at Missus Taylor's boarding house on Twelfth Street, so we can collect our stuff and settle up."

6

The scene was still pandemonium when Bo and Dutch arrived at the Union Square Bank. While Bo and Dutch were in his office, the commissioner had gotten word by telephone that Butch Cassidy and the Sundance Kid had robbed their first New York bank.

"Jesus H. Christ!" Bo said. Traffic was at a near stand-still, and the sidewalks were clotted with people who had nothing to do with the robbery and were probably not even in the bank at the time of the heist.

Four patrolmen stood in a line behind saw-horses to hold back the curious.

More uniformed men were posted at the bank doors.

On the bloodstained entrance steps of the bank was Sergeant Aloysius Mulligan from the Fifteenth. He was happy to see them. "We got two shot dead here and one expired inside. All three on their way to the morgue." He wiped sweat from his face. "It's ugly. We're keeping everyone in the bank so you can talk to them, but it ain't easy and a few ran off like scared chickens before we got here."

"Good job, Mulligan," Bo said. He followed Dutch into the bank.

The marble walls hushed sound, but there was no hushing the agitation. Dutch counted nine men, bankers and tellers. Four men in overcoats, patrons. A woman weeping.

Dutch announced: "Inspectors Bo Clancy and Dutch Tonneman. We're sorry to have kept you here, but we'd like you to tell us what happened, as much as you can remember, so that we can catch these villains."

"Butch Cassidy and the Sundance Kid," one of the bankers said. "Butch Cassidy shot Mr Phelps, our bank manager."

"Killed him in cold blood," from a man in an overcoat. "Said he wasn't moving fast enough."

"How do you know it was Butch Cassidy and the Sundance Kid?" Bo said.

"That's what they called each other," a banker said.

Dutch pulled out a small notepad. "We'll take a description now."

Each of the witnesses rushed to talk. Which is when everything fell apart.

"Butch had a long red beard."

"No, it was brown."

"No, it was Sundance who had brown hair. It was long. And he had a red patch over his left eye."

"No. The right eye."

"Both men were big as oxes and wore black cowboy hats."

"No, one wore a black derby and the other a grey cowboy hat."

"It wasn't grey. It was white. And dirty."

Between sobs, the weeping woman said: "A woman in a blue coat. She could give you a better description. She was standing right next to them."

A woman in a blue coat? Here was agreement. No such person.

"Hopeless." Bo shook his head. "Always the same. Mulligan, get everyone's name and where they live. We'll most likely need to talk to them again. Then send them home." To Dutch he said, "Flora's gonna hate missing this." Flora was reporter Flora Cooper, the girl Bo called a humdinger. She was in South Africa, covering the second Boer War for the *Herald*.

★

Outside, on the bank steps waiting for Bo, Dutch heard someone behind the wooden horses say, "You should tell them about her, Rose."

Dutch peered into the crowd as he moved down the steps. "Rose? Do you have some information for us?"

An old woman in a heavy blue shawl, her black hat resting atop wiry, grey hair, was pushed forward. "That's me. Rose Fleck."

"Don't be shy, ma'am," Dutch said. "What do you have to tell us?"

She paused, took a deep breath before she spoke. "Nothing. At all."

"Well, thank you anyway," Dutch said, watching Bo come out of the bank.

"Just a girl with one of them picture makers," Rose said.

Now Rose had Dutch's full attention. "A girl with a camera?"

"I think that's what they call them. She was holding the thing, then she got knocked down by one of them robbers. Two nice boys helped her up and found her picture maker and they left."

7

Delancey Street, not far from the Essex Street Market and the notorious Tombs, was the site of the proposed Williamsburg Bridge, construction due to start in 1902, connecting New York and Brooklyn.

All along Delancey Street were derelict taverns and basement oyster houses and tenement buildings. Some of these establishments were transient, the shopkeepers setting up, closing down, all within weeks, taking away what they could in push carts, even shopping baskets.

One of these newcomers was a narrow slice of tavern with a homemade sign nailed over the door. It said: PINKYS.

The proprietor was a reptilian little creature, whose height didn't quite reach forty-eight inches. Most of the time he could be found outside under the sign, luring patrons with the promise of a free beer.

He was born Francis Augustus Pincus. Or so he said. His first greeting to all and sundry was: "Call me Pinky." Pinky had a small pug nose that had been broken more than once. There were even stories, most likely self-invented, that he'd fought in the ring. At that size? Doubtful.

No matter. Pinky had several equalizers: a wooden box on which he stood when behind the bar; a shillelagh – his weapon of choice at any time during the course of an evening in the tavern and elsewhere – when and where needed.

And at times, Pinky had to resort to his third equalizer: a shiny silver and black .38 calibre Colt revolver, which he kept cleaned and polished in the embossed buffalo-leather holster hanging from the wide, thick belt around his narrow hips for all to see.

Not to be forgotten was Pinky's fourth equalizer: the woman swathed in red velvet, including her bright red turban with its large, white ostrich feather. Lorraine sat at an unsteady, round table reading tarot cards when asked. But her preference was a simple game of poker.

No doubt about it, Lorraine was Pinky's woman.

No family name. Simply Lorraine. Her talk was hard to follow or understand. As if, a time back, she'd bitten her tongue and it never healed right.

Even so, when she was the one standing outside under Pinky's sign saying hello, men ogled her, for she was a sight to see, and they followed her into the tavern without a second thought. One of the reasons was her size. The woman stood well over six feet. Fully unfurled, she had to duck her head to keep from smacking into wood beams.

When she stood next to Pinky they were a comical sight. But nobody ever dared laugh. They say opposites attract. That might be why the giant Lorraine and the midget Pinky were lovers.

*

It was just before noon on this cold December day when the news came shrilling down the street, passed from one pushcart to the next. Most of Pinky's tavern emptied out. Pinky didn't leave the bar, so the news was delivered to him by one of his drunken patrons, who stumbled back into the tavern, yelling, "Butch Cassidy and the Sundance Kid just robbed the Union Square Bank and killed twenty-two people."

8

Bequeathing the crime scene at the Union Square Bank to the precinct police sergeant and the medical examiner, Dutch and Bo walked the few short blocks to No. 5 Gramercy Park West, and declared themselves with the large brass knocker on the front door.

Wong peered out the small side window. If it was those two men who brought Miss Esther home, he would send them away. But it was Dutch Tonneman and Bo Clancy who stood on the steps, and Wong opened the door before Dutch could knock a second time.

"Miss Esther is resting in the parlour," Wong said. "She wrenched her knee, and I've made her a cold compress."

"Esther!" Dutch rushed into the parlour.

Esther was sitting on a chaise holding her Kodak camera. The parlour was warm as toast thanks to the blazing fire, and the spicy smell of pine cones filled the air.

Esther looked up, not really surprised. It was logical that the police commissioner would call up his special squad to investigate the bank robbery, as the robbers were Butch Cassidy and the Sundance Kid. And it was probable that someone had mentioned a girl with a camera.

Bo overrode his partner. "Esther. We'd like to talk to you about the bank robbery." He glanced at Dutch, who was already holding his beloved's hand. "That is, if you two love-birds can put your minds to something important."

"Sit down, please, both of you," Esther said. "I'm all right."

"You've been hurt," Dutch said.

"It's nothing. A sprain. Wong has me in an ice bandage."

Bo removed his derby, as did Dutch. Wong placed the hats on the tall stand in the front hall.

"Tea, Miss Esther?"

"Yes, thank you, Wong. And please bring me that parcel we prepared."

Before they sat, Bo said, "It has to do with the small matter of the Union Square bank robbery, which we think you may have witnessed."

"Yes. I was there."

"It's a pity," Bo said, "that you didn't wait a few more minutes until the investigating team arrived."

"I don't understand. If I did do anything wrong, I do apologize. But, what was it I did wrong?"

"Damn it, Esther—"

"John, please."

"Sorry, but this is serious. Three people are dead. We understand that you were seen in the company of two men who might have some connection with the robbery."

"Your understanding is wrong." Esther squared her shoulders and held her head high. "I did speak to two men. They were very kind to me when I was knocked down by one of the robbers, and they were in my sight when the two robbers ran off. They were proper gentlemen and saw me home. They went out of their way to help me, as they had planned to be on the road to Inwood."

"The man who knocked you down?" Bo said.

"His friend called him Sundance," Esther said. "And he called his friend Butch. I may have some photographs, but I won't know until they're developed. And, oh, I have something you might find of interest."

When Wong brought the tea, he also brought a brown-paper-wrapped parcel.

Esther handed it to Dutch. "Sundance dropped this when he fell on me."

Dutch unwrapped the parcel and whistled. A Colt revolver. He spun the cylinder and removed the bullets.

Bo said, "Esther, you got a good look at them. You think you and Sergeant Lowry – he's a good sketcher – can come up with what the two mutts look like? It'll get on the front page of every newspaper in the city. It's a good bet, even in the country."

9

Inwood Hill Park was desolate in winter. Evenings were formidable. Snow shrouded steep hills, and rocky battlements and sharp ridges jutted like monsters in brittle moonlight. When the prevalent winter winds weren't howling, a good listener could hear the crunch and rustle of wild animals prowling through the fallen twigs and branches.

Only in the summer was the desolation mitigated. The park became dense with vegetation, thick with a forest of tulip trees, hickory and oak, the air filled with bird song and the buzz of bees.

Because of the country atmosphere and the cool breezes in this northernmost corner of Manhattan, summer brought the owners of assorted mansions – boarded up in winter – to Inwood, and it was for the wealthy that, near where the Harlem and Hudson Rivers meet, the New York Central Railroad created the Dyckman Street stop.

The influx of the wealthy, and the rocky nature of the land, did not discourage the active fruit and vegetable and dairy farms in Inwood. These thrived in the summer when the slopes of the year-round farms became green, and corn stalks could reach the height of the abundance of fruit trees. Milk cows lowed, joined by the occasional na-na-na of goats.

It was to one of these farms that Robbie and Harry directed Jack West. "De Grout," Harry said.

The road had been treacherous due to the many ruts caused by run-offs from melting, then freezing snow and ice, but West had excellent control over his horses and the carriage. The bulky crates the men had collected at Missus Taylor's boarding house were tied to the roof of the carriage and served as good ballast. There was precious little daylight remaining when the horses pulled the carriage up the long drive, passing the weathered, two-legged sign that said: BOWERIE DE GROUT.

Only the carriage lamps and the thin yellow beam from a kerosene lantern near the gate marked their way to the front of the farmhouse. The house itself was weathered clapboard, turned grey from the elements over the previous century. Dutch style, in need of paint, and sprawling, with added-on extensions.

Smoke rose from three chimneys; light flickered in the windows. Beyond the house was a large barn and farther on, sheds and outbuildings, a fenced-in corral, and fields rising into the hills.

A grizzled old man came out of the barn as the carriage drove up the narrow road leading to the front of the house. He picked up the lantern and waited till Jack West reined-in the horses.

Harry was first out of the carriage and greeted the old man, "Evening, pappy." He opened the door and stepped into the house.

After unhitching the horses, Jack West slipped the old man two penny coins. "Feed them at the same time. The mare gets jealous. Some oats, but only a taste of water. I'll be out to see to them in a while."

Robbie had already begun unstrapping the crates from the roof of the carriage, and with Jack's help set them on the ground Harry, it appeared, had found something more important to do.

"A long sight easier than putting them up." Robbie pulled out his tobacco pouch and rolled a cigarette. He offered it to Jack, who declined.

"I'm a cigar man," Jack said, sniffing. The rich smell of roasting hens was spilling from the open door, where an old woman stood smiling. She beckoned them inside to the warmth of the great room and the hearty fire that burned in a huge old hearth.

Jack West was curious by nature. He liked to think that there was little he didn't know about his city. But he was less familiar with Inwood than he was with Brooklyn, where his wife and his daughter Mae lived.

Punch Jack West in the jaw and it didn't faze him, but freeze his saggy old arse on a winter's night and he'd be out of sorts for a week. So he took comfort in being surrounded by the warmth of the well-laid hearth and the rich smells wafting in from the nearby kitchen.

The walls were whitewashed, the beams heavy and rough-hewn, the great room being the earliest built part of the old Dutch houses. The furnishings were sparse, but, interestingly enough, there was a piano. Two old people, two young men, and the piano . . .

"You be staying the night, of course?" The old man came into the house, bringing with him a gust of frigid air. "Your horses are settled. There're some apples in the barn and some runty carrots, if you want."

"West is the name. Jack West. And I thank you."

"Mister West will indeed take supper and spend the night," Robbie said. He'd shed his coat. "The road is not fit to drive a carriage on in the dark."

West said, "I'll take you up on your hospitality and leave first light in the morning." To the old man, he added, "I thank you for giving me a hand with my team."

There were three horses in the barn and the arrival of two more was still being greeted by a lot of snorting and whinnying back and forth. Like they were talking to each other, Jack West thought. The old man had forked down hay, and water stood in a big oaken barrel, ladle attached. He stood by while West gave his team a brisk rubdown.

By the time he'd finished, gotten the horses settled for the night together in their one large stall, Jack West knew the old man was Samuel Hendricks. Samuel and his wife Annie had worked the farm for the de Grouts. In fact, Samuel was born on the farm. His father had been manager and his mother, housekeeper. Old Widow de Grout had died in September and now the farm belonged to her granddaughter Henrietta.

"Miss Henrietta, she come home as soon as she heard," Samuel said. "That girl was always adventuresome. She went out West and got herself a job teaching in school." He used a crowbar to open one of the crates.

Jack scattered hay for his horses. The gelding whinnied. Jack liked to think the beast was saying thank you. He turned to Samuel. "The boys? They're related?" The crate held a saddle. Well-ridden. The two had brought their saddles East with them.

"Mister Harry and Mister Robbie, you mean? Why Mister Harry is going to be Miss Henrietta's husband and Mister Robbie, he's his kin."

As they headed back to the house, the rousing sound of the piano could be heard and, when Samuel opened the door, Jack West saw Harry banging away on the piano-forte while Robbie whirled a tall, laughing woman around the great room.

After a substantial meal of roasted chicken and potatoes, the men settled down with their smokes.

"You boys fixing to stay in the city?" Jack West offered his companions cigars, which they took.

West studied them through half-closed eyes. Their colouring was wrong but they could be kin, because they seemed to have that thing brothers had of finishing each other's sentences.

Robbie lit his own, then his partner's smoke. "Maybe. Harry's the rancher here, but I'll be looking around, see if there's an opportunity or two. Though I'm guessing there's no work for rodeo riders in these parts."

⋆

A cot was made up for Jack in the kitchen. He was asleep the minute his head hit the pillow. Next thing he knew the old woman was firing up the stove. He'd missed feeding his animals. He frowned. Damn it, he'd told Samuel to fetch him in the morning. But no real harm done.

Outside in the crisp overcast dawn, Samuel had already brought West's horses to the carriage. Jack fed the two animals with the dried corn he always kept in the packet under his seat. They nibbled, but didn't act like they'd missed a meal.

"You'll have some eggs and porridge, Mister West, before you leave?" Henrietta de Grout stood in the doorway. She hadn't had much to say at supper, but she had a melodious voice with a tinge of the same soft drawl as Harry and Robbie. And she had a good humor. She was also a darn good-looking woman. The large fringed shawl she'd wrapped herself in didn't hide to West the fact that she was with child.

"I will, ma'am, then I'll be off before we get any more snow."

She took two coins from the small purse attached to her waist. "Two dollars, Harry said."

"Make that one dollar, with my thanks for the meal and bed."

She gave him the reeded-edged coin and went back into the house. Jack West pocketed the coin. When he was on the road, he took it out and held it up to the sunlight, admiring the sheen. Lady Liberty on the obverse and a bald eagle holding arrows and an olive branch on the reverse. Beneath the tail feathers of the bald eagle was 1890 and CC, for where it was minted. Carson City, Nevada. He'd seen one of these before and knew enough to recognize a Morgan silver dollar.

10

As the sun rose the palest yellow, they descended from the hackney at Merchants Gate on the west side of the Central Park, and entered the park. Though it was cold and the wind sharp, Esther Breslau was happy. The park under its blanket of snow was serene and beautiful.

"Winter birds," Professor Lazzlo Lowenstein said. "A great variety. Eh, Hughs?"

Professor Sidney Hughs mumbled assent.

They were costumed in long top coats that fell to the ankles; on their heads were shiny black top hats.

The little German had a full beard and moustache, while the large stout Englishman was clean-shaven. Lowenstein's teeth gripped a meerschaum pipe, which he had not lit for fear its fumes would worry the birds and spoil the pristine morning air. Hughs, a less meticulous man, chewed tobacco which he spat where he chose, staining the snow.

"*Zonotrichia albicollis.*" Professor Lowenstein pointed to the small bird. "Miss Breslau, you may proceed."

Esther made her picture. As the professors had felt that her tripod and glass plates would frighten away their quarry, her camera was her Kodak, which she could load in daylight with light-proof cartridges. It produced photographs that were two and a quarter by three and a quarter inches.

The two eccentric men amused her. Lowenstein had a soft, piping, almost bird-like voice. He wagged his head as if his own Hungarian-tinted German accent offended him. "This white-throated sparrow is usually one of our commonest winter birds. Last year's count was down. This year we are already up to fifty-three."

"Fifty-seven," Professor Hughs corrected.

Esther's feet were cold in her thin boots, and her knee still pained her, but she found the birds very interesting, and the work an education. She had never thought to make photographs of birds.

"Ach, Miss Breslau," Professor Lowenstein said. "You live so close to the Union Square where there was a bank robbery two days ago." He pointed to a small brown bird, then to her camera.

Esther made the picture a moment before the bird took flight. "I was on the sidewalk in front of the bank at the time. The one called Sundance knocked me down when he ran out."

"Oh, yes," Hughs said, with an odd chortle. "Dreadful, dreadful. Were they indeed the western outlaws Butch Cassidy and the Sundance Kid?"

Professor Lowenstein sidled closer to an oak where many of the birds were perched. "*Larus argentatus*, the Herring Gull. All through the winter, flocks often number as many as twelve hundred. They prefer to fly singly or in small clutches." He nodded his head and placed the index finger of his right hand at the side of his nose, posing. "Usually appearing in early October and ceasing by early November. Did you, Miss Breslau, happen to make photographs of these two outlaws?"

"I would have but Sundance knocked my camera from my hands."

A grumbling sound from Professor Hughs.

"Ah!" Lowenstein's exclamation startled several birds that flew off to a nearby birch. "*Carpodacus purpureus*." The professor showed brownish teeth. "The Purple Finch." The finch, as if it knew it was being talked about, flew away.

Hughs rumbled.

"Pity. The first I've seen this year. But you with your discriminating eye, of course, can describe these men."

Esther shivered. She felt weary in the cold with her testy knee. "Professors, you can call on me tomorrow and I'll have your photographs ready for you."

11

The woman in the blue coat stood on the pavement in front of the Bowery Savings Bank at the intersection of Bowery and Grand, looking up and down the busy street, gathering the courage to enter. The bank was a wonder to behold. Built in 1893, it was designed by the city's leading architect, Stanford White, and the leading architectural firm in the city, McKim Meade and White. To the woman in the blue coat on the sidewalk in front of the bank, it seemed a palace.

At last, appearing reassured, she took the step, passed the imposing Corinthian columns, and entered the bank.

"May I be of service?" A young man in a fine dark suit greeted her.

"I'm to meet my husband here." Her voice was small, and though she was taller than average, her demeanour was passive, almost apologetic.

"My name is Mister Cunningham. Come with me, please." He showed her to a formal waiting alcove with comfortable chairs. "I'll notify you when your husband arrives. He is Mister . . . ?"

"Place," she said, relieved to see the back of Cunningham, as he went off to greet another customer. Customer. That gave her a laugh.

The woman watched the activity of the bank, the men who came in to do business, and the bankers. The bankers took very good care of their customers. They came out of their offices to shake their clients' hands and greet them like much-loved relatives.

She noted the most obvious of these men: the bank manager. A stately individual with a protruding belly and an impressive grey goatee. She waited, growing uneasy, intimidated by the marble mosaic floors and the height of the ceiling with its art-glass skylight, and the well-dressed men coming and going, ready to do business with their fat wallets.

Standing so that she could see the entrance, she wondered

where they were? She didn't like being here by herself. What if Cunningham came back and asked questions?

By magic, they were there, near the entrance, guns drawn, yelling, "This is a robbery." They secured the double doors with a cattle-wrangling rope.

A shout: "It's Butch Cassidy and Sundance!"

Under cover of the commotion, the woman in the blue coat moved forward, ready to signal directions to her cohorts, but she didn't have to.

The bank manager hurried out. "Put down those guns," he ordered.

A shot. Shots. The bank manager collapsed. Blood spread across his chest staining his fine suit.

Time slowed. Sound became muffled.

Money bags were filled.

"Missus Place, Missus Place, get out of the way." Cunningham grasped her arm.

She shook him off. As she turned away, blood splattered her face. Her arms. Her coat. Cunningham cried out, clutched his shoulder and collapsed at her feet.

It wasn't what she wanted.

The shooters laughed as they grabbed up their money bags, released the doors, and ran off. The bank emptied of bankers and customers – and the woman in the blue coat.

12

The scene that Bo and Dutch found when they arrived at the Bowery Savings Bank was similar to the one five days earlier at the Union Square Bank.

Sirens, bells, chaos. Traffic-snarled.

The whole place was spinning like a top.

"We have a real live witness," Bo said, gesturing. "Let's go."

An ambulance was at the kerb, back doors open, horse snorting and pawing the street, while a doctor attempted to put a compress on the bare bleeding shoulder of a wounded man slumped in the open doors of the vehicle.

"Inspectors Tonneman and Clancy," Dutch said. "We have to talk to you—"

The attending physician shook his head. "This man has a serious bullet wound. He must be taken to Bellevue at once."

"No! No!" The wounded man struggled to stand but couldn't. "No!" His speech became a rasp. "I have to talk to the Inspectors first."

"We'll make it quick, doctor." Dutch's eyes narrowed as blood seeped through the compress. He wondered if the man would live long enough to tell them anything.

"Your name," Bo said.

"Cunningham. Clarence Cunningham III."

"You work at the bank?" Dutch said.

"I am a banker." Cunningham drew himself up in spite of the spasm of pain the movement caused.

"No disrespect, Mister Cunningham," Bo said. "Who shot you?"

"Butch or Sundance. I don't know. Couldn't tell which was which. But the woman—" He gasped, closed his eyes.

"Damn it, inspectors! This man is losing a great deal of blood."

Dutch leaned towards the injured man. "What woman?"

Bo's eyes twitched. The banker could go any minute. "The woman."

". . . blue coat—"

"Here we go," Dutch said. "That damned blue coat."

"Pretty woman. Tall, my height. Modest, almost shy. Said she was . . . waiting for her husband. Showed her to our waiting area, but she . . . kept walking back and forth. Fussing all the time." Cunningham coughed. Bloody spittle ran down his chin.

The doctor cleared his throat. "Inspectors, you promised to hurry."

"She came right out when the robbers appeared."

"Why are you telling us about her?" Bo said.

Cunningham moaned. "I tried to protect her when it started but she wouldn't let me. I had the distinct feeling that she knew them."

"That's enough," the doctor said. "Inspectors, help me."

Dutch gave the wounded man a hand-up to the stretcher on the floor of the ambulance. Flakes of snow came down in a sudden flurry.

"One last question, Cunningham," Bo said. "Did you get her name?"

"She said her husband's name was Place."

"As in Etta Place?" Dutch said, as they watched the ambulance drive off.

"We seem to have the whole kit and caboodle. Butch, Sundance, and Etta Place. Ripe for reward-collecting."

"Well, well, well; sure and I'm happy to see our police department has their best men on the job."

The speaker wore a heavy overcoat and a black derby and spoke with a rolling Irish accent. His bulbous nose was red with broken veins.

"As I live and breathe, it's O'Toole himself," Bo said. "What're you doing here? Did Tammany buy the building around the corner?"

O'Toole dusted the snow from his coat. "The Boss, he likes to stay in touch."

"The election didn't turn out so good." Dutch chuckled. "Did it, me bucko?"

The Tammany man flicked his finger at the brim of his black derby, raising it. "Don't mean a thing. We still got the influence."

"In other words," Bo said, "you know where all the bodies are buried."

"Now don't youse go putting words into me mouth, Inspector."

"So what do you want, O'Toole?" Dutch said. "We got a lot to do."

"One hand washes t'other, as the Boss always says."

"Does he now." Bo squinted into the snow. "Let's go, Dutch." They started off.

O'Toole came pussy-footing after them. "The Boss says youse might have a little gratitude for some information that's come his way, what with a new mayor and a new commissioner starting in a few weeks."

"And neither one owing you boys a thin dime," Dutch said.

"Never do know," O'Toole said. "But maybe youse want to take a look near where they aim to build another bridge to Brooklyn. There's a tavern on Delancey with a wee bit of colour. The fortune-teller there ain't half bad."

Dutch pulled his cigarettes out of his pocket and lit up. "How do you mean?"

O'Toole patted his lips. Dutch grinned and gave O'Toole his own ready-made smoke, and lit a second for himself. "Talk."

"Number one, she's a true beauty. A real pip."

Bo rolled his eyes. "What's number two."

"The fortunes she tells ain't no blarney. They're the real McCoy." O'Toole took a deep drag of his smoke, tipped his derby and shuffled off into the swirling snow.

★

"There's a bit of colour." Bo pointed to the swinging black-lettered sign ahead. "Pink it is."

Dutch sniffed. "Smells like Tammany to me. Is it possible Tammany's dirty fingers helped craft the Bowery Bank robbery?" He removed his hat, shook the snow off and put it back on his head. "Crocker can't steal an election, so he switches to robbing banks?"

"Robbing maybe. Killing? Not a good idea." Bo stopped to watch an ugly midget, swinging a small club, which he used to knock the accumulating snow from the sign that said PINKYS.

"A beer, gentlemen? Have your fortunes told? Who knows what secret pleasures the fates have in store for you?" The little man gave them a quick, studied, smile. "Not often I get coppers in my establishment. Pinky's the name."

"What say you, Dutch," Bo said. "A beer and a fortune?"

"Suits me."

"Whiskey would be my rathers, but . . ."

They followed Pinky into the narrow space. Two drunks were splayed on the crude bar. "Out, out," Pinky yelled, hitting the bar with his club. When the drunks didn't move, he grabbed the backs of their trousers, one pair in each hand, and cast them, howling protests, out the swinging doors. He barred the doors with planks crisscrossed on the door frame.

Dutch's eyes were drawn to a movement at the rear of the dark tavern. A white feather. The feather was attached to a red turban on the head of a woman swathed in crimson. She lit a candle, illuminating the small table where she sat and the two empty chairs opposite. Pinky nodded at the two policemen. "Have a seat, gentlemen. Lorraine! Fortune hunters." He exploded with laughter.

Bo took the chair to his right, opposite the woman, "Let's see what you have . . . Miss Lorraine."

With fast fingers she opened what appeared to be a fresh pack of cards, split the deck in two and spread the two halves into fans. Next, with a stylish and almost melodious ruffle, she melded the two parts back into the deck and offered the cards for Bo to shuffle.

"There a back door in this establishment?" Dutch edged past the table, noting the quick glance exchanged between Pinky and Lorraine.

Pinky cleared his throat. "Nothing out there, your honour. Maybe a beer barrel or two."

The rear door opened on to a narrow, rancid alley. Dutch stepped out, catching his coat on the metal band of a barrel. Flurries of snow danced round him. A white film covered everything, including that barrel and another. When he paused to inspect the damage to his coat, he saw under the few dark strands from his coat, a larger scrap of blue wool.

A bell went off in his brain.

He was careful in removing the bit of blue wool; he cupped his hand around it. An errant snowflake turned the remnant pink. Dutch smiled at the word pink, which seemed to colour everything in this place.

"Uh huh," he said, knowing Pinky was standing in the open door watching. He wrapped the cloth remnant in his handkerchief and placed it in his breast pocket.

Inside, Lorraine had laid out tarot cards and was making indistinguishable sounds and nodding her head. Bo yawned.

"Interesting out back," Dutch told Bo, patting his breast pocket.

"Beers coming right up, gentlemen." Pinky scurried behind the bar and filled two chipped mugs from the tap, wiped their heads clean of foam and thrust a mug at each inspector.

"Oh yeah?" Bo took a long swig and wiped his mouth on his sleeve.

"Bluth," Lorraine muttered.

Bo took off his derby, wiped the inside with his handkerchief, returned the derby to his head. "Say again?"

Dutch wet his mouth with the beer and set the mug on the small table near the cards. "She means blood," Dutch said. "And she sure is right."

Lorraine jerked her head round towards Dutch.

He said, "A woman in a blue coat. We've been told she was here, not too long ago."

Pinky shrugged, palms open. "She just ran through. What do we know?"

"More than you're saying." Bo stood, lifting the edge of the table. Cards and mugs came crashing down.

Lorraine gave a weak yelp and fell over backward. When Dutch offered her his hand, she pulled away.

Bo said, "We can close you down before you can fart."

Pinky showed his rotten teeth and ducked behind the bar. "We're protected."

"Don't think so. Tammany's already given you up." Bo laughed. "How do you think we got here?" He grabbed Pinky's collar with his right hand and lifted him out from behind the bar. His menacing left was poised close the little man's nose. Lorraine made a keening noise.

When there was no reply, Bo's right hand rose, dangling the little man in mid-air. Bo shook him. Not too hard. But hard enough.

"Madison Street," Pinky whimpered. "No. 7. Boarding house."

13

Madison Street, fewer than four blocks from the East River, was a cluster of tenements and cheap lodging-houses. This made it accessible to ships bringing the stream of poor immigrants, as well as to a number of piers where freighters heading for South America took on cargo.

The five-storied brick No.7 looked weary; were it not propped up by the tenement to the right and another grime-covered five-storey wreck to the left, it might slump to the cobble.

In spite of the cold, the street teemed with ill-clothed children, boys and girls of various ages, screaming, running, chasing sock-balls, trying to scrape snowballs from the thin, already grimy layer of snow.

One small boy in an oversized coat and newsboy cap stood on the steps leaning against the entrance to No.7. He watched Dutch and Bo as they came down the street and stopped in front of the house.

"You live here?" Bo said.

The boy stuck out his scabby chin. "What's it to you, copper?"

"Mouth-off again, and it's the Tombs for you. I'll ask you again, do you live here?"

The boy picked a scab off his chin and studied it before jerking his thumb in the direction of the tenement.

"So you're just resting here?" Dutch said.

"You got a problem with that?"

Bo said, "That's it. Let's take him in." He reached up and grabbed the boy's arm with fingers of steel. "Let's go."

The boy's nose started leaking. Even so, he wasn't giving in.

"Wait a minute, Bo," Dutch said. "What's your name, kid?"

"Mike." He tried to pull his arm from Bo, but Bo had a tight grip.

Dutch said, "You're a pretty tough guy."

"I hold me own."

"You behave nice and I'll talk Inspector Clancy out of sending you to the Tombs."

Mike chewed his lower lip. "Give me a nickel and we got a bargain."

Dutch suppressed a laugh as Bo dragged Mike down to the street level, keeping hold of his arm. "You little bastard."

"Easy, Inspector Clancy." To Mike, Dutch said, "Two cents."

Mike spat in his hand. Dutch did the same in his own. Then they slapped their hands together.

"Bargain," Mike said.

"Bargain." They shook on it. "All right, now, do you know a lady in a blue coat that lives here?"

"Let's see your money."

Bo agitated Mike's arm. "You need some persuasion?"

Dutch asked his question again. "The lady in a blue coat!"

"Top floor, back." Mike tried again to free himself, not expecting Bo to release him. When Bo did, he toppled over.

"Here you go," Dutch said, "Two cents and a penny more because you got grit."

Mike grabbed the coins and disappeared into the tenement next door.

The staircase in No. 7 was narrow and sloped to one side. Strident sounds of life could be heard behind most of the doors.

"Mother of God." Bo stopped at the fourth-floor landing to catch his breath. "It's a goddam Jesus-loving hazard to make two fine and upstanding New York Police Inspectors climb a goddam mountain to do their jobs."

"Funny, San Juan Hill didn't give you grief."

"I was a young spruce those years, as you was, Coz."

Dutch reached the fifth floor first and hammered on the door. "Open up."

A woman yelled, "What the hell?"

"Open up." Bo smirked at Dutch.

"Says who?"

"Says me."

"You and what army?"

"Me and Teddy Roosevelt. Open the blasted door or we'll break it down."

When the door opened a crack, Bo shoved.

"You got some nerve—" The woman was tall, her chestnut hair in a puffed up roll under a wide-brimmed hat. Around her shoulders was a long, fringed, black shawl. A bulging carpet bag lay open on the floor next to the narrow bed, which was positioned under the eaves of the tiny room. There was barely enough space for the three to stand without touching. Dutch kicked the door shut.

"A good day to you, ma'am," Bo said. "I'm Inspector Clancy. This is Inspector Tonneman. Are you Missus Place?"

"I don't know anybody by that name."

"We're here to talk to you about the robberies at the Union Square Bank and the Bowery Bank."

"You got the wrong girl." She turned, bent to close her carpet bag. The room was so small she had trouble masking her movements. "I'm an actress. I just heard about a job in Boston and I have a train to catch."

Bo grasped her by the arms and shifted her between him and Dutch, away from the carpet bag.

"Maybe you were at the Bowery Bank this morning."

"Maybe I wasn't."

"You own a blue coat?" Bo gave the carpet bag a nudge with his boot.

"Hey—"

Dutch said, "Ma'am, we need your help regarding those two bank robberies."

"I told you. You got the wrong girl."

"You were quick enough to open the door," Bo said.

"I am a law abiding citizen and you coppers have that certain smell."

"And what if you were wrong?" Dutch said. "You're not afraid someone might push their way in and rob you?"

She gave an uneasy laugh. "They wouldn't find much."

The floor creaked outside the room. Dutch eased his Colt from its holster. Bo, who believed in Dutch's intuition, drew his own weapon.

The woman tried to get around Dutch to the door, but Dutch blocked her.

Another creak. Hammers of their Colts back. The woman made a soft sound.

Bo took her wrist in his hand; she tried to pull away. "Quiet, or I'll break your neck."

They stood still. Silence. Sweat glistened on the woman's upper lip.

Bo motioned the woman to sit on the bed. He and Dutch exchanged looks. Bo gave the door a light push. Dutch stepped out, gun drawn. The hall outside the door was empty.

Dutch leaned over the stair rail, listening. Nothing. He went back into the room and shut the door. "Okay. It's clear. But I don't trust it."

The carpet bag caught Bo's eye. He picked it up. The woman jumped to her feet. "You put that down. That's private property."

"Private property? You don't say." Bo opened the bag and pulled out a blood-stained blue coat. "Look what we got here, Dutch."

"You have no right," the woman said.

Dutch found the tear in the sleeve of the coat. "I'd be more careful about my friends if I were you, Missus Place."

"Fire!" A cry from the hall. "Fire!"

Turning, they saw a burning piece of newspaper being slipped under the door.

With the distraction, the woman grabbed the carpet bag, scrambled to the door, threw it open, and ran.

Gunfire. From the hall. Six shots. Then: Click. Click. Heavy
steps on the stairs. The woman lay bleeding near the landing.
Dutch, closest to the door, stamped out the fire, then, Colt
drawn, hammer back, he jumped over her body to chase after the
shooter. More shots.

Weapon at the ready, Bo dragged the woman inside – he hoped
it was to safety, but Bo Clancy never deluded himself. He heard
Dutch's .38 calibre rounds. Quiet. He checked the woman for
signs of life. She was done.

Footsteps on the stairs.

"It's me," Dutch called. "Shooter's gone." Dutch entered the
room carrying the carpet bag. "Found this on the stairs." Blood
dripped from his cheek. "Dead?"

"No question. Let's see what all the fuss is about." Bo upended
the carpet bag on the narrow bed. Women's clothing scattered,
but the item of interest that came out last was a grey canvas bag.

A good shake of the canvas and out fell banded packets of
paper currency.

Dutch knelt by the dead woman and closed her eyes. He
paused. "Sorry, ma'am." He searched for hidden pockets in her
dress, her shawl.

Bo began to count the money. "Check her boots."

The dead woman's legs were slim, her stockinged feet narrow;
her boots were still warm. Dutch's big hands were ill-suited for
the search, but his fingers touched a piece of folded paper in her
left boot. He fished it out and unfolded it. He read it once, and
again. He rose and offered the paper to Bo.

"Her real name was Jenny McCracken. She was a Pinkerton."

14

"Holy shit!" Little Jack Meyers was standing on the corner of
Essex and Delancey across from PINKYS, watching for any
unusual activity, when who should show their Irish mugs and
head into the saloon but Inspectors Clancy and Tonneman.

He'd been wedged in the narrow entrance of Moishe's
Delicatessen since noon, trying to ignore the pungent smell of
corned beef. Moishe had chased him away twice before Little
Jack gave him two-bits for a sandwich to leave him be.

As he took a big bite of the sandwich, he saw Pinky tossing out a couple of drunks and had to smile. The midget could hold his own. The tavern door slammed shut. Little Jack gnawed another bite of corned beef and drifted across the street and up to the door of the saloon.

He stepped back, considering the door. Was there an alley? He could hear Big Jack in his head. "Drag your arse back and use the alley."

No, the coppers would check the alley. He played at pushing the door open – it was planked tight, all right. Big Jack always told him *never assume,* so he ran around the corner to check the alley, but Dutch Tonneman was there and just missed seeing him.

Little Jack returned to the tavern door. He pulled a small flask of rum from his back pocket and swallowed a mouthful. Eyes almost closed, lips slack, he let his body relax against the door. Couldn't see anything, but maybe he could hear what was going on. The voices inside were muffled. Lots of yelling. Not only was Bo Clancy a *bulvan,* he was also a good yeller who could scare the shit out of a statue.

It wasn't long before Little Jack heard the scraping sound of the plank being removed.

Shoving the last of the sandwich into his mouth, he sprinted back to the corner of Essex Street, dodging a horse and wagon, and colliding with a bearded man wheeling a pushcart full of roasting potatoes. The pushcart man cursed him: "*a broch tzu Columbus,*" which made Little Jack laugh because the man's curse was aimed not at him but at Christopher Columbus.

In front of Moishe's again, Little Jack saw the two inspectors leave PINKYS and head off east towards the river. Should he follow them? What would Big Jack think? Easy. Stood to reason, they'd learned something from Pinky; otherwise they wouldn't be moving so fast.

He might have followed, but out came Pinky from his tavern, looked around, and off he went, turning on to Essex Street. Little Jack held himself in check for a moment, then he followed.

All of a sudden, Pinky turned around and rushed back the way he had come, running smack into Little Jack, giving him a mean shove out of the way. So, Little Jack thought, Pinky had changed his mind and chosen to go towards the East River, after Clancy and Tonneman.

Rutgers Street was packed full of coppers, wagons, horses, and an ambulance. It looked like most of the neighbourhood was on the street, and those that weren't hung out the windows.

The area was blocked off by a sideways-parked wagon, with one patrolman standing guard.

"Uh oh," Little Jack said out loud, hanging back behind Pinky. He saw right away that he'd messed up because Pinky heard, turned and looked at him hard.

Little Jack shrugged and wormed himself into the crowd. Good thing, too. Tonneman and Clancy were coming out of the tenement. Blood on Tonneman's face.

"Hey, brass-buttons." Pinky pushed his way to the patrolman, keeping his head low. "Another bank get robbed?"

The patrolman shook his head. "No banks here. Woman got herself shot."

"Dead?"

The officer said, ". . . than a blessed mackerel."

Pinky looked around. He couldn't see Little Jack, who had ducked under a cart. Satisfied, Pinky shoved through the gawkers.

This time, Little Jack was more careful about being seen, and followed at a discreet distance. Pinky was heading back towards Second Avenue.

*

Pinky felt it in his bones. Someone watching him. "Don't stand out," Mister William liked to preach. "If you don't stand out you can slip through the world and never be caught."

Who was it? That *trumbanick* he'd bumped into? The one he'd seen again on Rutgers?

The school on Essex Street was letting out. Boys running, brawling, shouting. Pinky took off his cap, turned it inside out, and became one of them. He managed to blend with a group until Second Avenue, where he broke free. And at Second Street, he mounted the steps to the small three-storied brownstone. He lifted the heavy knocker and pulled it down hard against the oak door. A shadow appeared behind the diamond-shaped glass. The door opened; Pinky charged in.

The bearded man who'd opened the door removed the

meerschaum from his mouth, and raised his right eyebrow. "Another crisis?" His accent was German. He raised his voice. "Our friend has arrived again with another crucial moment, Hughs."

"Come in, sit down, my dear Pinky." Hughs was clean-shaven and spoke like a toff. "Lowenstein, give him a minute. He's a good fellow. Can't you see he's out of breath."

Pinky couldn't abide either of these fat-arsed snobs. They lived in this fancy house like their shit don't stink, while he and Lorraine was grubbers.

"I got important information. I got to talk to Chicago."

Lowenstein looked dubious. "What information?"

"The woman's been killed."

Hughs went at once to the candlestick telephone, cranked the ringer box, lifted the earpiece.

"Good afternoon," an operator said. "Number, please?"

"Please let me speak to Chicago operator PA 12." Hughs handed Pinky the telephone.

"One moment, please," the operator said.

Within seconds a man's voice came on the line. "Name and number."

"Pinky. Number 79."

"One minute, please."

*

Never in a million years had Pinky thought he would become a detective. He and Lorraine was happy playing three-a-day at Mick Sullivan's vaudeville house in Cincinnati, where they was billed as Pinky Pincus and the Pink Lady.

The two of them had started with Sam Smith, who had a magic act: The Great Smithsini. Sam taught both of them how to shoot, for a sketch he called "The Girl with the Vanishing Volumities," which was Sam's name for tits.

Pinky and Lorraine were both expert shootists. The big woman and the small man figured out almost at once that they were made for each other on and off stage. In their act, Pinky shot the Lady's clothes off until she was naked, or appeared to be naked – depending on the town they were in or the house they were playing.

Their encore presented the lady chasing Pinky off, stage

right. The velvet curtain billowed. Then the two of them would appear stage left, as the Pink Lady proceeded to shoot off Pinky's clothes, only to reappear – BIG-FINISH-ACCOMPANIED-BY-DRUM-ROLLS – naked, except for the large pink flower covering his private parts.

Everything changed on the night Mister William Pinkerton caught their act and invited them to work for the Agency.

"You on the line, Pinky?"

Pinky began to sweat. "Good to hear your voice, Mister Pinkerton."

★

Little Jack almost fell over backwards. He'd managed to hoist himself on to a window box, saw a broken pane and put his ear to the crack. Once more he said, but under his breath, "Goddam!" Pinky was actually talking to *the* William Pinkerton. Wait till Big Jack heard this.

★

Little Jack wasn't the only one to react. Another exclamation of surprise came from a man positioned more than a hundred feet away.

Davey Collins couldn't be seen by most people passing by. As a matter of fact, Davey, known as Davey Bear, was standing on spikes halfway up a pole that the telephone company had put up, off to the side of the street. The pole was masked by a tall tree with snow-laden branches.

The Boss had a lot of people around the city letting him know what was going on. When he used the information fast enough and in the best possible way, the bucks came rolling in and people like Davey Bear got walking-around money. He'd heard enough to make the Boss happy. Now, he had to disconnect from the brownstone's telephone so he could tap into another wire. "Boss, it's Davey."

★

Little Jack didn't know if what he had learned about Pinky was worth anything. But Big Jack would. And Little Jack was betting it was plenty. He turned west on Fifth Street and heard someone above him, talking. Goddam. Up the pole. Little Jack came to a dead stop.

★

"That little Jew, Pincus?" Davey told the Boss.

"What about him?"

"You sitting down?"

"Tell me right fucking now or I'll break your head."

"Pinky Pinkus is a Pinkerton Man. For sure; also, those two foreign bird gawkers. And the woman in the blue coat from the bank robberies? She's one of them, too."

15

All the doors of the houses on Gramercy Park house wore evergreen wreaths, studded with red holly berries and pine cones. Some of the wreaths had big red silk bows. In the park itself a plump spruce sparkled with tiny electric bulbs. A definite feeling of festivity hung in the air.

The winter sun cast frugal light, which Esther knew was ideal for the proper exposure she would need. The weather had turned mild. Esther unlocked the gate to the private park and held it open for Wong to pull in the wagon carrying her wooden tripod and her box of glass plates and her Scovill camera.

She motioned for the man and woman – who had come calling and commissioned a photograph – to enter, closing and locking the gate behind them.

"Wait here, please," Esther told them. She moved down the path, evaluating the light and the shadows, until she found a suitable space, then beckoned to them.

If Wong was surprised that morning to see on the doorstep of No. 5 Gramercy Park the men called Robbie Allen and Harry Kidder, who'd brought Miss Esther home after the bank robbery, and with them the tall and attractive young woman named Henrietta de Grout, he gave no indication. He was pleased, however, to see that Robbie Allen only stayed long enough to make flirting eyes at Miss Esther before he went on about his business.

Henrietta de Grout wore a long, green velvet coat with a high collar, white lace ruffle, fur cuffs, and flowing skirt. Pinned to her lapel was an elegant gold watch. Her thick dark hair was rolled, framing her oval face, ending in a topknot surmounting her head. She had removed her hat for the photograph. Standing close beside her, Harry Kidder looked handsome and serious in his broad-shouldered, black, single-breasted suit, high collar and narrow grey silk cravat, held in place by a diamond stickpin.

Because the photograph was to be in honour of the couple's engagement, Esther had put aside her Kodak and rolled film for her more reliable Scovill and the glass plates and fine lenses.

"Please stand perfectly still." After Esther focused the lens, she inserted a glass plate into a holder and placed it in the back of the camera. "Ready?" she said. "Do not move, please." The light was perfect, the weather benign.

"Ready." Miss de Grout's husky voice was steady, sure. She had a casual grace, standing there close beside her man.

Esther made the picture.

It felt right. But she removed the plate, inserted another and made one more picture.

★

Robbie Allen strolled down towards Union Square. On Fifteenth Street, he looked in the window of Tiffany's, where Harry had bought Henrietta a gold lapel watch and, for himself, a diamond stickpin. *Bought*, no less. Damn it all, they'd lost their voodoo.

Harry had anyway. He was all wrapped up in Henrietta and being a father, and now he was talking about ranching. In New York.

Goddam, in the old days they would have just held up Tiffany's and cleaned it out.

He had the itch, same as he'd felt as a boy in Utah. Still, there was time. He couldn't push Harry too hard just now. Another couple of weeks wouldn't hurt, while they saw a few vaudeville shows and enjoyed some of the night life. They'd taken rooms again at Missus Taylor's boarding house on West Twelfth Street, so they could celebrate the New Year and shoot the moon. Next week he'd get himself to the steamship lines on the East River and buy those tickets to South America.

He passed the Union Square Bank, which was open again; no sign that a robbery had ever happened. Those two had done another bank and gone to ground. Where were the bastards? He'd like to get his hands on them, all right.

All this thinking made his throat dry. He headed to Joe's Bar, a tavern on Union Square they'd been frequenting since they arrived in the city.

The streets were crowded with shoppers, workmen, servants carrying packages. Robbie was deep in thought. He failed to notice the two men on the opposite side of the street, who had stopped to talk.

These two men were studying the scene of the first crime at the Union Square Bank, when one said, "Look there, Dutch. If we didn't know they travelled together, I'd say that fellow there fits the description of Butch Cassidy."

"Yeah, Coz. Him and everyone else in city clothes and a derby. Cassidy has a moustache."

"Easy enough to shave off," Bo said.

"Forget it. You're clutching at straws. The shooters got away. The Pinkerton girl had a bagful of bank bills. She was with them, or not with them. They got cover from the kids in the tenement. And we have egg on our face."

16

January, 1902: Bo Clancy and Dutch Tonneman had once again been summoned to the Police Commissioner's office. There was a new commissioner, all the more reason for the two inspectors to be summoned.

Neither Dutch nor Bo wore top coats. Though milder than usual, it was still winter, but the new commissioner, Colonel John Partridge, preferred unlit hearths. "Good for the brain," he was known to say – and often. Too much heat wore him down, made him irritable. Therefore, to suit his taste, the interior of 300 Mulberry Street was like a block of ice.

On the staircase Bo took several pulls from the small flask he kept in his inside pocket. He knew Dutch well enough not to offer him a nip while they were on the job.

The welcome they received was sour, and weighed down by glares and reproaches, and no invitation to sit. Dutch wondered: did the Commissioner think they were tainted by the corruption surrounding the old Tammany regime? If so, he should know better. He and Bo were Roosevelt men. Rough Riders to the core.

"Report." The Commissioner had set down his cigar when they came into his office. It smouldered in the large ashtray on the Partridge's neat desk.

Bo had the rank; it was his place to answer. "No bank robberies in the past three weeks."

"And," the Commissioner replied, "no cases of sunstroke in Manhattan."

Dutch swallowed most of a chuckle.

Bo showed him his fist.

The Commissioner had his back to them. Dutch arched his eyebrows. "*It was funny*," he mouthed. To the Commissioner he said, "Their faces are splashed across the front page of every newspaper in the city."

The Commissioner lifted the cigar to his mouth and puffed pungent rings into the air. "Thanks to Miss Breslau and Sergeant Lowry. Damn it, men, where are Butch and Sundance? They can't have disappeared without a clue. Capturing them here in New York will get the press off our backs, put a twist in their long underwear. New York newspapers will have the best story since Tammany was squelched."

"Yes, sir," Bo said.

The Commissioner harrumphed. "Talk to me about the Pinkerton woman."

"She was going by the name of Etta Place," Bo said. "Her real name was Jenny McCracken. The Pinkertons claimed the body."

"And she had some of the bank money. Was she a thief? Or was she collecting evidence?"

"No way of knowing, sir," Dutch said. "The Pinkertons won't talk to us."

The Commissioner glared at Dutch. "Then what the hell good are you? I'd be better off with two trained monkeys, wiggling their pink arses." There was a noticeable silence. "Damn Pinkertons!"

So, Dutch thought, the Pinkertons weren't talking to him either.

Bo cleared his throat. "At least we recovered some of the bank money."

"I called the Pinkerton office in Chicago. Bill Pinkerton is never in. Damn it to hell and horse-shit! You do your job and show them up, you hear. They claim they never sleep. Well, we can do the same." The Commissioner concentrated on Dutch. "You're a descendant of Old Peter Tonneman who worked with Jacob Hays?"

"Yes, sir."

The Commissioner shook his head. "You'd think he would have passed something down to you."

Dutch's face reddened. "Sir."

"Don't 'sir' me. Get the hell out of here. Find the rest of the money. Find Butch Cassidy and the Sundance Kid. I want to be able to call Bill Pinkerton and tell him we caught Butch Cassidy and that we solved the murder of his operative and that, in the future, it would be more mannerly – and prudent – if he let us know when any of his operatives were working New York City."

The Commissioner's cigar filled the air with bitter smoke. He threw the stogy into the cold fireplace and lit a new one.

"Next time I see you two, I want results."

17

"I'm freezing my arse off here," Little Jack Meyers said, jigging from one foot to the other outside the shack, across the street from 300 Mulberry – where the reporters who covered police headquarters gathered, hoping for hot news. Little Jack had decided to stake out the Tonneman house on Grand before daylight to see what Bo and Dutch were up to this morning, and he'd followed them to the House.

Little Jack didn't get much sympathy but he did get a welcome taste from reporter Lem Borden's pint bottle.

All the scribblers watched the comings and goings of the coppers and police wagons. Some energetic souls crossed the street to ask their questions, then returned to the shack, no smarter than they'd been before.

Others followed after the goings, sniffing for a way to get behind the story. But the big story was Butch Cassidy and the Sundance Kid robbing banks and shooting up people in the city.

"You think they have something on Butch and Sundance?" Lem squinted at Little Jack. Little Jack was a wily one. He wasn't as sharp as his boss, Jack West, but he was smart enough.

Little Jack shook his head. "Don't know. Don't think so. Best guess is Bo and Dutch're getting a whipping. I'd like to get my ear to that door."

"No, you wouldn't. It'd get stuck to that block of ice. Then, all you'd have is an ear full of door."

Little Jack guffawed. "That's funny."

"As a corpse," the reporter said. "Hell would freeze in there, thanks to Partridge."

"Uh," Little Jack said. "Here they come."

"And I'd say you were right." Lem crossed the street with Little Jack and a half dozen other reporters on his heels. "Got a whipping."

"Jesus," Bo said. "The vultures coming to pick over the carcasses."

Dutch stepped out in the street and hailed a hack. As they drove off, Bo thumbed his nose at the reporters.

"PINKYS on Delancey," Dutch told the hackney man.

"You thinking what I'm thinking?" Bo said, yawning.

"If Jenny McCracken went to PINKYS after the Bowery robbery and Pinky knew where to find her, that would make him another of Bill Pinkerton's operatives."

"Couldn't have said it better."

But when they climbed down from the hack, all they saw was an old sot sprawled out on the icy sidewalk, blocking the door. Wound round his neck like a scarf was Lorraine's red turban, without its white feather.

The door to PINKYS was boarded up.

Bo grabbed the scarf, yanked the drunk to his feet and shook him. Putrid breath came forth with each snore. Dried blood covered the drunkard's forehead. His crusty eyelids fluttered.

"Where's Pinky?" Bo roared.

"Gone, gone, all gone." The sot screwed up his face and sobbed.

"When?"

"How's about a nickle for old Harvey? A piddlin' five cents, four-three-two? One?"

Bo dropped old Harvey to the sidewalk, dug a nickel from his pocket, and flashed it at old Harvey, who made a grab for it.

Groping the side of the building, Harvey lifted himself. On his feet, he belched, farted; spittle dribbled into his beard. "Middle of night, Pinky came with a wad of dough. Thought I was sleeping but I saw him show it to Lorraine. Gobswiped me with his club and threw me out on the street like garbage." Harvey tried to spit but only slobbered himself.

Bo let the nickel drop to the ground. Harvey scrambled for it.

Dutch pulled his whistle, which he kept on a chain next to his St Christopher's medal, and blew.

A patrolman rounded the corner of Essex. Old Harvey would sleep it off at the precinct – where at least he wouldn't freeze to death on the cold, cold ground.

18

Little Jack arrived at PINKYS in time to see that the two inspectors had failed again. Pinky was gone. What about the two Pinkertons that Pinky had reported to, the ones in the brownstone on Second Avenue? He saw the patrolman come to collect the drunk and used the distraction to skitter down Essex over to Second.

*

"You catch that?" Dutch said.

"What?"

"Sure looked like Jack West's boy. He's been tailing us since we left the House. He seems to know where he's going."

On Second Avenue and Second Street, they saw Little Jack stop in front of a shabby brownstone. A hackney with two passengers was pulling away; the driver coaxed his horse across Second Avenue and veered uptown. Bo and Dutch came to stand on either side of Little Jack as they all watched the hackney fade from sight.

Bo, amiable as a saint, crowded Little Jack. "You have something you want to tell us?"

"Shit."

"Besides that," Dutch said, crowding Little Jack on the other side.

Little Jack scowled. "I don't know nothing."

"You'd best tell us," Bo said, pressing in.

Little Jack rubbed his nose. He might as well share his information. "They was professors. Anyways, that's what they called each other; but sure as hell they're Pinkertons. I followed Pinky here after the woman got killed. They telephoned Chicago to report."

"They must have found Butch and Sundance," Dutch said.

"Doubt it," Bo said. "They would be shouting it from the rooftops by now, and Billy Pinkerton, he'd be bragging it all over the newspapers. Looks like those two professors made a mess of it and were told to get their arses back to Chicago."

Dutch climbed the steps to the brownstone and rang the bell. No response. Tried the door. It was open. He motioned to Bo.

"Beat it, kid," Bo told Little Jack.

"Yes, sir." Little Jack found a spot around the corner, and when the coast was clear, he hoisted himself up on the window box near the cracked window pane.

*

Dutch moved through the foyer. The house had a musty smell. The furnishings were shabby. Bo checked the other two floors, came back down.

"Nothing here," Dutch said. "You find anything?"

Grim, Bo held out a small card to Dutch. It was Esther's calling card.

19

The men who called themselves Butch and Sundance were holed up in a dingy lodging-house that let to sailors and dockworkers. It was convenient to the East River piers and taverns, and the rooms were cheap.

Butch climbed the rickety stairs to the third floor, stepping over the drunk collapsed on the staircase. He was carrying a newspaper, a bar of soap, and a honed and stropped straight razor. In the room, Sundance was lying on the bed snoring. Butch tilted the bed, sending Sundance crashing to the floor. "That goddam whore you knocked over at the first bank, the one stole your gun; done us in good." He dropped the folded newspaper on Sundance.

Blinking, Sundance sat up and unfolded the newspaper. There they were, right on the front page. "Pretty good likeness, I'd say." He scrambled away from Butch's kick, adding, "I always said I was a good looking hombre."

"It's in every newspaper, on the front page. We got to get out of here."

"One more bank," Sundance said.

"You looking to get hanged? Not me, pardner." He handed Sundance the soap and the razor. "Get rid of that ratty face-hair."

"How the hell will we get out? They'll nail us for sure if we get on a train." He brightened. "We could buy us a horse and wagon. We got the cash."

"We're going to need every bit of it. No telling where we'll end up." Butch peered out the grimy window. If you stood in the far right of the window, you could just about see the iced-up river that was locking all shipping in the harbour. "If we get lucky and there's a thaw, we can take one of them steamers." He laughed. "I hear South America is wide open for good businessmen with a little cash."

20

It had been a week since Robbie Allen and his friend Harry Kidder put Henrietta de Grout on the New York Central train to Dyckman Street, and the farm in Inwood. The men remained at Missus Taylor's boarding house, trying to come to a decision about their next move. The mild weather in the beginning of January had turned wicked, bone-chilling cold.

This morning they took a hackney down to South Street, got out and walked.

A sudden change in temperature, a slight warming, had shaken loose the solid field of ice on the rivers. Now huge blocks on both the Hudson and East Rivers were locking ships, freighters, tugs, and other boats, large and small, in the harbour. They kept walking, past the piers, past the shacks and warehouses along the waterfront.

Robbie stopped to roll a smoke. "So what do you say?"

A man on a bicycle, riding fast, pulled out of a side street and blocked their way. He jumped off, letting the bicycle fall, and confronted them. His two holsters were hung low like a gun fighter. "I know you!"

Never taking his eyes off the stranger, Harry smiled.

"Uh uh. Don't make no quick moves, neither. The reward poster says dead or alive." The stranger's guns came out of their holsters quick and slick.

Harry's Colts emerged, quicker and slicker. He fired both weapons. The stranger never got off a shot. He slumped against a warehouse wall, staring at his bleeding hands, stunned.

Robbie checked to see if anyone heard, but the waterfront was a noisy place, even with boats and ships out of service. He picked up the bicycle and righted it.

"If I was Sundance, stranger," Harry said. "You'd be dead and on your way to hell."

The would-be shooter sank to his knees.

Harry said, "You got anything to say to me?"

"No, sir. I'd be much obliged if you could leave me right here to die."

Robbie collected the shooter's weapons. Always good to have a couple extra. To the shooter, he said, "Hope you'll be feeling better real soon."

Untroubled, Robbie and Harry turned back the way they'd come, retracing their footsteps down South Street.

"So what do you say?" Robbie said.

"We couldn't do nothing now, even if we wanted to."

"Even?" Robbie looked at his friend.

"I'm thinking I might be ready to do some ranching."

"Ranching is good in South America, I hear."

"I mean local."

"I knew she would get to you."

Harry shrugged.

"I'm going to pick up a couple of tickets on one of those freighters. To Argentina maybe. She can come later with the kid."

21

Esther stared at her calling card. "They're scientists. They arrived the morning after the Union Square bank robbery – referred by Ernst Abbe, a German physicist and mathematician with whom I've been exchanging correspondence. Herr Abbe has been creating wonderful new camera lenses. These men engaged my services to photograph the diverse species of winter birds in Central Park."

"They're Pinkertons, Esther," Dutch said. "They were looking for information."

"How on earth could they possibly have known about my personal correspondence?"

"Pinkertons have sources all over the world." Bo said. "You did nothing wrong."

"They claimed to be ornithologists, called each other professor. They were well-dressed and spoke like scientists." Dismayed, Esther looked from Dutch to Bo, back to Dutch. "And now what do I have for my labours? A dark-room full of beautiful photographs that they never even came to see." She stopped, realizing the seriousness of the situation. "Oh, my goodness, they asked so many questions about the Union Square Bank robbery and what the robbers looked like, and what photographs I might have taken. I told them that I'd given all the photographs to the police. I thought they were, as scientists, inquisitive. I should have been more suspicious."

"You couldn't have known," Bo said.

"It's all right, Esther." Dutch took her hand. "You won't see them again. They ran off after the other operative was killed. Pinkertons make confusion out of the ordinary. It's their nature."

Bo agreed. "Their mission was a complete mess of their own making. On the good side, your description of Butch and Sundance provided us with fine likenesses." He smiled at her. "So fine, in fact, that there hasn't been a robbery in over three weeks."

Esther returned Bo's smile. She had it in her mind to tell them about the photograph she made for Harry Kidder and Henrietta de Grout's engagement, and the lustrous silver dollar the happy Henrietta had given her when she collected the photograph two days after.

But in that instant, a tremendous explosion blocked out all thought. The house shuddered. Shuddered again. In seconds, Wong was at the front door just ahead of Bo and Dutch.

The street was bathed in eerie light. Yellow smoke filled the sky from the direction of Grand Central Terminal.

"Stay inside, Esther," Dutch called. "Wong, close the door. And keep it closed." Dutch and Bo raced uptown, towards the explosion.

The devastation was evident even before they got to Fortieth Street. Shattered glass everywhere. The Murray Hill Hotel, reduced to ruins. The front of the Terminal facing Forty-second Street was a ravaged scar. Whistles and bells clanged. Ambulances, fire-wagons, and police. Firemen were working on wetting down the blazing remains of a wooden powder-house, as Bo and Dutch joined the search for survivors. The powder-house had contained over two hundred pounds of dynamite to be used for blasting the rocky schist in preparation for the subway dig. It had caught fire and exploded. The final tally: five people dead, 125 injured.

The tragic event in the building of the subway system that would transform the city, replaced the doings of Butch Cassidy and the Sundance Kid on the front page of every newspaper.

It would be a long time before Esther remembered what she had been about to tell Dutch.

22

After the Tammany candidates lost the election, Boss Crocker knew that he, Richard Crocker, was the man to rebuild his political machine. Crocker was still very much a part of New York politics, what with the construction of the subway system, the Interborough Rapid Transit, cutting and covering its way up Manhattan. He did not hold out much hope for the reformers.

"The voters will have their fill soon enough," he told his precinct leaders. "People get tired of reformers. Reformers don't give nothing to the people but words." He looked at their dejected faces. "New blood," he bellowed. "That's what I want. That's what we need. I want new blood, new faces, young bucks with fire in their bellies."

After Crocker sent them on their way, he set his top hat on his head and wrapped a heavy scarf around his neck.

In front of the Tammany headquarters waiting for him was his first automobile, a red Packard Model C runabout with leather seats and a wood body. It had arrived that morning all the way from Detroit, Michigan.

The vehicle had patent leather fenders and wire wheels, and, God bless us, running lights as well. What a wonderful time it was to be alive and living in this great and glorious city.

An awe-struck crowd, which included his precinct captains, was gathered around the gleaming red automobile. Mike Rafferty, his cousin's son, sat high behind the big steering wheel, like a goddam king.

Crocker had sent Rafferty out to Detroit to the Packard Motor Car Company to acquaint himself with the $2600 single-cylinder contraption. Henceforth, Rafferty would have the illustrious honour of chauffeuring Crocker around the streets of New York.

"Show me what you know, bucko." Crocker climbed into the buggy and donned the goggles Rafferty handed him.

Rafferty got down and cranked up the motor. The contraption sputtered and gasped, the whole automobile shaking to beat the band. While the on lookers cheered, Rafferty beamed and took a bow.

"Rafferty!"

Back behind the wheel, the chastised Rafferty waited for an opening to ease out on to the street. After a horse-drawn omnibus and several small delivery wagons lumbered past, he made his move. Put-put-put. He was on the street, free and clear.

"Where would you like to go, sir?" Rafferty wore a large black cap and a rugged black overcoat. He was thrilled to be sitting up in this fine automobile behind the steering wheel and next to Boss Crocker.

Crocker rolled a new cigar in his right hand. He didn't bite it or light it. "I want to see if the ice has freed up shipping in the harbour." He liked that people stopped what they were doing to watch as he and his automobile drove by. Like a God-loving prince, he began tipping his top hat to bystanders. "And, Rafferty, just so you remember whose vehicle this is, I'll be taking my turn at the wheel soon enough."

23

Robbie Allen left Missus Taylor's boarding house, passed the grubbers digging down in the hole, and sauntered east. At Union Square he bought a newspaper from the newsboy shouting out the headlines all about the investigation of the subway explosion near Grand Central Terminal.

He stopped at Joe's Bar for a beer and corned beef on rye – nice thing about New York, he thought. He might even miss the convenience. Seeking shipping news, he spread the newspaper out on the bar.

The British freighter *Herminius*, carrying freight and no passengers, was docked at Pier 32 on the East River, and was scheduled to leave day after tomorrow for Buenos Aires, with a stop in Montevideo, Uruguay.

Freight and no passengers. Robbie laughed out loud, knowing that though it was illegal to take on passengers, it was a good bet they would not refuse two cash-payers.

He patted his pocket, smiling when he felt the bank bills Harry'd found in the street after the first robbery. It would more than pay for their trip.

The blocks of ice that froze all shipping in the harbour had dispersed, and the violent gusts of northern wind eased. South Street, taking in the wake of the thaw, bustled with activity. Delivery carts and carriages and hackneys crowded the street, as an ocean liner took on supplies and passengers.

Because of the traffic jam Robbie, a copy of the *New York Herald* tucked under his arm, left his hackney some distance away from Pier 32, and walked along the busy street.

At the pier, the door to the booking office was held ajar by a brick. When Robbie pushed the door open, the hinges squealed. The ticket agent was asleep, his shaggy head on the unfinished wood counter, him snoring like a foghorn. A fired-up coal heater stood nearby.

Robbie slapped his hand on the counter; the agent snorted, shook himself, and lifted his head. His beard was full of drool, a chewed, spent cigar clenched in his teeth. He peered at Robbie. Under his wiry brows, his left eye was covered with a white film.

"Two passages on the *Herminius*."

The door squealed. Robbie didn't bother to glance behind him. He knew two men had entered. All he cared about at the moment was making sure Harry and he were on that freighter.

"The *Herminius* don't take no passengers." The agent spat into a battered spittoon and wiped his mouth with the back of his hand. "Freighters carry freight, not passengers."

Robbie laid some bills on the counter. "Passage for two. Robert Roe and Harry Doe." When the man didn't move, he put more bills on the counter.

Behind him, the door squealed. The two men probably got impatient and left.

The agent fingered the bills. "Sails day after tomorrow." He took a pad of tickets and a pen from under the counter, dipped the pen into the inkpot. "Robert Doe and Harry Roe, you say?"

"The other way around," Robbie said.

"Sorry, mate." The man's pen scratched for a bit. Finally, he pushed the tickets towards Robbie.

Robbie was pleased with himself as he ambled away from the steamship office.

The wharves were still crowded with lorries and hackneys, and the ocean liner was still boarding passengers. He crossed the street and walked down South Street towards the Battery, then cut over to Water Street.

At once, he felt himself jostled.

It was no accident.

He got grabbed, pulled into an alley, smashed in the face.

The sudden assault forced him to think, fight back, even with his nose gushing blood. Through bloodied eyes, he recognized the two bank robbers who called themselves Butch and Sundance. He reached for his Colt but both men slammed him, knocked him down, proceeded to kick and stomp him.

One extra sharp kick to the head and Robbie saw lights. Everything went to black.

24

"Here now, Rafferty, pull over. I'll take the reins." Boss Crocker was eager to sit behind that big wheel and play Roman emperor.

South Street crawled with traffic. Rafferty, being cautious, steered them over to Water Street. He rolled to the side of the street, careful to avoid a horse-cart coming from the opposite direction, and pulled the brake lever towards him.

The horse reacted, veering sideways, almost upending the cart. The cart driver worked at calming the horse and drove off damning automobiles and all who drove them.

"You watch where you're going!" Crocker shouted after the cart. He gave Rafferty's arm a punch. Hard.

With the motor running, they exchanged places.

Rafferty released the brake. "Make sure you're clear both ways, before pulling out, sir."

"You think I'm an oaf?" Crocker looked both ways, allowed a delivery van to pass, and steered them on to the street. "Glory be to God!" He adjusted his massive body and gripped the big wheel.

Rafferty covered his eyes. Crocker had just missed running down a black cat slinking across the road.

"I'm sitting on top of the world," Crocker yelled. The motor put-put-putted.

A man staggered out of an alley on to the street in front of them, waving his arms.

"Brake, brake." Rafferty grabbed the brake lever and pulled hard. But not soon enough. The Packard hit the man and threw him back on the sidewalk, where he lay prone, not moving.

"Jesus Christ Almighty," Crocker said. He knew enough to steer the Packard to the side. "Get down there and see what we've done." The Tammany boss looked about, but what with the noise of hooves and wheels on the cobblestones, and workers unloading goods from a warehouse down the street, no one was paying any attention.

Rafferty jumped down and knelt over the man. "He's alive, but not conscious. Looks more beaten up than what we did to him." He searched the man's pockets for his wallet. Nothing. "He must have been robbed."

"Well, don't just stand there. Get him up here. We'll have Doc Saperstein look at him. And make sure he don't get blood on my leather upholstery."

*

Robbie thought for sure he was dying, if not dead. Last time he felt this bad was when he was thrown from his horse and got his leg caught in the stirrup.

His head was killing him, but nothing compared to the rest of him. He groaned, tried to open his eyes. One was swollen shut; from the other he saw a thin slit of light. Voices rumbled around him. He was on a soft bed under sheets and blankets. His mind began to clear.

"What do you say, Doc?" a man said. "Why don't he open his eyes? Why's he still swelled up and groaning?"

"He's had a concussion, Mister Crocker. He's a lucky man. Sprains and bruises, but no broken bones. But he's not going to feel too good for a while."

Naa, Crocker thought. *I'm* the lucky man. "Thanks, Doc. You hear that, son? We're going to take care of you. What's your name?"

"Robbie Allen."

It came through thin from cracked and swollen lips, but Crocker heard what he wanted to hear. "Allen, eh? Irish Catholic?"

"Sure, and Ma and Pa came over from the famine." He'd been brought up a strict Mormon, but what the hell. He never took to it and had run off early on. So what could it hurt? He'd heard the Irish in Crocker's and Rafferty's voices.

"Good boy." Crocker continued, "You ain't dead and you're in my house and everything's going to be fine. I'll be back and we'll have a nice long talk. Rafferty, you stay with our guest while I see the Doc out."

A door closed, but not before Robbie heard the man say, "New blood. That's what we need around here, new blood."

Robbie tried again to open his eyes. Success at last with his good eye. The room was huge, lit by a chandelier up high. He moved his hand to his lips and pain stabbed through his shoulder. "Where the hell am I? Who shot me? What the hell happened?"

"You're in Mister Richard Crocker's house," Rafferty told him. "You ran out of an alley on Water Street and right into Mister Crocker's Packard."

"Hit by an automobile?" Robbie's rumbling laugh became another groan.

"We didn't know who you were so we brought you here and got Doc Saperstein to look you over. Why did you run out on the street?"

"How long I been here?"

"Two days."

Two days! It began to come back to Robbie now. Those bank robbers. "My clothes. I had money—"

"Your clothes were torn and bloody. And you had no money, no wallet."

"Jesus Christ, those bank robbers, Butch and Sundance. I recognized them. They jumped me and pulled me into an alley and beat the crap out of me. Took everything, including my steamship tickets." They must have been right behind him in the steamship office. Harry would think he went off without him.

Rafferty said, "My name's Rafferty, Mister Allen. You're lucky to be alive, but you're even luckier that Boss Crocker is on your side."

"Crocker? The man who called me son?"

"Yes. We all work for Boss Crocker."

"I'd shake your hand if I could, Rafferty. Only been in New York a couple of months; seeing the sights before I moved on."

"What do you do?"

"I'm a . . . prospector. Was heading for South America with a friend."

"The Boss already likes that you're Irish."

"I guess he's rolling in dough from what I see." I'm in a goddam mansion, Robbie thought. "Must be he's a railroad man."

"Boss Crocker runs Tammany."

"No railroad I ever heard of."

"Tammany is Democratic politics in New York. Boss Crocker runs it."

★

Harry'd been waiting at Missus Taylor's for two days now, and Robbie didn't come back and didn't send word. The newspapers had nothing to say about anyone being arrested, so what happened to him? For all Harry knew, Robbie could have fallen into one of them subway pits and ended up in the morgue.

What he *did* know was Robbie'd been in Joe's Bar two days ago. Joe said Robbie had a newspaper all spread out on the bar, then he paid up and left.

Harry had about made up his mind to pack his stuff and go to Inwood. Ask Missus Taylor to hold on to Robbie's things in case. As he headed back to the boarding house, that's what he intended to do.

A young man was stopped in front of the boarding house looking uncertain. "You coming or going?" Harry said.

"My name's Rafferty. I have a message for someone in Missus Taylor's boarding house."

"And who might that someone be?"

"I don't know if I should tell you."

Harry grabbed Rafferty by his coat and shoved him against the side of the brownstone; the man's derby hit the ground.

Rafferty was scared as a rabbit, shaking in his shoes. "Don't kill me, don't kill me."

"I only kill what deserves killing." Harry let Rafferty go, brushed off the stone dust from the man's coat, and handed him back his hat.

Rafferty said, "If you're Harry, Robbie Allen sent me."

25

Inspector Bo Clancy pointed his baton at the five ragged street urchins he and Dutch had lined up outside the tenement next door to No. 7 Madison Street. "Your damned spindly arses are mine. I'll have you in the Tombs before the day is out."

The smallest began blubbering and the other four turned on him yelling, "Baby shit, baby shit."

"Sweet Jesus," Dutch said.

"You'll cough up every penny you got from those two spalpeen killers."

Mike, their leader, spit on the sidewalk. "Like hell we will, coppers."

Bo caught himself raising his hand. He scratched the back of his head to disguise the gesture. "That does it, start marching."

It was all Dutch could do not to laugh at Bo's histrionics. "You better spill it, boys, or Inspector Clancy here will see you in the Tombs for sure."

"They's gone," one of the boys said.

"Shut your gob, Duffy," Mike yelled. He punched Duffy hard on the upper arm where it would be hurting for a week.

Mike stopped the guff when he saw the man who'd come up behind the two coppers.

"Imagine running into youse on this fine morning, Inspectors."

"O'Toole," Bo said, "The blarney rolls off your forked tongue like the devil's own music."

"Run on home, Mike, there's a good lad, and take your friends." O'Toole gave his bulbous nose a swipe. "And just remember that Tammany saved youse from life in the Tombs." He laughed as the boys ran off in different directions.

"You got a hell of a nerve, O'Toole," Dutch said.

"Before I bid youse good day, the Boss wants to help out with a wee bit of information come to him." O'Toole tilted his derby back. "For the good of the city. Youse might be interested in some passengers booked on a British freighter docked at Pier 32."

"What ship?"

"T'ought you'd never ask. The *Herminius*."

★

The shipping agent at the office at Pier 32 was padlocking his shed when Bo and Dutch arrived on the run. Though there were a lot of ships and boats docked at various piers, there was no sign of a freighter at Pier 32.

"That bastard O'Toole," Bo said. He turned to the shipping agent. "Inspectors Clancy and Tonneman here. Who are you?"

"Shipping agent. Calvin Yard."

"Where's the *Herminius*?" Dutch said.

The shipping agent stared at them, his white eye tearing. "The *Herminius*? She been and gone. Bound for Uruguay. Two hours now." He pointed out into the bay, crowded with ships and tugs. "You might be able see her steam in the distance. My eyes ain't so good."

"The passengers, who are they?"

"Ain't no passengers, Inspectors. Not legal."

"Okay," Bo said, "To the Tombs with you."

"That ain't right."

"Wait a minute, Bo. Maybe Mister Yard would tell us who booked passage, if we don't haul him off to the Tombs for being uncooperative. What do you say, Mister Yard?"

"Okay, okay. Two passengers. Robert Doe and Harry Roe. They booked for Buenos Aires. Robert Roe and Harry Doe."

Bo stamped his foot and yelled. "You blockhead! You booked passage for Butch Cassidy and the Sundance Kid, right out of our hands and out of New York."

Calvin Yard grinned. "I did? Well, how the devil could I know that?"

"Go on with you, Mister Yard," Dutch said. "What's done is done."

★

Early in the summer of 1903, when Jack West was going through old files, he found a packet of newspaper cuttings about the robberies committed by Butch Cassidy and the Sundance Kid that he'd ordered from a service in Chicago after the bank robberies in New York in 1901.

But by the time the packet arrived, Butch and Sundance had made their escape from New York and were somewhere in South America. So he put the packet aside and forgot about it.

Jack West had held on to the Morgan Silver Dollar Henrietta de Grout paid him for delivering her fiancé and his friend to Inwood. In fact, he planned to give the coin to little Mae in August for her ninth birthday.

But seeing the packet of clippings again awakened Jack West's curiosity.

Lighting a fresh cigar, he opened the packet. Newspaper cuttings of various and sundry robberies of trains and banks thought to have been committed by Butch Cassidy's Wild Bunch. West was ready to toss it all in the trash when he saw the list of items taken in the Tipton, Wyoming, robbery of the Union Pacific No. 3 train out of Omaha in 1900.

Part of the loot was a bag containing forty Morgan Silver Dollars.

Authors' Note

The story goes, that Butch Cassidy and the Sundance Kid were killed in a shoot-out in Bolivia in 1908. But what if it had been the bogus Butch Cassidy and the Sundance Kid – who robbed two New York banks, and sailed for South America on the British freighter *Herminius*?

We respectfully submit that Robbie "Allen" Parker – the real Butch Cassidy – was welcomed with open arms into the Tammany political machine by Boss Crocker. Robbie learned what Tammany already knew: that riches could be found in New York, not with a gun, but with a ballot box.

We would also like to believe that Harry "Kidder" Longabaugh – the real Sundance Kid – became a respected breeder of horses. And that he and Henrietta "Etta Place" de Grout, married and raised a half dozen children on their horse ranch in Inwood, New York.

Trafalgar

Charles Todd

From a husband-and-wife writing team to a mother and son. Charles Todd is the writing alias of Caroline and Charles Todd who, though both American, have chosen to set their novels in Britain. Their primary series features Inspector Rutledge, who has returned to Scotland Yard after the First World War but is affected by shell-shock, and is haunted by the memory of a soldier, Hamish, whom he had been forced to execute in the trenches. The Rutledge series began with A Test of Wills *(1996), which was nominated for an Edgar Award. The series has been praised for the authenticity of its characterization and post-war atmosphere. The following story takes Rutledge across the length and breadth of southern Britain to solve a murder, where the roots seem to go back over a hundred years to the Battle of Trafalgar.*

Mumford, Cambridgeshire, 1920

The old dog died at two o'clock, thrown unceremoniously out of his warm bed by the fire and on to the cold January ground.

And it was this fact that troubled Rutledge as he delved deeper into the mystery of Sir John Middleton's death.

It was the housekeeper-cum-cook, gone to the village for onions for Sir John's dinner, who found the old dog lying by the wall under the study window. Mrs Gravely, stooping to touch the greying head, said, "Oh, my dear!" aloud – for the old dog had been company in the house for her as well – and went inside to deliver the sad news.

Opening the door into the study as she was pulling her wool scarf from her head, she said anxiously, "Sir John, as I was coming in, I found—"

Breaking off, she cried out in horror, ran to the body on the floor at the side of the Georgian desk, and bent to take one hand in her own as she knelt stiffly to stare into the bloody mask that was her employer's face.

Her first thought was that he'd fallen and struck the edge of the desk, she told Rutledge afterwards. "I feared he'd got up from his chair to look for Simba, and took a dizzy turn. He had them sometimes, you know."

The doctor had already confirmed this, and Rutledge nodded encouragingly, because he trusted Mrs Gravely's honesty. He hadn't been particularly impressed by the doctor's manner.

Rutledge had been in Cambridge on Yard business, to identify a man brought in by the local constabulary. McDaniel was one of the finest forgers in the country, and it had appeared that the drunken Irishman, taken up after a brawl in a pub on the outskirts of town, was the man the police had been searching for since before the Great War. He fitted the meagre description sent round to every police station in the country. In the event, he was not their man — red hair and ugly scar on the side of the face notwithstanding. But Rutledge had a feeling that the McDaniel they wanted had slipped away in the aftermath of the brawl. The incarcerated man had rambled on about the cousin who would sort out the police quick enough, if he were there. When the police arrived at the lodgings that their man in custody had shared with his cousin, there was no one else there – and no sign that anyone else had ever been there. The case had gone cold, and Rutledge was preparing to return to the Yard when the Chief Constable came looking for him.

"Sir John Middleton was murdered in his own home," Rutledge was told. "I want his killer, and I've asked the Yard to take over the inquiry. You're to go there now, and I'll put it right with the Chief Superintendent. The sooner someone takes charge, the better."

And it was clear enough that the Chief Constable knew what he was about. For the local constable, a man named Forrest, was nervously pacing the kitchen when Rutledge got there, and the inspector who had been sent for from Cambridge had already been recalled. The body still lay where it had been found, pending Rutledge's arrival, and, according to Forrest, no one had been interviewed.

Thanking him, Rutledge went into the study to look at the scene.

Middleton lay by the corner of his desk, one arm outstretched as if pleading for help.

"He was struck twice," a voice said behind him, and Rutledge turned to find a thin, bespectacled man standing in the doorway. "Dr Taylor," he went on. "I was told to wait in the parlour until you got here. The first blow was from behind, to the back of the head, knocking Sir John down but not killing him. A second blow to the face at the bridge of his nose finished him. I don't know that he saw the first coming. He most certainly saw the second."

"The weapon?"

Taylor shrugged. "Hard to say until I can examine him more closely. Nothing obvious, at any rate."

"Has anything been taken?" Rutledge asked, turning to look at the room. It had not been ransacked. But a thief, knowing what he was after, would not have needed to search. There were framed photographs on the walls, an assortment of weapons – from an Australian boomerang to a Zulu cowhide shield – were arrayed between them, and every available surface seemed to hold souvenirs from Sir John's long career in the army. A Kaiser Wilhelm helmet stood on the little table under the windows, the wooden propeller from a German aircraft was displayed across the tops of the bookshelves, and a half dozen brass shell-casings – most of them examples of trench art – were lined up in a cabinet that held more books.

"You must ask Mrs Gravely that question. The housekeeper. She's been with him for a good many years. I went through the house, a cursory look after examining the body, to be certain there was no one hiding in another room. I saw nothing to indicate robbery."

"Any idea when he was killed?"

"We can pinpoint the time fairly well from other evidence. When Mrs Gravely left to go into Mumford, he was alive and well, because she went to the study to ask if there were any letters she could take to the post for him. She was gone by her own account no more than three quarters of an hour, and found him lying as you see him when she returned. At a guess, I'd say he died between two and two-thirty."

Rutledge nodded. "Thank you, Doctor. I'll speak to her in a moment."

It was dismissal, and the doctor clearly wished to remain. But Rutledge stood where he was, waiting, and finally the man turned on his heel and left the room. He didn't precisely slam the door in his wake, but it closed with a decidedly loud snap.

Rutledge went to the window and looked out. It was then he saw the dog lying against the wall, only its feet and tail visible from that angle. Opening the window and bringing in the cold, damp winter air, he leaned out. There was no doubt the animal was dead.

He left the study and went out to kneel by the dog, which did not appear to have been harmed in the attack on Sir John. Death seemed to be due to natural causes and old age, judging from the greying muzzle.

Hamish said, "There's been no one to bury him."

An interesting point. He touched the body, but it was cold, already stiffening.

Back inside, he asked the constable where he could find Mrs Gravely, and he was told she was in her room at the top of the house.

He knocked, and a husky voice called "Come in."

It was a small room, but backed up to the kitchen chimney and was warm enough. Cast-offs from the main part of the house furnished it, a brass bed, an oak bedside table, two comfortable wing chairs on either side of a square of blue carpet, and a maple table under the half-moon window in the eaves. A narrow bookcase held several novels and at least four cookbooks.

The woman seated in the far wing-chair rose as he crossed the threshold. She had been crying, but she seemed to be over the worst of her shock. He noted the teacup and saucer on the table and thought the constable must have brought it to her, not the doctor.

"I'm Inspector Rutledge from Scotland Yard. The Chief Constable has asked me to take over the inquiry into Sir John's death. Do you feel up to speaking to me?"

"Yes, sir. But I wasn't here, you see. If I had been—"

"If you had been," he said, cutting across her guilt-ridden anguish, "you might have died with him."

She stared at him. "I hadn't thought about that."

He began by asking her about Sir John.

By her account, Sir John Middleton was a retired military man, having served in the Great War. Rutledge could, of his own knowledge, add that Sir John had served with distinction in an HQ not noted for its brilliance. He at least had been a voice of sanity there and was much admired for it, even though it had not aided his Army career. Had he made enemies, then?

Hamish said, "Aye, it's possible. He didna' fear his killer. Or put up a struggle."

And that was a good point.

"Was he alive when you reached him?"

"Yes, I could see that he was still breathing, ragged though it was. He cried out, just the one word, when I bent to touch him, as if he knew I was there. As if, looking back on it now, he'd held on waiting for me. Because he seemed to let go then, but I could tell he wasn't dead. I was that torn – leaving him to go for the doctor or staying with him."

"What did he say? Could you understand him?"

"Oh, yes, sir. *Trafalgar*, he said. Clear as could be. I ran out then, shouting for help, and I met Sam on the road. He was willing to take a message to Dr Taylor, and so I came back to sit beside Sir John, but I doubt he knew I was there. Still, it wasn't until Dr Taylor was bending over him that I heard the death rattle. I think he tried to speak again, just before."

The doctor had said nothing about that.

"Are you certain Sir John spoke to Dr Taylor?"

But Mrs Gravely was not to be dissuaded. "I was in the doorway, facing Sir John's desk. He had his back to me, the doctor did, but I could just see Sir John's mouth, and his lips moved. I'd swear to that."

"Did he know that it was the doctor who was with him? Was he aware, do you think, of where he was?"

"I can't speak to that, sir. I only know he spoke. And the doctor answered him."

"Could you hear what was said?"

"No, sir. But I thought he was trying to say the old dog's name. Simba. It means lion, I was told. I can't say whether he was trying to call to him or was asking where he'd got to."

"How did Dr Taylor respond?"

"I don't know, sir. I could see the doctor rock back on his heels, and then came the death rattle. I knew he was gone. Sir John. There was nothing to be done, was there? The doctor said so, afterwards."

Rutledge could hear the echo of the doctor's voice in her words, "I couldn't do anything for him."

"And then?"

"Dr Taylor turned and saw me in the doorway. He told me to find my coat and go outside to wait for the ambulance. But it wasn't five minutes before he was at the door calling to me and telling me there was no need for the ambulance now. It might as well be the hearse. Well, I could have told him as much, but then he's the one to give evidence at the inquest, isn't he? He had to be certain sure."

Rutledge went back to something Mrs Gravely had said earlier. "Trafalgar. What does that mean to you?"

The housekeeper frowned. "I don't know, sir. As I remember from school, it was a battle. At sea. When Lord Nelson was killed."

"That's true," Rutledge told her. "It was fought off the coast of Spain in 1805. But Sir John was an army man. And his father and grandfather before him." He had seen the photographs in the study. At least two generations of officers, staring without expression into the lens of the camera. And a watercolour sketch of another officer, wearing a Guards uniform from before the Crimean War.

"Will you come down with me to the study? There are some photographs I'd like to ask you to identify."

"Please, sir," she answered anxiously. "Not if he's still there. I couldn't bear it. But I'll know the pictures, I've dusted them since they were put up there."

"Fair enough. The woman, then, with the braid of her hair encircling the frame."

"That's Lady Middleton, sir, his second wife. Elizabeth, she was. She died in childbirth, and the boy with her. I don't think he ever got over her death."

"Second wife?"

"He was married before that. To Althea Barnes. She died as well, out in India. He'd tried to persuade her that it was no place for a woman, but she insisted on going with him. Two years later she was dead of the cholera."

"The young man in the uniform of the Buffs?"

"His brother Martin. He died in the first gas attack at Ypres."

"And the old dog, outside the study window. That, I take it, is Simba? When did he die?"

"It was the strangest thing!" Mrs Gravely told him. "He was lying by the fire, as he always did, when I left for the village. And I come home to find him outside there in the cold. He was still warm, he couldn't have been there very long. I can't think what happened. I come into the study to tell Sir John that, and there *he* was, dying. I couldn't quite take it all in."

He thanked her for her help, and left her there mourning the man she'd served so long and no doubt wondering now what was to become of her.

Sam Hubbard, the farm-worker who had gone for Dr Taylor, had had the foresight to summon the rector as well. Rutledge found Sam standing in the kitchen talking to Constable Forrest and warming his hands at the cooker, mud on his boots and his face red from the cold.

He turned and gave Rutledge his name, adding, "I've buried the old dog under the apple tree, as Sir John would have wished. They planted that tree together. A pity Sir John can't be buried there as well."

"Did you find anything wrong with the dog? Any signs that he'd been harmed?"

Sam shook his head. "It was old age, and the cold as well, I expect. He was having trouble with his breathing, Simba was."

"Did you work for Sir John?"

"He sent for me when there was heavy work to be done. Mr Laurence, who lives just down the road, doesn't have enough to keep me busy these days. And, in my free time, I did what I could for Sir John. He was a good man. There weren't many like him at HQ. More's the pity."

"In the war, were you?"

"I was. And I have a splinter of shrapnel in my shoulder to prove it."

Rutledge considered him. He'd been coming up the road when Mrs Gravely had hailed him, but he could just as easily have been going the other way, turning when he heard her and pretending to know nothing about what had happened here in the house. And he'd taken it upon himself to bury the old dog.

"Where were you this afternoon? Before Mrs Gravely asked your help?"

Sam Hubbard's eyebrows flew up. "Do you think I could have killed Sir John? I'd have died for him, for speaking up during the war and trying to keep as many of us poor bastards alive as he could. They were bloody butchers, save for him. Caring nothing for the men who had to die each time there was a push or a plan. If it was one of the likes of *them* lying dead in the study, you'd have to wonder if I had had a hand in it. But not Sir John."

The passionate denial rang true but Hubbard had had time to consider the questions the police would be asking. Tell one's self something often enough, and it soon became easier to believe it. Like the rehearsals of an actor learning his part.

Mr Harris, the rector, was in the parlour. He had seen the body before the constable had got there, and he seemed shaken, standing by the parlour windows with a drink in his hand.

"Dutch courage," he said ruefully, lifting the glass as Rutledge opened the door. "I don't see many murder victims in my patch. And I thank God for that. How is Mrs Gravely faring?"

"She's a little better, I think. What can you tell me about Sir John? Have you known him very long?"

"I'd describe him as a lonely man," Harris told Rutledge pensively, "I encouraged him to take an interest in village affairs, to see the need for someone of his calibre to serve on the vestry. But he was loathe to involve himself here. It's not his home, you know. He was from Hereford, I believe, but sold up and moved here after the war. He said the house was not the same without his wife, and he couldn't bear the *emptiness* – his word. Elizabeth was much younger, you see. Sir John was married twice. Once early on in his career, and then again some months before the fighting began in 1914."

"Did he bring Mrs Gravely with him from Hereford?" He'd noted her accent was not local.

"Yes, she was taken on by Elizabeth Middleton just before their marriage, and she agreed to stay with him after her mistress died."

"I understand his first wife died in India. Of cholera. Is there any proof of that, do you think? Or do we just have Sir John's word for what happened to her?"

"That's rather suspicious of you!"

"In a murder case, there are few certainties."

"Well, I can only tell you that it's written down in the Middleton family Bible. It's on the bookshelf behind the desk. I've seen the entry."

But what was inscribed in the family Bible was not necessarily witnessed by God, whatever the rector wished to believe.

"Did they get on well?"

"I have no idea. Except that he described Althea Middleton once as headstrong. Apparently, she'd insisted on having her way in all things, including going to India."

"Did she also live in Herefordshire?"

"I believe she came from somewhere along the coast. Near Torquay. I went there once on holiday, and knew the area a little. Sir John mentioned her home in connection with my travels. The second Lady Middleton – he called her Eliza – was a love match, certainly on his part. He wore a black armband throughout the war and told me, if it hadn't been for his duty, he'd not have been able to go on without her."

"No children of either marriage?"

"None that I ever heard of. Which reminds me, speaking of family. You might include poor Simba in that category. I saw his body there under the window." Harris shook his head. "The dog was devoted to Sir John. I'd see the two of them walking across the fields of an afternoon, when I was on my rounds. I wonder who put him out. It isn't – wasn't – like Sir John. Odd, that, I must say."

"Odd?"

"Yes, he would never have shown Simba the door, not at the dog's advanced age. The dog had belonged to Elizabeth, you see. Sir John had been worried about him since before Christmas, when his breathing seemed to worsen. It got better, but it was a warning, you might say, that his end was near. Sir John would have gone outside with him, and brought him in again as soon as he'd done his business."

"But they walked the fields together?"

"Yes. I meant over the years, you know. Not recently, of course."

Which, Hamish was pointing out, could explain why the killer came to the house rather than accost Sir John on an outing.

But the dog had been with him today, Rutledge replied. *And the dog was put outside. Had the visitor arrived at the door just as his victim was preparing to walk the dog?*

Hamish said, "He was killed in the study, no' in the entry."

"Does Trafalgar mean anything to you?" Rutledge asked Harris.

"It was a great sea battle. And of course it's a cape along the southern Spanish coast. The battle was named from it, I believe."

"That's no' likely to figure largely in a military man's death in Cambridgeshire," Hamish commented.

Rutledge thanked the rector, and Harris went in search of Mrs Gravely, to offer what comfort he could.

There was a tap at the door, and Rutledge went to open it himself.

Dr Taylor had returned, and nodding over his shoulder to the hearse from Cambridge, he said, "If you've finished, I'll take charge of the body."

"Yes, go ahead. When will you have your report?"

"By tomorrow morning, I should think. It ought to be fairly straightforward. We have a clear idea of when Mrs Gravely left for market, and when she returned. And the wounds more or less speak for themselves. I don't expect any surprises."

Nor did Rutledge. But he said, "Have a care, all the same."

Taylor said sharply, "I always do."

Rutledge stepped aside, watching as the men collected Sir John's body from the study and carried it out the door.

As he walked with them to the hearse, one of them said to him, "I was in the war. I'll see he's taken care of." Rutledge nodded, standing in the cold wind until the hearse had turned and made its way back on to the road into Mumford.

As he swung around to go back inside, he saw Mrs Gravely at an upstairs window, a handkerchief to her mouth, tears running down her cheeks. Behind her stood the rector, a hand on her shoulder for comfort.

Rutledge was glad to shut the door against the wind, and rubbed his palms smartly together as he stood there thinking. Had the killer knocked, he wondered, and waited until Sir John had answered the summons, or had he come in through the unlocked door and made his way to the study?

Hamish said, "He knocked."

"Why are you so certain?" Rutledge answered the voice in his head. It was always there – had been since July of 1916, when Corporal Hamish MacLeod was executed for refusing to carry out a direct order from a superior officer. The price, Rutledge knew, of MacLeod's care of his men, shifting the burden of guilt from his own shoulders to Rutledge's. It had not been easy that day to send weary, sleep-deprived soldiers over the top again and again and again, knowing they would not survive. But orders were orders, and, although numbed to the cost, as the battle of the Somme raged on, Rutledge had done what he could to shield them. It hadn't been enough, he knew that, and Hamish knew it. And Hamish had broken first, willing to die himself rather than watch more men sacrificed. The machine-gun nest was impregnable, and every soldier in the line was all too aware of it. No amount of persuasion had shifted Hamish MacLeod from his determination not to lead another attack and, in the end, an example had had to be made.

And Rutledge, well aware that the young Scottish corporal would not see home again, had delivered the *coup de grace* to the dying man. But Hamish MacLeod did come back – in Rutledge's battered mind: an angry and vengeful voice at first, and then with time, a relentless companion who yielded no quarter, sharing the days and nights, and silent only when Rutledge slept, although dreams often brought him awake again, into Hamish's grip once more.

"Because the man was struck from behind. He wouldna' have let a stranger get behind him."

It was a very good point, and Rutledge agreed. A knock, then, and Sir John opened the door to someone he knew. They walked back into the study, and at some point the old dog was put out. Before or after Sir John had been attacked? There was no way of knowing. Yet.

He went into the study and began his search.

He saw the Bible at once, on the shelf just as the rector had told him. Opening it to the parchment pages between the old and new testaments, Rutledge scanned the record of family marriages, then turned the page to look through the listing of deaths.

There was the entry for Middleton's first marriage and, in darker ink but the same hand years later, his second. Entries also of his wives' deaths.

Althea Margaret Barnes Middleton, of cholera, he read, with the date and *Calcutta, India* after it.

And then, in a hand that was shaking with grief, *Elizabeth Alice Mowbray Middleton, in childbirth.* Under that, *John Francis Mowbray Middleton, stillborn.*

Putting the Bible back where he found it, Rutledge began to go through the desk drawers. Two of them held sheets of foolscap. He realized that Sir John had been writing his memoirs of the Great War. Glancing through the sheaf of pages, he saw that Middleton had just reached the Somme, in 1916. The next chapter was headed, *Bloodbath.* He quickly returned the stack to the drawers, then paused to consider the possibility that Sir John had been killed to stop him from finishing the manuscript. But if that was the case, why leave the pages here, to be found – and possibly completed – by someone else?

Hamish said, "Was it unfinished, or is part missing?"

"I can't be sure." He made a mental note to speak to Harris about the manuscript.

The rest of the desk held nothing of interest, and the bookshelves appeared to be just that – shelves of books the dead man had collected over a lifetime, with no apparent secrets among them.

He saw the small box on a reading table next to the bookshelves, and picked it up. It was very old, he thought, and inlaid with what appeared to be ivory and mother of pearl. Opening it, he looked inside. It was lined with worn silk, but otherwise empty.

As he was putting it back in place, a title in gilt lettering on the shelf by the table caught his eye, and he frowned. *A History of The Barnes Family.*

That was the maiden name of Sir John's first wife. He pulled the volume from the shelf and looked at the title page. There was an inscription on the opposite page: *To Althea, with much love, Papa.* The frontispiece was a painting of a house standing at the edge of what appeared to be a lake, Georgian and foursquare, with a terrace overlooking a narrow garden that ran down to a small boat-landing, jutting out into the water. Rutledge turned the book on its side to read the caption.

Trafalgar. Dartmouth, Devon.

He turned to the index, and looked for the name there. There were several references to the house as well as the battle. The house, he discovered on page 75, was built in Dartmouth in 1800, on the site of an earlier dwelling, and rechristened *Trafalgar* after the head of the family had served on HMS *Victory*, Nelson's flagship on that fateful day. The water in front of the house was Dartmouth Harbour.

Going in search of the rector, Rutledge found him having tea with Mrs Gravely. Harris stood as Rutledge came into the kitchen, saying, "What is it?"

"Just a few more questions," Rutledge said easily. "What do you know about Althea Middleton?"

"Very little," Harris admitted. "Only what Sir John told me over the years."

"Her family is from Dartmouth."

"Yes. As a matter of fact, I told you she had lived near Torquay. Not surprising. Her father was a Navy man – like his father before him apparently – and probably his father's father as well, for all I know." He smiled wryly. "Sir John told me once that her father was appalled that she had fallen in love with an army officer. He had felt that nothing less than a Naval captain would suit."

"One of her ancestors served aboard *Victory*."

"Did he indeed! I don't think Sir John ever mentioned that fact. Just that hers was a naval family and he'd enjoyed more than a few arguments with her father about sea power and the course of the Empire."

"Sir John also appears to have been writing a history of the Great War."

"He always said he was tempted to write about his experiences. I didn't know he'd actually begun. It would have been worth reading, his view of the war."

Mrs Gravely said, "A history? He liked to work of an evening, after his dinner. I wasn't to disturb him then, he said. He was a great reader. I never gave it another thought on mornings when I found the study floor littered with his atlases and notes."

Rutledge turned back to Harris. "Who lives in the Barnes house in Dartmouth now?"

"There's a house? I had no idea. Let me see, there was something said once, about Althea Middleton having had a brother. But, as I remember, he was disinherited. And Barnes himself died whilst his daughter was in India."

"Then it must have been his daughter who inherited the property, and it passed to Sir John at her death." He would ask Sergeant Gibson at the Yard to look into the matter.

"His solicitor is the same as mine," Harris told him, and gave Rutledge directions to the firm in Mumford.

"Would you care for a cup of tea, Mr Rutledge?" Mrs Gravely asked. "I was just about to make a fresh pot."

"Thank you, no," he said. "Has anyone come to call on Sir John in the past few weeks?"

"Not since before Christmas," she answered him. "And then it was a man who'd lost his foot in the war and had been given a wooden one in its place. I heard him come up the walk, because it made an odd sound. A thump it was, and then a lighter sound, as he put his cane down with the good foot. The old dog growled something fierce, and I had to hold on to his collar when I went to the door."

A cane. The murder weapon hadn't been found, the likelihood being that the killer had taken it away with him. A cane could have done the damage to Middleton's head and face, if wielded with enough force.

"Do you remember his name?"

"He didn't give it, sir. He said, 'Tell Sir John it's an old comrade in arms.' And I did as he asked. Sir John went to see for himself, while I took the old dog into the kitchen with me."

Was that why the dog had been put outside? Because he knew – and disliked – the killer?

Rutledge thanked her and went back to his search of the house. There was money in a wallet in the bedside table, but it had not been touched. Nor had the gold cuff-links in a box on the tall chest by the bedroom door. What had the killer been after, if not robbery?

Trafalgar? A property in Dartmouth?

The deed.

Rutledge left to find a telephone, and had to drive into Cambridge before he was successful. He put in a call to Sergeant Gibson at the Yard, and gave him a list of what he needed.

"I'm driving to Dartmouth," he said. "I'll find a telephone there as soon as I arrive."

"To Dartmouth?" Gibson repeated doubtfully. "You know your own business best."

"Let's hope I do," Rutledge replied. He left a message with the Cambridge police, and set out to skirt London to the southwest.

It was early on the third day that he arrived in Dartmouth, having spent two nights on the road after running short of petrol near Slough. Colourful houses spilled down the sides of the high ridge that overlooked the town and the water. Most of them were still dark at this hour. Across the harbour was the town of Kingswear, just as dark. He found a hotel on a quiet side street, a narrow building with three floors, its façade black and white half-timbering. The sleepy clerk, yawning prodigiously, gave him a room at the front of the hotel with a view of the harbour. He stood by the window for some time, looking down towards the quay and the dark water, dotted with boats silently riding the current.

The Dart River opened up here to form the harbour, and castles – ruins now – had once guarded the entrance to this safe haven. It was deep enough for ships, and wide enough for a ferry to convey passengers from one side to the other. Just whereabouts the house called Trafalgar was situated, he didn't know. He hoped the hotel clerk might.

In the event, the man did not. "Before my time, I daresay. You could ask at the bookshop on the next corner," he suggested later that morning. "Arthur Hillier is the person you want. Oldest man around. If there was a house by that name, he'll know of it. But I doubt there is. You've come on a wild goose chase to my way of thinking."

Rutledge found the bookstore just past the shoemaker's shop. It possessed a broad front, the tall windows displaying books on every subject, but mostly about the sea and Dartmouth itself, including works on the wine trade with France and fishing the cod banks. A bell jingled as he opened the door, and an elderly man looked up, brushing a strand of white hair out of still-sharp blue eyes.

"Good morning, sir," he said cheerfully. "Here to browse, or is there something in particular you're looking for?"

"Information, if you please," Rutledge replied. "I'm trying to locate a dwelling that was here some years ago." He had brought with him the volume on the Barnes family history, and opened it to the frontispiece. "This house, in fact."

Hillier pulled a pair of eyeglasses from his cardigan pocket and put them on. "Ah. Trafalgar. It isn't called that any more. For a time it was a home for indigent naval officers and, after that, it was a clinic during the war. Now it's more or less derelict. Sad really."

"Do you know anything about the former owners?"

"Well, you do have the Barnes history, don't you? But I knew the last of the family to live there. Not well, you understand. Fanciful name for the house. It was called that after an ancestor was wounded the same day Lord Nelson was killed. Quite the fashion to commemorate the battle with monuments and the like. Trafalgar Square in London was one of the last to do so; I expect they didn't know what else to do with that great patch of emptiness. At any rate, the house was River's End before that – just where the Dart opens into the harbour, you see." He gestured to the door. "Come with me, and I'll show you."

Rutledge followed him out of the shop, towards the harbour. "There's a boat," Hillier was saying, "that will convey you to the mouth of the River Dart. Where it broadens into the harbour, you can just see the rooftops of Trafalgar over that stand of trees. They weren't there in my day, those trees. You could see the gardens then. Quite a sight in the spring, I remember."

He could see where Hillier was pointing, but the morning sun hadn't yet reached that part of the harbour, and he had to take the man's word for it that the house was behind the trees. But then he looked a little farther along. There, just visible over the treetops, was the line of a roof.

"The boatman is just there, at the foot of the water stairs. Jesse is his name. He'll see you there and back without any trouble."

"You said you knew the last of the family to live there. What do you remember about him?"

"He was troubled with gout and often ill-tempered," the bookseller answered. "But catch him in good spirits, and he could tell sea-stories that were marvellous to hear."

Rutledge thanked Hillier, and walked on towards the harbour. He found the water stairs and the small boat tied up just under them. Jesse was nowhere to be seen. Rutledge turned to look back at the town, just as a man popped out of the pub on the corner, rolling down in his direction, a wide grin on his unshaven face.

"Morning," he said. "Going sommers?"

"I'd like to hire your boat for an hour or so. Are you willing?"

"I come with the boat," he said, close enough now for Rutledge to smell the gin on his breath. He began to cast off, gestured to Rutledge to step aboard, and sat down to pick up the heavy oak oars.

"Where to?"

"The house you can hardly see behind the trees over there."

"The clinic that was? Why do you want to go there? Not much to see, now."

"Nevertheless . . ."

Nodding, Jesse moved out of the shelter of the water stairs, pulled into the current, turned smartly, and headed upstream. "We're against the tide," he said. "It will cost you more to go up than to come down."

"I understand."

It was cold down here on the water, wind sweeping down the chute between the high ridge on which Dartmouth sprawled, and the lower one on the opposite bank. In the distance he could hear a train whistle, and, soon after, the white plumes of a steam engine could be seen coming into Kingswear. As they reached mid-harbour, Rutledge buttoned his coat up to his collar against the bite of the January air. But Jesse, in shirt sleeves, seemed not to feel the cold, plying his oars and glancing over his shoulder from time to time to take stock of any other river traffic that morning. A quarter of an hour later, Jesse drew up by what had once been a fine private landing, rotting now and slippery with moss.

"Going to explore, are you? Watch where you step or I'll be fishing you out of the river."

As he clambered out on what was left of the private landing, he saw that it would be precarious at best to make his way across the broken boards. Moving gingerly, he finally gained the tree-line and stepped ashore. The trees had grown unhindered for fifteen years or more, he thought. He needed an axe really, to fight his way through the undergrowth that blocked any semblance of a path.

Eventually, he'd made it to the garden beyond – itself a thicket of dead plants, weeds, and vines. Above it was a terrace, and he climbed the broad steps to the long French doors that let into the house. To his surprise, one of them was unlocked, and after the briefest hesitation, he went inside.

It was out of the wind, but the house was cold, only in a different way: unused, unheated, winter seeping into the very bricks. The room in which he found himself had once been beautiful, with a pale green paper on the walls – a pattern of Chinese figures in blues and reds and deep gold, sitting in a formal garden. But it was stained now, and torn in places. A temporary wall, still there, divided the spacious room in half. If there had been any of the original furniture here, it had certainly now gone.

He made his way to the door, found himself in a passage, and began to explore. The stairs had been battered and bruised by the comings and goings of staff and patients, and the only furniture he saw were the remnants of cots in a few rooms, mostly with legs missing or springs broken. Not worth removing, he thought, when the clinic was closed. He wondered if Sir John had been aware of the state of the house, or didn't care. He walked though the rooms, noting how they had been used, and how they had been left. A broken window on the ground floor had allowed leaves and rain to ruin the floorboards, and a desk in what must have been Matron's office lay on its side, a nest of mice or squirrels in one half-opened drawer.

He found nothing of interest – except for signs that someone had been here before him, footprints in the dust, a bed of worn blankets and quilts by the coal stove in the kitchen, and indications that someone had also cooked there; a dented teapot still on the cast-iron top, and a saucepan on the floor.

Who had been in this house? A vagrant, looking for shelter against the winter cold and happening on it quite by accident;

or someone who had come to this house because he knew it was there? A former patient? Or someone else?

Hamish said, "Look at the dust."

And he lit a match, studying the pattern of footprints hardly visible in the pale light coming through the dirty window panes.

The person who had been here had left his mark. Two shoes, one dragging a little as if the ankle didn't bend properly. And the small round ferrule of a walking stick. Or a lame man's cane.

Rutledge knelt there considering the prints, hearing again Mrs Gravely's description of how Sir John's December caller had sounded coming up the walk to the door. These prints were not recent. He would swear to that. Fresh dust had settled over them, almost obliterating them in places.

He went back through the house looking for something, anything, that might be a clue to the interloper.

All he found was a crushed packet that once held cigarettes. It had been tossed into the coal stove and forgotten. He smoothed it out as best he could and saw that it was an Australian brand.

Giving it up, he went back to the door on to the terrace and stepped out, shutting it behind him.

Jesse was still sitting in his boat, smoking a cigarette of his own.

"Where can I buy Australian cigarettes?" Rutledge asked the man.

"Portsmouth, at a guess. London. Not here. No call for them here. Why? Develop a taste for them in the war, did you?"

"No. I found an empty box in the house. Someone had been living there."

Jesse seemed not to be too surprised. "Men out of work in this weather take what shelter they can find. I came on one asleep in my boat a year back. Wrapped in a London newspaper for warmth, he was. I bought him a breakfast, and sent him on his way."

"Any Australians in Dartmouth?"

"Up at the Royal Navy College on the hill, there might be," Jesse told him, manoeuvring the boat expertly into the stream again. "But they'd be officers, wouldn't they? Not likely to be breaking into a house." The ornate red brick college – more like a palace than a school, and completed in 1905 – had seen the present king, George V, attend as a cadet. Jesse bent his back to the oars, grinning. "What do you want with a derelict old house?"

"It's not what *I* want," Rutledge said pensively, "but what someone else could very easily wish for." He turned slightly to look up the reaches of the River Dart, already a broad stream here as it fed into the harbour. "It wasn't always in disrepair."

But to kill for it? Hamish wanted to know.

That, Rutledge answered silently, would depend on what Sergeant Gibson discovered in London.

He found a telephone, after Jesse had delivered him back to the old quay in Dartmouth. Watching through the window as the ferry plied the waters between the two towns, he asked for the sergeant and, after a ten minute wait, Gibson came to the telephone.

"The old man, Barnes," the sergeant began. "He died in a freak accident. Slipped in his tub, and cracked open his head. Foot was swollen with gout at the time. There was some talk because the staff was not in the house when it happened. They'd gone to a wedding in Kingswear. The constable come to investigate thought there was too much water splashed about the bathroom. But the servants were all accounted for; the son predeceased his father, and the daughter was in India. The inquest brought in accidental death."

"The son was dead?"

"As far as anyone knew. He'd got himself drunk and wandered on to Dartmoor. They never found his body, but his cap was hanging on a ledge, half way down an abandoned mine shaft. A shoe was found at the edge. When the father was told, he cursed himself for disinheriting the boy. He was certain it was suicide."

But was it?

That was years ago, and should have no bearing on a murder in Cambridge in 1920.

"Sometimes memories are long," Hamish reminded him.

And Hamish should know, Rutledge thought grimly, for the Scots were nothing if not fanatical about revenge and blood feuds.

"Who owns the property at present?" he asked Gibson.

"It came to Sir John when his wife died."

Just as he'd thought.

He left Dartmouth for the long drive back to Mumford. Once there he located the offices of Molton, Briggs, and Harman, who were, according to the rector, Mr Harris, solicitors to Sir John Middleton.

Mr Briggs, elderly and peering over the thick lenses of his glasses, said, "The police informed us of Sir John's death. Very sad. Very sad."

"Since he had no children, I need to know who stands to inherit his property?"

"Now that's very interesting," Briggs said, clearing his throat. "He has left the cottage in Mumford to Mrs Gravely, for long years of devoted service." Taking off his glasses he stared at them as if expecting them to speak. "I doubt he expected to see her inherit so soon." Putting them back on his nose, he said, "There is a bequest to the church, as you'd expect, and certain other charges."

"And the property in Dartmouth? How is that left?"

"The one formerly known as Trafalgar? It was to go to a cousin of his first wife, but she died of her appendix. He made no decision after that. Until last December, that is, when he came in to tell me that the house was to go to the son of his late wife's brother."

"The brother died on Dartmoor. Years ago. After being disinherited."

"The brother fled to Australia for charges of theft. The death on Dartmoor was staged to save the family the disgrace."

"The brother was a convict?" Rutledge asked, surprised. Even Sergeant Gibson had failed to uncover that information.

"Yes. He gave the police a false name. His father went to Dartmoor and staged his son's death. To spare the then Lady Middleton. So Sir John told us in December."

"Then the son couldn't have returned to kill the father."

"The fall in the bathroom? He was drunk. He stayed drunk much of the time."

"Was Sir John quite certain this was his brother-in-law's son?"

"Yes, he had the proper credentials. It's quite in order."

And the son had gone to Dartmouth and slept in the house that would be his. Had he then decided to hasten that day? Or had he been given permission to begin repairs on the house?

Mr Briggs didn't know. "I was told to make the necessary changes to Sir John's will. I was not privy to any other arrangements between the two."

The house would require hundreds – thousands – of pounds to make it habitable again, let alone to restore it. The young Barnes, with his wooden foot, had been there and seen what was needed.

Had he come back, when he realized that the bequest was an empty promise and that the house would fall down around his ears, long before Sir John died a natural death?

"Where can I find this young Barnes?"

"I was given an address in London. I was told that he could be reached through it."

Briggs fiddled with the papers in front of him, found the one he wanted, and told Rutledge what he needed to know. "I expect it is a residence rather than a hotel," he added.

But Rutledge recognized the address. It was a small hospital where the mentally disturbed from the war were committed when there was no other course open to a doctor.

Rutledge thanked Briggs, and turned the bonnet of his motorcar towards London.

The street where the hospital stood was not far from St Paul's Cathedral. Two adjoining houses had been combined to form a single dwelling, and the main door was guarded by an orderly with great moustaches. Rutledge showed his identification, and was admitted. Reception was a narrow room with a long desk against one wall. Another orderly sat there with a book in front of him. He looked up as Rutledge entered.

"Sir?" he said, rising to stop Rutledge's advance. "Are you looking for someone?"

"Yes. A man by the name of Barnes. He was in the war, has a wooden foot, I expect he's a patient here."

"Barnes?" The orderly frowned. "We don't have a patient named Barnes. There's a Doctor Barnes. Surgeon. He lost his foot in the Near East."

Surprised, Rutledge said, "Is he Australian?"

"He is indeed."

"I'd like to speak to him, if I may."

The orderly consulted his book. "He's just finished surgery, I believe. He should be in his office shortly."

Rutledge was shown to a door where a middle-aged nursing sister escorted him the rest of the way, to an office behind a barred door.

"We must be careful with our patients," she said. "Some of them are very confused about where they are and why they are here. It's sad, really," she went on. "They're so young, most of them."

"What sort of surgery does Dr Barnes do?" he asked as she showed him into the drab little room.

"Today he was removing a bullet pressing on the brain of one of the men in our charge. Very delicate. But it had to be done, if he's to have any hope of living a normal life. The question is, will he ever live a normal life, given his confusion."

She sounded tired and dispirited. He thanked her, and sat down in the chair in front of the desk, prepared to wait.

When Dr Barnes finally entered the office, he wasn't what Rutledge had anticipated. Young, fair, intense, he seemed to fill the room with his presence.

Rutledge rose.

"What brings Scotland Yard to Mercy Hospital?" he asked, going around the desk and taking the chair behind it.

"I'm afraid I've come to give you bad news. Your uncle is dead."

The tired face changed. "Sir John? What happened? He was healthy enough when I saw him last."

"Someone came into the house when Mrs Gravely was in Mumford and killed him."

The shock was real. "Dear God!"

"It appears you'll be inheriting Trafalgar sooner than you expected."

Dr Barnes made an impatient gesture. "He was kind enough to leave it to me. I don't think he wanted it, come to that. But he could have said no. Still, I have no time now to restore it. Or even think of restoring it." He made a face. "Nor the money, for that matter. I'm needed here, anyway. For the time being. Well, to be honest, for some time to come."

"You went to call on Sir John in December. And you were in the house in Dartmouth then – or soon after that. You broke in."

The smile was genuine, amused. "Hardly breaking in. But I had no key. And it was to be mine. I decided it would do no harm. How on earth did you know? Did someone see me? Or the smoke from the fire in the kitchen?"

"Marks in the dust," Rutledge said. "Of a foot that dragged, and a cane."

"Ah. Have you found who killed Sir John? I hope you have. He was a good man."

"We have no leads at present," Rutledge said with regret. He hesitated, then added, "The last thing your uncle said, as far as anyone knows, was one word. 'Trafalgar'. It seemed likely that he was referring to the house. Why should that have been on his mind as he lay dying?"

Dr Barnes got to his feet and turned, looking out the high window. There was nothing to be seen from it, except for the wall of the house next door, some four feet away. "You think I must have killed the old man, don't you?" He turned. "I can probably supply witnesses to swear I was here – nearly round the clock, for the past month or more. But that isn't what matters. I didn't harm him. I told you, it would do me no good if I had killed him twice over. There isn't time to do anything about the house or the land."

"If he'd changed his mind and left it to you, one might wonder if he'd have been equally as easily persuaded to leave it to someone else."

"But to whom?" Barnes asked. "Who did I have to fear?"

"I don't know," Rutledge said. "But that one word 'Trafalgar' is damning."

Barnes sat down again. "There must be some other meaning."

"Yes. But what?"

Barnes shrugged. "My family wasn't the only one with a connection to the battle. Surely."

"Sir John had no connection to it. There was only the house in Dartmouth."

"There was the war. He made enemies there, very likely. I heard tales of what he did at HQ. He tried to bring reason to the decisions being made."

And Sir John had been writing his memoirs. It was possible.

Hamish said, "The blows. He couldna' ha' been thinking clearly."

"Yet," Rutledge replied silently, "yet he remembered the old dog."

Thanking Barnes for his time, he rose, saying, "I must have my men question the staff here. There will be statements to sign."

"Yes, to be sure. I have nothing to hide." As Rutledge reached the door, Barnes said, "I'd like to come to the services. Will you see that someone lets me know, when the arrangements are made?"

"Mr Briggs will see that you're kept informed."

As he was leaving, the heavy door to the stairs swung open, and a sister came out, carrying a tray of medicines. For an instant he heard the screams of someone in a ward above, and he knew what that meant. A living nightmare, the curse of shell-shock.

The screams were cut off as the door swung shut. Shuddering, he went through the other door and was in Reception once more, where he could breathe again.

Outside in the street, he walked for half an hour before returning to where he'd left his motorcar. It had been necessary to exorcise the memories those screams had reawakened.

"Do you believe yon doctor?" Hamish asked as Rutledge turned the crank.

"He'll have dozens of witnesses to prove that he was here at the hospital. So, yes, I believe he had nothing to do with killing Sir John." He got into the motorcar. "But that isn't to say that he didn't hire someone to do the deed for him." He considered the screams he'd heard. Was there a patient in the hospital whose fragile mental state might make him a perfect murderer? Who could be set in motion by a clever killer, chosen because he could be depended upon to do as he was told to do?

It was far-fetched. But, at the moment, Rutledge was running out of options.

Hamish said, "It comes back to yon dog, ye ken. Why was he put out in the cold?"

Would a damaged mind think to rid himself of the dog? Why had it been necessary? Simba was too old to attack and do any real damage. Although, Rutledge thought as he pulled into traffic, anyone with a dog bite in Mumford, or even as far away as Cambridge, would need treatment. And that would lead to discovery and questions by the police. Even Doctor Barnes would find it hard to explain how one of his patients could have been bitten.

Turning the motorcar around, he drove towards Cambridge. It was late when he arrived, but Mrs Gravely was still awake, a light on in the kitchen, and he lifted the knocker, letting it fall gently rather than imperatively. She opened the door tentatively, then smiled when she recognized him.

"I'm that glad of company," she said. "I don't quite know what to do with myself. There's no one to cook or clean for. The police tell me to leave everything be, and the doctor tells me poor Sir John's body hasn't been released, and, until it is, I can't begin the baking for the funeral. No one knows when there'll be an inquest." She gestured to the furnishings as Rutledge stepped into the house. "I haven't been told what I'm supposed to do with all Sir John's things. No surprise I haven't been sleeping of nights."

He wondered how she would react when the will was read, and she learned that the cottage was hers. Would she be pleased – or would the memory of Sir John's body lying in the study haunt her every time she walked into the room?

He let her make a cup of tea for him, and then said, "The man who came here in December, the one with the wooden foot, is actually the son of the first Lady Middleton's brother."

"My good Lord," she said fervently. "I'd have never guessed." She paused, measuring out the tea. "But why didn't he say so? Why tell me he was an old comrade in arms?"

"Perhaps he thought Sir John might refuse to receive him, if he used his own name."

Frowning, she shook her head. "I expect that was so. Still . . ." She left the word hanging, and busied herself taking down cups and saucers, retrieving the sugar bowl from the cupboard, then walking into the pantry for the jug of milk.

"You've cleaned for Sir John these many years. Did he have anything in this house worth stealing? I don't count money or gold cuff-links. Something of great value. Something that would make killing him worthwhile?"

Because Dr Barnes hadn't the money to restore Trafalgar, whatever he might claim about time.

"I can't think that there was. Some of his books? I don't know about such things, but someone else might."

"It didn't appear that there were books missing."

"That's true," she agreed. "I'm used to dusting them. They're all there save one."

Rutledge took the Barnes family history from his pocket. "My doing, that. I needed to show someone the photograph in the front."

"I'll see it's in its rightful place," she said, moving the book aside and setting down his cup of tea. "There's a bit of chocolate sponge cake, if you'd like that," she told Rutledge. "I made it for my dinner."

He thanked her, but refused. After a moment she sat down across from him. "There are the weapons between the photographs, in the study. But none of them was taken."

Not even all of them would raise the sum needed to restore Trafalgar. "It doesn't matter," he said. "If it were robbery, it would be for something worth thousands of pounds. Not a few hundred."

She nodded. "I worry, sometimes," she said, looking away as if embarrassed. "If I'd been here that day – or come back from the greengrocers a little sooner – could I have prevented what happened? I know you told me I might well have become a victim too. But it weighs on my mind, you see. I needn't have gone into Mumford that day. His dinner would have been all right without that onion."

"I doubt it," he told her bracingly. "Most killers would wait for their chance. If you hadn't left that day, you would have left on another."

Hamish said, "It's a kind lie."

He went through the study and the parlour again, looking for something missing – some explanation for why a man had to die – knowing very well that Mrs Gravely would have noticed and brought it to his attention long ago.

It was all as he'd seen it the first time. The tidiness of the soldier, used to Spartan conditions. The collector of books, most of them on warfare, Cambridge, even India. The husband, who loved his second wife and kept her portrait where he could see it, but who bore no grudge against his first wife, headstrong though she may have been. The fastidious man who was always freshly shaven and carefully dressed, judging by the body.

Rutledge went back to the bookshelves, and ran his finger down the line of titles. Nothing out of the ordinary. Several volumes: William the Conqueror, Henry II, Edwards I and III. Soldiers all

– in the days when kings led their men into battle. The tactics of the American general Robert E. Lee. The strategies of Napoleon.

He stopped and pulled out one of the books at random. As he opened it, something fell out and drifted lightly to the floor.

Stooping to pick it up, he saw that it was an article cut from a newspaper, yellowed and thin.

It was about the destruction of the Great Mews of Whitehall Palace. The stables of Edward I and his predecessors. This had been done early in the eighteenth century, when the ramshackle mews was more of an eyesore than it was useful. Rutledge glanced at the spine of the book and saw it was a biography of Edward I. The cutting was well before Sir John's time and, turning to the end covers, he saw that the name inscribed there in an ornate bookplate was that of Sir Robert Middleton. Father? Grandfather? Uncle?

He set the book aside and picked up the Bible. Searching the list of births and deaths, he realized that Sir Robert was a great-grandfather of Sir John's. Not a contemporary of the destruction of the royal mews, but Sir Robert had been alive in the first part of the nineteenth century when various architects, including the famous Nash, had taken on the task of creating a square that would fit into the overall view of a new and spacious London. The name given to the finished square came from the column bearing the statue of Admiral Nelson: Trafalgar Square. But as Hillier, the Dartmouth bookseller had said, it had been among the last of the memorials to Lord Nelson.

Interesting; but it was, as Hamish was reminding him, decades in the past. Hardly pertinent to a murder in 1920.

Glancing at his watch, Rutledge saw that it was half past one o'clock in the morning. The house was quiet, and he thought perhaps Mrs Gravely had gone up to her bed. Still, he sat down at a table in the parlour and read the faded cutting. It told him very little more. Picking up the book, he thumbed through the pages, looking for any reference to the Royal Mews. There was nothing of interest. He went back to the study, searched for other books on Edward I, and carried them into the parlour. Had it been only coincidence that the cutting was in that particular history?

It was close on five when Mrs Gravely came in with sandwiches and a pot of tea. He ate absently, his mind on the hunt. When she came to take away his plate and cup, she said, looking over his shoulder, "He must have loved that book. I can't count the times I'd find it on his desk when I was dusting."

Rutledge turned to see what she was pointing to. A slim volume bound in worn leather, printed a hundred years ago.

It was written by a man called Baker, and it purported to offer an account of the crusade the then Prince Edward Longshanks made to the Holy Land. He had already turned homeward in 1272 when he learned of the death of his father, Henry III, and that he was now King. He was two years in reaching England to be crowned. Legend claimed that with him he brought a small gold reliquary, encrusted with precious stones and containing a piece of the True Cross. It remained with him through the early years of his reign – although it was more common to give such relics to a church in thanksgiving for a safe return. As he'd been sickly as a child, it was thought he kept the relic for his own protection. But when it failed to save his dying Queen, Eleanor of Castile, in a ferocious fit of temper, he ordered it buried in the largest dung pit in the stables.

According to Baker, it had been lost to history from that time forward, until a workman had discovered it during the demolition of the stables in the eighteenth century. The man had shown it to his brother-in-law, a yeoman farmer in Kent, who paid him handsomely for it, and the object had remained in the farmer's family, passing from father to elder son in each generation. It had become known, Baker went on, as the Middleton Host, although the family had denied any knowledge of it, and with time, the Host and the family itself had been lost to history. The remodelling of the land once occupied by the stables had revived the tale, but Baker had been unable to prove whether the tale was true or not. He had contacted a number of families by the name of Middleton in Kent and elsewhere, but had failed to find any trace of the story.

Rutledge sat back, considering what he'd just read. Then he rose and went back to the study to look at the small wooden box by the bookshelves.

There was no way of knowing what it had contained. Even Mrs Gravely, when questioned, had no idea what had been kept inside – if anything. She had dusted it, but never opened it.

But suppose – just suppose – it had held the Middleton Host.

That would match with the message that the dying man had tried to pass on to his housekeeper.

Trafalgar. Not the name of his late wife's home, but the square in the heart of London. Would he have told the secret to Althea Barnes? A great joke, that, one she might have appreciated and passed on to her father and her brother.

What would such a reliquary be worth? Monetarily and intrinsically.

What would it be worth to Dr Barnes, working daily with men whose minds were destroyed by war? Had he come, in December, to ask for the use of the Middleton Host? And instead been pawned off with promises of the house in Dartmouth? A house he had no use for and couldn't afford to keep up? An albatross, compared to the cure the reliquary might achieve in men who could be brought to believe in its power.

Rutledge went to the door, called to Mrs Gravely that he would be back shortly, and hurried to his motorcar. Driving into Cambridge as dawn was breaking, he went to the telephone he'd used before and put in a call to the clinic where Barnes worked.

He was informed that Dr Barnes was with a patient and couldn't be disturbed.

Swearing under his breath, he walked out to his motorcar and was on the point of driving to London when another thought occurred to him. Even tired as he was, it made sense.

The old dog.

Mrs Gravely had claimed that Sir John had spoken to Dr Taylor just before he died. She had nearly been sure that he'd asked about his dog. And the doctor had responded with a single word, *No.* She had thought that the doctor was telling Sir John that the dog was dead.

Turning the motorcar around, he drove back to Mumford. He searched the High Street of the little town, then looked in the side streets. Shortly after nine, he found Dr Taylor's surgery, next door but one to the house where the doctor lived – according to the nameplates on the small white gates to both properties.

Hamish said, " 'Ware." And it was a warning well taken.

Knocking on the surgery door, Rutledge scanned the house down the street. He could just see a small woman wrapped in a coat and headscarf, standing in the back garden, staring at the bare fruit trees and withered beds as if her wishing could bring them into bloom again. The doctor's wife? That told him what he needed to know.

The nurse who admitted Rutledge was plump and motherly, calling him *dearie*, asking him to wait in the passage while she spoke with the doctor. "His first patients of the day are already in the front room. It's better if you come directly back to the office."

"It's about his report on the post-mortem of Sir John."

"He has already mailed it to the Yard," she said. "I took it to the post myself."

Rutledge gave her his best smile. "Yes, I've been in Dartmouth. It hasn't caught up with me yet."

She nodded and bustled off to tell the doctor that Rutledge was waiting.

Dr Taylor received him almost at once, saying, "Mrs Dunne tells me you haven't seen the post-mortem results." He sorted through some files on his desk and retrieved a sheet of paper. "My copy," he added, passing it across the desk to Rutledge. "You're welcome to read it."

Rutledge took the sheet, scanning it quickly. "Yes. Everything seems to be in order," he said, glancing up in time to see the tension around Dr Taylor's eyes ease a little. "Two blows, one to the back of the head and the second to the face. Weapon possibly a cane." He handed the report to Taylor. "There's one minor detail to clear up before the inquest. Mrs Gravely told me that Sir John spoke to her as she was coming into the study. Was that possible, do you think?"

"I doubt if he was coherent," Taylor said easily. "A grunt. A groan. But not words as such."

"She also reported that he spoke to you. And that you answered him, just before he died."

Taylor frowned. "I thought he was asking if the old dog was still alive. I told him it was dead. I wasn't sure, you understand. But I thought if that was what he was trying to say, I'd ease his mind."

He had just contradicted himself.

"I don't think that the dog's death was something that would comfort him."

Taylor shrugged. "I wasn't in a position to consider my answer. As I told you, he wasn't coherent. I did my best in the circumstances."

"Actually, I think he was probably asking if you'd use the Middleton Host to save the old dog. And you refused. You had to, because Mrs Gravely was standing there in the doorway."

Taylor flushed. "What host?"

"He must have told you at one time or another. A medical man? That a king had found it useless and thrown it in a dung heap. But then Eleanor of Castile was probably beyond help by the time the reliquary reached her. She died anyway. King Edward loved his wife. Passionately. Everywhere her body rested the night on the long journey south to London, he built a shrine. The wonder was, he didn't smash the relic. But I expect he felt that the dung heap was a more fitting end for it. A fake, a sham."

"I have no idea what you're talking about, Inspector. And there are patients waiting."

"It was a story that must have touched Sir John. He hadn't been able to save either of his wives, had he? The host was, after all, no more than a pretty fraud."

The doctor's face changed. "That's an assumption that neither you nor I can make. Sir John was a soldier, a sceptic; hardly one to take seriously legends about relics and miracles. Where is this taking us?"

"I'm trying," Rutledge returned blandly, "to establish whether or not Sir John loved Elizabeth Middleton as deeply as – for instance – you must love your wife. Because it was for her you did what you did. Not the patients out there in the waiting room." It was a guess, but it struck home.

Taylor opened his mouth, then shut it again.

"Why did you put the dog out? Did it attack you? If I asked you to have another doctor look at your ankles or legs, would he find breaks in the skin to indicate you'd been bitten? Even if it has begun to heal, the marks must still be there. Would you agree to such an examination?"

Taylor rose from behind the desk. "Yes, all right, the dog was dying when I got there. Sir John was kneeling on the floor beside it when I opened the door and called to him. He told me he was in the study, and to come quickly. Still, the damned dog growled at me and got to its feet as I struck the first blow. I had to get rid of it because Sir John was still alive and I needed to hit him again. The cold finished it off, I expect. It's breathing was shallow, laboured." He moved to the hearth. "My wife has just been diagnosed with colon cancer. I'd already asked Sir John if I could borrow the reliquary. To give her a chance. He told me it had done nothing for his wife, dying of childbed fever. But I didn't care. I was ready to try anything. I just wanted to *try*. But he was afraid that, if my wife recovered on her own, Mumford would be swamped with the desperate, the hopeless, believers in miracles. He said it would be wrong. Time was running out, and yet that afternoon he begged me to do something for his *dog*. It was obscene, I tell you."

He reached down, his fingers closing over the handle of the fire tongs. Lifting his voice, he shouted, "No, no – you're wrong! Put them down, for God's sake."

And, before Rutledge could stop him, he raised the tongs and brought them down on his own head, the blow carefully calculated to break the skin but not knock him down. And as blood ran down his face, he dropped the tongs and cried out, "Oh, God, someone help me . . . *Mrs Dunne . . . he's run mad.*"

And in a swift angry voice that only reached Rutledge's ears, Taylor said, "She's ill, I tell you. I won't be taken away when she needs me. Not by you, not by anyone."

He rushed at Rutledge, grappling with him.

The door burst open, Mrs Dunne flying to the doctor's aid, pulling at Rutledge's shoulders, calling out for him to stop.

Rutledge had no choice. He swung her around, and she went down, tripping over the chair he'd been sitting in. He turned towards the hearth, to retrieve the fire tongs as Taylor reeled against the far wall, calling, "Stop him—"

Mrs Dunne, scrambling to her feet, must have thought Rutledge was about to use the tongs again, and she threw herself at him, carrying him backward against the hearth, stumbling over the fire screen.

Her screams had brought patients from the waiting room, pushing their way through the door, faces anxious and frightened as they took in the carnage, drawing the same conclusions that Mrs Dunne had leapt to. A woman in a dark green coat gasped and went to the doctor's aid, and he leaned heavily against her shoulder. Two men put themselves between Rutledge and his perceived victim, one of them quickly retrieving the fire tongs from where they'd fallen, as if afraid Rutledge could still reach them.

It was all Rutledge could do to catch Mrs Dunne's pummelling fists and force her arms to her sides, so that he could retrieve the situation before it got completely out of hand. Hamish in the back of his mind was warning him again, and there was no time to answer.

In a voice used to command on a battlefield, he said, "You – the one in the greatcoat – find Constable Forrest and bring him here at once."

Taylor said, stricken, "He's trying to arrest me . . . for murder . . . I've done nothing wrong, don't let him lie to you. For God's sake!"

They knew Taylor. Rutledge was a stranger. The man in the greatcoat hesitated.

The doctor swayed on his feet. "I think I'd better sit down." The woman helped him to a chair, and his knees nearly buckled under him.

She said, "I'll find your wife."

He gripped her arm. "No. I don't want to worry her." Taylor took out his handkerchief to mop the blood from his face. "Just get him out of my office, if you will."

Rutledge crossed the room, and the man with the tongs raised them without thinking, as if expecting Rutledge to attack him. But he went to the door and closed it.

"You'll listen to me, then. I'm Inspector Rutledge, Scotland Yard." He held up his card for all of them to see. "I've just charged Dr Taylor with the murder of Sir John Middleton. As for those tongs, he himself wielded them, I never touched them, or him."

"I think you'd better leave," Mrs Dunne snapped. "He's a good man, a doctor."

"Is he? I intend to order Sir John's dog exhumed. I expect to find shreds of cloth in his teeth." Hamish was reminding him that it was only a very slim possibility, but Rutledge ignored him. "What's more, I intend to ask a doctor from Cambridge to examine Dr Taylor's limbs for healing bites. And the clothing he was wearing the day of the murder will be examined for mended tears."

He saw the expression on Mrs Dunne's face. Shock first, and then uncertainty. "I mended a tear in his trousers just last week. He'd caught them on a nail, he said."

"Then you'll know which trousers they were. If the shreds match, he will be tried for murder. We can also look at those tongs, if you will set them carefully on the desk. The only prints on them will be Dr Taylor's, and yours, sir. Not mine."

"Can you do that?" the man holding the tongs asked, staring down at them.

"There are people who can."

He moved to the desk, putting them down quite gently. Dr Taylor reached for them, saying, "He's bluffing, look, it's my blood that's on them."

Rutledge was across the room before Taylor's fingers could curl around the handle of the tongs, his grip hard on the doctor's wrist, stopping him just in time.

The man in the greatcoat said, "I think I ought to fetch Constable Forrest after all, if only to sort out this business."

He left the office, and they could hear the surgery door shut firmly after him.

The doctor said, "I tell you, it's not true, none of it is true." But even as he spoke the words, he could read the faces around him. Uncertainty, then doubt, replacing belief.

The woman in the dark green coat said, "I really must go—" and started towards the door, unwilling to have any further involvement with the police. The other man, without looking at the doctor, followed her in uncomfortable silence.

Taylor called, "No, wait, please!"

Mrs Dunne said, "I'll just put a sign up on the door, saying the surgery is closed," and hurried after them.

Rutledge turned to see tears in Taylor's eyes. "Damn you," he said hoarsely. "And damn the bloody dog. I love her. I wanted to save her. Do you know what it's like to realize that your skills aren't enough?" He turned from Rutledge to the window. "Do you know how it feels when God has deserted you?"

Rutledge knew. In France, when he held his revolver at Hamish's temple; he knew.

"And what would you have done if the reliquary failed you too?" Rutledge asked.

"It won't. It can't. I'm counting on it," he said defiantly. "You won't find it, I've seen to that. By God, at least she'll have that!"

But, in the end, they would find it. Rutledge said only, "What did you use as the murder weapon?"

Dr Taylor grimaced. "You're the policeman. Tell me."

Hamish said, "He did the post-mortem. Any evidence would ha' been destroyed."

And there had been more than enough time for Taylor to have hidden whatever it was, on his way back to Mumford before he was summoned by Sam Hubbard.

When Constable Forrest arrived, Rutledge turned Taylor over to him, and warned him to have a care on their way to Cambridge. "He's killed once," he reminded the man.

He watched them leave, and Mrs Dunne, who had come to the door as the doctor was being taken away, bit her lip to hold back tears.

Rutledge walked to the house next but one to speak to Taylor's wife, and it was a bitter duty. Her face drawn and pale from suffering, she said only, "It's my fault. My fault." And nothing would dissuade her. In the end, he had to tell her that her house would have to be searched. She nodded, too numb at that moment to care.

He left her with Mrs Dunne, and went to tell Mrs Gravely that he had found Sir John's killer.

She frowned. "I'd never have believed the doctor could do such a thing. Not to murder Sir John for a heathen superstition. Poor Mrs Taylor, I can't think how she'll manage now."

He left her, refusing her offer of a cup of tea. Then, just as he was cranking the motorcar, she called to him, and he came back to the steps where she was hugging her arms about her against the cold wind.

"It keeps slipping my mind, Mr Rutledge, sir! And it's probably not important now. You asked me to keep an eye out for anything that was missing, and I wanted you to know I did."

"Is there anything? Besides the reliquary?" he asked, surprised.

"Oh, nothing so valuable as that." She smiled self-consciously, feeling a little foolish, but no less determined to do her duty. "Still, with the old dog dead, and Sir John gone as well, I never noticed it missing until yesterday morning. It's the iron door-stop, the one shaped like a small dormouse. Sir John used it these past six months or so, whenever Simba needed to go out. To keep the door from slamming shut behind them, you see, while he walked a little way with Simba, or stood here on the step waiting for him. He never cared for the sound of a slamming door. He said it reminded him too much of the war. The sound of the guns and all that."

Rutledge thanked her and drove to Cambridge to ask for men to search the sides of the road between Sir John's house and Mumford.

As they braved the cold to dig through ditches, and push aside winter-dead growth, Rutledge could hear the doctor's voice again.

You're the policeman. Tell me.

Three hours later, he drove once more to Cambridge to do just that. A few black hairs still clung to the dormouse's ears, and on the base was what appeared to be a perfect print in Sir John's blood.

Dead of Winter

Richard A. Lupoff

From the aftermath of the First World War to events leading up to the Second World War. As with the previous story, the following is based on certain characters and events that really happened. It concerns Nazi activities in the United States in preparation for the war effort in Europe.

Richard A. Lupoff is as well known for his science fiction as for his crime and mystery novels. His first book was a study of the works of Edgar Rice Burroughs, Master of Adventure (1965), and Lupoff became something of a master of adventure himself, but never with anything formulaic. Such books as One Million Centuries (1967) and Sacred Locomotive Flies (1971) rang the changes within science fiction, whilst Into the Aether (1974) was one of the early works of steampunk. A number of his books have been pastiches or tributes to some of Lupoff's favourite authors, such as Lovecraft's Book (1985), and readers will, of course, recognize the origins of his detective, Caligula Foxx, in the following story. Another Foxx story, "Cinquefoil" will be found in Lupoff's collection Killer's Dozen (2010).

Almost anyone would have been embarrassed to answer the doorbell wearing Buck Rogers pyjamas. Andy Winslow, however, felt no shame. His attitude was that anybody who sounded the brass gryphon knocker on the front door of Caligula Foxx's house on West Adams Place had better be prepared for whatever sight he encountered. Especially if said caller arrived on a Sunday morning and sounded the knocker at the ungodly hour of – Winslow checked his Longines wristwatch and decided – well, it might not be such an ungodly hour at that, but it *was* Sunday morning.

Foxx was upstairs in his Colonial-era four-poster. The entire house was furnished with antiques, none of them dating from later than 1789 – when James Madison was said to have written the Bill of Rights on the polished maple desk that now served as Foxx's daily working surface.

Reuter had prepared Foxx's daily ration of steel-cut Irish oatmeal, moistened with a dab of freshly churned butter and a dash of heavy cream, and sweetened with a touch of maple sugar and cinnamon. A huge mug of Jamaican blue mountain coffee, seasoned with ground chicory root, Louisiana style, rested steaming on the tray beside the bowl of cereal. An array of Sunday newspapers covered the goose-down quilt on Foxx's bed, the colourful comic pages set neatly in one pile, the rotogravure magazines in another, and so on through the various news sections of the papers.

No one interrupted the great detective while he was at breakfast, nor while he was reading his newspapers.

Hence, Andy Winslow to the front door.

He peered through the small fan-shaped window in the door but the caller, whoever that was, was nowhere to be seen. A light, early-winter snow had dusted West Adams Place during the night, painting the street itself a sparkling white, turning the graceful elm trees that lined the street into illustrations from a Currier and Ives print.

An automobile sped away, headed west, its exhaust rising in the crystal-like air. Winslow caught only a glimpse of it. He was pretty sure it was a LaSalle coupé and that it had a sticker of some sort, possibly an American eagle, in the back window. But it was gone before he could make a definite identification. Its licence plate, in any case, was obscured by snow.

Winslow opened the door.

A uniformed figure slid into the foyer. It was that of a youngster, garbed in military cap, tunic, and boots. As the newcomer collapsed on to the broad-plank floor of the foyer, a narrow streak of blood was drawn the length of the door. Winslow noticed a neat hole in the wood, then turned his attention to the uniformed figure.

He turned the newcomer over, face up. The military cap, knocked askew by the fall, still clung to dark, wavy hair, held there by rubber-tipped bobby pins. Winslow carefully removed the bobby pins and the cap. The hair fell free. The corpse – for there was no doubt in Andy Winslow's mind that the newcomer was deceased – was that of a young woman, hardly more than a schoolgirl, garbed as a messenger for the Postal Telegraph Company.

A tiny hole, apparently the exit wound of a small-calibre bullet, formed a black circle just above the bridge of her nose. Winslow lifted her head, found a small section of her dark hair stained even darker with blood. Winslow had found the entry wound of the bullet.

A chilly gust swept a sprinkling of snow into the foyer. Winslow set the catch on the front door so he would not be locked out, then stepped on to the rounded brick porch. A bicycle stood leaning against the handrail. A few snowflakes had accumulated on it and more were continuing to do so.

Winslow touched the hole in the door, put his eye to it, and discerned a bullet therein. Apparently the messenger had been shot from behind just as she sounded the knocker. The bullet had penetrated the back of her skull, travelled through her brain, exited via her forehead, and come to rest a half inch deep in the antique polished oak.

A trail of fresh footprints in the new-fallen snow led from the opposite side of the street to the house, and back to the empty space at the curb where the LaSalle had stood. There was also a narrow furrow in the snow, obviously laid down by the bicycle that now leaned against the railing.

It appeared that the shooter had fired from the LaSalle and then walked – or, more likely, run – from the car to the brick porch. Then he had returned to the car and driven away.

Winslow stepped back into the house and closed the door. He could hear the voice of his employer bellowing out a demand. "Come up here, confound you, and tell me what all the abominable racket is about down there!"

Eschewing the small elevator that Foxx had ordered installed for his use, but concealed behind a *faux* bookcase of Colonial vintage, Winslow sprinted up the broad staircase. He gave Foxx a quick, breathless summary of the occurrence.

Foxx narrowed his eyes, fixing Winslow with a sharp stare. "You have a talent, my boy, for drawing trouble as a bar magnet draws iron filings. All right, phone Dr McClintock. I suppose we'll have to bring the police into this as well, but let's get Fergus on the case before those busybodies come snooping around."

Winslow phoned the doctor and sketched out the situation for him. Fergus McClintock, MD, said that he'd be right over. Andy said, "You'd better drag your carcass out of that bed, Caligula, and put on some clothes before the doc gets here."

Foxx took a large swallow of coffee, gave out a sound that was a cross between a sigh of pleasure and a grunt of resignation, and began the process of climbing from his four-poster. "You'd better get out of that funny page-outfit yourself," he growled at Andy Winslow.

Winslow was out of his pyjamas, into street clothes, and back downstairs before Foxx was fully out of his bed. The casualty lay unmoving where she had fallen just inside the front door. Musing that it never hurt to be certain, Winslow laid his fingers on the messenger's neck, expecting no pulse and cooling, clammy corpse-flesh. Instead, he felt warmth and detected a faint pulse.

He ran to fetch a blanket and laid it over the messenger, leaving only her face uncovered. He lowered his cheek to a point a fraction of an inch from her face and detected a faint susurrus of breath from her nostrils. He ran to the bathroom and brought a damp cloth to lay across her forehead, covering the ugly black circle where the bullet had emerged.

By the time Dr McClintock arrived, Caligula Foxx had completed dressing and arrived on the ground floor via his personal elevator. He strode to the motionless form on the polished wooden floor.

The door knocker sounded. Andy Winslow, who had been kneeling beside the wounded messenger, sprang upright and admitted the iron-haired, red-cheeked doctor. Andy took Dr McClintock's homburg and winter coat. Reuter had also arrived, emerging from the kitchen. He accepted the doctor's accoutrements from Winslow and disappeared.

Dr McClintock made a cursory examination of the supine messenger, then rose to his feet. "This is truly amazing. Not unprecedented, but still most unusual."

Foxx sputtered. "Never mind the commentary, Fergus. What have you found? Is she alive? Dead? Speak up."

Dr McClintock shook his head in disbelief. "This woman has been shot. Not from very close range – there are no powder burns around the entry wound. I would say that the bullet was a .22 calibre. So small a round punched a hole in her skull. A larger bullet, a .38 or .44, would have smashed the skull at point of entry, but this .22 or whatever it was punched cleanly in."

Andy Winslow interrupted the doctor's monologue. "Is she alive, though?"

Dr McClintock nodded emphatically, his steel-wool eyebrows working up and down. "Absolutely. Mr Winslow, summon an ambulance at once."

The call was made quickly.

While they awaited the arrival of the ambulance, Dr McClintock asked Andy Winslow what had happened and Winslow repeated his story. "I think the driver of that LaSalle automobile shot the messenger. The double set of footprints that you mention would fit with that, Mr Winslow."

Andy Winslow rubbed his chin, his eyes still fixed on the softly breathing woman. "But you said that the shot was not fired from very close to the victim."

"I did indeed." Dr McClintock pursed his lips. "Most likely the miscreant fired from across the street, then ran to the house, performed some brief task, ran back and drove away. Would there have been time for that, do you think? Did you hear the shot fired?"

Andy Winslow said, "No, I was in the lavatory brushing my teeth. I only came to the door when I heard the knocker sound. A .22 fired from across the street might not have been audible even though the door knocker was."

Caligula Foxx had found a seat in an antique ladder-backed chair, from which he observed the proceedings. Now he gestured Andy Winslow to him, murmured a rapid series of instructions in his ear, and sent him on his way.

Winslow left the house. In moments, the doors of the two-car garage behind the residence – once a Colonial-era carriage house – were opened and a yellow Auburn roadster, its folding top and canvas side-windows in place against the cold, rolled forth. The

428 Richard A. Lupoff

roadster disappeared up West Adams Place, Andy Winslow at the wheel.

Back in the house Dr McClintock tilted his head questioningly at Caligula Foxx. "Is that correct procedure, Caligula? I imagine Lieutenant Burke will be arriving shortly, along with the ambulance. Shouldn't Mr Winslow have stayed here?"

But by now Andy Winslow had reached the office of the Postal Telegraph Company not far from Caligula Foxx's house. He drew his roadster to the curb, leaped from the car, ran up a short flight of terrazzo steps and burst through the door. He demanded to see the manager and was introduced to one Oswald Hicks, a Cuban-looking individual wearing a business suit, a Clark Gable moustache, and wavy black hair.

Andy Winslow identified himself and described the incident at West Adams Place.

Hicks's eyes widened. He raised a carefully manicured, mahogany-coloured hand to his face. "Come with me!"

He led Andy Winslow back to the public office, asked the clerk on duty to tell him who had carried messages in the past hour and had not returned. The clerk didn't have to look it up. "Not much business this morning, Mr Hicks. Martha's the only messenger on duty. Martha Mayhew. She went out" – he checked his log book – "forty minutes ago. Night letter going to a Mr Foxx on West Adams."

Hicks turned to Andy Winslow. "You're sure she's alive?"

Andy grunted an affirmative.

"And you summoned an ambulance?"

Andy repeated the sound.

"They would probably take her to St Ambrose's. Let's go there, sir." He left the clerk in charge of the office and they headed for the street. Andy Winslow led the way to his roadster and piloted the Auburn through quiet, Sunday-morning streets, to pull in at the hospital. Martha Mayhew had been admitted and taken on a rolling gurney to the newly established radiology laboratory, pride of St Ambrose's medical staff.

There was little for either of them to do at St Ambrose's.

While Dr McClintock stood by, a young intern explained, they had taken X-rays of the patient's head. The foreign object – the intern did not refer to it as a bullet – had entered at the rear of the patient's skull, had passed through the channel between the two lobes of her brain, and had exited through her forehead.

It was a thousand to one chance, the intern said, then corrected himself, a million to one chance. A fraction to the left or right and severe, possibly fatal, brain damage would have resulted. But, as it was, the only concern was possible infection. The patient would be monitored, the entry and exit wounds kept clean, sulpha drugs applied if necessary. The entry and exit wounds were small enough to heal without further surgery. Barring the unexpected, she should be released in a few days, with only a small round scar on her forehead to show for her near encounter with the grim reaper.

Hicks asked, "How can that be? Thank heaven Miss Mayhew is alive, but as you describe the wound, Doctor – this is incredible."

The intern, looking almost like a child costumed to play doctors, looked from Hicks to Winslow and back. "You know the brain is composed of two hemispheres. They're quite separate from each other, connected only by a sort of bridge or highway, the *corpus calossum*. It seems that the object passed between the hemispheres and above the, ah, bridge. It's not unprecedented, sir. We studied a far worse case in med school. Back in 1848 a poor fellow named Phineas Gage was tamping down an explosive for a construction project. The dynamite went off and drove the tamping rod through his cheek, up through one eye, through his brain, and out the top of his skull. You'd think he was a goner for sure but he recovered and lived a normal life."

★

Shortly, the patient was in a private room. She had regained consciousness but had no recollection of being shot. "I parked my bike and climbed the steps. I remember I had the knocker in one hand and Mr Foxx's night letter in the other. Then I – I don't remember anything until I woke up in this bed."

"You had the night letter in your hand?" Andy Winslow asked.

"Yes, I remember distinctly. I had it in my hand and—"

At this point the door of the hospital room swung open and Lieutenant Adam Burke strode into the room, followed by a couple of uniformed officers. He glared at Andy Winslow. "You left the scene of a crime, Winslow."

Andy looked innocently at the cop. "I did?"

"You know damned well you did. Who the hell do you think you are, letting a corpse into the house and then leaving her there on the floor to die."

Andy grinned. "What corpse would that be, Lieutenant?"

"This one!" Burke jabbed a thumb at the slight figure on the bed.

"You mean Miss Mayhew, Lieutenant? I don't think Miss Mayhew is dead. Are you dead, Miss Mayhew?"

The slim woman managed a wan, tiny smile. "I don't think I'm dead. I don't even feel sick. I do have a dreadful headache, though."

Andy Winslow grinned, "You're entitled to that." Then, to the cop, "It's true that Miss Mayhew was shot at Caligula Foxx's house. I thought it was more important to make sure that she was all right, than to wait around for New York's Slowest— er, pardon me, I mean New York's Finest – to arrive."

Burke frowned. "You rode in the ambulance with her?"

"No, I took my car." He didn't mention his detour via the Postal Telegraph office, but then he hadn't exactly lied, either.

"And you, sir?" Burke whirled towards Oswald Hicks.

Hicks identified himself.

"The victim worked for you?" Burke asked.

"Yes, sir."

"What was she doing at Mr Foxx's house on a Sunday morning?"

"Postal Telegraph prides itself on its service, Lieutenant, seven days a week. A night letter came in from London, England, and Miss Mayhew was despatched to deliver it to the addressee."

Burke stared at the slim figure beneath the bedclothes, then turned back to Hicks. "You always use girls for this kind of work? Isn't it dangerous?"

Hicks said, "Would that bullet have bounced off the messenger's skull if he'd been a boy instead of a girl?"

Burke growled. "All right, never mind. We'll need statements from all concerned. That's all for now."

He strode from the hospital room, followed by his retinue. As soon as the police detachment was out of earshot, Andy Winslow asked Martha Mayhew if she'd mind his looking through her

Postal Telegraph uniform, hanging now in the closet. Martha Mayhew managed a barely audible assent.

Winslow checked out the clothing, then turned back to her and to Oswald Hicks. "It isn't there."

"What isn't there?" Hicks asked.

"The night letter. The message that Miss Mayhew was attempting to deliver to Caligula Foxx."

"Could she have dropped it at the house?"

"I would have found it when I answered the door."

Hicks rubbed his chin thoughtfully. "I don't suppose she would have left it in the basket of her bicycle."

Winslow said, "I'll check on that when I get back to the house but I doubt it." He hadn't told Hicks specifically about the LaSalle coupé that had pulled away from the house just as he answered Martha Mayhew's knock, but that had been part of his narrative to Lieutenant Burke. "I have a feeling that whoever shot Miss Mayhew escaped in that LaSalle car. And I have a feeling that he committed the crime in order to prevent her from delivering it to Foxx. Most likely, he has the night letter now."

Oswald Hicks said, "In any case, I think I'd best get back to my office. There will be paperwork to do, both for the company and for the police."

Andy Winslow offered him a ride back to his office. As they made their way through the quiet streets, Hicks volunteered, "We'll still deliver the night letter, you know. Postal Telegraph takes pride in its reliable performance."

Winslow was startled. "How can you do that?"

"Oh, we have a copy of the message on file at the office. Two, in fact. It's standard practice. And if we didn't have it, there would be the original in London. They'd have to retransmit it to us, but that wouldn't take very long."

At the Postal Telegraph office Hicks located the night letter. It had been typed out and a flimsy sheet remained in the overnight file folder.

Winslow stared at it. The message was a lengthy one. "I'll need to take this with me."

Oswald Hicks assented.

By the time Winslow pulled his yellow Auburn into the garage at West Adams Place and entered the house, a police evidence team had removed the .22 calibre bullet from the front door. The ever-competent Reuter had filled the hole with quick-hardening putty. He was already at work staining the putty to match the surrounding wood.

Caligula Foxx, resplendent in his usual glaring aquamarine silk shirt, flannel trousers and foulard-pattern dressing gown, was seated behind his gigantic glass-covered desk, reading the Sunday funny pages. A bottle of Teplitz-Schonau ale stood at his elbow.

He lowered the colourful newsprint, tipped the bottle of ale into a tall glass and sipped judiciously. He wiped his lips with a bandanna and looked at Winslow.

"Tell me everything."

Winslow repeated his story, reporting on the condition of Miss Mayhew.

Foxx nodded approvingly. "She is an innocent child, Andy. Whatever deviltry is afoot, she did not deserve to be attacked in this manner. It almost gives one to believe in divine intervention to learn that she could take a bullet through the skull and suffer nothing worse than a headache."

"Almost," Winslow said. "But, if God got into the act, he could have made the gun misfire and blow off the shooter's hand, couldn't he?"

Foxx grinned sardonically. "I should know better than to engage in theological speculation with you, my boy. And Lieutenant Burke's man said that it was a steel-jacketed bullet, so it didn't break apart in the victim's brain. And it must have had an extra load of propellant to make it punch its way out and penetrate into our door."

He leaned back in his oversized chair and drew a breath. "All right then; I detect from your manner that you are holding something back. Spill it, Andy, spill it."

Winslow reached into his pocket and withdrew a large envelope. It bore the Postal Telegraph logotype – the company's name set in large, jagged letters that suggested bolts of electricity – in the corner. "This is the message that Miss Mayhew was attempting to deliver when she was shot. I couldn't find the original in her clothing. I even searched her messenger's bicycle. I've asked Reuter to put it in the garage. They'll have to come for it themselves if Lieutenant Burke doesn't want it."

Foxx nodded and made a humming sound.

Winslow said, "Oswald Hicks, the manager at Postal Telegraph, gave me this copy. I guess the shooter didn't realize that Postal Telegraph keeps copies."

Foxx nodded impatiently. "All right, Andy, all right. Read it to me."

He took a sip of ale, lowered the glass to his desktop, leaned back in his chair, closed his eyes and laced his fingers behind his neck, his elbows extending like the antennae of a giant butterfly. To any casual observer, it would appear that Caligula Foxx was treating himself to a nap, but Andy Winslow knew that the rotund detective's incisive brain was fully on the alert.

"'Dear Cousin,'" Winslow read, starting on the night letter. "'I apologize for my dilatory response to your previous communication, but I have been deeply immersed in sensitive work for the crown and for the government of this nation. A personage has asked me to convey his gratitude for the assistance you so brilliantly provided, even from the distance of three thousand miles. The crown and sceptre have been recovered and restored to their proper resting place, and the scoundrels involved in their temporary abduction are in custody.'"

A smile played around the lips of the detective.

Andy Winslow continued to read. "'You are surely aware that the situation on the Continent continues to deteriorate, as madmen and villains vie for the title of Most Evil Man in Europe. You own country has, to date, escaped involvement but I assure you, cousin, that this will not be the case for very much longer.'"

Winslow paused for breath. Foxx unlaced his fingers and without opening his eyes gestured for Winslow to read further.

"'You may not have heard of Heinrich Konrad, cousin. Or, come to think of it, I am certain that you do know of him, as he is a native of Maffersdorf bei Reichenberg in Bohemia. Not far, as I recall, from the seat of your own branch of our family, and the place of your birth. Konrad was the leader of the Sudetendeutsch Partei and a campaigner for the recent, vile treaty that led to the dismemberment of Czechoslovakia and the annexation of the Sudetenland by Germany. The Sudetendeutsch Partei no longer exists as a separate entity, and Konrad is now a fully fledged Nazi.

" 'His Majesty's government, as reported to me by our mutual relative in the Diogenes Club, believes that Konrad was involved in the planning of the recent misfortune at the Tower. He had been in England as a minor functionary of the German embassy. He is no longer in this country. It is my belief that he has entered the United States of America in the guise of a businessman. He travelled as a first class passenger aboard the North German Lloyd liner *Leipzig*. The name under which he travelled is Bedrich Smetana.

" 'I do not know his mission in the United States, but I would suggest that you contact the American authorities and set them on the *qui vive* for this man. In fact, I am of the distinct impression that you are already acquainted with him, so I will not attempt a physical description. It is not entirely impossible that he will be in contact with his nation's embassy in Washington or its consulates in other cities. Our mutual cousin has also suggested that Konrad is involved in Germany's war preparations, and her relationship with her Asiatic ally. It is thus possible that Konrad will proceed from New York to the American State of California. He may also have contacts with such groups as Herr Fritz Kuhn's German–American Bund or the Ku Klux Klan. You are doubtless aware that there are also a number of supposed German–American Friendship Societies or social clubs that are actually dens of fifth columnists.

" 'Be careful, dear cousin. This scoundrel is totally ruthless. Feel free to call upon me at any time if you feel that I can be of assistance.' "

Andy Winslow folded the document and laid it on his employer's desk. "That's it," he announced. "Oh, and the signature—"

Caligula Foxx grumbled. "I wondered if you would bother with that bit of information. Shall we play a guessing game, or would you be so kind as to tell me."

"Sorry, Mr Foxx. It was signed, *Sexton Blake*."

Andy Winslow ran his finger down the sheet of paper. "That's a lot of words, Caligula. Must have cost Blake a bundle to send it over the cable."

Foxx pursed his lips, then sipped at his ale. "I wouldn't worry about Cousin Sexton's financial status. He drives that wondrous bullet-proof Silver Ghost, keeps his man Tinker on call, and feeds his bloodhound ground porterhouse. He can afford a few extra pounds sterling." Foxx studied the golden beverage remaining in his glass. "Very well, Andy, here are your instructions. No, you will not need your pad and pencil. Just pay close attention to what I tell you, and then we shall take a break from our labours and sample Reuter's no doubt excellent Sunday luncheon."

★

Following a light meal of lobster bisque, spinach salad, and steak tartare garnished with tiny cherry tomatoes and topped off with espresso and biscotti, Winslow set to work. He telephoned Jacob Maccabee, whom both he and Foxx regarded as the premier legman in the City of New York, as well as the best-connected with the shadier elements of that metropolis's demi-monde. They agreed to meet on a bench beneath the statue of one-time Senator Roscoe Conkling in Madison Square Park.

Despite the distance involved, Andy Winslow chose to walk from West Adams Place to Twenty-third Street. The light snowfall had ceased and a bright December sun shone in a sparkling blue sky. When Andy reached the appointed spot, Maccabee had already arrived and brushed the accumulated snow from the bench's green-painted wooden slats.

Maccabee was a man of less than average height, dark complexion, heavy eyebrows, huge dark eyes, and a distinctly Semitic nose. He wore a nondescript overcoat, slightly scuffed shoes, and a grey fedora that was starting to show its age. He was perusing a black-covered copy of *Mein Kampf*, in the original German. He looked up at Andy Winslow. "You seem intrigued by my reading-matter, Andy."

"Was I so obvious?"

"Know thine enemy, Andy."

Winslow sat down beside Maccabee.

Maccabee slipped a bookmark into *Mein Kampf* and turned his full attention to Winslow.

"We had an attempted murder on our doorstep this morning, Jacob."

"So I heard."

"Really? So quickly?"

"Word spreads fast around here. You know that New York is just a small town. Maybe the biggest one in this hemisphere, but it's still a small town at heart. Western Union messenger, wasn't he?"

"Postal Telegraph, and *he* was a she."

Maccabee said, "Oh." He drew it out into two long syllables. "And the victim survived?"

Winslow nodded.

"That's nice. Always happy to hear of a victim coming through alive. He – I mean she – going to be all right?"

"I think so."

There was a momentary silence as a young couple, out to enjoy the sunny afternoon despite its cold, paused to look up at Roscoe Conkling.

Once they walked on, Maccabee said, "Still, I imagine this would be police business. Does Lieutenant Burke know about it?"

Winslow said, "He does. I'm sure his excellent men will pursue the matter appropriately. It's the message that the girl was trying to deliver to Foxx that matters to us."

"Don't tell me. The message mysteriously disappeared and the sweet girl messenger has no idea who took it or where it went."

"Exactly."

"And you want me to find it."

"No. We have the message. Postal Telegraph had a copy in their files. Foxx has it now." From memory he summarized the Sexton Blake "Dear Cousin" night letter.

"And so . . . ?"

"I want you to find Heinrich Konrad, aka Bedrich Smetana. Do you think you can do that?"

"What, find one bad Czech in the City of New York? How long do I have to locate this character? And how much is your ever-generous employer willing to pay for my services?"

"Oh, Jake. Wait a minute." A teenaged girl riding a bright red Schwinn and holding the leash of a black Labrador retriever pedalled past.

"Okay. We need Konrad as fast as we can get him. And you know that Foxx has never quarrelled with you over a bill."

Jacob Maccabee stood up, slipped the fat copy of *Mein Kampf* into a copious overcoat pocket, and folded his hands behind his back. "Andy, let's walk."

They started along the tarmac path. The early snow had melted off the macadam but it remained on the grassy areas and the trees that surrounded the pathways. The effect was a chiaroscuro landscape punctuated by marble plinths bearing statues of half-forgotten statesmen.

"This Konrad fellow is an unpleasant individual, Andy. You know, some of us have more reason to follow events in Europe than others. I've seen pictures of Konrad in his Gauleiter's uniform. I've seen the look in his eye."

He paused, looking up at a statue of Chester Alan Arthur, a rotund former President. "But why is Foxx after this guy? Isn't that the feds' business? I imagine J. Edgar Hoover would be interested, to put it mildly."

Winslow nodded. They started walking again. "I'm not sure what kind of passport Konrad is using now, since the powers sliced up Czechoslovakia and started giving away the pieces. Foxx was born there, you know – in what would become Czechoslovakia, while that country existed. He's pretty cagey about the details, although there has to be an English branch of the family Foxx says that Sexton Blake is his cousin, and another famous English sleuth is in his family tree. But he does admit that he was born in Bohemia and could even claim that citizenship if he ever wanted to."

A breeze came sweeping through the park and a shower of snowflakes dropped from an elm tree on to Winslow and Maccabee.

"Konrad could be a citizen of – what do they call it since the treaty? the Protectorate of Bohemia and Moravia. Or he could just have decided to call himself a German. It hardly matters now, Jake, does it?"

Their conversation was interrupted by a thump. A squirrel, losing its grip on a wind-swept tree limb, had fallen on to the footpath not ten yards from Winslow and Maccabee. The squirrel shook its head in comical imitation of a stunned man, looked around – could a squirrel be embarrassed? – and scampered up a nearby oak.

"Poor creature," Maccabee grinned. "Doesn't he know he's supposed to be happily curled up inside a hollow tree by now?" Then to Winslow, "You mean this is personal?"

Winslow nodded. "I know Caligula Foxx about as well as any living person, I think. After all, I work for him, I live in his house, we dine together. On those rare occasions that he's willing to leave West Adams, he likes me to drive the Packard. I've offered to take him in my Auburn but that's beneath him, 'don't you know'."

He paused, then added, "Anyway, he still has feelings for the land of his birth. I'm certain of that. He feels that Konrad has sold out their mutual homeland to the Nazis and he's determined to find out what Konrad is doing in the US. And to stop him!"

Jacob Maccabee exhaled, his warm breath turning white in the frosty air. "I'll get on to it, Andy. I'll get some men working on it today. I'll call a couple of pals on the daily rags and get photos of Konrad. You know, my pal Barney Hopkins got hired away from the Brooklyn *Eagle*; he's working for the *Herald-Trib* now. Or maybe Del Marston at the *World-Telly*. Well, don't you worry about that. I'll get photos made and send some over to you at West Adams."

The men shook hands. As they parted, Winslow said, "Remember, he entered the US under a false name. I don't think he'd be calling himself Konrad."

Maccabee said, "Got it. Relax, pal. Bedrich Smetana. Good Czech name."

Maccabee headed east from the park; Winslow, west.

Back at West Adams Place Andy Winslow peered into the garage and noted that the Postal Telegraph messenger's bicycle had been removed. Apparently Lieutenant Burke's men could do something useful. Andy let himself in, wiped the snow from his shoes, and found Caligula Foxx in the parlour seated before a roaring fire. A Steinway grand piano, its size proportionate to Caligula Foxx's great bulk, was situated well away from the fireplace. A snifter of cognac stood at Foxx's elbow. The stack of Sunday papers had migrated from his down-filled comforter to his more than ample lap.

Winslow never ceased to be amazed at Foxx's ability to absorb the content of every paper from the staid *Times* and *Post*, to the wild tabloids – one of which was uppermost on Foxx's lap. It was the *Sunday Mirror*. A huge photo of a burning building filled most of the front page, a headline announcing an explosion and fire at a synagogue on Essex Street.

Foxx turned his massive head to greet his assistant. "Ah, Andy. How went it with Mr Maccabee?"

Winslow gave him a report on his meeting with the investigator. "I'll look forward to seeing the photos of this bozo," he concluded.

"A nasty piece of work. I have not previously mentioned that I crossed paths with *Pan* Konrad – I suppose he would prefer Herr Konrad now – towards the end of the Great War. He was serving in Emperor Franz Josef's army at the time. It was then that I got to know him quite well. One's loyalties are often strained by the exigencies of war." Fox rubbed his massive forehead contemplatively. "And of politics," he added.

Uninvited, Andy sank into a chair facing Foxx. "I didn't know you'd served in the war."

Foxx removed the papers from his lap and set them aside. He took a sip of brandy. "Would you like some, Andy? No? Well, not to bore you with excessive detail, but I will say that I did not serve in the war in an official capacity. Or, well, perhaps not exactly in the capacity in which I seemed to serve." He grinned. "I hope that is not too convoluted an explanation for you."

Winslow ignored the dig. "But unofficially?"

Foxx smiled. "Yes. I like to think that my modest talents were not entirely wasted. I was a mere lad, you understand. And *Pan* Konrad was another. We are of an age, you know. In fact, I believe that at one time we competed against each other in schoolboy athletic contests. I disliked Konrad even then. When the war broke out – that was the summer of '14, of course – I was ready to enlist and offer my services to Franz Josef, he of such tragic memory. But, instead, a court official – I imagine at the instigation of our village priest, but one can never be certain of these things – gave me a ticket to Prague. A ticket to Prague, that lovely city, and an address at which to report."

Foxx had a faraway look in his eyes.

"Imagine, Andy, a mere stripling lad, a *vysoko škola u enic* – nowadays we would say, a high-school scholar – entrusted with missions that would have resulted in my immediate execution, had I been captured by the Tsar's men."

"And you met Konrad then?"

"Andy, I thought that *Pan* Konrad was a loyal subject of the Emperor – as I was. Little did I know, my boy. I carry a scar to this day – you have never seen it, nor will you, I trust – but I bear that scar to this day, and I will carry it with me even when I go to meet my maker. A scar, courtesy of Heinrich Konrad."

"And now he's calling himself Bedrich Smetana," Winslow supplied.

Foxx held his brandy snifter and gazed through it at the dancing flames. He was in the habit, Andy Winslow knew, of changing the subject at any time, with little or no notice. And yet, when one reviewed the conversation afterwards, a relevance in Foxx's words was always apparent. Now he asked, quite suddenly, "Did you happen to pass by Wanamaker's on your way home from your meeting with Maccabee?"

"I did, Caligula."

"Have they put up their light display? Surely they would have done so by now. I had not yet got to the customary photographs of it in the rotogravure sections when I was so rudely interrupted this morning."

"Yes, it's up. It's truly magnificent, Caligula. I would have been home sooner but I stopped to admire the lights. And the children, of course. Swarms of them, with beaming parents, come to look at the colourful lights, and wreaths, and trees. And of course, the presents."

"Well, Andy, I'm glad that it snowed today. That would add to the children's pleasure. But now,"– he lifted an inch-thick sheaf of papers off the larger stack – "to return to the unpleasantness of Heinrich Konrad. I have here a list of events in the city, planned by Herr Kuhn's German–American Bund, and other organizations of its ilk. I want you to study these and coordinate your efforts with those of Jacob Maccabee. Surely *Pan* Konrad will be at some of them. You will need to be there as well."

"Then we're not giving this to Jacob Maccabee?"

"Andy, Andy." Foxx heaved a great sigh. Considering his bulk, it would have done justice to a rugby squad. "I have the greatest admiration for Jacob and his little band of merry men. And women."

He paused to lace his fingers, this time across his bulbous abdomen.

"But I believe in casting more than one line into the stream when I set out to catch a fish. Yes. Heinrich Konrad is a very slippery and elusive fish, but I mean to catch him if I can. Jacob will do his work. You will do yours."

He shuffled the papers in his lap. You'd have thought there was no order to them, and perhaps there was not; but, shortly, Foxx's surprisingly sensitive fingers emerged with a slickly printed section of a Sunday publication.

"Here is a list of events over the next few days, Andy. Most of them are society dances, weddings and birth announcements. But there are also cultural gatherings. Buried among the concerts and art exhibitions are events scheduled by groups with which *Pan* Konrad would surely be in sympathy, and to which I would be astonished if he were not invited."

He fixed his assistant with a sharp look.

"Do you think you could pass for a Nazi sympathizer, Herr Winslow?"

Andy Winslow leaped to his feet. He clicked his heels, gave a mock stiff-armed salute, and barked, "*Sieg heil!* "

Fox said, "Pretty good, Andy. You might want to practice a bit more. But that wasn't bad." Then Foxx made one of his lightning-like transitions. "Have you seen the lovely Miss Rose Palmer lately, my boy?"

"Of course." Winslow paused. "Of course," he repeated. "We see each other from time to time."

"A most competent and talented young lady," Foxx said. "And quite attractive, I should say."

"I wouldn't quarrel with that."

"Very well, then. Here's what you are to do. I am planning a little holiday supper for tomorrow evening. While you were conversing with Jacob Maccabee this afternoon, I met with Reuter and planned the menu *du soir*. A very small gathering, you understand. Strictly informal, no need to dress. You will invite Jacob and an associate of his choice. I trust you to communicate with Jacob. And of course Miss Palmer and yourself will be present. Eight o'clock promptly, cocktails and supper."

Andy Winslow said, "Okay. I'll take care of that. What else?"

Foxx rattled the slick section of the newspaper. It was part of *The New York Journal-American*. He poked a carefully manicured finger at a column of event notices. " 'The Beethoven–Wagner Cultural Institute is holding a luncheon meeting at the Blaue

Gans Restaurant on Duane Street this Wednesday: reading of the minutes, a *heimatlich* meal, good Cherman *bier,* and the introduction of a special guest-speaker from the *Heimat.*' I have a feeling that the special guest-speaker will be Herr Konrad. The meeting is open to all like-minded patriots."

"Sounds pretty dull to me. You know Count Basie and Billie Holiday are more my speed. I just don't understand that longhair opera stuff, Caligula."

Foxx lowered the newspaper and lifted his brandy. He took a sip of the beverage, then returned the snifter to its place. "Andrew, your musical taste, execrable though it may be, is your own concern. I will not engage in debate over the matter. But the Beethoven–Wagner Cultural Institute is not a music appreciation society. I assure you of that. When you get there you will find out what I mean. You still carry that little popgun that I gave you, do you not?"

Winslow tapped his chest. "Sweet little Beretta 1934. Not that I've had to use it very often."

"Nor would I wish you to. But when the time comes, do not hesitate. And now," Foxx stacked the Sunday newspapers carefully beside his chair, drew a golden turnip from a pocket and examined it, then repeated, "and now, I shall retire to my greenhouse and assure myself that the dear roses are safely enjoying their winter hibernation."

★

Martha Mayhew was sitting up in bed when Andy Winslow entered her hospital room. She looked about a thousand per cent better than she had the day before. Which is to say, she looked like a young woman with a bandaged forehead rather than a wax dummy or a corpse waiting to be transported to the morgue. She was holding a movie fan magazine, slowly turning the pages of photos of Greta Garbo and Myrna Loy, Gary Cooper and Robert Montgomery, stopping in between to study ads for cosmetics and shampoos.

Winslow reminded her of who he was and she managed a smile of acknowledgement. She said that she was feeling better today. She also told him that she was starting to remember the previous day's events. "I was trying to deliver a night letter to your house."

"Yes. To my boss."

"I'd come from the Postal Telegraph office on my bicycle. I'm trying to save enough money for college."

"You were shot on our doorstep."

"Next thing I knew, I was here." She laid her hand on the bed-sheet when she said *here*. "But I can remember what happened before I was shot."

Winslow nodded encouragement.

"I was pedalling carefully because the new snow was slippery and I didn't want to skid. There was hardly any traffic, so I steered over near the curb. I noticed a car parked across the street with somebody sitting in it, and the motor running – I could see the exhaust."

"Did you notice what kind of car?"

She started to shake her head but stopped and raised a hand to her temple. "Wow, that hurts!" She drew a couple of breaths, then went on. "It was a closed car, I think a coupé. A dark colour. I didn't notice the brand."

"A LaSalle?"

"I'm sorry. I really didn't notice. But I saw inside a little bit. There were two men. They were talking to each other, but when I pedalled up they stopped, and one of them rolled down his window and talked to me."

Winslow waited.

"He asked if it was cold enough for me. You know the old joke. 'Cold enough for you?' 'Hot enough for you?' 'Wet enough for you?' I'm from Indiana, Mr Winslow. I know all about cold and hot and wet. I said it was just fine, I love winter and snow. The man said, 'How about a ride, we can put your bicycle in the trunk, you'll be warm.' I said I was nearly there, but thank you anyway. And I *was* nearly there. I was looking at the house numbers on West Adams and I turned up the footpath and leaned my bike against the railing and reached for the door knocker; that was the last I remember until I woke up in here."

Andy Winslow started to ask another question but Martha Mayhew dropped the movie magazine and lay back in her bed. "I'm very tired."

Winslow said, "That's all right. You're doing very well." He started for the door, then turned back. "One more question, Miss Mayhew, and I'll leave you. Could you identify either man? By his appearance or anything else?"

She closed her eyes and he thought she was going to sleep, but she opened her eyes again and said, "He was wearing glasses. Round glasses with metal rims – the one who talked to me. And his hair; his hair came down to a point, a . . . a . . . what they call a widow's peak, you know? And he spoke with an accent. Some kind of European accent."

*

Andy Winslow had picked up Rose Palmer early at her Sutton Place apartment. She wore a pale green chiffon dress that set off her white shoulders and flaming hair; darker green, elbow-length gloves, a silver fox jacket, and high-heel pumps completed her ensemble. They stopped at the Carlyle for cocktails and a medley of Cole Porter melodies, then proceeded to West Adams Place.

By the time they arrived there, a full moon shed ice-cold light on the frigid scene. They hurried up the steps to the front door. Earlier in the day Reuter had laid a fire. Jacob Maccabee and his companion were already present. The fire was crackling. Longhair music – the kind Winslow disliked – oozed from concealed loudspeakers in the corners of the room.

Jacob Maccabee and his companion were seated on the brocade sofa near the fire. Jacob wore a pinstripe suit, white-on-white shirt, maroon diamond-patterned tie. His dark complexion and saturnine features looked positively satanic in the light of dancing flames.

Foxx made introductions.

Maccabee's companion was a broad-shouldered woman of middle years. She wore her blonde hair in long braids, wound around her head, and had on a brown dress that did little to hide her full figure. Rubies, or at least red, gem-cut stones, sparkled at her ears and throat and wrists. Her name was Lisalotte Schmidt.

Reuter's wife, Helga, served *hors d'oeuvres*. Foxx himself rose from his favourite chair to offer beverages – a rare event, Winslow noted.

After a time Helga Reuter returned to announce the meal, and the party moved from the parlour to the dining salon.

The meal consisted of alternating hot and cold courses: a red-pepper soup of Reuter's own devising, a cold asparagus salad, small portions of fillet of sole in lemon sauce, tiny portions of sherbet to clear the pallet, *noisettes d'agneau* with small roasted potatoes and legumes, and for dessert Reuter's own apple pie served hot with home-churned vanilla-bean ice cream.

During the meal it had become obvious to Andy Winslow that Lisalotte's English, while fluent, was not that of a native speaker. Her accent bore a distinct North German harshness.

When the meal had ended, Caligula Foxx offered a humidor stocked with dark red Cameroon Diademas. Jacob Maccabee accepted one – as did Lisalotte Schmidt, to Andy Winslow's surprise. Rose Palmer declined the smoke, as did Andy. An ancient Bodegas Gutierrez Oloroso sherry was also served.

Foxx blew a stream of blue-grey smoke towards the room's high ceiling. He turned to the investigator. "Jacob, you have prints of the photographs provided by our friend Barney Hopkins. Would you be so kind as to pass them around."

The photographs were crisp and glossy. One was apparently a studio portrait. It showed a man apparently of Foxx's age. He wore a dark suit, white shirt, dark tie. A small swastika pin was visible on his lapel. The face was long and not altogether unhandsome. The most notable feature was his jet black hair, which he wore cut short. The hair had receded from his brow above the eyes but protruded forward in an extreme widow's peak. He wore round, steel-rimmed spectacles. A point of light was reflected sharply in each lens.

The second photo was neither as formally posed nor as sharply focused as the first; in it, the man in the first photo could be seen standing in a small group. All were similarly garbed in grey military uniforms with peaked caps. All of them were smiling as if they had just accomplished an important and rewarding task. All of them wore swastika armbands on their uniforms.

"This is a news photo," Maccabee explained. "Came from Barney Hopkins's paper's photo library. It's our boy and some comrades celebrating the reunion of Sudetenland with the Fatherland just a few weeks ago. Aren't they all a happy little crew?"

"The fellow with the devilish hair is one Heinrich Konrad," Foxx stated. "He and I were comrades – after a fashion – in the Great War. He is now my mortal enemy. He arrived in the United States using the *nom de guerre* of Bedrich Smetana."

"Dopey name," Andy Winslow commented.

"Not really," Foxx corrected him. "I would say, rather, that *Pan* Konrad is thumbing his nose at me. He must have known that I would find out he was in New York, and he has chosen a name that only a fellow Bohemian would recognize. Or a lover of fine music. Being neither, Andy, you could hardly be expected to get the joke."

"Okay, Caligula, so I don't know this Bedford Stuyvesant guy or whoever he is, but I *do* recognize the gink in the photos."

That created a sensation.

"Blast you, Andrew, why didn't you say so?"

"Caligula, I just did."

"Double blast you! Out with it! You recognize Heinrich Konrad? Had you seen his photo in the newspapers?"

Andy Winslow shook his head. "I was up at the hospital earlier today visiting Miss Mayhew. She's getting her memory back. She described two men in a car who offered her a lift on her way here from Postal Telegraph. One of them was this bozo."

He picked up the portrait photograph and snapped Heinrich Konrad on the nose with his fingernail.

Jacob Maccabee made a humming noise. "Mr Foxx, this is all very interesting, but you haven't given me my assignment."

Foxx repeated the information he'd given Andy Winslow about the planned luncheon at the Blaue Gans. "I want Heinrich Konrad in this house. I want to confront that man. I want to find out his mission in this country and I do not want him to be able to accomplish it. Do you understand me?"

Andy Winslow asked, "Why don't you go to the meeting yourself, Caligula? I'll warm up the Packard and—"

Foxx's frown and his angry growl were all the answer Winslow needed. He already knew how much Foxx hated to leave his home. "All right, Caligula. Then why not just invite him over?"

"He would ignore my invitation. No, Andy, we must lure the rat from his hole and into our trap. That will be Miss Schmidt's job. I have known Konrad for a quarter of a century. I know his taste in many things, including women. He is drawn to women of – pardon me, Miss Schmidt – a certain size and appearance. Large women with long blonde hair worn in braids."

He turned to the woman in the brown dress. "Did Jacob Maccabee explain your assignment to you? Is this agreeable to you, my dear?"

Lisalotte Schmidt laid a large fist heavily on the table. "He is one of Hitler's men, this I know. You know they kill people. Mostly Jews they kill, but also others – anyone they choose. My brother Heinz, he was – how do you say it – slow. He was like a child. He did not understand everything but he was a sweet man. He harmed no one. He wanted only to please."

She shook her head. "They came for him, the Nazis; they said they were taking him to a hospital to make him better, to make him like everyone else. He trusted them, my Heinzie; he went with them, smiling back at me and merrily waving, but it was not to a hospital they took him. It was a camp. They killed him there. Hitler's men. Men like this Konrad. Yes, I will lure him here, Herr Foxx, *Pan* Foxx; I will bring to you this foul Nazi rat."

*

It might have drawn too much attention had they arrived together, so Andy Winslow and Rose Palmer, Jacob Maccabee and Lisalotte Schmidt walked into the Blaue Gans a few minutes apart. December night falls early in Manhattan. Duane Street was a small thoroughfare, running from West Broadway to Church Street. The lighting was poor.

A cold wind carried a hint of sleet. Andy Winslow and Rose Palmer scurried through the cut-glass doors of the Blaue Gans into a merry world that could have come from Mad King Ludwig's Bavaria. The restaurant was decorated with stuffed hunting trophies. Bartenders seemed to compete for the title of Largest Belly and Biggest Moustache. Serving-girls carried foaming steins of beer.

Winslow asked a waiter where the Beethoven-Wagner Institute was holding its meeting, and he and Rose Palmer were directed up a flight of stairs to a meeting-hall filled with oversized tables set with white linen and shining china. There must have been a couple of hundred members of the Institute at least – the majority of them males – gathered in groups, exchanging conversation in a mixture of German and English.

Half a dozen oversized portraits decorated the walls. Winslow assumed that the fierce-looking individual with the shock of dark hair was Beethoven – at least, he thought he'd seen that image on the cover of a record album in Foxx's collection. Then the other old-timer in the fey-looking outfit must be Wagner. Winslow nudged Rose Palmer. "Who's that gink next to Wagner?"

"Johann Wolfgang von Goethe," she whispered back. "Don't you know anything?"

He recognized Otto von Bismarck from a herring-can in Reuter's kitchen. The guy in the fancy uniform and trademark moustache was the old Kaiser, no question about that. And then there was the biggest portrait of them all. *Der Führer.*

Andy Winslow and Rose Palmer drifted from group to group. Rose drew more than her share of male attention and not a few suspicious glances from females. They kept well away from Jacob Maccabee and Lisalotte Schmidt. Jacob's features might be a little too obvious in this crowd, Winslow mused, but he could handle himself.

Most of the men in the crowd – in fact, Winslow realized with a start, every one of them – wore unobtrusive pins on their lapels. They depicted an angry raptor not unlike the old NRA blue eagle. But, when Winslow got a closer look at one, he realized that instead of holding lightning bolts in one claw and a cogwheel in the other, the pins substituted a swastika for the cogwheel.

The symbol was everywhere. There was even a table near the door where a couple of functionaries proffered sign-up sheets to new arrivals, and sold eagle-and-swastika pins and *lavallières*. Andy bought a pin for himself and a *lavallière* for Rose. The insignia stood out against the tasteful lavender of her silk-covered torso. She leaned against Winslow and whispered in his ear as she lovingly attached the pin to his lapel. "If we ever get out of here alive I'm going to have to take twenty showers before I feel clean again."

The chairman, a thin-faced, thin-haired individual, whose personality matched his slightly shabby grey suit, rapped for attention and asked everyone to take their places. He stood at a speaker's lectern decorated with the eagle-and-swastika symbol. Andy and Rose found seats at a table far from the centre of action. Jacob Maccabee and Lisalotte Schmidt placed themselves near the head table.

They sang *The Star-Spangled Banner* and then *Deutschland Über Alles*. The chairman gave a half-embarrassed-looking Nazi salute and everyone sat down. A beefy individual at their table seemed determined to dominate the conversation. That was fine with Winslow. The beefy guy was an importer. All he could talk about was how great the newest Telefunken and Blaupunkt radios and phonographs were. He could get you a deal, he could get you a great deal on either brand. You've never heard anything like it. The music made you believe you were in the Berlin Opernhaus. *Ach,* Schumann, Von Suppe, Abel, Johann Sebastian Bach and all his sons, Praetorius, Gluck. And opera – why, you would think you were at Bayreuth in person! And did you know what was coming soon? Yes – he wasn't supposed to tell you about this yet, it was very hush-hush, but . . . the German engineers under the inspired leadership of the *Führer* were developing television; yes, television, and soon you would be able to see great drama and important political rallies in your own home. Yes! It was true!

Winslow ate *Kavalierspitz mit Sauerkraut und rote Kartoffel* and drank a couple of glasses of *zweigelt umathum*. Rose Palmer nibbled at a *frisée* salad with a poached egg. The importer kept talking and Andy hung on every word, relieved not to have to say anything except for an occasional *Ach, ja?* or *Nicht wahr,* or *Wunderschön!*

They'd just started on coffee and Schnapps when someone stood up and started singing. Andy Winslow blinked in astonishment. It was Jacob Maccabee. He was swaying drunkenly, leaning on Lisalotte Schmidt's shoulder, singing "*Es zittern die morschen Knocken*".

Lisalotte joined in, then a couple of people at Maccabee's table. The grey-suited chairman stood up and rapped his gavel a couple of times, then realized it wasn't going to work and started waving the gavel like a conductor's baton. Now the whole room was singing. When the song ended, Jacob swung into "*Kampflied der Nationalsozialisten*". The songs came to a roaring conclusion, followed by men jumping up at one table after another giving the stiff-armed salute and *Sieg heil*-ing.

Jacob sat down to a round of applause.

Rose Palmer leaned over and whispered in Winslow's ear, "I thought he would try to make himself inconspicuous in the middle of all these Aryans."

"Leave it to Jacob," Winslow whispered back. "Right into the lion's den, and challenge anybody to call him out on it!" He couldn't help grinning.

Once the singing had died down, the diminutive, grey-suited chairman rapped his gavel again. "Ladies and Gentleman, *Damen und Herren, Kameraden*—" a round of applause at the last word. He went on like that, mixing English and German, and all the while it was obvious that he was leading up to the boffo introduction of the special guest of the evening.

"But, first, a special treat!"

He reached under the speaker's lectern and came up with something the size of a movie poster. He studied it himself. The side turned towards the audience was blank.

"In case any of you missed this recent newspaper, I want you all to see it."

With a grin, he turned the poster towards the audience. It was a huge enlargement of the *Mirror* front page with the photo of the Essex Street synagogue, blown up and burning. He made a clucking sound with his tongue, the kind your mother does when you're just mildly naughty. "Isn't that a pity."

The audience howled with laughter and applause.

"And now, *Damen und Herren,* the noble leader of our movement in Sudetenland, a comrade-in-arms in the great National Socialist revolutionary movement, the man who led our separated brethren from the false and artificial state of Czechoslovakia back into the welcoming embrace of the Fatherland. May I introduce to you – Herr Heinrich Konrad." He hadn't bothered to use Konrad's *nom de guerre*.

Andy Winslow felt Rose Palmer grab his hand under the table. Her nails were sharp and her fingers were like ice. He returned the squeeze, heard her exhale a held-in breath.

No question, these guys went for drama; and give 'em credit, they did it well. Up to now the room had been filled with so much *Gemutlichkeit* you could choke on it. Now the atmosphere was completely changed. You'd think that Joe DiMaggio had just been introduced to a room full of rabid Yankee fans.

Where the heck had Konrad been? Maybe in a back-stage room, Winslow decided. Certainly not in the dining room. Now, as the chairman finished his introduction, the houselights snapped off and a spotlight blazed on. Striding from the rear of the room came Heinrich Konrad decked out in full Nazi regalia: swastika armband, jackboots and all. The spotlight followed him to the microphone, then dimmed a little as a second spot hit the oversized portrait of the *Führer* behind the podium.

Oh, he was good. The flashy uniform, the black hair in its widow's peak, even the silver-rimmed specs to add just a touch of the intellectual, took away just a bit from the brute in the fancy get-up. The speech was the usual palaver that these gangsters had been peddling. Stuff about the master-race, the New World Order, the brilliance of the *Führer*, the greatness of the world's most advanced civilization, the pinnacle of humankind in painting, music, poetry, industry, literature, blah-blah.

And then he got into the really nasty part. The part about the subhuman vermin who needed to be exterminated. Oh, the Jews. Of course he had it in for the Jews. But the Slavs were not far behind. Caligula Foxx would get a kick out of that. Surely he fell into that category.

Come to think of it, didn't Konrad, too? Wasn't he some kind of Czech by birth, same as Caligula Foxx? But, no, he was a German, a true Aryan. Too bad he wasn't a blue-eyed blond, but then neither was the *Führer, nicht wahr?*

For a few minutes Andy Winslow felt himself caught up in the flow of Konrad's words. The man's English was fluent if lightly accented, and he painted pictures of a bright future of towering cities and glittering machines – and then he would leap back to his theme of racial purity, and armies marching like robots across a landscape.

They loved it. Oh, they loved it. Konrad could have been elected Mayor if he'd wanted. As soon as he finished, the boobs in the audience went nuts.

∧

When it was all over, Andy Winslow and Rose Palmer made their way out of the meeting-room. The main restaurant downstairs was filled with diners – happy New Yorkers celebrating the holiday season, and out-of-towners come to see the bright lights and the tall buildings of the big city.

A hand came down on Winslow's shoulder and another on Rose Palmer's. They turned to see Jacob Maccabee. His tie was askew, his overcoat was buttoned wrong and his homburg was on the back on his head. Winslow was a tall individual and Rose Palmer was proportionately sized. Maccabee grinned at them. He was shorter than either. Before Maccabee could speak, Winslow said, "That was brilliant, Jacob. Crazy brilliant, but brilliant."

Rose Palmer asked, "Whatever gave you the idea of singing those disgusting songs?"

They had moved away from the restaurant now. The meeting was breaking up and Winslow recognized some of the people from the upstairs room wandering off to find cars or cabs.

"Come on, I don't want to see my friend the importer again. If he tries once more to sell me a Blaupunkt radio I think I'm gonna punch him in the shnozzola."

Rose Palmer said, "Where's Lisalotte?"

Maccabee said, "Did you watch that thug Konrad? Did you see the way he looked at her? I made it a point to light a cigarette for her while he was making his speech, and he spotted her and his eyes lit up. Man, he looked at her the way my cat looks at a slice of raw liver."

"But where is she now?"

"They're together. I don't know where Herr Konrad is staying while he visits our burg. Maybe uptown at the German consulate. Maybe in a hotel or some safe house they've got set up. We'll find that out."

Winslow fingered the Beretta inside his jacket, snug in his armpit in its holster. "I was tempted," he said. "A couple of times." He pulled the automatic partway out of its resting place, far enough to show it to Maccabee. Rose Palmer already knew where he kept it.

"Bad idea, Andy."

"But . . . that man . . . even if Caligula hadn't said anything about him, you could tell Konrad's a disgusting animal. And a dangerous one. And you just left her there to go off with him?"

Maccabee made a growling noise deep in his throat. "Fräulein Schmidt is a tough cookie, Rose. Don't you worry about her. When Konrad finished his rant, all those Nazis started in on *Deutschland Über Alles* again and Konrad started working the crowd like Al Smith at the Easter Parade. He cut through that mob like a hot knife through butter. Every thug got a handshake and a *Sieg heil,* and then the big cheese moved on to the next bunch of suckers. Till he got to Lisalotte. You could tell that was his plan all along, from the first time he laid eyes on her."

A Checker cab rolled past, throwing up black slush from the gutter. They were nearly at Church Street now.

"Jacob," Rose persisted, "I still want to know what gave you the idea of singing like that. You weren't really drunk, were you?"

"Jews don't get drunk."

"You don't know everybody I do."

"Anyway, it was this." He laid a finger across the bridge of his nose and swept it down to the tip. "Put me in a lineup with a Chinaman, a Choctaw, and a Hottentot, and ask anybody to pick out the Jew and they'll get it right on the first try."

"But "

"But nothing, Rose. It's the old Poe gimmick. Hide in plain sight. If a Jew tried to infiltrate that bunch of Nazis, what's the obvious thing to do? He'd head for the darkest corner he could find, he'd keep his head down and his trap shut and hope that nobody'd notice him. And do you think that would work? In a pig's ass – pardon my French, Rose – they'd catch him out in a minute. So I stood up and acted drunk and sang Nazi songs. No Jew would do that; so they just figured I was an unlucky Aryan who managed to pick up a bad gene from a wandering ancestor. So maybe this drunk wasn't quite one hundred per cent pure Aryan, but he was obviously a good Nazi, so let him be. At least for now."

Rose wasn't satisfied. "What now? Do you think Lisalotte will actually spend the night with that – that person?"

"Ah, Rose, Rose, don't be so squeamish. This isn't a Mary Roberts Rinehart romance. Lisalotte may not enjoy staying over with that thug but, believe me, it isn't a fate worse than death. It's bad, but death is worse. And she'll get more information from him in a few hours than I could get in a month in my bed."

He took off his homburg, punched out a dent in it and set it back on his head. He straightened his tie and rebuttoned his coat. He said, "I'm headed for the subway, kiddies. My beloved helpmeet and the offspring are calling to me."

Winslow said, "Wait, I've got my car. We'll give you a lift."

"Not necessary. Thanks all the same. I'll see you at West Adams Place tomorrow. Lunch-time unless you hear different. I'll lay a double sawbuck that Schmidt will show up and she'll bring the bacon with her."

*

Maccabee was right. Andy Winslow and Jacob were completing their reports to Caligula Foxx when the brass knocker sounded. Foxx himself wore his usual aquamarine shirt with hand-painted tie and comfortable grey flannel suit. Winslow knew that Reuter was busy in the pantry preparing the day's luncheon so he answered the door himself. He had already placed a silver tray with coffee urn and cups and pastries on Foxx's oversized desk.

Lisalotte had changed her outfit to a stylish toque hat of forest green and a matching winter coat. In the foyer she doffed the coat to reveal a dark grey dress set off with mild yellow trim. To Andy Winslow she looked simultaneously weary and energized, as if she had followed a hard night with a brief rest and a refreshing shower.

Ever courtly, Foxx rose and took Lisalotte's hand. He escorted her to a seat and poured coffee for her. There was a low table beside her chair and she placed the cup and saucer on it carefully.

"I am no blushing schoolgirl," Lisalotte announced, "but, in all my life and all the men I have had dealings with, no one comes close to that beast. I just hope the filth and the stink of him is off me." She held her hands before her and studied them. She exhaled.

"He is staying in a hotel in Yorktown. The Rotfrauhaus on Eighty-Sixth Street. He is registered under the name of Antonin Dvorak."

Caligula Foxx burst into laughter. His belly shook with merriment. "Oh, that is too good, too good, Lisalotte. That alone makes my day, and it's hardly mid-morning yet."

Andy Winslow said, "I don't get it, Caligula. What's so special about that name?"

"Why, Herr Konrad entered this country under the name Bedrich Smetana. My cousin Sexton Blake warned me of that. I don't imagine a person whose musical tastes are as – shall we say, as limited as your own – would get the joke. Nor the punch line of becoming Antonin Dvorak once he'd arrived in New York. Oh no, Herr Konrad is a despicable individual, but he is neither stupid nor ignorant."

He leaned forward, studying the assortment of pastries Reuter had provided. He selected one and transferred it to a Dalton dish, cream-coloured with maroon-deckled trim, circled in gold. He sliced a wedge-shaped morsel from the pastry and popped it in his mouth, consuming it with obvious pleasure.

He turned to Lisalotte Schmidt. "You have my gratitude, my dear. You have done a greater service, I imagine, than you realize. But now we need to know what information you gathered from Herr Konrad-Smetana-Dvorak. Why is he in this country? Surely not just to address a room full of ne'er-do-wells and malcontented bully-boys."

"He is going to Long Island, to the village of Carrolton Beach. Do you know that place? I do not, Mr Foxx."

Foxx nodded. "I know the place. Yes. Go on."

"There is an aeroplane factory there. They are developing a new kind of aeroplane for the government. I do not know the details, but Konrad says Hitler wants it for his own forces. He says that Hermann Goering is eager to see the plane, to see its plans, and to build a copy of it for the Führer."

She paused to down a heavy draught of coffee, wiped her lips with a linen napkin, and resumed.

"He has a spy in the aeroplane factory. He is going to see him tomorrow, to get a set of blueprints from him and take them back to Germany."

Foxx steepled his fingers on his chest. "I don't suppose you know his spy's name?"

"He said it was Richard Strauss." She gave the name its proper pronunciation. *Reek-hardt*.

Foxx shot a look at Jacob Maccabee. "Well, Jake, what can you add to that?"

"Only aircraft factory any where near Carrolton is Sapphire-MacNeese. Good company."

"Connections?"

"Mr Foxx – how long have you known me? Of course!"

Foxx sliced another wedge of pastry. For a man of his enormous appetite he was a fastidious eater. He nodded to Maccabee, signalling him to continue.

"Aaron Lieberman. Chief designer there. Reports directly to Carter MacNeese. MacNeese bounces between Long Island and their California plant. Flies his own plane every time he wants to hit the other coast. Seems to me it would be a long commute, but who am I to say?"

Foxx pursed his lips. "Tell me about this Lieberman."

"We grew up in Brownsville. Went to William Seward High together. Aaron was a brainy kid. We used to build model aeroplanes together. All that Aaron ever cared about was aeroplanes. Aeroplanes and rocket-ships. He used to read the funny papers: Brick Bradford, Buck Rogers, Flash Gordon. He couldn't get enough of that crazy stuff."

Foxx shook his head. His dark brown hair was overdue for a trim. It whipped back and forth. "Never mind that. Are you still close?"

Maccabee raised his hands, clasped like those of a prize-fighter celebrating a knockout victory. "Like this."

"When did you last see him?"

Maccabee grinned. "We both got out of Brownsville a long time ago, but we're still pals. Our wives go shopping, kids all play together. We just had a big Thanksgiving dinner Chez Lieberman. He's done well. Has a nice house out on the Island, a little goldfish pond in the backyard, shiny new car."

"All right, Jake. Good. Now, do you have any idea what Lieberman would be working on that Goering and Hitler are so eager to get their hands on? Jack? Lisalotte? Did Konrad say anything last night – think hard, my dear – that might give us a hint?"

Lisalotte Schmidt said, "He had a bottle of Schnapps. He'd had a couple of drinks at the Blaue Gans and he drank a lot more at the Rotfrauhaus. He fell asleep after . . . after he fell asleep, he woke up half in a stupor. I had to help him to the toilet. A pig he is. He looked into the bowl and he said something very strange, Mr Foxx. He said, I give you his words exactly; he said, *'Fliegend kommt es aus der Toilette.'* I thought he was just babbling. But something maybe it means, yes?"

"Yes, it does," Foxx said.

Maccabee said, "Yes."

Andy Winslow said, "Not to me it doesn't. I don't understand kraut."

Foxx said, "It means, 'Out from the toilet it comes flying,' Andy."

Winslow said, "I get the picture. But do I want to?"

Foxx said, "Jake, what do you think?"

Maccabee said, "I saw something in Lieberman's house on Thanksgiving, Mr Foxx. It was a model aeroplane, I thought. Only it looked more like a spaceship. I figured Aaron was up to his old tricks again, building toy aeroplanes and spaceships for his kids.

"But he said, 'Come outside, I'll show you something.' The girls were making dinner in the kitchen and the kids were all down in the basement playing hide and seek. He picked up the model aeroplane, rocket-ship – whatever – and we went outside. It was pretty chilly, but the goldfish pond wasn't frozen or anything. He clicked a couple of switches on the model and set it down in the fishpond. At first it sank but I could still see it – the pond is only a couple of feet deep. Some lights went on in the model, a couple of propellers started to whirl around, and it came right up out of the water and flew around over our heads, and then it circled back and landed in the pond. It started to sink but Aaron got a hold of it and we went back in the house and had our dinner."

Foxx had dropped his chin – all right, his *chins* – down on his chest as Maccabee told his little story. You might have thought Foxx had fallen asleep but he hadn't. He was listening to every word. Now he said, "'*Fliegend kommt es aus der Toilette.*' It came flying out of the toilet. But it didn't, it came flying out of the fishpond. Jacob, do you see what your friend has invented? Andy, don't you see it? Miss Schmidt? No one?"

He heaved a great sigh.

"This little toy of his – imagine a dozen of them – a hundred – packed in a submarine. Imagine the submarine approaching the enemy coast. It could send one of these little machines up to circle over an enemy force. It could carry one of those small motion-picture cameras that are all the rage. It could take pictures of the enemy army then fly back and dive into the water. Or . . ." he turned his massive head to the ceiling as if he could see fleets of tiny aircraft circling there ". . . or, they could be packed with explosives instead of cameras. They could be used in naval battles to attack enemy ships. Miniature flying torpedoes."

He shook his head. "No wonder Hermann Goering wants to get his hands on this thing." To Lisalotte Schmidt he said, "When is Konrad going out to Carrolton? You say he told you he is going tomorrow. What time? Does he have an appointment with Strauss?"

"No, he didn't say. He was from the Schnapps, too much he drank, drunk and sick. But he said in two days. *Zwei Tage.* He said that."

Foxx pointed a carefully manicured finger at Jacob Maccabee. "Tomorrow morning. Crack of dawn. Here, Jake."

"Okay."

"And make sure your friend Lieberman knows we're coming. Andy, make sure the Packard is gassed up and ready to roll. Miss Schmidt, will you join us?"

"*Mit Vergnügen, Herr Foxx! Donnerstag hele und früh!*"

*

Thursday bright and early. Reuter had prepared a breakfast for Foxx of oatmeal, fried eggs with bacon, Russian-style rye bread, lightly toasted and covered with fresh home-churned butter plus half a grapefruit roasted with honey. A pot of chicory-flavored coffee with heavy cream accompanied the meal.

Andy Winslow had a glass of orange juice and a toasted bagel.

Jacob Maccabee and Lisalotte Schmidt stated that they had breakfasted at their respective homes. More to the point, Maccabee told the others that he had reached Lieberman by telephone on Wednesday night. They'd discussed the miniature fliers.

Lieberman told Maccabee that he'd been suspicious of Strauss for some time. He was a good worker, a talented and intelligent man, but he had a habit of poking through other people's files. He often carried work home with him. That wasn't a bad trait in itself. But he tended to overdo it.

Didn't he have any private life? Maybe he did, but, if so, he didn't share it with anyone. Everybody else at Sapphire-MacNeese seemed to have family photos on their desks: pictures of themselves on vacation, evidence of hobbies. Not Richard Strauss.

Still, there was nothing there that shouldn't be. Only it seemed that, beyond his slide-rule and his drawing board, Richard Strauss wasn't even there.

Jacob Maccabee said that he'd warned Lieberman to keep an eye out for anything that seemed suspicious today, especially unexpected visitors. But, speaking of visitors, would he arrange a set of passes for Caligula Foxx and companions.

★

A uniformed guard checked a sheet of foolscap on a clipboard, asked to see identification, and waved the Packard through the gate. Andy Winslow pulled the big car up to a visitors' spot and they all climbed out.

"Uh-oh!" Winslow grabbed Caligula Foxx's elbow. He pointed. "Take a gander at that!"

Foxx followed Winslow's pointing finger. "Yes, what is it, Andy? Confound you, what am I supposed to be looking at?"

Winslow ran half a dozen steps to a dark-coloured LaSalle coupé. It might or might not have been snowed upon in the past few days, but it was spotlessly clean now, sparkling in the bright sunlight of a December morning.

In the corner of the LaSalle's rear window was a sticker. It depicted an American eagle, a cluster of lightning bolts in one claw and a swastika in the other.

"Konrad beat us here, Caligula."

"All right. Let's get on with this." Fox turned. "Jacob, are you ready? You and Miss Schmidt? Your friend Lieberman is expecting us? Right, then into the lion's den we go!"

★

The Sapphire-MacNeese Aircraft Company loomed like a grey rectangle against the bright blue sky. A smartly dressed receptionist asked them to wait while she phoned Dr Lieberman. The reception area was decorated with oversized photographs of past Sapphire-MacNeese aeroplanes. There were single-engined pursuit craft, both open-cockpit biplanes and streamlined closed cockpit monoplanes. There were also a couple of bombers, huge, lumbering, four-engined aerial behemoths. There was even a modern airliner, silvery and glistening, that looked as if it could give the latest Boeing and Douglas models a run for their money.

Aaron Lieberman arrived and shook hands all around. He was red-haired and freckle-faced. He looked more like a schoolboy than one of the leading aviation designers of the era. He put his arm around Jacob Maccabee's shoulders. "Mr MacNeese is in town this week, Jake. I'll introduce you. Mr Foxx, I know he's heard of you. He'll be thrilled to meet the famous detective."

Maccabee said, "I've told my friends about your little robot flier, Aaron. I know they'd like to see it."

Lieberman said, "We need to talk about that. Come on, this will only take a little time."

He led the way to a conference room. When they entered they were confronted by a pair of uniformed figures, one in the heavy forest-green outfit of an army major, the other in the dark blue of a navy captain. A third man, wearing civilian garb, was also present. The newcomers were ushered to seats at a polished table. The naval officer promptly took charge of the meeting.

"Mr Foxx, Mr Winslow, Mr Maccabee, Miss Schmidt," the captain nodded to each in turn. "I'm afraid there has been a serious breach of security. I'm not blaming Dr Lieberman or anyone else here at Sapphire-MacNeese. Oh, I don't suppose you know Mr Carter MacNeese. It's his company." He allowed himself a small, rather icy smile.

"Dr Lieberman has confessed that he took home a test model of the OR-X1. That he actually demonstrated it to at least one of you. Ah, Mr Maccabee, I see you're joining in the confession."

"I wouldn't call it a confession," Maccabee responded. He was angry, that was clear.

Lieberman's reaction was milder but similar. "I acknowledge that I took it home. I showed it to Mr Maccabee. I wouldn't use the word *confess,* though, captain."

Now Carter MacNeese took a hand. "Captain, I understand that the government wants the OR-X1 kept secret. That is what they want *now.* And we are implementing every possible precaution to keep this device out of the hands of any potential enemy. But, we started this development on our own; *then,* there was no government contract. We've been offering the OR-X1 to the army and navy for three years. They finally decided they wanted to give us a contract for the device. You can't hold Dr Lieberman responsible for a breach of security before there was any security to breach!"

They went on that way. By the time the conference broke up there were armed soldiers and sailors patrolling the halls.

Aaron Lieberman spoke to Caligula Foxx and his companions. "I guess there won't be any demonstration of the model today. We've been running tests from a navy submarine in Peconic Bay.

I wonder what the local wildlife think of our little flying gadgets. Or the local fishermen! Jake, you won't talk about this to anyone, I hope."

"Of course not. I love the way those military stuffed-shirts act as if they were high muck-a-mucks."

Now Lisalotte Schmidt spoke up. "What about Konrad? He was going to come out here today!"

Lieberman grabbed the nearest telephone. He got an extension. He asked a question, waited for an answer, then exclaimed, "Gone? Both of them gone? Call the gatehouse." He turned to the others, aghast. "They've left. I don't know if they took anything important with them. A working model or a set of blueprints."

Andy Winslow sprinted for the door. He raced to the visitors' parking lot. He turned around and walked back into the building. "Come on, everyone! The Packard is still there. The LaSalle is gone."

Caligula Foxx sank into a visitor's chair. He dropped his head into his hands, held the posture briefly, then shook himself like a dog emerging from a duck pond. He pushed himself to his feet and suddenly, for the first time since arriving that morning, he was clearly the man in charge of the situation.

"Mr MacNeese and those uniformed popinjays will have to be informed at once. Someone needs to telephone the FBI right away. Probably the general and the admiral will draw straws to decide who gets to do the job. Konrad and Strauss must have caught on, they know their gaff is blown. I expect that they're headed back to Manhattan and straight to the German consulate on Park Avenue. Either there or to Bund headquarters in Yorkville, but they'll have extra-territorial rights at the consulate. That will be up to the FBI.

To Lieberman he said, "I'm sorry about all of this. My apologies, sir."

Lieberman shook his head. "Not your fault, Mr Foxx. Not your fault."

Andy Winslow was practically jumping up and down with impatience. He ran for the door, followed by Jacob Maccabee and Lisalotte Schmidt. Caligula Foxx brought up the rear, puffing like a winded dray-horse. Winslow held the Packard's passenger door open for him. He had the big sedan in gear even as Foxx pulled his feet from the running board.

They headed out of the parking lot, blew past the little guard-station, and headed for the new roadway that would lead to Manhattan. They caught sight of the LaSalle just as it pulled on to the Grand Central Parkway. It must be a special model, perhaps modified from the modest little car that it appeared, for it accelerated furiously away from the Packard and headed back towards the city.

There was considerable traffic in both directions; commuters headed for their homes and shoppers and celebrants speeding into New York. The sky had turned grey and heavy, wet flakes were falling, threatening to make the roadway dangerously slippery. The Packard's windshield started to ice up and Andy Winslow turned on both the wipers and the defroster.

He caught sight of the LaSalle forty or fifty yards ahead. He could see the eagle insignia in its rear window. He floored the Packard's accelerator, and the big car leaped forward. Reaching into his jacket, he pulled the Beretta from beneath his arm.

A convoy of bright yellow school buses loomed ahead of the Packard; the LaSalle blasted past them, the Packard following. Andy Winslow caught a glimpse of children's faces, peering out the windows of the buses, watching the two speeding cars as if they were piloted by Barney Oldfield and Eddie Rickenbacker.

A figure leaned out the passenger window of the LaSalle and pointed something at the Packard. Andy Winslow saw a yellow-red flash and heard a metallic sound as a small-calibre bullet bounced off the Packard's fender. The LaSalle swerved in front of the first school bus, the Packard following, drawing alongside the LaSalle, and Winslow caught sight of a hand as the passenger leaned across the driver and fired again at the Packard.

Winslow handed his Beretta to Caligula Foxx. Out of the corner of his eye he saw Foxx roll down his window and get off a shot at the LaSalle. From the back seat of the Packard, Winslow heard a loud report. He inferred that it was a .38 or even a .45, fired by Jacob Maccabee.

A circle appeared in the driver's-side door on the LaSalle, which swerved, its bumper clipping the corner of the Packard, swerving back again into its own lane. Another shot came from the LaSalle and Winslow felt the Packard lurch to the side. He fought the wheel, struggling to keep the big sedan from going into a 360-degree spin, finally managing to bring it to a halt on the shoulder. The LaSalle swept past, the convoy of school buses close on its tail.

Andy Winslow climbed from the Packard and walked once around the car. He let loose a string of obscenities that would have made a longshoreman's ears burn. Jacob Maccabee climbed from the car, and the two of them jacked up its front end and replaced the destroyed whitewall tyre with the spare.

When Winslow and Maccabee climbed back into the car, Caligula Foxx said, "A pity, Andy. If only we'd acted a little sooner we'd have caught them before they ever got out of the parking lot."

Winslow shook his head. "I don't know. I just don't know." He inhaled deeply. "All right, boss. What now?"

Foxx said, "Of course that was Konrad and Strauss. They're probably headed for the German consulate."

"Okay. We'll catch them there."

Foxx shook his head. "The consulate is technically German territory. We can't enter without permission, and you can be sure that we'd not get that." He looked dejected, a rarity for the huge detective. "Back to West Adams, Andy." He laid a massive arm on the back of his seat and swung around to face Jacob Maccabee and Lisalotte Schmidt. "Reuter will fix us a light supper and we'll plan our strategy."

By the time they reached West Adams Place, an early winter dusk had fallen and the heavy, wet snowfall was turning streetlamps into glowing lanterns. They trooped up the steps to the old house, Foxx in the lead, and lifting the brass gryphon's head to let it fall against the strike plate. He pulled his watch from his vest pocket and studied it.

"Where the devil is that fool Reuter? You'd think he'd know enough to answer the door."

Andy Winslow said, "He's probably busy in the kitchen, Caligula. You know when he gets involved in a new recipe, he just goes into a world of his own."

"All right, all right." Foxx slipped his watch back into his pocket. "Blast it, I never even carry a key. Why would I need it when I never leave the house? Andy, you must have one, the way you gallivant around all night and wander home at all hours like an alley-cat."

"Right." Andy Winslow tugged at his keychain and found a key to the front door. He inserted it in the lock and turned. The door swung open. They all entered.

The foyer was dark. "Reuter!" Foxx shouted again, "Reuter, confound you; what does it take for a man to be admitted to his own home!"

There was no response.

"All right." Jacob Maccabee hung back, closing the door behind the others. Caligula Foxx advanced, followed by Andy Winslow and Lisalotte Schmidt.

Music was coming from Foxx's study. The massive detective smiled. He turned to the others, said softly, "*Liebestod.* The Wagner piano transcription. Of course. One must credit even the monster Konrad with taste."

He signalled Andy Winslow, pushed open the door to his study and took a cautious step across the threshold. He recognized Heinrich Konrad seated at Caligula Foxx's grand piano. His touch on the keys was skillful and surprisingly sensitive. A Walther pistol lay on the music stand; clearly, Konrad knew the piece by heart.

Konrad looked up, an icy smile on his lips. He said, "Come in," addressing Foxx by a name other than Caligula Foxx.

"You remember—" said Foxx. He advanced several more steps. Again, there was a fire on the hearth, although a smaller one than on prior days. A man's body dressed in a dark suit lay before the fire.

"Your chef is in the wine cellar, *Soudruh.* Or would you prefer *Genosse*? Or simply Comrade? We were comrades long ago, were we not, Herr . . ." Again, he used the name that was not Foxx.

"Call me what you will." Foxx stood over the prone figure. "We were comrades at one time. I would not call you Comrade now, *Pan* Konrad. Herr Konrad."

"No. Nor I you, save, perhaps, for old times' sake. It is time for revenge, then, *Soudruh.* What is it that Monsieur Sue said in his novel? '*Revenge is a dish best served cold.*' It has been twenty years, *Soudruh.* Twenty years since you betrayed me."

"Betrayed!" Foxx snorted. "You would have sold us out to the Serbs had I not stopped you."

"They were advancing. We were outnumbered. To fight on would have made no sense!" Heinrich Konrad rose from the piano bench, reaching for the pistol that lay on the music stand. He lifted the pistol and pointed it briefly at Caligula Foxx but then he lowered his hand and sat once more, holding the pistol in one hand, caressing it with the other. "Too soon, *Soudruh,* too soon. We must settle our ancient grievance first."

"There is nothing to settle, Heinrich. You fixed a handkerchief to your bayonet and started from the trench. I merely did my duty."

"Duty. *Pah!* What duty? You toadied to the officers so they made you a sergeant and you became a veritable martinet."

"I did my duty, Heinrich. I was a soldier in the Emperor's army. As were you. And when I reached for your token of shameful surrender you—"

"I know what I did, *Soudruh.* Yes, I turned my bayonet on you." Foxx made an odd gesture. "I carry the scar to this day."

"My only regret is that I didn't kill you on the spot."

"Ah, but you did not. And we held off the charge."

"And I was cashiered and imprisoned. For that there is no forgiveness. None."

Foxx turned away from the other. He knelt beside the body on the floor. Then, to Konrad, "I take it that this is Mr Strauss."

"He served his purpose. I could not take him back to Europe with me and he would have been dangerous to our cause in America. I knew him. He was weak. He would have revealed too much, too soon, to the wrong persons. Anyway, already he was wounded in the car. I am not a nursemaid. He is a problem no longer."

"So you shot him. In the back of the head, I see. Clearly your preferred form of murder. Will you do the same to me? Here, I will make it easy for you." He struggled to his feet, puffing as he lifted his great bulk from the floor. He swayed, then reached for the edge of his desk to steady himself.

He stood with his back to Konrad. Over his shoulder he said, "Well, Heinrich? I see you find it most convenient to shoot when you do not need to look them in the face. You shot that poor child whose only crime was to deliver a telegram."

For a time there was no sound in the room other than the crackling of the fire and Caligula Foxx's breathing as he slowly regained his equilibrium.

Then strangely, Foxx heard the music resume. He turned. Heinrich Konrad had placed the Walther pistol back on the music stand and resumed playing the Wagner melody. So softly at first, that his voice could barely be heard, Konrad began to sing.

Mild und leise
wie er lächelt
wie das Auge
hold er öffnet
seht ihr's, Freunde?
Seht ihr's nacht?
Immer lichter
wie er leuchtet,
stern-umstrahlt
hoch sich hebt?
Seht ihr's nicht?

And from the doorway, advancing slowly into the room, a hand extended before her, the other concealed behind her back, came Lisalotte Schmidt. She sang, also, in harmony with Heinrich Konrad, Wagner's lines rendered into her own accented English.

Softly and gently
how he smiles,
how his eyes
fondly open.
Do you see, friends?
Do you not see?
How he shines
ever brighter.
Star-haloed
rising higher.
Do you not see?

Heinrich Konrad rose to his feet, his hands resting on the piano above the keyboard. The Walther pistol still lay on the music stand.

Lisalotte Schmidt brought her hand from behind her back, pointing Andy Winslow's Beretta at Heinrich Konrad.

Konrad started for the Walther, but Lisalotte Schmidt fired a single shot. He slumped back on to the piano bench, bleeding from the shoulder. With his other hand he reached for the Walther but was stopped by a single word from the bulky woman.

"Lisalotte," he murmured. "Lisalotte. After ... after our night ... after our night of love ... Lisalotte. How—?"

"Sie haben meinen Bruder ermordet." Her voice had become an angry growl.

From the doorway, Jacob Maccabee whispered the translation to Andy Winslow. "You murdered my brother."

Lisalotte Schmidt carefully aimed the Beretta, pointing it at Konrad's heart.

Konrad lunged for the Walther but Lisalotte Schmidt's second shot sent him reeling backward. The piano bench caught him behind the knees and he crashed to the floor. A final syllable hissed from his lips. *"Sieg ..."*

Lisalotte Schmidt hissed, *"Mein Bruder ist revenged."*

Andy Winslow said, "There's no need to translate that, Jacob."